PRAISE FOR
And Still Her Voice

"A wildly inventive novel about a half-Mexican young woman, Anna LeMar, whose dead grandmother takes residence inside her head from birth. *And Still Her Voice* tackles issues of identity, class, and belonging in wholly original, often hilarious, ways. What a pleasure to follow this feisty heroine who never stops fighting for love and freedom despite her meddling grandmother—and the odds stacked against her."

—Cristina García, author of *Vanishing Maps* and *Dreaming in Cuban*

"Ruthie Marlenee's debut novel, *And Still Her Voice*, follows Anna LeMar on a journey of escape and return—a quest to rediscover herself. Guided (and sometimes goaded) by the voice of her spirited grandmother Phoebe, Anna ventures into her own wilderness: through cities and across rivers, encountering allies and adversaries alike. With echoes of *Huckleberry Finn* and *One Hundred Years of Solitude*, Marlenee weaves a lyrical tale where reality blurs into the magical. With a knife strapped to her leg, a guitar on her back, and Phoebe's voice in her ear, Anna learns when to listen, when to resist, and how to trust the quiet power of her own inner voice."

—Julia Park Tracey, author of *Whoa, Nelly!* and *The Bereaved*

"*And Still Her Voice* by Ruthie Marlenée is a daring and deeply imaginative novel that blends the grit of a runaway's journey with the surreal weight of inherited memory and unresolved legacies. Sixteen-year-old Anna LeMar's search for freedom becomes a battle for autonomy as her privileged, deceased grandmother clings to life through Anna's consciousness. Set against the vibrant, chaotic backdrop of 1960s America—from Haight-Ashbury to Woodstock—the novel delivers both a coming-of-age odyssey and a layered meditation on family, identity, and reconciliation. Marlenée's prose is soulful, sharp, and unafraid to explore the strange places where trauma, love, and selfhood intersect."

—Lillian Ann Slugocki, *The Erotica Project* w/Erin Cressida Wilson, *How to Travel with Your Demons.*

"A wildly original, soul-stirring ride through the Summer of Love. Also, an unforgettable coming-of-age story with heart, humor, and a ghost in the backseat—*And Still Her Voice* is a radiant, fearless exploration of identity, legacy, and the voices we carry with us—this book completely swept me away. A hauntingly beautiful, genre-bending novel that lingers like a song you can't shake—bold, tender, and unforgettable."

—Lori Rosene-Gambino, Screenwriter and Producer, "Anniversary"

". . . Marlenee's writing is beautiful and lyrical, and each word seems to be written with such care. If you enjoy historical fiction and characters that will stay with you long after you've finished the book, read *And Still Her Voice*."

—Leslie A. Rasmussen, award-winning author of *When People Leave*

And Still Her Voice

A Novel

RUTHIE MARLENÉE

Sibylline
DIGITAL FIRST

Sibylline Press

Copyright © 2025 by Ruthie Marlenée
All Rights Reserved.

Published in the United States by Sibylline Press,
an imprint of All Things Book LLC, California.

Sibylline Press is dedicated to publishing the
brilliant work of women authors ages 50 and older.
www.sibyllinepress.com

Sibylline Digital First Edition
eBook ISBN: 9798897409679
Print ISBN: 9798897409686
Library of Congress Control Number: 2025938372

Cover Design: Alicia Feltman
Book Production: Aaron Laughlin

This is a work of fiction. Names, characters, places, brands, media, and incidents are either the product of the author's imagination or are used fictitiously. Any resemblance to similarly named places or to persons living or deceased is unintentional.

HUMAN AUTHORED: Any use of this publication to train artificial intelligence (AI) technologies to generate text is expressly prohibited.

Sibylline
Press

AND STILL HER VOICE

BOOK ONE

CHAPTER 1

The Bloody Knife

I stabbed my dad Easter Sunday, 1967, the day Jesus rose from the dead so that we might live forever. At least I thought so, not that I ever had it in me to kill him, or anyone. Plus, I didn't mean to.

Decades later, I still feel the knife, heavy in my hand and stained with his blood, his shocked face, the whites of his watery eyes, salmon pink now, the irises camouflaging into a metal grey, a look like he couldn't believe me capable of such an act. The whole scene would haunt me until the day I died which, at the time—because of the whole Jesus resurrection and my grandmother's transfer to me of her consciousness—I believed meant for eternity.

Even now, I sense the vibrations of Grandma Phoebe's cigarette-raspy voice rattling inside my young head with every step I take. And by voice, I mean, sometimes it's something more thought-like, other times it's literally out loud and I have to be careful not to be around anyone who might think I'm some looney kid talking to an imaginary rabbit. Grandma's emotions come in an aura of different colors. "Anna, go back home," she says in an anger-tinged mauve, a color that tastes like cigarettes. I hum out loud trying to drown her out, but still her tone cauterizes my brain and I think I can almost smell it. "Darling, he'll be fine," she says in a soothing green, tasting of menthol cough drops.

Except, I'd seen all the blood. How could he be fine? I wouldn't be going back, even if I stayed out past sundown in this part of Glendale's all white community, where, according to my father, a "darkie" could still get lynched should she be out after the sun slips behind the dusky Verdugo's. Half Mexican on my mother's side, but also cloaked in Dad's whiteness, the last thing I worried about at the moment was passing.

Looking back, I see my sixteen-year old withered self, twigs for arms and legs elongated in the shadows over the moonlit asphalt. Cold, sallow skin, darkness circling, fever-shined, hazel-green eyes, I'm too dizzy and weak to move, yet I'm a survivor filled with adrenaline from a lethal combination of fear and rage as I push myself on the run of my life. Knife strapped to my leg, guitar bouncing on my back, wild auburn hair flying behind me as the sound of sirens gets closer. Except, I'm not alone.

★ ★ ★

There'd be no outrunning my looming migraine, much less Grandma, a royal pain in the cabeza who'd also hitched along for the ride. *If you had a body of your own, maybe I would've stabbed you, instead.* Every step I took down the street felt like a hammer to my skull. My period usually brought on the headaches, also leading to memory lapses, but since I'd lost my baby fat and my boobs, I hadn't had a period in a while. So, now headaches were a signal I needed to eat.

I slowed down. *Am I having a heart attack?* The metallic taste of blood rose up from my heart beating louder than the sounds of the emergency vehicles blaring up Cañada Boulevard. Some nosy neighbor must have called again. After a bit, I stopped to catch my breath. Hands planted on my knees, pulse-pounding and panting; I became disoriented. Under the zigzag lights beaming from the Glendale swastika-designed streetlamps, my eyes throbbed as I tried to focus on my watch. The wiggly little hands pointed to just past midnight. I looked up to see that I'd only made it as far as the park near our house. Verdugo Park where just yesterday, after the anti-Nazi protest, the community had held its annual Easter egg hunt complete with a giant Easter Bunny whom I knew to be our old pro-Nazi neighbor, Mr. Krüger. I'd recognized his voice when he talked to Dad about how our neighbors the Blumenthal's people had killed Jesus. Mom hated Dad hanging around someone who'd "killed the Jews." "Who next?" she'd ask. "The Mexicans?"

Through the moon's muddled reflection on the stagnant puddles, I could see I'd escaped home still in my pink nightgown underneath the white sweater I'd worn to Mass earlier. When will it all stop? Carrying my pillowcase like a knapsack on my back, I'd had enough sense to stuff it with a change of clothes and my diary. I wasn't your normal sixteen-year-old so definitely I'd die— irony of ironies—if I were to leave behind my crazy thoughts for anyone to read. Morbid stuff like: *I've been wearing sadness like my heavy sweater for a long time. Being terrified only interrupts the ongoing unhappiness. I hate my parents. I wish I were dead.*

I cut through the park, head throbbing, tears streaming down my cheeks, my gown getting bunched up between freshly shaved thighs. Slowing to reach down and fix myself, I realized

I'd at least had the sense to pull on a pair of thick knee-socks, good for hiding things like money and the six-inch Bowie knife, the one I'd used to—to stab my father. *I stabbed Dad! But, how could I?*

Under a labyrinth of leafy shadows, I weaved through the sycamores, squirrels taking cover as I recited out loud the Act of Contrition. *Oh my God, I am heartily sorry for having offended Thee, and I detest all my sins because of Thy just punishment . . .*

My shoes punished worse than any Catholic penance, as if my feet wept the Hail Mary Janes through the three teardrops cut out of the leather sides. I shouldn't have put the white patent leather Sunday shoes I'd worn for Mass earlier back on, except I only owned one other pair of sneakers which would have been better to run in, but obviously I wasn't thinking so straight. Who could think straight after doing what I'd done? *I firmly resolve, with the help of Thy grace, to sin no more and avoid the near occasion of sin.* The sin in my heart rushed up and ran away from my eyes. I wiped my tears with my sleeve.

Deep in the belly of the park, sirens blared far away. Squaring my shoulders, I lifted my chin and took off until I got to the edge of the mossy arroyo.

And still her voice, burbling like the creek, the liquid sound rushing up through the loops and whirls against the dark snail-shaped spirals in the walls of my inner ear. "We're okay." The water babbling over the polished pebbles sounded soothing, hypnotic, but then even over gurgling, there'd be no drowning out the voice in my head, a drone, neither young nor old, just timeless; neither high nor low, just sort of neutral like the murmur of a hornet, unless she had something to prove which was pretty much all the time. She'd say I needed shaping and fine-tuning as if I were her stupid piano or my guitar. *We're okay? Oh, I'm so damn tired of we.*

"Turn around, Anna. He was drunk," Grandma muttered without emotion, as if being tanked excused everything. "Darling, he was angry with me, not you."

Dad had been pretty pissed with his mother for a long time. Even before I ever came into this world. "Yeah, so why am I always the one to suffer?" I massaged my thumping temples as a withered sycamore leaf drifted down the creek. I wished I could hop on and sail down to the ocean.

"You're not the only one," she said as if that was any consolation.

"But I *am the only one* who killed him." The leaf stuck to a river stone. "With my hands."

"Oh darling, you didn't kill him."

"What? How do you know? Now, you're psychic?"

"I just know he isn't dead—at least, not yet."

"Not yet? Like I should turn around and risk spending the rest of my life in jail? And then I'd surely be stuck behind bars with you."

"You do have a point, my dear."

My molars clamped together. Unfortunately, there'd be no escaping the voice and she wasn't about to butt out now.

"He hates me, not you," Grandma said.

"And he was angry with you, so why should I give a fuck!?" I stopped again to catch my breath. "So, what's your plan, Grandma?"

"It's a dangerous world out there." I could just imagine her checking her luminously painted nails. "You'll get hurt."

"Like you care. Like I haven't been hurt enough at home," I snapped back, dashing through the park like a scared coyote escaping a hillside fire.

"Anna?" Her sound raised a few notes on the second syllable of my name.

"Shut up!" I slid my guitar off my back and across my chest. Except for church, I didn't go anywhere without my guitar. My thinking was that it was my best defense against that stupid voice in my head. I twanged the strings and sang out loud as I ran, hoping the noise would make her go away. *I want to skip naked through the park!* I sang until I reached the tunnel cutting underneath the street. I stopped to rest on a nest of leaves and branches that had gotten snagged up on the higher ground. Cold all the time, as if the furnace in my soul had stopped burning due to lack of food fuel, now I froze. I pulled my knees into my chest and waited for my galloping heart to slow to more of a trot. In between each beat and breath, I knew. Grandma didn't have a plan. *I've. Been. Betrayed.*

I pulled out the little book of matches I always carried in my pocket in case of an emergency. As a little kid, besides liking the sulfury smell; I also liked to believe it scared away the bad stuff and now I thought I might burn leaves for warmth, but the box was empty. The night loomed, long and scary. Darkness absorbed the sound of my breathing. I'd told Grandma to shut up, but now I needed to hear her voice. Strange, as a kid I'd never imagined living without her voice to calm me, so much like one of Brahms's lullabies. But sadly, there in the dead of night, what I did know was that she was the root cause of all of my turmoil. I knew that even though she said she'd only been trying to help, to make up for the sins of her past, she'd been the source of my family's chaos.

★ ★ ★

Grandma believed she knew best for everyone. Even though my Mexican mother—a former migrant worker who picked grapes and lettuce up and down the California farmlands—had taken home economics as she finished up her GED during night school, Grandma, like one of those Pilgrim colonists from the old country, thought it was her job to educate me on such things as "please" and "thank you," on how to write a thank-you card and which fork to use at a dinner party—as if we were invited to such shindigs—how to be polite and pleasant even though most of the time, I thought my life pretty much sucked. In her day, she'd been a refined classical musician and part of the Los Angeles Bluebook Society as am I because of my auspicious birth. I became her second chance. She'd pretty much fucked up with my father in that department. She wanted to teach me how to act civilized, how to play the piano and sing pretty so as to fit into her society; all things Dad had obviously rebelled against. There was plenty wrong with Dad, i.e., his Navy medical discharge, for one thing, or his drinking problem, for another. Rather than getting knifed, wouldn't it have been better to eat him when he was young like some members of the animal kingdom did to remove their inferior offspring?

The stabbing incident wasn't the first time Grandma had used my voice box and gotten us into trouble. And to be clear, not only did she talk to me all day long, but she also spoke through me in a smoker's voice an octave lower than mine. She'd died, rather, she'd left her body before my birth then took up residence inside my head by transferring her consciousness before I ever took my first breath. It's part of an Eastern religious thing she learned in India, sort of a shortcut toward enlightenment. Anyway, she moved in non grata, then started to decorate my headspace, filling it with so much crap, I could've had a huge junkyard sale.

But while Grandma and I'd shared a consciousness, we didn't exactly share a conscience. And while there'd certainly been justi-fication and plenty of motivation for the stabbing, besides the fact that I was so tired of Dad and Mom fighting day and night and me getting stuck in the middle of the three-ring circus—well, four-ring, since I happened to share head space with Grandma—and even as angry as I got, I wasn't vengeful. I didn't think I had it in me to squish an ant much less stab my father. But I began to wonder about Dad's mother, Grandma Phoebe, who'd hijacked my body in order to "protect me," she'd say, and while she was at it, rewrite some history, re-right some wrongs, and carry out her warped sense of what she deemed appropriate or not, justifiable or not. Now, it was she I wanted to kill.

CHAPTER 2

I Am a Consciousness

In death, there is no concept of present, past, or future, so as Anna tumbles into sleep, allow me this opportunity to step in and give some background about the little-known practice of transferring one's consciousness, Phowa. I will also endeavor to clarify how, even living with the consequences of a transfer gone bad with her father, my son, who quite honestly might have been a bad seed (and Anna does have a point about the animal kingdom eating their young, but we humans do have other choices), I still chose to move into my granddaughter's space at her birth.

It hadn't been my plan to leave this realm yet, for I still had so much music in me that the world needed to hear, but then as my lung disease got worse, I realized my life had not been as pure as it should have been in order to gain entrance into the pure realm of Amitabha, so I summoned my lifelong opera friend, Marie, from Mills College, to help me prepare for my transfer. But then I took a turn and as I lay dying, I learned that Charley would be a new father. I could not help but think I had made so many mistakes raising him and saw this as my last chance to try and square things with my conscience. As it would turn out, Anna, truly a gifted musician, and quite a prodigy, rekindled my soul, and so protecting her would become a priority.

Quickly, before she wakes, I can tell you that years prior, in 1908, so distraught over the death of my dear daddy, a kind and gentle soul, inimitable, I prayed he'd find a better place. Devilishly handsome, too, I might add, I was his princess. I'd never known nor would I ever be with a man who lived up to his virtuosity; none of my beaus, neither of my husbands, and certainly not my Charley. And so, I traveled to India, chaperoned by sweet Marie, to learn how to stay connected with my father. I learned about death as a continuum of the spirit. While visiting the Theosophy headquarters in Adyar, I had the opportunity to study many religions, including the ancient Eastern religious practice of Phowa. Still, not too many people know about conscious dying, much less mindstream transference. The belief is that at the time of one's death and even after, with proper assistance, one can live on by transferring his consciousness over to a pure realm. I prayed for my father to find his pure happy place. As for me, babies are pure at birth, hence my own transfer to my granddaughter.

As I lay dying, Marie came up to my bedroom and put a recording of my music on the Victrola. Ah, those were the special moments. Music had been my connection to everything—the balance that had always set the scales.

I remember how my sweet Marie, a true love until the end, leaned over me and pierced the crown of my head with a needle. As a droplet of blood dripped into my ear, I heard the music trickle in as I drifted in and out of consciousness, or might I be remembering as I picture the sky, a golden light of the Holy Spirit—the wisdom, and compassion of all the enlightened beings—my thoughts scattering like startled birds darting through a dark forest as I fly over. "Open your heart to their presence and trust they are there," Marie whispers, as I sink like a dead weight, entering a dreamlike state and yet this process of death gives me a certain diaphanous clarity.

"Through your guidance and blessing, through the power of the light streaming from you," Marie sings the prayers lovingly. "May all the negative karma, destructive emotions, obscurations, and blockages be purified and removed . . ." A joy so intense washes over me, filling my heart. "May she know the time has come to let go into the process of taking a new rebirth. May she know this life is over and whatever mistakes may have made have been forgiven and cleansed. May she know her family and friends love and appreciate her and want her to move on without regret, and with confidence and ease . . ." I hope this is true. "May Phoebe be guided towards a new and beneficial birth in a place where she can accomplish all of her virtuous aspirations."

A silence falls over me as I soak it all in. I feel Marie's warm breath on my face. "Phoebe, can you see the rainbow light from the heart of all wisdom?" And the light pulsates. She takes my cooling hands. "The light is streaming into your heart. Pray with me, Phoebe. Oh, Magnificent King of boundless light, I lay down before you. I take refuge in you. Please bestow upon me your countless blessings."

And I envision the process of transferring my consciousness up through the tiny pinhole in my skull, into the pure realm and down through the fontanel of my grandchild.

Unfortunately, there would be a problem with the transfer. Accordingly, one must first prepare by letting go of earthly possessions; one must die with a pure, clean mind in order to die a happy, joyful death. In other words, I should have lived a better life, been a better person, spent more time with my son. But, as a human, I'd made some mistakes. My son would have preferred that I had died. I should not have resorted to this shortcut toward enlightenment.

While dying, there is no concept of time, no separation of moments, but what seems like only moments later, I hear a favorite concert finale of mine: Beethoven's Ninth Symphony. I'm at my piano in the chamber room built for me by Anna's grandfather, my husband Dr. Wesley LeMar. The audience, all the movers and shakers of Los Angeles, is so moved by my performance, I soak in the energy of their applause and am lifted higher.

As the dawn of a new century warbles, I sense the bones in her soft skull vibrating, and then from somewhere even deeper, the music becomes more critical. A vast spectrum of sound pulsates all around. The pounding of a heart, like a summer thunderstorm, blood coursing through veins and arteries, the sloshing of fluids. Lightning strikes again and the sound of skin stretching, and then more lightning and the zapping of electricity somewhere out there jolting us and . . .

Things speed up like a menuetto, a pace so lively, lightning and rain coming faster and heavier until . . . Adagio. I hear a suctioning, and a peal of thunder so fierce startling me out of my quiescence, jolting me from my serenity. The violins vibrate beginning in the key of G. Gradually more notes and more instruments are added and suddenly . . . from somewhere deep within a warm, dark place, as if under water, I strain to hear the low sounds of a man, e enfine, he shouts, "Push, Teresa, push!" But Anna doesn't want to be born and the poor dear tries to crawl back up into the womb. She is breech.

Allegro molto e vivace. Yanked by her feet, she recoils. She doesn't want to leave her warm world, but as the music finally enters her, she flips, allowing the melody to lure her out of the comfortable, wet darkness and carry her out toward the light, to the blinding cold surface. She can't open her eyes, but I can hear, "It's a girl!" And together we scream in the key of C major.

And *we* would continue to sing a beautiful duet until that fateful Easter night.

But again, this is Anna's story and I promised to let her tell it using her own voice. Unfortunately, it will prove to be quite difficult since I am a consciousness who doesn't sleep. I share thoughts, ideas, and memories with my granddaughter. Except, you see, a child doesn't form a memory until around age three, but retains a different, more mysterious sort of memory—in Anna's case two sets of memories—that will last a lifetime. I only want to step in to fill the gaps when and where necessary; for instance, when she is too young to remember or when she's asleep, or when she needs clarification for some of my memories, or sadly, when she is passed out. And when it comes to my son's stabbing, I want to assure her that it had to be done. She thinks she has thick skin, but under the surface, she has an elastic heart that stretches until it bleeds, and on this journey which we are about to embark, she'll need to believe she has the courage of a lioness in order to defend herself as she takes on the world. After all, there are two of us with souls at risk.

Shhh! She is waking.

CHAPTER 3

Growing drowsy, I hid inside that dark, womb-like tunnel in Verdugo Park, resting my head on my knees, but then for a moment, I wondered if La Llorona might come find me to drown me in the creek. I hugged myself, crying now like the weeping woman of Mexican folklore and sounding like some sort of wild animal.

The howling music of coyotes sounded a little too close for comfort inside the park, so chilly, damp, and dark. Hidden deep in the pit of the burrow, I felt a lump underneath where I sat and I rolled onto one butt cheek to reach down and pick up something small, smooth, and roundish. Wiping my eyes that had finally made peace with the dark, I held the object up to the tiny globe of light seeping in from one end of the tunnel—a foil-wrapped Easter egg from yesterday's hunt. What parent would let their kid wander into this scary, dark place all alone to look for Easter eggs? Mine, obviously. I shoved the egg into my pocket.

I shivered. How long can I stay away? Forever? I'd miss my dog, Bella. I should've brought her with me, if not for company, then to keep me warm. She'd been a puppy when Dad rescued her and brought her home—the day after he'd accidentally broken my arm—something that had slipped my mind until now, something else I didn't want to think about and tried to push back down, something never talked about because really he didn't mean for my arm to break when he yanked me, or was it Grandma he'd wrenched off the piano during a rendition of "Ode to Joy"? He'd been drinking and the song reminded him of bad stuff, like the mysterious deaths of his own father and a stepbrother, he told me after I came home from the hospital in a cast. But then he gave me Bella, a short-haired beagle mutt who barked too much, especially when anyone got too close to me. I loved her. Bella couldn't stand Dad. Maybe that's why he got her for me, for protection around him. She'd been my best friend and because I was homeschooled, she was my only companion except, of course, for Grandma. Dad said every kid needed a dog. *Son of a bitch. Oh Dad!* Please don't die, but if you do, please don't rise again. I sobbed for my dog and buried my head like I wanted to bury the past.

But the memory pushed up through the grave, or maybe it was a dream, hazy and fickle. I floated up weightless and heard music in a mishmash of color. Just before I got Bella, I sensed something super weird about Grandma, but I couldn't put the uncomfortable feeling into words like I could with a tummy ache or a wiggly tooth. I'd been too young to understand that Grandma wasn't the be-all and end-all she'd led me to believe. She used big words that roughed up my throat and ached my gums. *Psychology Today* magazine had yet to be published, besides I'd have been too young to comprehend the psychiatry of narcissism much less the future concept of Stockholm Syndrome. The distinguishing moment came into focus.

I'm four years old and seated at the grand piano we inherited from Grandma, in the chamber room. Trying to master Beethoven's "Ode to Joy," my small hands stretch across the keyboard, while my two little sisters twirl around the room, leaping from one embroidered flower to the next on the Oriental rug, another hand-me-down from Grandma. Sitting behind me, next to the fireplace, Mamá cradles baby Michael as she keeps talking about me to Dad who remains silent. "She has your mother's ear para la musica."

As I played the piano, Mamá kept making these comparisons about Grandma and me—as if it might endear us to him or them—like the color of my peach skin or auburn hair, "tambien pelirroja." I knew when my mother spoke Spanish, for emphasis, she was either super mad or trying to please my father, like it made everything sound a little more pleasant, made her sound more like one of those submissive wives from the Bible that Father Reynoso talked about at Mass. Plus, she didn't think Grandma understood Spanish, but we did. And they wouldn't stop yakking about her. Dad finally spoke up. "She's got Phoebe's eyes." He always referred to his mother as Phoebe, or worse, anything but mother. He referred to me as Mouse because my ears stuck out like his, the better to hear with. Lucky me.

"Igual de misterioza," Mamá whispered low enough, but I still caught on. The one disadvantage to talking about Grandma, in Spanish or English, was that her voice became more acute in my head, like a screeching rat. I stopped playing, swiveled around on the piano bench, and, in a sound unfamiliar to me outside of my head, the voice asked, "Are you talking about me, darlings?"

My parents' faces turned paler than a couple of Vikings. Dad then beelined it for the kitchen, probably for a beer. At that moment, more than what I said, it was how I said it. Neither "darling" nor "querida" were words in our home's vocabulary, much less that of a four-year-old, but Grandma had spoken up through me. Again, it's not that I hadn't heard her before, but only inside my head, thought-like. Never out loud. Funny, I'd never thought about how the voice in my head sounded out loud. Did it really matter to a four-year-old? Was it so abnormal? But when the strange sound spilled out of my mouth, it felt a bit freaky, to say the least.

Mamá must have figured I was old enough or ready to learn about my condition because, as if one thing connected to the other, she got up to take a seat next to me on the piano bench. "You know what I've told you about La Llorona?"

"You mean the crying Mexican lady who drowned her niños?" The story was one she'd tell us kids to keep us in the house after dark.

Mamá nodded and then shook her head. "There's no such person."

Whew, that's a relief—no Llorona. I plinked a few notes on the keyboard. But then, as if the truth about the crying woman was meant to soften the blow, Mamá leaned in and whispered, "Mija, oigame." I stopped playing and turned to see her eyes darting around like she wanted to make sure we were alone, like La Llorona hadn't snuck into the room.

"I'm listening."

"There's no old woman out there." She cupped my face, tapping her index finger on my temple. "But there's one in your cabeza. You were born with your abuela's mente . . ." She released her hands and my suddenly heavier head dropped.

"Que? Her mind in my head?" I couldn't quite follow. Besides, did I really need to know? I mean, I barely knew that my favorite color was rainbow and that I loved chocolate and that smell of comfort when you strike a match, but I couldn't say why I loved Ludwig van Beethoven as much as Elvis Presley. So, Grandma lived in my head. So what? I mean, did I even know that everyone in the world didn't think the way I did? How should I know most people entered this world alone and died alone?

"Y, a veces su voz comes through, tambien," Mamá added.

Her voice, too? My lips parted, stale air swathing my heavy tongue, as Dad staggered back into the room slugging down a beer. I pursed my mouth, folded my hands in my lap, and sat quietly, the metronome ticking back and forth, my eyes in unison, as I waited.

Dad chugged the last drop and burped. "Is *she* finished talking?"

She? I licked my lips and swallowed. So, this wasn't the first time they heard her noise spilling from my lips. Is this why my tongue felt so tired like stretched-out bubblegum? This was just the first time for me to put one and one together and still come up with only one, the first memory of Grandma and me as a single person. I raised my hand to my mouth and gnawed the skin around my thumbnail until it bled, listening as the grownups went on discussing my situation. I wiped the blood onto the hem of my dress and then pounded down on the keyboard to try and drown out the noise and that's when Dad grabbed my arm, yanking me off the piano.

He was sorry, but the only solution my parents would come up with was to not talk about it, not the voice; later, not the broken arm. It's no wonder I became silent, slowly losing my own voice. In kindergarten, my teacher reported to my mom that I seemed to have lots of conversations with someone named "Phoebe" and how I wasn't interacting with the other children. It didn't take long to realize that none of the other kids had grandmas who talked to them. Mamá sat me down, stared me in the eyes, and asked Grandma to please leave me alone. That didn't seem to work, and by middle school, I sat alone to eat lunch, having lost any friends. Even my words left me alone. Keeping me home was for my own protection. Yeah, right.

Around the age of nine, I'd been seated at the piano practicing Beethoven's "Hammerklavier." No one else was around, so Grandma took this opportunity to speak up using musical terms to describe the process of the transfer. Sometimes when she spoke in her lyrical way, like some sort of lethal lullaby, I'd fall asleep, but this time she had my full attention. I continued to play the piano, acting like I wasn't interested in the story of my birth, but I wanted to hear more about it. I couldn't remember being born, of course, but she said it had been worse than her own death. Never mind the pain Mamá went through carrying me around like a bowling ball for nine months before trying to push me out. Never mind the pain I went through being born.

There's a reason you don't remember these sorts of traumas, like when you stab your dad. I had to believe the whole birth process had to be the first worst day of my life, the second would be Dad's stabbing.

From then on, Grandma and I would sing a discordant duet. She would use music to try and bridge our generational gap and I would keep jumping razor-wire hurdles.

After she'd trespassed and then moved in, literally taking up space—never bothering to knock before entering—her sharp sound insistently scraped against my skull, my ambitions dulled into a haze. As I got older, during moments of clarity, I never questioned *how*, but only *why me?* It's not just because I had two sets of realizations or the mindfulness of two people, it's that it got to be too much, especially when it conflicted with my own agenda. I mean, what teenager wants her grandmother's nonstop, two-cents, for God's sake! You've got to wonder how many other grandmas or grandpas in the world out there were fueled by such an egotistical desire. Everything would've been better if I could have found a way to disappear Grandma, once and for all.

Unfortunately, out of all of the research I'd done about my condition, including some of Grandma's old pamphlets on the subject stashed in our library (before I set the fire during a botched séance when I was ten to try and send her back to wherever the hell she came from), I wasn't so sure this religious thing hadn't gone a little haywire somewhere from the start. I mean, I'd read that if a transfer's done wrong, like if the prayer isn't clear or if a person isn't ready, there could be terrible consequences. So, there you have it. Talk about fucking up. If there was anyone in this world I hated more, it was her.

CHAPTER 4

A Love-In

Good Friday, 1967: Two days before the Easter stabbing.
My parents are at it again and I hate them! I hate my grandmother worse. I know "hate" is a strong word, but isn't "love" stronger? And what are those two emotions anyway? All those songs about love, and how much it hurts, I hate how much I hurt. The Bible says that we should love one another as God the Father loves us, but if God is anything like my father, there's a major problem. Love thy neighbor as thyself. Well I got news for you: I don't like my neighbor, Mr. Krüger, much less myself. And yet, I really want love. I'm confused. I mean, how horrible a person can I be if love is something I crave? Dear God, if you exist and I deserve even more than the air I breathe, can you please, please help me find love? If not, I believe I'll just die.

The arguing stopped. Maybe they finally killed each other. I set down my pen, still feeling hurt, but now also feeling that old Mexican Catholic guilt for having written about my feelings. It was as if I suffered from diabetes like some of my relatives who weren't allowed to have any of the candy on the giant Easter egg hunt called life.

* * *

Easter morning arrived a couple of mornings later carrying a basket full of hope. My parents had reached a truce. Usually, I saw the world more whitewashed, but this morning I woke up in a room swimming in a soft shade of morning light, the color of a baby chick. Feeling all cozy and warm, curled up in bed, I listened to the starlings serenading the rising lemony sun as the breeze, bitter cold but sweet, snuck in through my window. Not exactly a Pollyanna, but no matter how bad things seemed, I always felt better after a good night's sleep, like what happens when a jury returns the next morning with a *Not Guilty* verdict. The scent of gardenias and jasmine marched in stronger than the scent of the damp Verdugo hills, a sign that spring had sprung into full bloom. Yawning, I stretched my arms to the ceiling, and as I turned, I noticed my hairy armpits, like the shredded paper grass I'd stuffed into the Easter baskets the night before for my siblings. Someone had to fill them, and I hoped the day might also be filled with the sweet pastel promises of better things. After all, it was a time for renewal, Father Reynoso would preach at the ten o'clock a.m. Mass at Cristo Del Rey Church, a time to be more loving.

I slipped my spindly hairy legs out of bed to get ready for the day, and then rushed into the bathroom, ahead of everyone else. When I glimpsed at my skinny self in the mirror, I could almost see the love in my heart smiling through my ribcage. I grabbed Dad's razor. I decided to shave my armpits. Feeling a little daring, I decided to shave my legs, too. Why not? I asked my reflection before opening the cabinet door. I'm sixteen, so it's about time. Starting at the ankle, I scraped all the way up past my knees, up my thighs, feeling sort of sneaky and sexy at the same time. I finished the other leg and went back to my room to put on the sleeveless pink and chartreuse-colored A-line dress that I'd had to alter since losing so much weight. Mom bought it from "the JC Penney," as she referred to the department store, after I'd shown her the ad and we both agreed it was tasteful, not too grown up—jeez in the old country I'd already have been married by then with a couple of mocosos underfoot!

In the dim hallway, I bumped into Mom and backed away, my whole body prickled at the sight of her unusually puffy morning face hidden in the shadows. "You should have taken in more material, mija, but I do like how you're losing your baby fat." What about my boobs? I'd given up sweets for Lent and hadn't been trying to lose weight but then I'd come to a place where I couldn't tell if I was hungry or not. Grandma told me I was unconsciously trying to become untouchable and disappear into thin air. Could be.

"Where are your socks?" I didn't think she'd noticed my nicked-up legs, so now I was in for it. "Who gave you permission to shave?" She stared into my eyes, something she rarely did. Her eyes were so dark I couldn't see her pupils, but I could definitely see she had a black eye. "Was it Phoebe said you could?"

"No." I'm capable of making my own choices, sometimes.

"And why did you give Dad permission to hit you again?"

"Sin verguenza." But I felt no shame that morning, turning to face her, standing my ground, the opaque light streaming in from a window behind me cloaking me with a false sense of power. Just because she didn't shave, much less do other things until she got married, didn't mean I needed to wait. Why should I? My face burned when she raised her hand. I thought she might take a swing at me, but instead, she said, "Que la fregada. Anna, you can't go barelegged in la casa de Dios. Wait here." Noticing the limp as she stepped back into her bedroom, I immediately felt sorry for causing more drama. She returned to hand me a pair of her silk stockings and a garter belt, something else for me to try and figure out.

I did learn a lot from Mom, especially when she shared what she learned in her GED night classes which proved challenging because Spanish was her first language. But for the most part, especially as the oldest, I had to figure a lot of stuff out for myself. Driving was one of those things I had to teach myself. Mom never learned and because we lived in the rural part of Glendale and the closest mercado and our church was more than an hour's walk away, leaving us with blisters every time, she was happy when I learned to drive. Plus, I could drive her to school without my father ever knowing. So, it was my decision as to when it was time to shave or kiss boys.

But when you're stuck at home all the time, what does it matter? You really don't even get a chance to talk to the cute boy who lives around the corner unless you sneak the car out of the garage again when your parents have locked the door to their bedroom after they've finished fighting. Then you're terrified of getting caught so you don't even slow down when you see him standing in his front yard tossing a football with his dad, Mr. Krüger, who wore the Easter Bunny suit over at the park, and you make your tattletale sister sitting shotgun swear she won't tell and you know she won't because she's already kissed three boys and Mom would kill her if she were to somehow find out.

The stockings, so satiny and shimmery over my newly naked legs, made me feel grown up. And then just before we left for Mass, I pushed my luck even further by refusing to wear a silly hat like my sisters'; that flowered bonnet with an elastic string under your chin in case you don't have enough sense to hold it down should a strong wind blow in during the Gospel of Paul. "Cover that red hair!" Mom yelled like it was an even bigger sin to have hair color the same as Mary Magdalene—like I asked to be born with the same hair color as a puta, like I asked to have something else in common with Grandma. There'd been a feud between my mother and my grandmother since before my birth and I was just about done being stuck in the middle. As far as she was concerned, I was too much like Grandma. More and more, I wished I'd never been born.

"Acuérdate de donde vienes," Mom would say whenever she thought I forgot where I came from or if I acted too white or if my head got too big as if it were some helium filled balloon that needed the heft of my Mexicanness to weigh me down. This confused me because she always pushed me to do better than she had with her limited education, with her limitations period.

"Si Mamá." She didn't like being called "Mom." Too gringo.

"Remember you're also a Verdugo." As if that made us Spanish royalty or something. "And we were landowners here long before any white man, before the LeMars."

Curious, because my mother also told me more than once that her Mexican people had owned this land first as part of the Verdugo Land Grant of the 1700s. I spent a lot of time in the library reading everything I could about our local history and the people who inhabited this land going back thousands of years before the Spanish settlers arrived, and then how we came to live on it.

"We were Tongva long before we were Verdugos," my mother told me.

Verdugo or not, as far as white Grandma was concerned, my mother could be doing a better job making my father happy. Mom should have been more grateful. I mean, just look where we lived. Look at all we'd inherited. Look at all Grandma had sacrificed. If there were a way for me to sacrifice Grandma to the god of her choice, I'd do it.

Mom handed me a lacy white mantilla to cover my head and I felt guilty for making so much trouble. With all of her kids and my angry Dad, she probably didn't have any more energy to deal with a rebel and a heathen in the making, plus it was Easter and she'd just been to Confession, so she didn't want to start sinning already before stepping into church and taking Communion.

Mostly, I wanted to make Mom happy, plus I did like going to church where I could breathe uninterrupted for at least an hour every week. I loved the sulfury smell of incense. To me it represented comfort. It also canceled out other unpleasant senses. Grandma despised it worse than church—not a fan of Catholicism and all of its rituals. She didn't believe in the concept of heaven or hell, the transformation of blood into wine, much less Jesus's resurrection on Easter Sunday from the dead, but she thought it was better than nothing as far as religion went. And so, for sixty minutes every Sunday, she checked out, leaving me in peace. Except for some of the liturgy and songs that seeped in like an earworm, the space in my head was so quiet, you literally couldn't hear a church mouse, and at least for a space in time, I didn't have to sit through hell. All angelic-like in our best Sunday outfits, we slid into our wooden seats for the ten o'clock Mass, Mom in a belted, peachy flowered-dress and one of Grandma's old fancy hats, the one with fake crepe orchids attached to it. Around her neck and jawline, she'd been extra generous with her Maja face-lightening powder and cologne, a blend of citrus, spice, flowers, and woods. With her Coty red lipstick, I thought my mother looked pretty even under a pair of cat-eye sunglasses to hide the fresh bruise Dad had given her on Good Friday. If only someone had kept her mouth shut and I don't just mean Mom.

Michael, my seven-year-old brother, a little man and Mom's pride and joy after having birthed only girls, much to Dad's disappointment, hair all slicked back with Mom's Dippity-do, showed off in the same starched white shirt and pressed pants he'd wear, as long as he didn't get mas gordo, for his First Holy Communion coming soon.

My sisters sparkled in their new white patent leather shoes that were supposed to last until the next Easter, lacy socks, hats with plastic flowers and an elastic band stretched under their chin.

Three-year old Josie, the product of the rhythm method I'd heard Mom complain about on the phone to Sister Bernadette, wore the frilly pastel-colored dress first worn by me before it got passed down to Maggie, eleven months younger than me, and then Patty, three years younger than me. Behind her coke bottle glasses, Maggie already had her eyes on my outfit from the JC Penney.

My father wasn't always Catholic—his mother had tried to bring him up as a Unitarian or a Scientologist or in some Hollywood "cult" like Mom called it—but to make Mom happy and to keep her quiet after an awful weekend where he crashed the car into the "Welcome to Glendale" sign, and ended up in jail with a DUI a couple of years ago, he got baptized. We had a few good months of not tiptoeing over too many eggshells after that.

For this special Easter Sunday, though, as penance for another bender and a sign of his contrition, he didn't just sleep off the hangover in the car while waiting for us. He attended Mass with us wearing the white guayabera shirt Mom bought for him in Mexico and set out for him, the one with the pocket to hold his cigarettes.

Afterward, we hopped into the yellow Ford Falcon station wagon. I'd barely shut the door when Dad, a Camel dangling from his lip, fired up the engine and sped across the parking lot. I lurched sideways when he turned right onto Brand Boulevard. Obviously, we weren't headed home.

"Donuts?" Michael asked, leaning forward in between the two front vinyl bucket seats. Sometimes when Dad messed up, we also made out with treats.

"No, Piggy," he said, reaching around to muss Michael's hair.

Michael bawled, smoothing back the do he'd worked on so hard making sure the sides stayed down.

"We're going to the park, you little sissy. Quit your bawlin'. Sons of sailors don't cry."

Michael hadn't yet learned to cry without making a splash.

"I'm not a sissy. I'm a boy," he shouted, ducking to take cover in the backseat. I might have defended him, but I was still sort of sitting in the afterglow of church and besides, it was too early to start any trouble.

Dad burst out laughing, slapping the steering wheel. "We'll see about that, sissy."

Maggie laughed and Michael punched her arm. "Leave gordito alone," Mom said (as if "fatty" was a better name), throwing a shoe that sailed past my head all the way to the backseat, landing smack in the middle of Patty's giggling face, but Josie, on Mom's lap was the one who wailed. Dad, in rare form that morning, blasted the radio. Mom must have given him some special candy or slipped him an extra teaspoon of sugar in his coffee like she did some mornings when she sensed he'd woken up feeling down again. She'd visited curanderas to prescribe special cures made of herbs and prayers. But it was Grandma who shared the trick with her about the candy. How'd that work out for you, Phoebe?

"But this is the wrong way," Mom said.

"There's some good shit happening over at Griffith Park," Dad said, our bodies jerking up a bit as he shifted gears. She turned to face him, her left eye bulging now like a purple Easter egg, as if to say, *We just got out of church, watch your language.*

By now I was very familiar with the park because sometimes on Sundays after Mass, if he even made it to church with us at all and depending on how bad his hangover was, we'd head over to ride the carousel or the miniature trains. But, once we got there, if Dad ended up napping in the shade, we knew not to wake the monster to ask for anything like money for popcorn or cotton candy, much less a trip on the merry-go-round.

"Yay, the horsies," Josie squealed. She loved riding the carousel, the same as I did at her age when everything seemed magical about the shimmery, bejeweled horses. Unable to see the happenings around me, the faster we went around, if not for the belt strapping me down, I'd fly away. Like they could take off to some castle in the sky filled with ice cream and lollipops and loads of new, sparkly toys. Mom rode with us once until she screamed for the operator to stop; like she'd screamed for Dad to stop.

"Hay no! Not today. Estás loco?" Mom said. "I read in the papers that it's gotten kind of crazy with all those hippies."

"Shi–oot, Teresa. They're love-ins. Tell me, how can that be bad?"

Love-ins? That didn't sound like a familiar term in Dad's vocabulary. The only thing he seemed to love lately was his Pabst Blue Ribbons and his smokes. So there had to be something else drawing him, but Mom tried hard today on el Domingo de Pascua to put into practice what Father Reynoso had preached according to 1 Timothy 2:12: "I do not permit a woman to teach or to exercise authority over a man; rather, she is to remain quiet." Besides, she already had one black eye.

★ ★ ★

We pulled into Griffith and parked as a parade of motorcycles roared up carrying young wild-haired men in black leather vests with girls hanging on behind, their long hair whipping in the wind. Except for the paint splattered across their breasts, some of the girls were topless.

Mom, peering through her sunglasses, sucked in a breath, quickly reaching around to cover Michael's innocent eyes.

"Hijos, stay in the car!" She pushed the button to lock her door.

But as he exited, Dad yelled at us to get out.

What were we to do? Dad strode already twenty steps ahead of us by the time everyone spilled out of the car, Michael and Josie with their Easter baskets in tow. We knew who the boss was today. Dad seemed buoyant, like Jesus walking on water, the way he drifted across the park. Mom followed, scooping three-year-old baby Josie onto her hip, her kitten heels spiking the grass. I trembled, yet felt exhilarated to be out of the comfort zone of my house, which wasn't so comfortable. I didn't know what freaked me out more, Dad's sudden mood change or all the Hell's Angels on choppers or the chill looking hippies in psychedelic paint.

We followed Dad toward the merry-go-round and soon we were in the midst of a bunch of longhaired, and big Afro-haired "hippies," young people of all races, full of happy faces. I noticed a couple kissing hard like right out of a movie scene. It was the first time I'd seen kissing in public, or just the first time. Immediately, I knew what had been missing in my life.

"Sin verguenza." Mom gave me a sideways look, yanking my arm.

"Escandalosos."

Was it sinful because they were out in public or was it because the girl was white and the boy was Black? I'd just watched the news about how an interracial couple from Virginia had been arrested, but then a higher court ruled that the law was unconstitutional.

"Selfish people," Mom grumbled. "They're obviously not thinking about how their children will suffer."

Even I could see the irony. Did she think a white/Mexican relationship was better than a Black/white one? Still, I didn't see my parents as a mixed couple and I couldn't see how it might be a reason for my suffering. Had I gone to a regular school, maybe I might have noticed a difference. Mom always said how bad it was for her as a Mexican in the white world. Even in Glendale where I couldn't imagine things were as backward as places like Virginia, I did notice the looks the other fancy housewives gave my mother when we were out, whether it was at the park or church. I'd stick out my tongue at them.

I remembered the time down at the pharmacy when a yellow-haired lady smiled at my siblings and me and then asked if Mom was our nanny. Holding her newly coifed head high, she responded, in flawless English. "No, they are mine." The pale woman backed away but still stood close enough for me to notice the difference in their skin color, even with Mom's ivory face powder. Incidents like that were why Mom mostly took the bus to do her grocery shopping at the Mexican market on the edge of town. It's why she made sure to be back in the house by sundown. Dad loved to tease her about being so dark.

"No soy negra!" she'd yell at him.

Like being Black was a bad thing. Mom also talked about some of her own family who were super dark and how she never would have married anyone darker than she.

The love birds finally stopped kissing and skipped away, hand in hand. The organ music from the carousel lured Michael up the hill and Mom gave chase, dragging Josie behind like a rag doll.

Surrounded by bodies glistening in the sun, I sniffed incense mixed with BO and then I whiffed the stuff that lingered in the garage after Dad had been in there working on his motorcycle awhile. With Mom out of the picture, Dad crouched down, cupping his hand to take a puff of a cigarette some guy had offered him. I may have been sheltered, but I knew it was marijuana.

Dad pulled out his wallet and I panicked hoping Mom wouldn't witness this transaction, too, or there'd be hell to pay, and we were already in debt up to our ears.

My pulse quickened, fluttering in my throat until, in an accent not my own, the voice I wished I'd never been born with; the voice echoing the sound of scratching, splashing, and stomping in the hallway of my cochlea, now yelled, "Charley!" —a grey-purple light pulsing all around me.

Dad shot up, glaring at me. "What the hell, Phoebe! Mind your own goddamn business."

"My family is my business, Charley," Grandma Phoebe said, and I squeezed my throat, running my hand up to cover my mouth. She'd been silent all morning especially while I sat in church. "How can you bring the children here amongst these heathens?"

Dad lunged for me. "Shut the fuck up, Phoebe."

I backed away, clamping my mouth shut, because even though Grandma Phoebe was more scared of my father than I was, she needed control and wasn't afraid of getting in the last word, especially when she could use my body as a shield.

I ran up the hill to catch up to the others and then after the little ones took a few spins around the carousel, we walked back through the park. Balloons and bubbles floated in the air and girls wore flowers in their hair. A kaleidoscope of color—a sign Grandma also dug the music—pulsated to the beat of the intoxicating music as people in psychedelic body paint danced, swaying and bouncing to the beat of bongos and tambourines. Young painted people pirouetted around us handing out jellybeans that Mom quickly confiscated. Someone handed me a daisy and Baby Josie a balloon. Michael gave chase again when someone blew bubbles.

Others sat in circles within circles chanting, snapping small finger cymbals, peacefully celebrating life. I strolled by a girl with long red-brown hair like mine, except straight. She said, "Hello pretty one. Peace and love to you."

I tingled inside. "Thank you," I said, mesmerized by her smiling face, her wondrous wide eyes the color of the water at the city pool. Glancing down through her gauzy blouse, besides her brown nipples, I could almost see the love in her heart. She'd been weaving a wreath of flowers. She reached out to crown me and a transformation took place inside me, like the time I got confirmed taking the name of Joan of Arc, my patron saint. But at once I became weak and self-conscious in my Sunday armor—all of us in our finest clothing as if we were some sort of missionary family entering the park to save lives or something.

I didn't know whether to "cleave" like it said in the Bible or to break away from my family and run for the hills. Mom snatched my arm, pulling me into her.

"Find your father."

Are you sure? Couldn't we just leave him here, or better yet, just leave me.

Mom swiveled her head searching for Dad before handing me the baby. "Let's get back to the car," she said, grasping Patty and Michael with her free hands.

As Maggie and I trailed behind her, a longhaired, fringe-vested boy around my age appeared facing me as he back-stepped along. He stood tall and skinny with stringy light hair, and small squinty mysterious eyes, but still sort of cute. He turned to stride in step with me and something inside me stirred. I handed Josie off like a bride's bouquet to Maggie. I'd always imagined I'd end up marrying (yes, I was already thinking of marriage and the sooner the better so I could move out. I hadn't yet thought of running away) someone more clean-cut, dark-haired with a pretty boy face and big eyes like Tony Curtis or Elvis Presley. And then a young couple ran across us and disappeared up the hill into the sycamore trees where I pictured their passionate kisses like what

I'd seen in the movie *From Here to Eternity* where they rolled around on the ocean shore. I imagined rolling around in the hills on a soft carpet of grass and leaves with this young wild-haired boy that walked beside me. We'd share kisses. I was ready for love. I wanted to be loved.

"Anna, hurry up," Mom shouted, probably wishing she'd learned to drive so that she could get us home quickly to wash out our eyes.

Dad finally made it back to the car and we swerved off to the sound of the Beatles' "She Loves You" on the radio, Mom yelling at him the whole way home even after he'd put his hand over her mouth, squeezing it so hard her Coty lipstick smeared across her cheek. I panicked. I wanted to jump out of the car and run back to climb up on one of those carousel horses and gallop off somewhere, anywhere.

Mom wiped her face with her embroidered church hanky and turned to stare out the window. "We're never going back," she said. "It's a wonder God hasn't sent us all to hell by now." She turned a cheek to my father, crossing her arms over her chest. "That place was a modern day Sodoma y Gomorra—un infierno."

Dad grumbled, "Yeah, yeah, yeah," before switching stations.

With a love like my parents had, I wasn't very glad.

CHAPTER 5

Not a Love-In

I grew up in a lonely space, and yet not alone inside the walls of my crowded tiny headspace, within a big cold house that definitely didn't feel like a home and for sure not a love-in. How I hated having to return later that Easter afternoon. But as we pulled onto our sycamore-lined street, the blooming buds cheered me up a bit as we came up the drive to our mini-mansion, Grandma's *Graceland*. Supposedly, Dad's rich father, Dr. Wesley LeMar, built the replica of a French castle for Grandma back in the twenties, filling it with all sorts of antiques and a real nine-foot Steinway grand piano so that Grandma could hold concerts in the chamber room while butlers served Champagne and caviar to their guests; where my grandfather could entertain celebrities, politicians, and even his brothers from the Masonic Temple. That was a long time ago, before he was killed by greedy partners who stole his part of the company and took him for all his worth—according to my father—leaving Grandma a broke widow with a newborn. And then worse, his best friend, George, married Grandma Phoebe and took over. I'd seen the saved newspaper articles about his suspicious death. Nothing was ever proven, but I continued researching all of this down at the library.

Nowadays, the house needed a lot of work. Some of the screens were torn and the shutters on the windows hung on by a nail and the roof leaked upstairs in the hallway between our bedrooms. Just like a big family, a big house needs a lot of attention and money, but lately our family lived from paycheck to paycheck. Sure, we were left the house, but no money to maintain it. Some Friday nights we'd wait for Dad to bring home his pay from the Lockheed factory so we could eat something heartier than meatless chile rellenos, or peanut butter sugar sandwiches, or the buttered tortillas like we had on Good Friday before things really went to pieces, when Mom told Dad she'd taken a job cleaning houses, a job she let me help with because I could drive. A job that was supposed to be a secret from Dad until she let it slip. And there'd been hell to pay for that with Dad's violence trickling down through Mom to me somehow. I'd miss that job and all the clean smells of Pine-Sol and lemon Pledge that came with it. I'd miss getting a glimpse at how other people lived. I'd miss reading their issues of *Life* magazine, *Ladies Home Journal*, and *Psychology Today* while Mom and I were on lunch break.

But honestly, even though it was dilapidated, our home, bordered by river stones the size of dinosaur eggs, stood more beautiful and unique than some of the newer ones we cleaned, even the ones with pools. Cookie-cutters is what Mom called them, "nada especial" like all of a sudden ordinary was a shameful thing. I thought her goal for us all was to assimilate and be like everyone else. But our home, built in 1923, was supposedly a replica of a chateau in Normandy, together with a little creek (who needed a pool?) that ran along the property and all the way down to Verdugo Park. I was lucky enough to have my own bedroom to escape go to. So, after the adventure earlier that day at Griffith Park, my brother and sisters went to their rooms to set out their uniforms for school the next day. I didn't have to and I guess some might say that's the cool thing about being homeschooled, getting to stay home, but honestly, I was pretty lonely except for Grandma's voice in my head, which ironically was the reason I was stuck at home in the first place.

So, as my sisters laid their things out for school the next day, I read another chapter of *A Wrinkle in Time* to Michael. He liked to imagine he was Meg's little brother on an adventure to save their scientist father. "But we're gonna save ourselves, right?" Michael said. Poor Mikey, neither he nor my sisters knew the exact reason for the strangeness in our family, including me.

"Right." I kissed him goodnight and went down to the den to find something else to read before bed.

Back in Grandma's time, the den used to be the library that housed shelves full of books—everything from *Rebecca of Sunnybrook Farm* to my grandfather's books on optometry, *The Clansman,* and even a big black book titled *Mein Kampf.* Mom kept a copy of the Catholic Bible, which Grandma said was the wrong version. Still, I read it from Genesis to the Book of Revelation, including the seven extra books that I couldn't find in the Protestant version like the book of Wisdom and the Maccabees. The den library was where I got most of my education, except for what Grandma tried to shove down my throat. It's where my curiosity about the outside world grew and what I couldn't find in there, I would find a couple of blocks away down at the Glendale Public Library.

I reached up and pulled out the *Dream of the Red Chamber* and I also snatched the Sunday paper off the big mahogany desk where Dad hid his key to the safe in the garage full of his booze and a pistol. I climbed upstairs to my room and plopped onto my bed.

The front page of the newspaper read: "LBJ Plans Twice a Year Strategy Conference on Vietnam Struggle." Why are we even in Vietnam? Could the war be any worse than here at home where the dictator constantly battles with the queen of the kingdom?

I flipped onto my back and turned the page. "In Griffith Park today, hippie tribes expected to gather today for a Love-in." Wow! My body tingled. I'd been there. I'd been a part of something meaningful, part of history. These human be-ins were taking place all across the country.

I popped open a can of beer stolen earlier from Dad's stash in the garage and took a swig. I'd been sneaking sips since I was about fourteen. Sometimes there was something a little stronger like Thunderbird wine, but I could barely choke that down. He had a hard time keeping track of his hooch he'd bring into the house, and if he happened to notice anything missing at all, he'd blame Mom for pouring his stuff down the drain, which she did a lot of times. Last Friday she told me to do it. I liked how it took the edge off, mellowed me out. Grandma, of course, freaked out every time. But the good thing about being pleasantly buzzed— besides water and the Communion wafer, which is about all I'd had all day—was that I didn't care as much. I found her laughable. She had a hard time understanding that she couldn't do anything to stop me.

I slugged another mouthful and then lay in bed where the scented smoke-ring memories of the day's experience at Griffith Park swirled through my head. There'd been so many people my age, whites, Blacks, Asians, Mexicans—all so happy-looking like those beautiful glass-eyed creatures going around on the carousel. Everyone seemed to get along. Nothing like at home where Dad used to scare us with the threat of some Japanese or Russian or even Martian invasion. Or he'd march around like some Nazi soldier, making Michael salute, "Heil Hitler!" and then laughing and saying it was a joke. (I remember Mom once telling me that Dad's stepfather used to take him to Nazi rallies up at Hindenburg Park.) Griffith Park was sort of like a universal love-in. I needed to go back. I hoped they'd be there every Sunday and if so, I'd find a way to get there. So inspired by the day's experience, I jotted down the start of either a poem or a song. Soon, a tune popped into my head.

Stop this merry go round, it's spinning too fast
No time to feel sorry about the past
I want to skip naked through the park
Tired of living alone in the dark
Think of tomorrow beginning at dawn
Come back to reality and today is . . .

Suddenly, a loud crash and a thud like an earthquake shook the house and my hippie daydreams were interrupted. It boomed from my parents' room. They were yelling at each other again, picking up where they'd left off Good Friday night after Dad had been out "en una borrachera." He'd gone out straight after work and spent his paycheck on booze without leaving Mom anything for groceries or the bills; another Friday night when we'd had to fast whether it was Lent or not, whether we had a choice or not.

"God damn it!" I heard cussing from all the way down the hall. "You had enough to buy all that Easter shit!" Dad yelled.

Mom yelled back. "No skin off your nariz. I bought the kids things with my cleaning money." Oh no! My stomach flipped. I brought my hands to my mouth, squeezing my lips. Why did she have to go and bring that up again? Dad had made it clear that there was enough work in our own home. "I told you I didn't want you working outside of the house, much less cleaning the neighbor's houses."

"Your mother never minded when my family cleaned her house," Mom said, and then the shouting and cursing escalated to the point I slapped my pillow over my head.

I wondered if I should call Mom's brother Teodoro to come and get us. Last time, there'd been too many of us to stay over like before at his tiny house in Monte Vista with his wife, all of his kids and Abuela Antonia, so he'd dropped us all off at a motel over on Colorado Boulevard. I sort of missed those earlier times at his house, even though the circumstances of us being there were embarrassing. I liked hanging out with my older cousin Teodora "Teddie," named after my uncle. And even though she was "big, brown and beautiful" —she liked to say—she terrified me. The good kind of terror. The oldest sister of all boys, she didn't take anyone's shit, not even her father's. I wished I had her power.

I thought it sort of sick how Mom equated terror with love, like power was sexy? I couldn't muffle the sound of her crying now and I wanted it to stop. Maybe I should drive her away from here myself. I sprang out of bed and rushed down the hall, crashing through the door into their bedroom and accidentally kicking over a can of beer which rolled across the floor toward my parents where my dad, now in his white T-shirt and skivvies, had Mom pinned to the floor, holding a knife to her throat. Her one eye was still swollen from Friday night, the other bloodshot and glazy. Why couldn't she learn to play dead like me? She screamed, "Anna, llama la policia!"

"You call them and I'll kill her," Dad yelled, Mom arching and kicking until her garter belt snapped.

"Hijo de puta." Mom spit at him. Oh, no! Didn't she know she only pushed his buttons harder by calling him a son of a whore? I noticed a run in her stockings. The helpless look on her face embarrassed me. I felt pity for her when I so needed to feel respect. "Call the police!"

But it wouldn't have done any good to call the police. They never helped. I was too afraid, besides Mom told me it was worse if you were a woman and even worse if you were a Mexican woman. I didn't know what else to do, inching forward like a lion tamer, as if I could reason with him. I popped open the can of beer and held it up as if I could lure him away. "Is this what you want?"

But then in her smoky pianissimo voice that Grandma sometimes used to try and calm Dad down, she spoke out, "Charley, you're better than this. Put down the knife." His eyes pierced through to my core and Grandma spoke a little louder, in her scarlet mezzo-forte voice, "Charley, you need help."

"Shut up, bitch!" Dad yelled fortissimo, tears streaming down his cheeks. "The only help I need is for you to get the fuck out of my life!"

Mom yelled. "Anna, te dije que llamaras a la policia."

"Phoebe, get out of here. Leave me alone," he shouted, lunging at me with his knife, slashing the air beside my face. I threw the can to deflect the weapon as he raised it for another stab at me, and then with the strength of St. Joan of Arc, I grabbed his wrist with my right hand. Only because he was so drunk, was I able to snatch the knife away with my left hand before knocking him down. He grabbed my leg. "No Daddy, please. Don't hurt me!" were the last words I heard as he pulled me down, my back slamming onto the floor, knocking the wind out of me. His weight crushed me as Grandma's red and purple rage flared, her screeching for him to stop. I saw stars before blacking out.

My head throbbed when I came to, finding him curled up next to me on the floor. I panicked, wondering if he might have hurt me even worse than I could tell, but then I noticed him clutching his stomach as blood and other squirmy stuff squirted out between his fingers, seeping onto the old, already-stained carpet.

"Ay, no!" Mom turned, glaring at me. "Bueno para nada! Now look what you've done." She crawled over to kneel by him, throwing me off to the side. I was good for nothing.

I got up and ran to my bedroom where I cried without making noise. Still holding the knife, I noticed the slash and bloodstains now on my JC Penney Easter dress. *You see, Grandma.* I stripped out of the dress and tossed it into the wastebasket. *This is all your fault!* I had no choice except to escape this hellhole.

Suddenly, I wanted to get back to that girl in the park with long red-brown hair like mine, the one who said, "Hello pretty one. Peace and love to you." I needed to find the girl in the mirror looking back at me with the love in her heart shining through.

CHAPTER 6

Pretty Girl, Cease to Exist

I thought about calling my cousin Teddie, but I didn't want to wake a sleeping bear. I'd wait until daylight.

"Darling, no need to air our dirty laundry once more," Grandma said. "Go home."

"Talk about dirty laundry. You never minded when Mom's family washed and ironed your clothes or polished your silver or took care of the child you practically abandoned. And then you had them all deported!"

"Anna, that's not true."

But in my search for the truth about my grandfather's death, after the Crash of '29, I'd learned how my dad's family did have something to do with my mother's family getting deported to Mexico during the '30s "Repatriation" of Mexicans and Mexican-Americans. My mother told me the story of the morning she'd been in their Glendale kitchen having breakfast with her mother Antonia and brother Teodoro. My mom, little Teresita, only five at the time, had been in kindergarten, her brother in second grade.

The morning started the same as any other weekday beginning with Abuela Antonia hand-making tortillas for breakfast before they all headed up to the big house to fetch little Charley LeMar, and then taking them all to school. My father and mother had grown up together and were now in the same kindergarten class.

My Mexican grandparents Antonia Verdugo and her husband Pedro Marquez had worked for my white grandparents, the LeMars, for many years, at first to pay back a loan for land taxes. Apparently, the property, once part of the big Verdugo land grant, had been purchased in 1921 by my Grandfather LeMar, a small attached portion still owned by the Marquez family. Even after the loan got repaid, because Grandpa Marquez loved working the land and tending the orchards, he stayed on in Grandpa LeMar's employ, even after Grandpa LeMar's untimely death. If you asked me, Grandma Phoebe remarried George way too soon. After that, my abuela Antonia practically raised my father.

Anyway, Grandpa Marquez had been working in the orchard the morning when some armed men in uniform approached him and told him to get in the car. At the same time, Teresita had just bitten into her tortilla, butter dripping down her chin, when men in uniform stood on the porch shouting at Antonia and her children to come out and get in the car. From the backseat, Antonia was confused. "But we're legal," she said. "We were born here. This is our property. We work hard. We pay taxes."

Antonia was horrified because, at the same time, she knew her husband had not been born here. Teresita, terrified, asked what they'd done wrong. It wasn't until a few days after they got out of a crowded jail cell with no food or toilets that my mother saw her father again. Reunited, they were all put on a train and deposited somewhere south of the border. Teresa never saw Charley again until some fifteen years later.

Not until she was older did my mother learn that it had been my father's stepfather George who had reported the Marquez family to the authorities. He then subdivided the property where they lived, selling it to pay off his gambling debts. Allegedly, Grandma Phoebe had been dealt out of George's shenanigans. Apparently, when she learned what had happened, she sent the family money in Mexico—only to assuage her guilt, my mother would say later. "He was your husband," Mom retorted, as if she'd ever been able to control her own husband, my father.

But then, in the '40s, the Bracero Program issued temporary US work permits to millions of Mexicans to come back and work due to a labor shortage caused by the war. Except for my Uncle Teodoro, everyone returned to Salinas, "the Salad Bowl of the World." That's where my parents reunited one day, my dad having just been discharged from the Navy and needing work.

Of all the strawberry fields in all of the world, he ran into Teresa, in a Salinas strawberry field, but that's another story written before this one, a story that might have ended differently, had my grandfather not been killed.

★ ★ ★

A squawking mockingbird jangled my nerves before the first light. In the bowels of Verdugo Park, perched on a huge river stone inside the cold tunnel, I'd snatched at a stingy sleep, shivering until dawn, my head throbbing the whole time. I stood, hiking my gown before squatting to pee over the sound of frogs and then, emerging like a tadpole, I adjusted my eyes to the new day and sidestepped a spider's web at the exit. Grandma spider lady already had me in her web.

A brown bunny scampered across a bed sheet of white frost covering the ground. I stomped my feet to get my blood going, and as I blew to defrost icicle fingers, I could see my little puffs of breath. My hands were freezing; my nail beds were blue. I panicked. Am I dying?

"No, you just need to eat," Grandma said, "so we can live."

I'd rather die. I grinned, thinking I still had control over whether I ate or not. I stuffed my hands into my sweater pocket and felt the little chocolate Easter egg I'd saved and reluctantly popped it into my mouth, the juices coming alive in my mouth when I realized I was still in my nightgown. Reaching into my knapsack, I grabbed the hand-sewn maxi skirt and slipped it on over my gown. I then trudged over onto the highway to wait with my guitar and knapsack strapped to my back. How hard could it be? Stick out your thumb, a car stops and, it's strawberry fields forever.

"Anna, you're a smart girl—not so street smart. Let's go back. This can all be fixed."

"Like I'm your little pot of liquid gold used to repair our broken family and make us stronger. I'm not one of your fancy antique vases."

I decided not to call my cousin—at least, not yet. I stuck out my thumb.

★ ★ ★

After a while, a dusty green Ford Econoline van pulled over. Behind the wheel sat a young woman. Her long frizzy braids swung pendulum-like across her lap and a cigarette poked out of the skinny leather band tied around her forehead. In the passenger seat sat a girl with long, licorice-colored hair, probably around my age. A hand pulled back the curtains on a small porthole-type window on the side of the van. Through the smudged glass I made out some others in the back gawking at me like tiny goldfish inside a giant fish bowl. The driver's bangled arm reached across to tap the passenger who rolled down the window. "Dig the maxi. Where you headed, babe?" the driver asked, leaning toward me.

Flattered out of any good sense, I answered, "Griffith Park."

Inside, I heard someone say, "Us, too." The hand closed the curtain and the side door slid open, blasting out a haze of smoke. The interior reeked of body odor and pot, that same skunky smell in Dad's garage. "Hop in."

Gurgling crept up my windpipe. "Anna, call Teddie. Don't get in! It's all my fault."

No argument there. But there was no swimming back upstream for this little salmon. As I climbed in, the oyster light on the ceiling went out. I took a moment for my eyes to make friends with the dark before finding a spot amongst the others. The van lurched forward and I stumbled to the floor, landing directly across from a dark-haired man seated cross-legged on the floor.

"Meet Charlie," the driver said.

Somewhere in his thirties, maybe my father's age, he sat between a raven-haired girl and an acne-faced boy. Across him sat a blonde Barbie-look-alike. Every cell in my body sparked at the sight of the man in the dark with my father's name. I had the burning sensation I'd just jumped out of the proverbial frying pan into the fire.

"What's your name?" Charlie asked. I dared to look through the curtain of my hair as the light from the windshield bounced off his dark, searing eyes.

Alarms sounded in my gut, signaling my brain something wrong. So far out of my element, I felt as if I'd been hit by a tsunami of oddballs, choking and drowning inside this sinking ship. Grandma Phoebe had always been super sensitive to these signs, something she always nagged me about. *Anna, trust your instincts,* she shrieked white in my head now. I shouldn't have been here. I reached into my pocket to feel for my packet of matches. *Don't talk to this man. He could be dangerous.*

But he looked scrawny, under a white T-shirt, baggy jeans, and black boots, like I could take him. Patting the knife under my skirt, I tried to calm down and stop shaking. Being homeschooled hadn't prepared me for this. I had no social skills or any practice on how to have a proper conversation with most humans, much less a man. If only people were as easy for me to diagram as those sentences Mamá had me work on—mostly so she could understand subject and predicate. *See Dick Run.* Anything I'd learned about relationships came from witnessing my parents' twisted interactions and those sneak peeks at the Million Dollar Movies when they left me home alone. Wasn't everyone a macho mobster? Didn't everyone talk like Bogey and Bacall in *Key Largo*?

"Your name?" he asked again. "I heard you talking to Caroline, so I know you're not deaf." So that's the driver's name.

I remembered Nora in *Key Largo* did a lot without saying much. "What's it to you?" I replied, stiffening like a petrified clown fish, yet trying to appear self-assured and shark-like powerful, as if I could go it alone without Grandma. And then he laughed, spittle splashing my face, the crevasse in his chin growing wide enough to swallow a minnow.

"Anna," I murmured, before adding, "you have my dad's name." Immediately, I regretted volunteering this unnecessary information.

"Hear that everyone, her old man's name is Charlie."

"Her old man's name is Charlie," Pimple Boy repeated, trying to light a joint.

Smirking, Charlie leaned in a little closer. "If Dad's anything like me, it's no wonder you're inside this van. Is he the reason you're running away?"

It felt like a bucket of ice cubes got dumped down my back. "I just want to go enjoy the music," I responded, tapping my guitar, my heart thrumming.

The crack of his laugh could have pierced my eardrums. "How sweet. You dig music. Child, play us a tune."

"I'm not a child." A little unruffled duck on the surface, but beneath, I kicked my Mary Janes frantically.

Sneering now, eyes like a measuring tape, he sized me up. "Oh, no? Shouldn't you be home playing with your baby dolls?"

"I never played with dolls."

He laughed. "How old are you, anyway?"

Grandma spoke. "Old enough to know better."

But I wasn't old enough, and I didn't know better. Worried, I sat straight, and suddenly, my skin didn't seem to fit. "Eighteen," I lied, as if that would have made a difference to him. I hugged my guitar closer, a not-so-subtle indication that I wouldn't be taking the stage today. He reached out and plucked the guitar from my hands. I had no choice but to let it go. A peg caught the hem of my skirt as I handed it over, exposing the knife poking out of top of my knee-sock.

A wicked sneer spread across his face. "Smart girl," he said, pointing to my weapon.

I pulled down my skirt, sensing he somehow had the ability to smell fear.

"You know how to use that thing?"

"The knife?"

He nodded, giving the others an exasperated look.

I still wasn't quite sure how I'd managed to stab my father, but truly it didn't take a genius to know how to use it. "I didn't know it came with instructions."

A smile that didn't match his steely cold eyes spread above his stubbly chin. "You're funny," he said, whipping a pocketknife out of its buckskin sheath.

Charged, I kept my wits about me. "Classic Buck knife manufactured after the Japanese attacked Pearl Harbor. (I knew my knives, part of Dad's homeschooling lessons—knives and guns.) It's actually been around since—"

"For the love of God," Charlie said. "What are you?"

I couldn't stop my mouth or the rush I got conversing with this stranger. "And, what are you, a cop?" I'd been treading deep waters, but now I'd sunk pretty deep.

He spit out a bitter laugh. "No, kid," he said. "The only thing fascist pigs are good for is protecting society against niggers and Mexicans."

Those words skewered my bleeding heart. "My mother is Mexican," I said, defensively, reaching for my knife.

"You don't say. You can pass for white." He laughed, as if that made it all better.

No longer just trembling, my mixed blood heated up and I sensed an urgency to get the hell out of there before it was too late. It was the sort of talk I'd heard in my messed-up home—Dad always badmouthing the police, society and yelling at Walter Cronkite on the television news. He despised anyone who was different than he was. Marrying my mom, according to her, a Mexican, only softened him a little while giving him a false sense of superiority. It made me sad to hear the way my father talked about others and it sickened me to think he was referring to that half of me that was my Mom, never mind the part of me that was also my Grandma. I couldn't believe I'd merely traveled a couple of miles only to run into someone like Dad. Were all men the same? Mom said they were. Compared to my father, though, this Charlie seemed saintly. I knelt and leaned toward the cab of the van. "Say, Caroline. Can you pull over and let me out? Anywhere's fine."

"Sort of hard to do on the freeway," she yelled, cigarette dangling from her lips.

She smiled into the rearview mirror and I sat back to find Charlie strumming my guitar. "Here's a little ditty I've been working on," he said.

Pretty girl, pretty pretty girl
Cease to exist
Just, come an' say you love me
Give up, your world . . .
My blood froze.

"He's meeting some music people in LA," Barbie said, passing me a joint. "Remember the name Manson. He's going to be bigger than the Beatles."

Anna, don't! Grandma screamed inside my head. I hated her telling me what to do, but the last thing I needed right now was to lose control of my senses. I turned down the weed, besides the van reeked enough for me to get high, anyway.

. . . Submission is a gift

Go on give it to your brother . . .

Bigger than the Beatles, huh? Charlie finished his song, everyone clapped, Barbie swooning over him as if he was Elvis. He handed back my guitar. "So, what did you think, Guitar Girl?"

Me? I think I want to get out of there. I covered my mouth, feeling Grandma coming on like a sneeze, but nothing I could do would stop her. "Colonel Scott would be quite proud."

My hands tingled and the hair on my arms went into shock. *Who's Colonel Scott?*

Charlie opened his mouth like a bottom-feeding flounder before turning white as cod. "How'd you know about the Colonel? How'd you know my father's name?"

Just as surprised, I covered my face with my hands and shook my head. There's no way I could have known about his father, much less his name, but apparently Grandma did. I looked around at the curious faces staring at me as the words dumped out of my mouth. "Oh, darling, I know lots of dead people."

"What the fuck!?" Charlie yelled.

What the fuck!? I held up my guitar to shield myself from what might come.

"What else? How do you know about my old man?"

"Nothing else, honestly."

Charlie cocked his head, peering at me as he leaned in. I thought he'd try and shake information out of me, like I was a box of Cracker Jacks or something.

"What kind of freak show did you run away from?" he asked.

Grandma spoke up in a mauve-colored voice. "We're a little tired right now. Perhaps, we can schedule a little tête-à-tête another time."

"We?" Charlie backed off, slowly, looking at us sideways. "You got a mouse in your pocket?"

I snapped my eyes closed. *Grandma, shut up.*

Things got quiet. He returned to his singing and strumming. *Pretty, pretty girl.*

★ ★ ★

It's sure taking an eternity to get to Griffith Park. I rested my head on my knees, imagining Grandma and I had freaked Charlie out when we talked about his father, and that was why he left us alone to work on his tunes which caused Grandma to tune out for the next several miles so I got some time to myself to try and figure out my next move. I worried about my family. I'd miss helping Michael get ready for his First Holy Communion ceremony. I'd told him not to be scared and that it was no big deal, that I'd be right there if he got too nervous. And then, I cast my mind back to my own special day, remembering how sad I was that Dad, too hungover, wasn't there for me. And now I wouldn't be showing up for Michael.

But then the dam broke, tears soaking my maxi dress as I wondered if Dad was okay. Just because Grandma said he was fine didn't make it so, unless she could see the future, but what about the past? Couldn't she see the damage her husband, my grandfather, had caused everyone by transferring over, including and most especially, my dad? How many lives were lost or ruined because of Grandpa's selfish desire to live on through his own son so he could be with Grandma and also get revenge over his death. Couldn't he simply wait for her to die and then join him wherever he ended up? And once you're dead, do you really care about getting revenge? And now what about me?

"Grandma, how did you know about Manson's father?"

"It's just another of the gifts I was born with—the ability to send messages to loved ones from the other side. It's one of the reasons I know your father is still alive. He hasn't contacted me."

I felt some relief, but still some skepticism.

"Why, people used to come to the house all the time and ask to talk to their mothers, fathers, sons, daughters, even their pets, but unfortunately it doesn't work that way. It's only a one-way street."

"So, Colonel Scott wants to say something to his son?"

"He wants to warn him."

"About what?" I asked.

"Oh, darling, I don't know. Just because we die doesn't mean we become clairvoyant. Had I been given the special gift of knowing the future, surely we wouldn't be sitting in the back of this filthy motor wagon with this Wisenheimer."

True. And had she known, maybe she wouldn't have hijacked my body in the first place. I sensed danger up ahead and needed to find a way out through the doorway and not just the one at the back of my mind.

I got on my knees to peek out the small window and sensed a bigger storm brewing on the horizon.

★ ★ ★

After a while, I couldn't keep my eyes open. Besides not getting any sleep the night before, the fumes were getting to me and finally I drifted off. I dreamed I was dead and woke up in a bus full of angels headed to heaven. Piercing through big fluffy clouds, a peaceful feeling came over me until a dark-haired man I believed was Jesus took the wheel and turned the bus around, headed to hell. Ready to scream, I heard, "Pit stop. Who's got money?" Caroline asked.

Without thinking, I reached into my knee-sock to hand her most of what I had.

The side van door opened and everyone piled out. I noticed a payphone just beyond a gas pump outside a general store. I wanted to call home and ask about Dad, but then I felt a tug on my blouse and turned to see Charlie's hand clutching it. Heart stopped, I looked up. "Take the crazy girl with you and get her something to eat," he told the dark-haired girl. His eyes latched onto mine. "Although the closer to the bone, the sweeter the meat."

Shoulders shrugged, the girl escorted me to the restroom.

"How much longer until we get to Griffith Park?" I asked, shivering as I opened the door to the stall.

"Oh, we passed there hours ago," she said. "We're headed to San Francisco."

What!? San Francisco? "I thought he was meeting some music people in Los Angeles."

"Charlie has to meet someone up there first."

As I exited the bathroom and headed toward the phone booth, I heard Caroline shouting, "Everyone back in the van." The girl grabbed my hand, pulling me back.

"But I want to call home."

"Next stop," she said.

Inside the van, Caroline handed out a brown bag full of food. My stomach gurgled. "We're taking the scenic route," she said, and we were off again, but the only scene I had was in the back of the stinky van with the communal snacks and drinks.

We continued rolling on through velvety green hills of mustard seed plants and fields of cows. Poppies erupted along the road, but then after a few more miles of twists and turns, I felt crummy. The front windows were rolled down and I could feel the crisp ocean breeze and smell the mix of sweet pine and briny air. But it didn't help. "I'm going to be sick," I yelled, clapping my hand over my mouth. Caroline swerved off the road and as soon as the door was opened, I threw up. Too weak to run, I still thought about it.

"Why don't you ride up front with me," Caroline said. I reached for my guitar and backpack, readying for the next chance I'd get to run away. "Keep your eyes on the horizon."

Wiping a tear away with the back of my hand, I wanted to go home.

"Yes, darling. Let's go home. I'm sure they miss you," Grandma thought-whispered. "I'm sure they have learned their lesson."

I had my doubts. "If you'd learned any lessons back when you were alive, you wouldn't have come back to bother us," I thought back. I didn't think taking up space in my head and butting in on the family gave her any more insight and our situation certainly wasn't anything she could fix. "From what I read of your religion you're supposed to let go of earthly possessions."

"Oh, but I did, darling. I left everything to the family. I left you the piano."

"But, I think that meant all earthly relationships, too. When you die, isn't the end goal to be happy and have peace at last? Didn't you suffer enough—with Dad, especially?"

"Oh, dear, I'm a mother. You never stop worrying."

"Well, if that's the case, trust me, I'll never be one." I stared through the bug-splattered windshield, the sun setting behind the ominous dark mountain we were climbing. "I have enough to worry about."

About an hour later, except where the headlights shown, everything turned pitch black. "We're not going to make Big Sur tonight," Caroline said, pulling off the road. "We'll sleep here tonight." I remembered seeing a book of matches on the dashboard. I grabbed them.

My heart nearly blasted out of my rib cage. I'm not sleeping anywhere near this scary man. Caroline walked around to the back of the van and gathered some blankets. "Follow me," she said, and we trailed her to a patch of grass where she spread the blankets. I sat down, struck a match, and inhaled to calm myself while looking back at the van and feeling sorry for Barbie who'd chosen to stay behind. Maybe she hoped he'd buy her a dreamhouse someday.

"She's made her bed," Grandma said.

CHAPTER 7

Be Sure to Wear Flowers

At dawn, I woke to the sound of seagulls, and waves crashing onto the rocky shore. A memory surfaced of our family vacation one summer to Big Sur. Dad's booze had kept him warm while the rest of us practically froze to death in cheap sleeping bags. I'd climbed out to go pee along the creek running through the campground. In the creek, a water snake slithered by. I bolted up midstream pee and ran back to the campfire. Dad said it was a killer electric eel. He told me that instead of using their eyes, they emitted a weak electric signal like radar to find a mate or prey. I dove back into my sleeping bag.

The ache in my head had dulled, but I felt damp, cold, and needed to pee. Giant pines spiked through a thin mist like tall, skinny witches cloaked in hoary shawls. The others were still asleep as I got up to go squat behind a tree. I hoped there were no eels out there. I'd held so much in, I thought I'd wake the others with the loud sound streaming from me, but then I saw the flash of twin electric lights and I heard the sound of an engine. A Volkswagen bug pierced through the fog, appearing like an alien spacecraft out of the *Wizard of Mars*. It pulled over to the side of the road. The engine stopped. Squeezing the last drops, I yanked up my underwear and hurried back to grab my things.

Running toward the little yellow car, I had no time to worry about what kind of Martians might be in the vehicle.

A young tow-headed couple sat in the front seat and by the time I reached the Beetle, the woman had emerged holding a baby and then walked around to the trunk at the front of the car. She appeared to be a little older than me, at least I assumed so since she had a baby.

Panting from the frantic dash over, I announced myself so I wouldn't scare her. "Hello ma'am?"

She looked up, still clutching a diaper pin in her mouth. Smiling, she removed it. "Ma'am? I'm not that old. Although today, I feel ancient."

"I'm sorry. Please, I need a ride," I said, turning to look behind me. I didn't see anyone stirring just yet, but there was no time to waste by explaining my situation.

She stabbed the pin into the diaper and then picked the baby up out of the trunk. "As you can see, there's not that much room with the baby and all."

"Please. I just need to get away from here." I hooked a shaky thumb toward the van. "From them."

She peered at me before looking beyond my shoulder, nodding. "Far out, I'll tell Ben."

In the back seat of the cramped Beetle, there was more room to breathe than in the van I'd just escaped. Betsy's blue eyes, hard to miss, called attention even behind the quiet, almost invisible eyelashes. Tiny colorful beads strung onto gold chains dangled from her ears as she moved her head, constantly. I'd learn she couldn't talk without moving her body and she couldn't sit without talking; boy could she talk.

"Again, I'm Betsy and this is—" She giggled. "Well, I already said, Ben." With a blond buzz cut, Ben, now holding the baby, looked like he might only be a year or so older than Betsy. She turned toward Ben, unbuttoned her blouse, exposing full breasts, and then reached for the baby. My face burned as if flames the size of dollar pancakes had flown out of her nipples. I'd seen my mother nurse my siblings, but she'd always been very discreet. The baby latched on as if she hadn't eaten for days. "She's Poppy. Almost a year old," Betsy said, kissing the top of the baby's head, a shock of translucent white hair sticking out like a scared dandelion.

"That's a cute name. I'm Anna."

"Far out. Nice to meet you, Anna."

"So, this is not a test but, how old are you and where are you from?"

"Eighteen. Glendale. It's in Los Angeles."

"Yeah, I know. I was born in Beverly Hills before we moved to Arroyo Grande where my father opened a medical practice." She cleared her throat. "Well, a psychiatry practice. Ben's from Oakland. We met in Ethnic Studies at Cal Poly."

"Good ole Cal Poly, the most conservative college in the world," Ben chimed in. "I had no idea how hayseed SLO was. Man, I should've gone to Santa Cruz or UCSF where all the action is."

"But then we wouldn't have met," Betsy said, reaching out to caress his arm. "Besides, you only have one more year," she said, turning toward me. "He's going to be an engineer."

"If Nam doesn't get me first," Ben said, turning the dial on the radio.

"Talk about action. And that's why we're headed up to San Francisco. To protest the nasty war," Betsy said, as if she had the power to move mountains, stop bullets.

"Are you communists?" I asked, recalling how my father called draft dodgers commies. Even though he hadn't volunteered. Grandma had simply given him no choice but to join the Navy on his seventeenth birthday.

They laughed and Ben slapped the steering wheel. "We're conscientious objectors," Betsy said, switching the baby to her right breast. "We can no longer remain silent in the face of such cruel manipulation of the minorities." She sounded like she'd been rehearsing a speech, like she was Mrs. Martin Luther King, Jr., or something.

This young fair, blue-eyed couple didn't look like minorities, per se. They weren't dark-skinned like Mom or my cousins or the families at Cristo Del Rey or those singers like Diana Ross and the Supremes.

"You're very beautiful," Betsy said, peering at me. "Isn't she Ben?" My whole body ignited like church penny candles.

Ben, still fiddling with the radio, glanced at the rearview mirror. "Sure."

I looked away.

"Exotic. What's your background?" Betsy asked.

"American."

"I mean—"

Even though I could be quite naïve, I knew what she meant. "My dad's white. My mom's Mexican."

"A mixed-marriage. Far out." She said "far out" a lot and for just about everything like if I'd have said, my dad's Martian and my mom's Klingon, she'd have said "far out," and then in that case it might apply.

Far out, if you say so. The jury is still out on that one. Mostly, when I went out with my parents, some people just stared at us. Mom would get angry and whisper things like "Gringos estupidos, trailer trash," or "Okies." She'd read *Grapes of Wrath*, but for some reason she had some bias against the poor white people from Oklahoma who'd also migrated here looking for work during the Dust Bowl.

"Do you know how many Mexicans or African-Americans are enrolled at our school?" Ben asked. "How about Harvard? Berkeley? What about just poor people in general?"

I shrugged. As far as I knew, there'd been no plans for me to go to college. My parents couldn't even afford to give me a quinceañera party. But what did it matter? I was that special daughter groomed to either get married or take care of them into old age.

"How many of them do you think have been drafted?"

More than the educated, rich white people? "I have no idea."

"We've been following the teachings of Dr. Martin Luther King," Betsy said, and I nodded to show interest. "He talks about how racism is still deeply rooted all over America." She placed the baby on her shoulder to pat her back. "His wife Coretta says women are the backbone of the Civil Rights Movement. Have you heard them speak?"

I'd just heard King on the television last week, but before I could answer, the baby burped, spitting out breast milk and thankfully taking Betsy's attention away for the moment to clean up the mess. I looked out the window, remembering.

Holy Thursday meatloaf and mashed potato night, the night before Good Friday fishsticks and fries. My family had gathered around the dinner table with the evening news blaring in the background as usual. "Didn't Johnson just sign that Civil Rights bill?" Dad said as I finished setting the table. He took his knife and stabbed into the meatloaf. "And they got their voting rights. Now what do they want?" he asked as Mom walked in from the kitchen carrying a pot of mashed potatoes.

"Didn't I just see another warning sign down on Harvey Drive saying, 'Darkie, don't let the sun go down on you in our town'?" she asked, and I sensed the leading question—leading to trouble.

"As long as you're home by dinner, you should be fine," Dad snickered.

"Cabrón," Mom said, slopping down a spoonful of mashed potatoes onto his plate, splashing his face. Dad didn't know yet about her GED classes. He thought she'd been hanging out at some Bible study meeting. She'd have me drive her to the high school once a week and wait for her.

She marched back into the kitchen just before Dad threw his plate after her. The plate crashed against the wall, the ketchup like blood dripping down.

"Teresa, come back here," he yelled, wiping the food off his face, the chair scraping the floor as he got up to follow her into the kitchen. "Just joking."

I tried to swallow the noise. Every night an explosion of words or an eruption of more of the same old vitriol about how Dad thought he was better than Mom. "Son of a bitch," she yelled from the kitchen. Fighting words.

"Don't you call me that!"

I went and sat in front of the "boob tube," as Dad called it.

"Dammit Anna, come sit back down. And eat!" He returned with a can of beer. It was only Thursday; he wouldn't be waiting until the next day to get drunk.

"I'm not hungry and I want to listen." I dared to stand up for myself. I wanted to understand what we were doing in Vietnam and what Dr. King said about the connection between the war and the struggles in America. *Like home.*

"Turn that shit off." He popped open his Pabst Blue Ribbon, his fat stomach bulging, like a bowl of mashed potatoes, under his white T-shirt.

Mom took her place across from him. "Anna, get over here and clean up this mess."

★ ★ ★

The inside of the tiny car felt toasty. Even through the static on the radio, I heard bits and pieces about Vietnam, sensing a certain irony. The war had seemed so foreign to me from inside the four walls of our violent family room in Glendale and yet that's where Mom and Dad argued over every little thing, where you had to duck and cover, step lightly so as not to set off a grenade. I traced a smiley face on the back steamed-up window.

The baby fell asleep, and as I helped settle her in the back seat next to me, her little mouth puckered as if she was still nursing.

"They're killing babies," Betsy said, switching off the radio dial.

"What?"

"War is the enemy of the poor," she added, twisting around to look at me.

"Lord, I thought she was done talking," Grandma said.

"What?" Betsy asked.

I fake coughed. "You were talking? Who's 'killing babies'?"

"They're using children as soldiers. There used to be hope but now the government is focused on Vietnam and it's taking our young people. Sucking away their money and skills. So, you see, the war is an enemy of the poor. Americans speak of peace and yet continue to drop bombs on the poor, weak nation. What this does is take the focus off the poor, disenfranchised people of America." Betsy barely took a breath in between sentences. "They're killing babies," she said again.

I perked up. Had I heard correctly?

Ben reached over to tap her thigh and said, "Babe, make love not war." Betsy looked at him adoringly. "Enough of the news broadcast, let's listen to some music for a while."

"Sorry," she whispered, reaching over to turn the radio back on.

"I thought she'd never be quiet," Grandma whispered as the engine purred along.

I wiped the smiley face off the window to look out. That song about silence being golden came on. Ben and Betsy looked at each other, laughed, and then sang along. So much for silence.

* * *

They were a nice, smart, and beautiful couple who would give me so much to think about. On this short road trip, I'd learn more about everything from family, peace, the pill, and the state of affairs than I would from my parents or the television world news. Even though they spoke of war, their tone toward each other calmed me. It sounded as if she were the melody and he the harmony. And even though they were strangers whom I'd only traveled with for a couple of hours, they made me feel safe. Now I could get a different perspective on the world, and even a different take on how to have a civil discussion—meaning just continue to let others do most of the talking—without any bloodshed.

But maybe I should go back and try harder at this peace thing, starting at home, I thought as I balled up my sweater making a pillow to lean my head on.

"Yes, good idea. Let's," Grandma said.

Back home, Grandma always talked about how making peace with the past would make us all better, and yet she continued to drop bombs on me by bringing up her bygone days, like when Dad was put in the Navy hospital after an attempted suicide. "Oh, darling, he was never meant to go to war."

And what Betsy had said about the poor also made me wonder about how I'd grown up poor, Mom having to take a housecleaning job behind Dad's back. And yet we were surrounded by so many fancy things and—Grandma bubbled up now inside my head interrupting my thoughts for the millionth time. "Yes, darling, and don't forget your grandfather and I worked hard for everything you inherited." She meant my murdered grandfather, not Dad's stepfather George. "We created a better world filled with opportunities for the family. You should be thankful and feel privileged."

What I felt was anger and also the shame of not being appreciative for being so much better off than those poor people I saw on the television every night. At least I had a roof over my head, never mind it was a head where Grandma also dwelled. But Mom and Dad worked hard, too. Mom's family worked very hard.

"Oh yes, of course, they worked for us; such humble people. Antonia was the best cook and there was nothing Pedro couldn't grow or fix." Grandma was talking about my other set of Mexican grandparents.

I wondered if Grandma was upset because my Mexican mother was now the queen of what used to be Grandma's castle. Besides love, one of the perks of marrying Dad, Mom told me, was that she became queen of a castle built on land once owned by her people, the Verdugos.

"Don't be silly, Anna. I loved your mother."

"Before or after you stole their land and had their family kicked out?"

"Darling, I've told you, I had nothing to do with that," Grandma said, her internal tone pulsing an exasperated magenta.

"But when you found out what George had done, what did you do to fix things?"

Betsy, eyebrows knitted together, turned a sidelong look. "Fix what things? Who's George?" I fake coughed again, turning my head toward the window, and tried to silence Grandma.

"I divorced him. He went to prison. I had a son to raise. It wasn't easy."

"Oh, like it was easy being his daughter?"

"I know it's not enough, but it's my goal to make living amends."

"Except that you're sort of dead." And unfortunately, that's where I'd come into the story sixteen years ago. Just a little collateral damage, I'd say.

"I promise. You'll see once we go home."

But going home was not a possibility if the police were after me.

★ ★ ★

After some time, I woke to the sound of the car door slamming. The engine was off. I heard the wind whistling. Through the window, I saw Betsy fighting the gust as she set food out on a picnic table at the edge of a cliff. In the center of the table, wildflowers sprouted from an empty soda bottle that served to anchor down part of a tablecloth. They were making a family holiday out of their trip to protest a war.

Feeling like an uninvited ant at a picnic, I hesitated to join them until my hunger finally won out. "There's plenty," Betsy said, handing me a bologna sandwich. I thanked her, taking a seat across from Ben as she ate standing with the baby at her hip.

Ben then relieved Betsy of her motherly duties. "Having a baby, sure changes things," he said, bouncing Poppy.

I smiled, appreciating the fact that he talked to me like a grown-up.

"My draft number was twenty-three, but I have another year until my deferment takes effect. I'll get to be here for her first birthday."

Betsy finished chewing. "I missed my birth control pill one day and voila, she's what happened." She gazed at her daughter. "It was my decision to go forward with the pregnancy. Not everyone gets a choice."

"We did discuss it," Ben added with a smile. "But in the end, it's still your body."

"My parents are so upset, but mostly because we put the cart before the horse."

I peered at her, tilting my head. "We aren't married," she said, holding out her left hand. "Mother always dreamed of a big wedding at the country club."

"We don't need a piece of paper," Ben said. "Why marry only to get divorced? What we need to do is divorce from society."

"Oh, but wouldn't Poppy make a cute flower girl?" She reached up to pinch Poppy's chubby cheeks. "Oh, wouldn't you?"

As their attention turned to their daughter, I finished my lunch and walked over to the edge of the cliff, gripping my hair as the wind swept up, my head spinning as I imagined what Mom would've said about me hanging around this "immoral" couple with a child out of wedlock. "Tan disgraciados." I knew how the church stood against birth control, and even more against sex outside of marriage. And I also knew how Mom followed the church's teachings, picking and choosing from a divine smorgasbord those beliefs that worked best for her.

"What I never understood about your mother was why she had so many children," Grandma said suddenly. "Those Mexican Catholics just love a big family."

"Grandma, remember I'm also half!" I recalled the moment she'd compared my light skin to that of my siblings. It made me sick being separated from the fold.

"After your brother, the doctor, warned her not to have any more."

"Anymore what? Brownies? Jesus, can't I just have this moment to think to myself? I'm sure she would have stopped if she could have," I said, wondering, if it hadn't been for that foam stuff and that red douche bag Mom had hanging in the shower, who knows how many more she might have had.

"All it did was burden my Charley further."

"Oh, for God's sake." As if it weren't bad enough sharing Grandma's mind, sometimes I imagined what my mother might say. I wanted to explode when I found myself constantly taking up her defense against Grandma Phoebe, against the white world. "Like he didn't have a part in all of this? Like he's the one who had to carry heavy bowling balls in his stomach around five times, go through morning sickness. Swell up like a blimp. Be cut open with Josie. I never even saw him change a single diaper. He was the one who cried when I was born a girl and then he wouldn't let Mom give up until she gave him a boy!" My heart raced.

"He was never fit to be a father."

"And maybe that was just a reflection of you!"

Grandma went cricket silent.

How could Mom let him be in charge of her own body, like she was his property. When it came to the number of children, Grandma and Mom were both wrong. If I were to have children, which I wasn't, I'd have only two, one for each hand, not five for each . . . what . . . finger? Who needs more than five fingers on one hand anyway? And, definitely not an only child, one is an accident like Dad. One is the loneliest number, but then again, one of five can be even lonelier. A strong gust nearly lifted me off the ground. I moved away from the cliff, hugging myself and rubbing my arms to get warm.

"She had a choice." I couldn't believe my ears. "Charley was not equipped to be a husband, much less a father. You were born and I had to do something."

Did Grandma honestly think she could do something by moving into my headspace to try to protect me and control her son? Suddenly, I wanted to jump off the cliff, but I wasn't quite sure about the consequences of suicide, like I knew it was a sin and sinners go to hell—but then, again, I might have been better off.

"She never should have had anymore. She could have left. From the beginning, I tried to warn her but she thought by giving him a boy, it would change things."

"Like what?"

"Like how to be the father he never had."

"Oh yeah?" Now I fumed. I looked up to see if Ben or Betsy might see smoke puffing out of my ears, but their eyes were seared onto Poppy. "And what I never understood was why you waited thirteen years to have my dad—an only child. What kind of birth control did *you* use, Grandma?"

"If the pill had been around, believe me, I would have taken it."

"What? Really?"

Grandma hushed after dropping this little bomb, as if she'd planted the seed, no pun intended, for me to learn more about the "pill." And since I already decided I'd never bring a child into this world, and I could never be a nun like Sister Bernadette, it was time to learn more. I'd take complete control of my own body. And now maybe, like Betsy, I'd never have to get married. Maybe I didn't have to be a wife! Maybe I'd be a lesbian!

"Darling, it's not something one chooses, like buying a new frock."

★　★　★

I wiped my eyes tearing from the cold and spotted some sea otters or dolphins out on the ocean. My mind cast back to the book I'd read as a child, *Island of the Blue Dolphins*, about a young Native American girl caught in between two worlds. I imagined what it would be like living by myself on an island but then I realized there'd always be Grandma like one of the fur trappers who'd invaded the tiny place. Sadly, the true story of the woman of the island was that she ended up dying within weeks of her capture. Free at last.

Above me big clouds cast giant inky shadows blanketing a sea of grey. Dad's accusatory electric eel eyes broke through and I turned away. In the distance, Ben and Betsy packed up.

Back in the car, Betsy, who loved to chat and mostly about herself and her view of the world, filled me in on everything without my ever having to ask. But I supposed that when you had a baby, there was no time for any sort of repartee, which was just fine by me. And then just as I thought how great that she hadn't even asked anything about me, except for my name and age, so that I wouldn't have to lie too much, she said, "So, tell us a little about you. Where did you say you went to school?"

I raised my voice over the sound of the car's engine. "I didn't say. I was homeschooled." I hoped this would be the end of the interrogation.

She shook her head. "Far out. I had to drop out myself. But I'm only twenty-two, so there's still time to take over Dad's practice someday. I wouldn't change a thing."

"And we won't bring another child into this world until there's peace," Ben said.

So different from how my father wouldn't let my mother stop bringing kids into the world until he got his boy. I looked at the cute baby girl, a shock of fine downy hair like her father's, deep serious eyes, inset like her mother's. I thought of all of my siblings and how we fought so much. There was no peace in our home, even after Michael, the boy, was born.

"Children are the future," said Betsy, patting Ben's lap, gazing out the window as if she'd swallowed a secret.

"I'd wager she's carrying another child," Grandma whispered. "After all, children are the future."

Grandma drove me crazy! What a contradiction after she'd just told me that if the pill were around when she was younger, she'd have taken it.

"But what kind of future will there be for her?" Ben said. "Unless we change things."

The baby, asleep now, whimpered, her brow furrowing. "She's chasing angels," Grandma said. "Oh, you used to be that small. I had so much hope for you. Big plans."

So that's what babies are for? Empty vessels raided by disappointed souls to fulfill unfinished dreams of a better life, a better future. I was the mirror Grandma held up to see her forgotten self.

"There's still time to change," Grandma said.

"What are you gonna change?" I blurted out loud.

"The world," Betsy said, not reacting to the voice. She pushed a loose strand of hair behind her ear. "We want to be a part of something bigger. Stand for something greater. Protest more than just the local supermarket for selling non-union grapes. Ben's going to be shipped off to Nam once he graduates, unless we can somehow stop the war. Stop the baby killing, rescue the child soldiers."

Child soldiers? Suddenly, I worried about my little brother, only seven, but if this war didn't end soon, or World War III got started, might he be drafted someday as a child soldier, too? Suddenly my problem with Grandma wasn't as big. I might figure out a way to handle her, but I wouldn't be able to save my little brother unless I did something, but I didn't know what just yet.

"The rally is next week. In the meantime, we're staying at Ben's family home in Oakland. His folks are vacationing in Acapulco. You're welcome to tag along," Betsy said.

Maybe I could make a difference?

CHAPTER 8

Dead Babies

We arrived late in the evening. Ben parked the car at the top of a steep hill in front of a three-story Victorian home with a gabled roof and a round tower that I imagined Rapunzel might pop out of to let down her hair. I crashed as soon as my head hit the goose feather pillow in an upstairs bedroom belonging to Ben's sister.

The next morning, in a cozy study across from the foyer, I paced the squeaky floorboards waiting for an answer on the telephone. A thin beam of sunlight cut through the window, illuminating rows upon rows of books like back home. I followed the trail of dust motes floating in the sunbeam's wake and landing upon *Wars I Have Seen* by Gertrude Stein.

"Hello? Is that you, Anna?" my little brother Michael hollered. "You went on a galaxy adventure without me?"

"Sorry." I heard my own breath fill the receiver before a clunk.

Maggie came on the line, breathless as if she'd raced Michael and lost. "Anna, where are you?"

"I'm in Oakland." I cut to the chase. "How's Dad doing?"

"He's all right. Just a little sore, but he's been much nicer to everyone lately. Even Mom is singing and dancing around the house."

I was happy for Mom, but hearing that hurt. Wasn't she worried about me? "So, then it's a good thing I left, huh?" I twirled around, the cord wrapping me serpent-like.

"Yeah, it seems like," she answered softly.

"Can I talk to her?"

"She's at work." So now Dad doesn't mind her working? "Wanna talk to Dad?"

"Yes," Grandma interrupted.

"No. Maybe later," I added quickly, untangling myself. I wasn't ready. I just wanted to know if he was okay. "Are the police looking for me?"

"I don't think so. Why?"

Well, first of all, because I'm a missing person and a minor, except that Mom obviously isn't missing me. "Because of Dad."

"Because he was so drunk, he fell on his own knife?" Maggie asked.

"Is that what he told the police?"

"I guess so," she said. "Anyway, I don't blame you for running away from this crazy house. I'll be out of here next. Where's Oakland, anyway?"

"Near San Francisco."

"That's so far away. When are you coming home?"

"I'm not sure. Please let Mom know I called."

"Okay. But in the meantime, can I borrow your Daniel Boone jacket?"

"Sure."

By the time I hung up the phone, the sun shone brightly on the lake's face, its rays filling the room with lots of natural light. But the city beyond sat in fog.

"Well, this is wonderful news. Now we can go home," Grandma said. "I told you he would be fine. I just sensed it."

Good news for sure and knowing I hadn't killed Dad certainly brought me a sense of relief. Now maybe I could focus on what to do with the rest of my life. I felt no urgency to return home, especially if my family didn't miss me, besides I still wasn't sure someone hadn't reported me missing, a runaway minor child, after all. I liked the idea of exploring a little more and even being in charge of my own destination, despite butting heads with Grandma.

"Let's go."

"You go. Why don't you just give me a break for a while? You owe me." I stepped toward the bookshelf and borrowed the book by Gertrude Stein.

"Ah, yes, good choice. I recall the time with Miss Stein and her girlfriend Alice in France when we all worked as volunteers during the First World War."

Of course, you did.

★ ★ ★

I volunteered to watch Poppy while Betsy and Ben were downtown working on a campaign to mobilize the big rally happening the next week. I had plenty of experience watching kids, but it wasn't my career path of choice, not that I had one.

By late morning, I discovered she loved going for walks where I pointed out the flowers, the cats in the windows, the dogs in the yards. Kitty says "meow." Doggie says "ruff." She repeated after me.

Back at the house, I played with her on the floor, read to her, and strummed my guitar, singing as many nursery songs as I could remember. *Twinkle, twinkle little star . . . Mairzy Doats and doazy doats and liddle lamzy divey . . .* She reached out for my guitar and plucked at the strings as I sang. *The wheels on the bus go round and round.* Finally, I let her hold it. *Frère Jacques, ding ding dong.*

By noon, I'd run out of songs. As soon as she yawned, I took her upstairs to her room where she fell asleep in my arms. I removed the rubber nipple from her mouth, her little lips still puckering, and dared to imagine what it might be like to have a baby of my own someday. Just as quickly as I envisioned this idea, I set her into her cradle and then stepped away, making sure to keep her door open so I could hear her. I tiptoed downstairs, noticing the upright walnut piano in the main parlor. I walked in, took a seat, placing my hands onto the cool smooth keys.

"Don't you miss your music?" Grandma asked.

I wouldn't admit that to her. She knew, anyway. I pushed off and left the room to wander.

The house, not as spacious as ours, certainly seemed grander with its fill of riches from all over the world and modern art that had been part of the "degenerate" art confiscated from the German museums by the Nazis. "So the story goes," Ben had told me as he gave me a tour of the house the night before, "the Nazis linked avant-garde art with disorder, democracy, and pacifism. The pieces were supposedly the culture documents of the decadent work of the Bolsheviks and Jews."

Ben told me his parents had purchased the paintings at an auction in Switzerland. "Turns out, part of the money was used to finance the Nazi party," he'd said. "But my parents said they honestly didn't know. They thought the money would go back to the museums from where they were stolen." He parked his hands on his hips, shaking his head. "Oh, the stories we're told."

I thought about all the fancy furniture and furnishings back home wondering where they came from and then I remembered Dad telling me how as a kid, he went with his stepdad to a meeting at the Nazi headquarters in a secret Glendale location.

I'd been a kid myself when he told me, and I didn't understand anything about Nazis and how their goal had been to eliminate Jews in Hollywood. I stared curiously at a vivid painting where naked Israelites danced like crazy in front of a golden cow. I remembered the Bible story of Moses who led the Israelites out of Egypt. Apparently, after Moses parted the Red Sea, he left to get the Ten Commandments and when he got back after forty days, his brother who'd been left in charge, created this golden cow to appease the followers who needed a new god to worship. Oh, the stories I was told.

"Don't you miss home?" Grandma asked.

"World traveler that you were, I'd have thought you'd like getting out."

"Oh, indeed, and it was my music that took me places like New York or Paris, even Bombay, but I was always chaperoned."

"Well la-di-da! Lucky for me I've got you as my chaperone."

"Your grandfather eventually built me the house and I made it our home."

"Somewhere he could keep the old lady in the shoe except without all the kids so you could keep your music career. Dad told me the story."

I stepped into the kitchen to fix myself some lunch. I opened the refrigerator and scrounged around.

"Anna—"

"Oh, I thought you were finished." I reached in for a juicy, ripe tomato.

"I'd like to talk about something I never shared with anyone. It's not something one talked about back in those days, much less with an immature, troubled son."

"You mean how you were a lesbian?" I set out two slices of white bread, a slice of ham, the tomato, and picked up a jar of mustard. "It's all starting to make sense. Your choices."

"I was pregnant a couple times before I had your father."

The jar slipped, shattering to the floor, speckling gold all over my shoes. *Dammit!* I grabbed a towel and dropped to my knees to clean up the mess. "Go on, I'm still listening," I said, wiping my Mary Janes.

"The first went full term. She died after a week. Heartbroken, I didn't want to go through that again. It would be up to me to decide if or when. Too soon, and barely healed, I found myself pregnant again. Wesley supported my decision to end the next one in an abortion."

I'd taken a seat and found myself staring at the glistening, pink ham. This was a topic we for sure didn't discuss at home, so I didn't know very much about the subject matter. What I knew was that it was a sin against God. "Wait, was abortion legal back then?"

"No, but it wasn't uncommon. It just wasn't talked about. Though we were silenced, it was a way for a woman to have control over her own body. It used to be legal until all the men in the medical profession banded together to decide what was best for all females."

I'd been taught that God was in charge of his church, and like God, husbands were in charge of their families. So, for sure, I thought Grandma had taken too much control on matters such as to who gets born or not, and especially whether or not it's time to die.

"Unbelievable," I said.

"Well, believe me, an abortion isn't the best form of contraception—which, by the way, was also illegal back then—and if there'd been the pill, I would never have gotten pregnant again."

"But then you had Dad."

"I rest my case."

I detected purple sarcasm. "Why didn't you abort him?"

"I was already pretty far along. Besides, I was older and established in my music career. Besides, if I hadn't had him, we might never have had you."

"Well lucky me. I can tell you I wish I'd never been born. Besides, who cares?"

"Oh, darling. They care. A mother never stops aching over her missing child."

I thought of the story about the woman from the *Island of the Dolphins*. When she realized her son wasn't on board the ship that had captured her and her people, she jumped off and swam back to shore. Suddenly, I felt a tug in my womb, and an ache in my breasts. I cradled my stomach, rocking myself as I imagined what it might have been like for Grandma to deliver her baby, to hold her, care for her, love her, but then lose her after only a week.

"Did you name the baby girl?"

A dark shade of blue tinged the room as she whispered, "Aria."

I choked, trying to swallow my tears before they made it up to my eyes. Damnit! I didn't want to feel sorry for Grandma because I needed to keeping hating her if I were to survive.

CHAPTER 9

Mothers for Peace

Ben carried a sign: "Children are for loving not burning." He pushed the stroller with his free hand. Betsy marched alongside holding a sign: "Mothers for Peace."

By early afternoon, I'd fallen into step with other demonstrators, male and female, both young and old, as we paraded peacefully toward Kezar Stadium. "Stop the War," we chanted to the beat of drums and tambourines. I had nowhere else to be, except that Grandma, with her daily mantra, insisted on going home. I swung my guitar off my back and strummed along and even though I was swept up in this march, I felt like at last I'd taken control of my own destiny.

A young Black man marching next to us carried a sign: "Peace now, Viet Cong never called us nigger."

I came up with a simple tune and chanted: *Peace now, Children are for loving*. Soon, others joined, the collective vibration echoing between my ears and filling me with such emotion as we continued on toward the promise of something I could only trust was meaningful and good. I strummed my guitar, every stroke charging the air with so much anticipation that I could no longer hold back the deluge of tears dropping like little wet bombs onto the asphalt. Not even in church, surrounded by hundreds of parishioners had I ever felt such a connection. Uncomfortable with such a public display of feelings, I didn't know what to do with myself except to play through the tearful blindness. Soon, someone had wrapped their arms around me.

"Let it out," Betsy whispered. In that moment, I realized this was something missing in my life; something very foreign to me and yet so vital. The soft human touch. I'd seen such displays of affection on TV, never in our home. I felt a release of tension and broke into sobs.

Once we got into the stadium, there was talk of burning draft cards. Ben took out his shiny, brown leather wallet and pulled out a card. He then tore the paper in half, letting the breeze carry it off with a passionate speech by an actor I recognized at the podium. "The primary reason for our being in Vietnam today is our refusal to admit a mistake," he said. "In our attempt to make Vietnam a Pro American, anti-communist state—"

A counter-demonstrator shouted out, "Don't listen to him!"

Swept up by a tide of passion, I also knew first-hand what it was like to be invaded by an intruder. Grandma was America and I was Vietnam and the time had come to get strong and stand up to this foreign enemy who'd dug into the trenches of my brain, part of which was still ripe and ready to be fertilized with new ideas.

And then a beautiful Black woman with a white corsage pinned to her lapel came to the podium. I recognized the wife of Martin Luther King, Jr., and when Coretta Scott King got to the part of her speech, "When the heart is right, the mind and the body will follow," I knew it was a matter of listening to my own heart, something I didn't share with Grandma. I wanted my heart to beat as one with this movement. I wanted to take control of my body.

"Let's go home," Grandma said.

"No," I said digging in my heels. I saw certain parallels and a connection that might give me strength to take charge of my own destination. There were so many choices to consider and probably just as many battles with Grandma to conquer. It felt as if I were being called to climb a steep mountain and with every step, I would get stronger. Again, it felt as if I had a bigger purpose than the whole Grandma thing. I just needed to find it.

Lazarus Rising, a band I'd never heard of, took the stage. The lead guitarist blew me away. All the vocals were done by the others. There were no females in the band, which wasn't unusual, but it might have helped, if you were to ask me. The last two bands came on, again groups I'd never heard of like Steve Miller or Country Joe and the Fish or the Big Brother and the Holding Company, and then we left.

★ ★ ★

Sitting in the parlor back at the house, Poppy being down for the night upstairs, Ben opened a bottle of wine and poured us a glass. "Cheers!" he said, clinking Betsy's glass and then mine. When Betsy started talking about the events of the day, Ben got up and excused himself to go upstairs to do some reading. He kissed Betsy goodnight and took his glass. She got up to pour the rest of the bottle, offering me some. I shook my head. There were still a couple of swallows left in my glass. I already felt a slight buzz. She poured herself the rest and I sat back looking up toward the ceiling thinking about the day as she kept talking about this and that. She scooted next to me, placing a hand on my lap. "What a day," she said, twisting toward me.

"I'd say it was pretty *far out*."

She laughed. "And you, you've been holding out on us."

I took a sip of my wine, preparing to have to talk about Grandma. It might be a relief to tell someone.

"Not just a pretty face, but you have a beautiful voice. You can go places."

"Thank you." I knew I was good on the piano and even the guitar, but I never thought my singing was so special.

She then put both hands on my cheeks.

"Such a face, so innocent." I was only a few years younger than she was. She kissed me and as it lingered, she slid her arms around me. Human touch. I didn't know how to react, but I didn't do anything to stop her. She tasted like warm grapes, like I could have plucked and devoured her kisses one by one. But as soon as I put my arms around her, it was over, leaving me utterly confused. I mean, Betsy and Ben are a couple, but they aren't married. But they have a child. Why would she kiss me like that? Earlier in the park, there'd been talks about free love; talks about making love not war.

"Goodnight, Anna. Sleep tight." She vanished upstairs, leaving me alone to wonder what the hell had just happened.

How am I supposed to sleep? I lay in bed still buzzing from the day ending with a kiss. Grandma wanted to go home. Home? I began feeling more at home running away from it, besides I'd started to develop somewhat of a girl crush on Betsy and thought it needed more exploration. Totally confused about my feelings, at first, I'd thought of Betsy as a big sister or a mother, or even a shrink of sorts—one who didn't let the patient talk. Mixed up about relationships, both female and male, and then after what just happened downstairs, I was thoroughly baffled, maybe if I read more Gertrude Stein.

"I'm not ready." Besides, I wanted to be a part of this change, be a part of something bigger than myself, bigger than us. I felt I must fight to end the war and for equal rights and for women's freedom.

"Anna, you're still so young. Young people are idealistic and full of passion."

"But I'm not stupid."

"Nor are you naïve, and I am simply trying to protect you from a lifetime of struggles. I don't want you to repeat my mistakes. I'm so tired of them all."

"Seriously? So, then just die already! This is my life! You had yours to fuck up."

"Indeed, Anna, and I learned so much—some good information and some bad. I know the difference now and that's why I want to guide you in the right direction."

"Oh my God! How do you know what's right or wrong for me? What do you know?"

"I know history repeats itself. But sometimes it's more like a pendulum swinging so hard one way and then even harder the other way. I don't want that for you."

"Well, I don't want to go home and turn into a subservient suburban housewife like Mom or like her mother before her."

"Darling, that's not your only choice."

"Oh yeah, what do you know?" I rolled over and put the pillow over my head, an act in futility.

"I was once just a young woman giving piano lessons to support myself. I, like other women, wanted suffrage, but why should I have to marry in order to have any rights? Why did men have all the rights? Women had already been fighting for nearly one hundred years. I belonged to the Votes for Women Club in Los Angeles. We were part of mobilizing over ten thousand local supporters, including teachers, college women, wage earners and veteran suffragists to carry out the drive. We spoke wherever we could find an audience, to voters in the streets and from automobiles. We distributed a million pieces of literature and thousands of 'Votes for Women' buttons in Southern California alone."

Surprised. Was this Grandma talking? I pulled the pillow off my head.

"We used electric signs and billboards and even lantern slides at night to flash the message. And yes, we marched and even held mass rallies like the 'monster rally' in San Francisco, followed by fireworks and a band concert, much like today. Oh, the blisters on my feet from canvassing. Imagine, California finally gained suffrage in 1911."

I rolled back over. "Yeah, but mostly white women gained the right to vote."

"True, but we were making progress. My future looked bright. For once I felt invested in myself. And then the war came. In the end, it served to strengthen the cause. But we're still fighting. Imagine, that was almost fifty years ago. I do hope we continue to see more changes in women's rights soon, certainly within the next fifty years."

2017 seemed so far away. Surely all of this would get resolved by then. "Wait, didn't you get married fifty years ago?"

"Yes."

"And so, all you believed and fought for flew out the window. Why did you end up marrying?"

"It was complicated."

"Mom told me you don't get married unless you're in love, or pregnant. Were you pregnant? She also told me a woman needed a husband to co-sign for property or credit cards."

"And then after Wesley died, you married again. George, of all people. Dad told me George had something to do with the death of his own father, Wesley."

"Charley needed a father figure. I didn't know until it was too late."

"Well, I'm never getting married."

"Anna, you don't have to marry, you can aspire to be wise. You can learn all you can. Education is the key to freedom."

"What better way to get educated than to see the world—like you did."

"True, but my views have changed with death."

"What do you mean?"

"The world is different now."

"Different, not better. Have wars ended? Have women gained equality? Or only for rich white people like you."

"Not exactly, but there's another struggle you must consider."

"Uh huh, like what?"

"Wherever you go, I go, too."

"Well maybe you should have thought of that before you invaded my body."

"I know that now. Unfortunately, once I started the transfer, I knew I'd made a mistake, but it was too late."

"Now you're telling me?"

Grandma suddenly changed lanes on me. "I do miss my music. Don't you, too?"

★ ★ ★

The next morning, Ben and Betsy with wilted flowers stuck in her hair, announced they were headed home. "Ben has finals so we do need to get back," Betsy said.

From the surprised look on my face, she added. "You're welcome to come home with us, maybe help out with Poppy. I can't believe how in just this short time, she's grown so attached to you."

I'd learned to love this little family and suddenly panicked at the thought of being on my own again, but grew even more terrified at the thought of what home would look like in the middle of Betsy and Ben. My gut told me it wasn't a good idea.

After I declined the offer, she got up to get a pen and a piece of paper near the yellow wall phone and wrote something down. "Our phone number and address in case you change your mind, or, if you just want to talk. I know I talked so much, but I got the sense you didn't mind." She winked. "Besides, I noticed, on the ride up, you carrying on your own conversations a lot. They seemed pretty deep. At first, I thought you were asleep." I felt my face flashing red. "My father used to talk about some of his cases. Schizophrenia is such a fascinating subject. I've never really . . ."

"Wait. What? I'm not schizophrenic!" Although, I'd heard talk about it being part of my father's diagnosis, the reason for his Navy discharge. Was it hereditary?

"I'm sorry, of course not." She smiled apologetically and then took in a sorry breath. "I really feel if you stayed, I could make a difference."

Like what? I wondered. As your little lab rat? "I'll be okay."

Grandma added, "Of course. Besides you're a mother and a wife, well a mother, whose responsibility is her family. That's a job you have until you die."

Betsy stared at me, open-mouthed. "You sound hoarse. Are you getting sick?

I shook my head.

"I guess you're right. My place is next to Ben." She then took my hands and looked into my eyes. "We all have our challenges, and I get the sense there's something heavy on your mind." I couldn't hold back the tears. "I know you're running away, but maybe you're running toward something," she said, sounding wiser than her twenty-two years. "But remember, wherever you go you take yourself with you."

Betsy looked down at my shoes. The march had given me blisters and one of my straps from my Mary Janes had ripped, flapping along as we marched up Fulton Street toward the stadium. "But you can't get keep running in those," she said, peering closer. "Is that mustard?" She handed me her boots and told me I could hang out in the house as long as I liked, but that Ben's parents would be home in a couple of days.

"Thank you," I said, wiping my nose with the back of my sleeve.

It didn't take long for them to pack up. "Stay safe." Betsy pulled me into the middle of a group hug with her and Ben and Poppy. As we said our goodbyes, I felt my heart tearing apart. I missed family.

★ ★ ★

Before deciding my next move, I called home. At last, my mother came to the phone. She sounded upset, of course, but Dad was fine, like Grandma told me.

"So, the police aren't looking for me?"

"No. How would I explain that it was your dead grandmother who caused her son to get stabbed?"

"I'm so sorry this happened, Mom."

"Why should you be? It wasn't your fault." She didn't sound mad. "Anna, you've always been stuck in the middle." She understood my dilemma? "Just come home."

Now she'd really given me something to cry about. Without saying so, I knew she missed having me around while everyone was off at school. She missed her ally, her helper, her partner in crime. Mom sounded sweet which made it harder to explain that I wasn't ready to come home yet. I tried to describe how I was changing. And just as quickly, she harshened her tone. "I'm sure you are, traveling around with those big ideas in your head. Desgraciada. Como tienes sangre azul. I'm sure your high-society Grandmother is so happy she finally pulled you away from us."

"She didn't pull me away, I ran away after I stabbed Dad, remember? He would have killed you if I hadn't stepped in."

"He wouldn't have touched me if your grandmother hadn't been such a metiche. Anyway, it was nothing any different. He needs me too much to actually kill me."

So, she'd risk getting beaten to death. "But needing isn't the same as loving, Mom."

"What do you know about love?"

Not much, except that it's obviously truly blind. Mom had never seen the frightened little Anna standing in front of her.

I wondered if the reason she constantly engaged in arguments with Dad, a sort of sick game to her, was to prove some kind of love. Still on a high from marching for peace, singing songs of freedom and unity, chanting words of hope, I wouldn't let Mom bring me down.

"Anna, what are you trying to do? Get killed? You don't understand what it's like to be a minority. You weren't around during the riots."

"You're right, Mom." But we've come a long way since the Zoot Suit Riots. I'm marching for change. We need to end the war."

"Aye dios, your father would be shocked to hear this."

"And your father might be proud. Where would we be if not for Dolores Huerta and her family? Don't you see the good that came of her?"

Mom laughed and I could picture the sneer on her face. "You're no Dolores Huerta."

No, I'm Anna LeMar and I'm not coming home. I hung up the phone.

★ ★ ★

Neither Mom nor Grandma were happy now about my decision. With Grandma's disapproval about my choices came her silence—which I sort of dug. Aside from losing control over me, it seemed the stronger I became, the weaker she became, which ironically seemed to give me strength. But I also waited for the other boot to drop. She'd also become more silent the more she learned about this new world, its troubles overwhelming her. She thought the best place for me to be was at home. If only she'd stayed out of our family matters, then maybe we might have had a chance at a happy, normal home, and even though stabilizing the situation had been her challenge, she'd failed miserably to bring peace.

Getting caught up with everything happening around me also served to educate me. I couldn't wait to see what else I might discover, besides being kissed by a girl. Finding a way to make Grandma go away became secondary to finding love. There was no turning back now.

CHAPTER 10

Never Take a Knife to a Gunfight

I'm nine, Dad stands behind me, his arms over mine guiding the cocked rifle, target within sight. "Pull the trigger." But I won't shoot the bunny and I step away.

We'd been on a camping trip up to the local mountain forest. Dad had even worn his old garrison cap with the Boy Scout insignia from his Eagle Scout days. He'd seemed so happy, like his scouting days were some good times. But later that night, using his Bowie knife to cut kindling, he's unable to start a fire to cook a rattlesnake he shot. I pull the book of matches from my pocket and think I've saved the day. He also should have paid attention to the weather reports because after finally pitching the tent with help from Michael and me, a gust of wind blows it down just before the rains dump on us, dousing our fire. Mom yells at him. "What kind of scout were you? Can't even tie a knot!" At the risk of being beaten, Mom still manages to blow Dad down, like a tent in a rainstorm. Grandma tells him to calm down when he flashes his knife. But he drops it at the sound of me cocking the gun.

* * *

Caked in mud after another night sleeping on wet grass in Golden Gate Park under a blanket, borrowed from Ben's parents' house, I remembered that stressful time with my family before the rains came and how we packed up and went home all muddy and shivering wet.

That was then. I wasn't ready to give up and go home yet. I slipped into the park bathroom and tried to clean up, finger-combing my matted, tangled hair. I dried my face with paper towels that I'd gathered from the floor, and noticed my face in the mirror's reflection. Dark puffy circles cradled my eyes like little purple aprons. A new pimple sprouted on my cheek and a cold sore had erupted on my upper lip. I was a mess.

Even over the street noise, I heard my stomach rumble as I strayed into the city. I'd given Caroline most of my money, so I knew I needed a job if I were to continue to survive on my own. Maybe today I'd find a job.

Betsy's boots were a size too small for me and by the afternoon, my feet blistered from clunking along the sidewalks; my guitar swung across my back as I slipped in and out of shops asking if anyone needed help. No luck finding a job. No one wanted another "lazy hippie" working for them. Weary and famished, I dropped the blanket to the curb to sit. Pretty soon I heard people shouting, "Free Food. Free You. Digger!" An old truck full of young happy-looking people came around the corner. I stood as a yellow-haired boy jumped out of the bed of the truck and ran up, pressing a flier into my hand advertising a place where I could get free food. But I needed to find a job.

I followed the truck traveling up the street. And then, as I stood at the intersection of Haight and Ashbury, Grandma spoke up. "Music!" I heard the piano. Not just any piano. "It's a Steinway," Grandma said. "Pre-Depression era."

My sense of smell seemed more acute at the moment than my hearing. The rich aroma of coffee wafted out of a shop with a sign that read *Steinway Café*.

Dust motes floated in the light streaming in through the windows as I stepped in to look around a cavernous space filled with cozy-looking chairs, mismatched tables, and nooks where one could curl up with a book and a hot cup of coffee. My stomach growled at the thought of curling up with a cheese sandwich. But then, out of a shadow in the middle of the shop, glowing at the end of a ray of sunlight, my heart wanted to sing when I laid eyes on an ebony grand piano. I'd heard the music from the street, but now I didn't see anyone playing it. The piano looked so lonely. When I got close enough, I noticed a lock on it.

"Do you play?" someone asked. I turned around, coming eye to eye with a round-headed older man—probably around thirty—boyish and yet balding with a thin ponytail. Pudgy and pasty-looking, he looked like he'd never seen the California sun.

In a movie, I'd be the sort of nice and naïve girl who barely makes it out alive. Dilbert Moss was the sort of man—so far, all men were the sorts of men—who made my stomach hurt. He was also like all of those bad guys in the movies who don't usually make it in the end. And my gut sent up warning smoke signals.

"Well, do you?"

Feather-like tickles skipped up my throat. "I used to," Grandma answered, before I could say anything.

"Who was playing before I walked in?" I asked.

"Must have been the radio," the man said appraising me as if I were the FBI. "So, you play?" I nodded. "Only customers who can play well are allowed to play it," the man said sternly, his eyes flickering in the dark as if he were tapping out a code of warning.

"I used to play very well," Grandma said in lyrical yellow as I turned to leave. I wanted to shut her up but there'd be no stopping her when it came to her pride, her ego, or her music.

"Some even called me a virtuoso," Grandma added.

The man looked at me dubiously and the next thing I knew I sat at the piano playing Beethoven's *Piano Sonata 14*. At once, it felt like I'd returned home. "Don't you just miss it?" Grandma asked.

When I finished, I heard clapping and finger-snapping. A crowd had gathered just outside the window.

"You obviously can play classical," the man said, "but can you play something from this century?"

"Darling, show the man what we've got."

And with that I broke into Chuck Berry's "Roll Over Beethoven." Within moments, the crowd had come in and gathered around the piano.

"Encore!" someone shouted.

"Are you hungry?" the man asked. He probably fed all the young, wayward kids around here who could play for their supper.

I nodded, and he yelled. "DeeDee!"

A young golden-haired girl appeared out of the dark. "Bring— what's your name?"

"Anna."

"Good to meet you, Anna. I'm Dilbert Moss, this here is DeeDee."

DeeDee bowed like a blonde Geisha girl.

"Bring Anna here a sandwich and a cup of coffee. You drink coffee?"

"Yes." I took a seat at one of the little tables and poured cream and sugar into my cup. DeeDee quickly returned to the table with my food. "Thank you."

"So, I take it you're not from around here. Where you staying?" Dilbert asked.

I stopped chewing and held up my index finger. "First things first. I need to find a job and then I can worry about finding a place."

"How old are you?"

"Eighteen." I took another bite and swallowed the lie.

He looked away as if considering something, then turned and peered at me. "You can work here."

Practically inhaling the cheese sandwich, I thought of Oliver Twist. *Please sir, may I have some more?*

"And, you can take the room upstairs," Dilbert said, following DeeDee. "It used to be Mother's."

The juices in my gut soured. I'd gone to see *Psycho* with Mom down at the Alexander Theater when I was way too young to be watching the likes of Bates and the exhumed corpse of his mother upstairs. Mamá had jumped up, squeezing my arm during that infamous shower scene. I'd calmed myself down, reminding myself it was only a movie.

"And this is real life, Anna. You can't stay here," Grandma whispered.

"But you're the one who had to go and show off and play the piano. What was that all about?"

"That was a mistake."

"Another one? Besides, isn't this how you once supported yourself?"

I was confused and too exhausted to look for another place. "Grandma, you're not always right about all your premonitions. After all, remember, you're not clairvoyant."

"True, but wisdom does give one a certain amount of transparent foresight necessary to make sure all escape routes are clear; to look at the best worst-case scenario, and the best," Grandma whispered. "I've been around long enough to know that when I think something bad is going to happen, then it will."

Dilbert returned. "Well, actually, you'd have to share the room with DeeDee."

Relieved. I made the decision to try things out. In the meanwhile, I wouldn't be taking any showers and I'd sleep with my knife under my pillow.

* * *

Around six-thirty, a few mornings later and just before the shop opened, while it was still dark, quiet, and empty, I sat at the keyboard practicing a new song I'd been hearing on the radio lately, the same one playing on the radio driving up with Ben and Betsy. I had no idea what the lyrics meant—something about *turning cartwheels across the floor* and *sixteen vestal virgins leaving for the coast.* I smelled the coffee brewing and then out of the corner of my eye, I saw Dilbert enter the room. I kept playing, hoping he'd leave me alone. He'd been creeping me out even more lately the way he'd slither past and brush up behind me with his fat jelly belly. *And although my eyes were open, they might just as well have been closed.*

"I like that. You have a good voice," he said, and I felt his hands on my shoulders, squeezing like an accordion. "Do you like this?"

I shook him off and he backed away. I continued to play, my fingers trembling, the blood draining from my body as the memories filled in the fissures.

I'm eleven years old again, seated at the piano back at home. Mom had asked if I might audition for the church music director. "Be nice and remember to smile," she says before disappearing into the kitchen. What does smiling have to do with playing piano?

I didn't like how Mr. Fletcher sat so close to me on the piano bench. He set up the sheet music to *Hosanna.* As I played, he reached up, ready to turn the page. I could smell his toilet breath as he let his hand fall into my lap and then quickly slid it further up in between my legs. "Do you like this, Anna?" he whispered. "Take your God damned hands off us!" Grandma screamed in black. I quickly scooted off the piano bench and landed on the floor. I heard Mom in the kitchen, rattling pots and pans, but now she stopped. "Get out!" Grandma yelled, and Mr. Fletcher raised a hand to his mouth, obviously alarmed at the strange guttural tone of my voice. Staring at the kitchen door, he lowered his voice. "You tell anyone and I'll say it's you who has a crush on me. I'll say you tried to kiss me!" *What?* I picked myself back up and took my place at the piano as he scurried like a sewer rat out the front door. Mom came back into the chamber room. "What did you do?" I wouldn't end up getting to play for the church.

★ ★ ★

Dilbert pressed up against me and I could feel his hardness in the small of my back. Arching away, I stopped playing before pushing off from the piano, and turned to run. His body blocked mine. "Please let me pass." He didn't budge, but then over his shoulder, I could see a couple of customers just outside the door. "It's time to open up," I said, pointing to the front window. He turned to look and backed off.

Still in shock, my body spiraled one way, my head spun the other way. My heart pounded out the loudest key in the lowest octave of my body. Feeling suffocated, I opened the door and a gust of fresh air blasted me, not with any common sense, unfortunately, but with just enough oxygen to clear my head. I stepped out as all kinds of ideas ricocheted inside the walls of my skull, bruising Grandma's hair-brained schemes. To bolt now would be to admit failure.

"Yes, run away!" Grandma shouted inside my ears. "What's there to prove?"

I walked up the street and sat on the curb. Maybe I sent the wrong signals again, probably a miscommunication of some sort. I can fix this. I can handle it, I thought. Just in case, I reached down the inside of my boot and pulled out my knife. The weight of it felt so light, but the need to survive felt stronger and a power rose up from my toes. I stood up, ready to return to the shop.

"What would stabbing him solve?" Grandma asked.

"Well, I need this job to live and I'm not going to be a victim. I've done it before."

"No, you haven't."

"Yes, I have. I stabbed Dad."

"No, dear. That night you passed out."

"I do remember seeing stars."

"I did it," Grandma said.

"You what!?"

I slumped down onto the curb to rest my forehead on my knees. I'd been having trouble putting the pieces together from that night, but honestly, my goal had been to just put it out of my mind and keep running. This news was a huge revelation. "How could you?" My anger mushroomed into nuclear bomb proportions. I sprang to my feet. "And, why didn't you . . . when were you going to tell me? Do you even know . . . understand . . . Do you care what this has done to me? To my family? To Dad? Your son!"

"Anna, it's not that easy."

"What's so difficult about telling the truth?" I yelled, pacing the sidewalk, pedestrians staring, but standing clear.

"Darling, here's the truth. That night as you raised the knife—with no intention of using it—you lost consciousness when he fell on you, but I stared into his vacant eyes. He was out of his head. 'Charley, stop' I yelled. 'I'm so sorry Mother,' he cried. 'Please kill me.' I saw the pain in his soul, the same pain he's had to endure his whole life. All because of my choices. I just wanted to keep him away from you and Teresa. But when he grabbed your throat, I had no choice but to plunge the knife into him, but it didn't kill him. You didn't kill him. You would never be able to do it."

"But you could?"

"I know death."

"Except when I took off running, you had me believe I did it. Why?"

"How would you explain to the police that it wasn't you? That it was your Grandma, like your mother said. Besides, we all needed some space. I suppose it seemed refreshing and a bit thrilling to get out of that house for a bit. But as soon as you stuck your thumb out, I knew the canary could not be returned to her cage. I couldn't have you believing you couldn't take on that rogue in the van. And you did a fine job handling him."

"So, you've let me believe the police are looking for me."

"But they're not, so we can go home. Your father knows it wasn't you, darling."

"Don't *darling* me!"

I wanted to kill Grandma about now.

"So now you know the truth, let's go home."

★ ★ ★

More than an interloper, Grandma was dangerous enough to stab her own son. Who else? I wondered if there might have been other times that she'd used my body against my will. I mean, what else happened when I was asleep or scared out of my mind?

I shoved the knife back into my boot, turned around, and trekked toward the cafe. Knowing I hadn't stabbed my father filled me with a weird, dizzy sort of joy mixed with anger, like I'd stepped off an emotional spinning carousel.

★ ★ ★

After a long day on my feet, I freshened up. If he made a move, I wouldn't go inside myself this time. I wouldn't run away. Next time I would speak up. I'd defend myself. I'd watched plenty of movies. What would my favorite *femme fatales* like Crawford or Stanwyck do? I put my apron on and stepped into the kitchen to start the coffee before taking my seat at the piano, with a smile.

"Let the show begin," Dilbert announced, taking his place behind the counter. Pencil behind his ear, he crossed his short arms over his fat belly.

I looked into the lively audience. "Any requests?" I asked.

Over the shouting, I heard someone yell "Eartha Kitt" —a strange request from such a young crowd, except that Eartha had just been cast as Catwoman in the *Batman* series. The request intrigued me and immediately I remembered the Eartha Kitt songs on records my mother had at home like "Santa Baby" and "C'est Si Bon." There were other older albums in Mom's collection, including Grandma's recordings with her ex-husband George singing opera, but it was Eartha Kitt's music that truly moved me with that spicy voice of hers. The definition of sexy.

After riffing one of her songs, I realized the piano and my voice wouldn't do her justice. I looked into the audience. "Who asked for Eartha Kitt?" In the back, a young Black girl, a little older than me, waved her slender arm, shiny golden bracelets slipping to her elbow. She smiled at me and I swear I'd never seen a more beautiful human. Well-dressed, she wore a half-sleeve, satiny A-line dress with a teardrop cutout below the neckline, sparkly earrings, and a swept-up French roll hairdo. She stilettoed up to the piano, leaned in and asked in a voice so lush, I melted. "Do you know *I want to be evil.*"

A force of nature, she stood statuesque as if she'd been carved out by Michelangelo, yet slinky as a cat. She inhaled before opening her ruby-lacquered lips to purr the intro, breathy and seductive. As the Black beauty sang the first sultry bars, skin glowing radiantly under the dimmed house lights, she could have been Eartha Kitt in the flesh, the way she pulsated her root beer-colored eyes without closing them, the way she fluttered her arms like graceful butterfly wings. I wanted to stop and reach out to hug her. I wanted to be her best friend. And even though she was a girl, I wanted to kiss those lips like cherries—after all, I'd been kissed by Betsy and I liked it. I mean, maybe, what if boys won't turn me on?

The crowd dug it as they snapped their fingers, clapped their hands, whistled and, most importantly, filled the tip jar. I could get used to this. Encore! And then after "Champagne Taste," Dilbert slithered over and whispered into the girl's ear. Abruptly, she walked back to her table, grabbed her matching coat, and followed him to the back.

Just finishing up the next song, I noticed her clutching her bag and coat close to her chest, one hand over her face, as she ran out the front entrance. What had he said to her? What had he done to her? I wanted to run after her. Take me with you!

After my shift, Dilbert handed me an envelope. "What's this?" I asked, peering into an empty envelope.

"The arrangement was that you'd work for tips," he said.

"Yes, but the tip jar was full of bills earlier."

"You're still on probation. Tomorrow, you'll get more. In the meanwhile, here's a tip for you," he said. "It's best you remember which side your bread is buttered on."

"I—" Biting my tongue, I wouldn't quit just yet, not until I came up with a plan.

★ ★ ★

That night, DeeDee told how she handled Dilbert. Basically, she kept clear of him, spending spend most nights sleeping at other places. Later, after I'd locked my door, I drifted off to sleep angry and confused. I dreamed about strangling Dilbert as the mysterious girl with cherry lips sang in the background, "I Want to Be Evil." I woke up wondering if it was evil to want to kiss her? Was I some sort of lesbian?

"Darling, just because you kissed her doesn't make you a homosexual."

"Oh my God, Grandma! You butt in even in my dreams?"

"Only when you're curious about something."

"That's why there's a library."

"I told you when I was your age, I got to travel. Paris was the biggest thrill," she said in a shade of lavender.

"Grandma! You kissed a girl?" I asked, shocked.

"But I wouldn't label myself Bessie Smith. Darling, we're all looking for love."

"So, is that a bad thing?"

"Absolutely not. Love is the most beautiful thing in all the realms."

★ ★ ★

Seated at the piano the next morning, a slice of dry toast and a cup of coffee off to the side, the lyrics still ran through my head, the thought of that girl exciting me. *I wanna be evil, I wanna spit tacks.* I wondered if she'd come back. What had Dilbert told her? The hairs on my arm rose like miniature red flags when I heard him approaching. He handed me an envelope, again, with only a few bills.

I wanted to spit tacks, I was so pissed. I got up and stormed out. "That's right, Anna, just keep walking," Grandma said. "Let's find a bus."

"Grandma, leave me alone. I gotta think."

★ ★ ★

The Haight and Grandma had something in common in that they didn't sleep and kept me company throughout the night. On the streets there was plenty to keep me distracted. Lost kids bumbled around as music blared and poets recited on sidewalks. "They call that poetry?" Grandma asked. The night was full of sounds and stink.

After roaming the streets all night, I returned to the shop, planning to work through until the end of my shift and this time get my tips. I snuck up to my room to rest.

Later, I took my place at the piano. There were already a few patrons seated at tables waiting to be entertained.

Livid, Dilbert's nostrils flared like a racehorse. "Where've you been?"

"None of your business. You don't own me."

I stood my ground as he walked up and slammed the keyboard cover, just missing my fingers. The customers hushed. He glared at me as I opened the lid to play. As he stormed off, I knew I'd have to face the consequences.

After the last call, all of the other workers finished their clean-up and said goodbye. DeeDee hung up her apron and approached me. "I'm headed over to a party on the next block. Don't stay here by yourself. Join me."

"As soon as I'm done, I'm out of here."

I finished the last song just as Dilbert approached and grabbed my tip jar.

"No. You can't do that!" I yelled.

He laughed. "This is my place. I can do whatever I want, and whoever I want."

"Let us go!" Grandma yelled as he grabbed my wrist, twisting it around my back, throwing me face first into the piano. With my free arm, I reached into my boot and whipped out my knife, slashing him in the leg.

"What the fuck!" He tried to grab my knife.

We struggled. My backside created a strange cacophony on the piano and then finally he backed away with a limp.

"Psycho bitch. You're fired," he yelled, massaging his leg. "Get out!"

I held the knife as I backed away and turned to take the creaky stairs two at a time.

"Anna, no! Let's get out of here!"

Of course, I should've run away when I had the chance, but I wasn't thinking straight and I couldn't leave without my guitar. As I gathered the few items I owned, I heard footsteps on the stairs. My heart pounded.

"Oh, Anna, he's coming!" she screamed in brown, the taste of bile.

Bursting into the room, he held a gun. I held up my knife, David to Goliath. Panicking, with my free hand, I grabbed the back of a chair putting it in between us, like a lion tamer. He jerked the chair out of my hand and soon nothing stood in his way. I backed up and fell onto the small bed.

"That's right," he said.

"If you get any closer, I'll cut off your balls!"

He laughed. "Drop the knife or I'll shoot!"

I sat up and, as if I were surrendering to him, I dropped my knife. But when he inched closer, I pulled my legs in toward my chest and then, pumped full of adrenaline, I catapulted them straight into his gut. He went flying backward, tripping over the chair, hitting the ground with a thud and releasing the gun that landed across the room. We both scrambled to get it, but he reached it before I could, my hand over his grasping tightly. As he pulled, I couldn't hang on to it and let go. His hand snapped back, the gun flashing the instant before any sound. I gasped, suppressing a scream. He went limp in front of me, blood seeping from a hole in his neck. I scooted away, looking toward the door to make sure no one was coming. He lay there, not breathing, eyes stuck open, right hand still gripping his gun. I wanted to check his pulse to make sure he was dead, but I obviously couldn't press on his neck like I'd seen them do in the movies. As I reached over to move the gun in order to check the pulse on his right wrist, Grandma shouted. "He's dead! Don't touch anything! Darling, it will look like suicide. No one will ever know."

Oh my God! I gathered my things, careful not to step in the blood seeping into the floorboards. "Don't forget your tip, darling." I squatted down, rummaged through his pockets and then stepped over his body to leave. I remembered the lyrics to "I Want to Be Evil," but I forgot all about grabbing my Bowie knife. Just before exiting the room, I reached into my pocket to pull out a packet of matches, *Steinway Café* engraved in gold, craving the smell of sulfur.

I struck the match and inhaled, remembering how Dad first shot the rattlesnake, then as overkill, he took out his knife and chopped off the head and tail. He lobbed the head into the bushes, and then tossed me the rattle. "For your musical pleasure, Phoebe."

CHAPTER 11

Asphalt & Patchouli

The fog shrouded the streetlamps, wrapping around them like a damp gray scarf. I stopped underneath to hug myself and then rubbed my chicken-skinned arms to get warm. "Darling, you mustn't stop now." My heart raced faster than my feet could carry me and as I looked up the street, I felt a migraine coming head-on. Twin flames of fear and guilt seared into my brain. And because I had two different consciousnesses, the fires doubled in size, blue, white, red, and yellow, even though Grandma didn't seem worried.

"It was self-defense, darling," she said.

Shards of glass zigzagged across my eyes. My period would be here soon with the debilitating cramps. I hoped it wouldn't be as bad as times when everything went black. I needed to hurry and find a place to crash before I doubled over like a heap of trash.

I trembled at the thought of Dilbert Moss and hoped he wouldn't be discovered until at least the morning. DeeDee would probably be out all night again. So far, I didn't see anyone following me.

As if stumbling through the middle of a funhouse, I bumped into young wayward pedestrians. Some serenaded, playing their guitars, while others huddled around dumpsters blazing with garbage on the side of the street. Some offered their food, their drink, their marijuana, their needles, and their bodies (bread for head) for comfort, warmth, or dollars, but I needed to keep going. I needed to keep my wits about me.

Finally, I made it to out of the amusement park back into Panhandle Park where Grandma and I argued about me going home. At last, except for the chorus of snoring, all was quiet. An orgy of bodies strewn all over the grass like a soggy braided carpet of youth smelled briny and sour. I found an abandoned tattered blanket and swooped it up, finding a place to crash under a sycamore tree next to some bushes. My knapsack made for a lumpy pillow, my guitar, a lonely companion.

I dreamed about the mysterious singing girl with ruby lips. Then I was that girl, running in high heels across the snow, a growling polar bear chasing me. I tripped, skidding along some ice, the membrane between dreaming and waking ruptured to a morning, cold as the inside of a frosted over freezer.

The sun burned through, blinding me even more than the lingering migraine. I didn't know how much time had passed when I heard Grandma whispering. "Darling, it's time to return. Please, before you find yourself in more trouble."

I yanked the cold, clammy cover over my face as if I could smother her voice. More trouble? Are you kidding me, like I could go home after what had happened to my father? At least I hadn't killed him.

"It is truly a shame what happened to Mr. Moss," Grandma said. "But some people just deserve to die."

"Are you for real, old woman? What happened was totally wrong. Even if you say it was in self-defense." I stood up and gathered my belongings.

"Ah, the agony of a bad conscience is the hell of a living soul," Grandma said.

"You're the *bad conscience* and why don't *you* go to *hell*," I yelled, and it felt like a jackhammer to the inside of my skull.

"I didn't raise you to be like this, Anna."

I stopped, curled my hands into fists over my aching stomach. "But that's just it—you didn't raise me. You have no business in my life!" I lowered my head, closing my eyes. "Why can't you just leave me alone? Go away. Just die already." Full of rage, I finally stopped screaming when I looked around and saw sleepy-eyed people staring at me and then I heard a gentle voice.

"Are you lost, my friend?" I opened my eyes to see a pair of sandaled feet planted in front of me.

I looked up, but through my shattered-glass vision, it was hard to make out the haloed vision of a woman. Probably in her twenties, she wore silver bracelets and a crown of flowers in her fuzzy butter-crème colored hair. She wore a long gauzy dress and held up what looked like empty coffee cans.

"I don't think so," I responded. "I just need to rest."

"Who do you want dead?"

"What?"

"You said, 'Just die already.'"

"Oh," I answered, sliding my guitar across my chest. "Lyrics. I'm working on some lyrics for a new song." I picked up my guitar to strum a few notes. "*You have no business in my life! Why don't you just leave me alone. Go away—*"

The woman looked at me skeptically, but then started clanking the cans together like cymbals, bracelets jingling. "Catchy lyrics. *Die already. Leave me alone.* So anti-establishment."

The clanging hurt my head.

"My name is Mary. Are you hungry?"

I nodded and she handed me a chunk of bread that I inhaled as she pulled out a canteen to pour me a cup of water. "There's more if you want to follow me," she said. "And then we can treat that cut on your forehead."

I reached up to touch my brow, remembering how Dilbert had slammed my face into the piano. Maybe that explained the headache. Mary seemed safe enough and Grandma wasn't saying anything to stop me as I followed behind.

I tried to ignore my aching head but then it felt as if I might throw up. Along the way on either side of the street hundreds of young people already milled around in a sort of dreamy haze. The cloying aroma of marijuana and incense, pee, asphalt, and patchouli hung in the fog hovering over hippies, strolling back and forth without any destination. My brain was on sensory over-load, sharp pains pricking me in the pit of my stomach, and my headache threatened to explode with a vengeance as we climbed Clayton Street. I threw up and slumped onto the sidewalk before blacking out.

★ ★ ★

A man in a white coat and wire-framed glasses handed me a green bottle of 7Up as I awoke. Mary sat on the curb next to an orange bucket. Water had been splashed onto the mess I'd made. I felt better and thanked the man as I stood.

"Take it easy, young lady," he said.

"I'll take care of her," Mary said.

★ ★ ★

The sun hovered just above the buildings lined up like jagged teeth as I followed Mary to a dilapidated three-story place that seemed to have barely withstood all the earthquakes I'd read about. Except for the modern mind-blowing paint job, it looked like it came straight out of *The Strange Case of Dr. Jekyll and Mr. Hyde.* A three-storied Victorian that, I imagined, had been splashed with every color of leftover or donated paint. There were a couple of kids sitting on the steps leading to the entrance smoking joints. "Hi Mother Mary." The skinny girl with long limbs who was not much younger than Mary acknowledged her as we climbed up and over a few potted spiky, leafy plants on the stoop.

The inside smelled like the Pan Dulce bakery back home over on Cañada, with just a hint of marijuana and incense. And then as I trailed through a narrow hallway toward the kitchen where I smelled something so mouth wateringly delicious, my stomach did cartwheels in anticipation. The empty coffee cans clinked when Mary set them down on a long stainless steel counter top.

"Not many donations today," I said, squeezing my legs together, as if I could hold back the inevitable.

She tilted her head, looking at me curiously. "Money is an unnecessary evil. People hoard money blocking the free flow of energy and when it's trapped, it causes so much pain and chaos."

"Is there a bathroom I can use?" I felt blood snaking down my chafed-from-running inner thighs.

She hooked a thumb, first door on the right. I went in, cleaned up, and then stuffed my soiled underwear with toilet paper. I washed my hands, splashed my face, and returned to the kitchen smelling like chicken soup.

I smacked my lips as Mary ladled me some broth from a huge pot simmering on the stove. I slurped a few spoonsful as I searched the inside of the bowl. "Wish soup," Mom would call it. I wished there was some meat. "Thank you," I said, mopping up the bowl with more bread.

Others came in and out of the kitchen, some with coffee cans full of money that they counted out. The kitchen felt warm and I found myself nodding.

"You can crash with us tonight," she said. "Until you figure things out."

"Thank you." It would take more than a night to figure stuff out.

I followed her out of the kitchen and up some worn, creaky stairs lined with psychedelic music posters of bands I wasn't familiar with. There was one of a pink girl with green, Medusa-like hair for an event held at the Avalon ballroom with Big Brother and the Holding Company. And then there was another green and red poster of some sort of horned demon for a Grateful Dead and Moby Grape event.

"This is the community bathroom," Mary said. "Help yourself to the soaps, toothpaste, towels."

"Do you have a pad I could borrow?"

"Borrow?" She laughed.

"I mean—"

"Under the sink, there's a box of Tampax."

I hesitated, remembering what Mom had said about losing my virginity if I inserted it wrong. I'd ended up at the library doing my own research on the matter and learned how once a month, the ovary produces an egg that either gets fertilized or shed. I felt like that little egg, fertilized with weird ideas and discarded into the world. But I'd also learned I wouldn't lose my virginity that way.

Mary's bedroom was across a narrow hallway where she parted a curtain of colorful beads before entering. Up against a wall was a small bed with a bright madras bed cover and a similar cloth used as a window shade. Already dark outside, she turned on a small lamp on a table loaded with candles, soda bottles dripping with wax, more incense and a small stack of books: *The Doors of Perception, Strangers in a Strange Land, The Autobiography of a Yogi, Be Here Now, Siddhartha, I Ching,* and the *Tibetan Book of the Dead.* On the wall were more wild posters. Spread across the floor were piles of colorful pillows and blankets.

"Three of us share this room," she said. "You don't wiggle too much, do you?"

I shook my head.

"Good. I had a roommate back at the university. We didn't share a bed, but when she rolled around, the whole dorm shook like a seven point five on the Richter scale."

"I'm maybe only a one point five," I said.

She laughed, turning to leave. "Where are you going?" I asked. She seemed trustworthy, but I wasn't so sure someone hadn't discovered Dilbert's body yet. There could have been a search party out for me with some kind of reward for my capture. But by then I was so tired, the thought of running was the last thing on my mind.

"It's still early. I've got to get things ready for the morning," Mary said. "Just save me room on the edge. Okay, get some rest."

After washing up, I struggled to insert the tampon and not too deep. I mean, I'd already figured out so many things like how to shave my legs, how to drive, how to use a garter belt, so how hard could this be? Pretty difficult, as it turned out, but thank goodness, the box had illustrated instructions and contained more than just one tampon for practice. I could only hope there'd be a how-to for the other challenges I was about to face.

I returned to the room and sat on the bed. I'll just lie down for a few minutes.

The bedspread smelled of Sta-Puf fabric softener, reminding me of all the nights when Mom would come to my room and make me scooch over in my twin bed to give her room. She and

Dad would have been fighting again. I'd tried to sleep, but the sound of him begging for her to come back to their bed caused me insomnia—and nightmares.

Now, the pillow soft murmurs and sheets of laughter floated up from the kitchen below, mixed together with the comforting aroma, sounded like a sensory lullaby.

"Mother Mary seems like a fine young lady," Grandma whispered, disturbing my peace.

"Yeah, she does." Even though I was still mad at Grandma, my anger, like my migraine, had gone away for now, but I was too tired to talk. Grandma, in her pink aura, was not.

"She was right about money and the flow of energy," she said. "You know what happens when energy is trapped."

"Yeah, she causes lots of pain and chaos."

★ ★ ★

If heaven had a bakery, it would smell like what came wafting up from the kitchen the next morning. I got up and stepped over the mounds of blankets, careful not to crush anyone, before coming down to find Mary already up and standing amongst several young girls all busy working with dough. There were stacks of two-pound coffee cans everywhere. The kitchen felt toasty warm and my stomach somersaulted with the smell of fresh bread.

"Morning, Sleeping Beauty," Mary said cheerfully, hands stuffed into a couple of oven mitts. "There's some hot water on the kettle for some tea and there's some honey on the table."

"Thank you." I walked over to the stove to pour myself a cup. I sat at the long wooden table. As I stirred in a teaspoon of honey, I watched her pull a two-pound Chock Full o'Nuts coffee can out of the oven.

"We're making the bread today," she said, as a brown muffin top rose from the lip of the can. "I learned how over at All Saints Church when we were helping out the Diggers. Thought I'd give it a try here."

"The Diggers?"

"A bunch of actors who started by wanting to create a society free of money and capitalism. In the meanwhile, they've ended up trying to feed the hungry while also providing some medical attention to those in need," Mary said.

"That sounds very Christian-like."

"It's about being a good human," she said, turning the can upside down. A fat tube of steaming wheat bread slipped onto the table. "Voila! Get it while it's hot." Smiling, she removed the mitts before slicing a couple of pieces and handed one to me.

"Can I help?" I asked.

"Not on an empty stomach. Help yourself to as much as you like."

"Thank you," I said, and then bit into the bread, even better fresh out of the oven.

"Hi, I'm Willow," said a young girl with a spring in her voice befitting her name, and a long slender arm used to slide over a jar of golden jam.

"Try it with honey," another dark-haired girl named Indigo said.

I finished chewing. "Thank you, but I think it's pretty tasty without it."

The girls all reminded me of my sisters whom I hadn't thought I'd miss so much.

"How many loaves are you going to make?" I asked Mary.

"This week, I'm going to shoot for around two hundred loaves. Lots of kids come up here and have nothing to eat so we provide food, not just bread."

I looked over to the stovetop where there were more giant pots bubbling up deliciousness.

"Ready to start?" Mary asked, slapping down a mound of batter onto a floury surface. "Work it with the heels of your hands, pushing and stretching it. Keep just enough flour on the board and your hands to prevent it from sticking. Until it's shiny and pushes back like an elastic rubber band."

Suddenly I'm back in the kitchen with Mom. She's trying to teach me how to make tortillas, her hands all a blur as she pats out the little ball of dough into a flat pancake. I roll mine out into the shapes of Rorschach inkblots. "What kind of Mexican are you?" Mom asks. I shrug my shoulders, grinning. "The tasty kind?"

"When you're finished, you'll stuff it into one of those coffee cans," Mary said. "This whole process should take you about ten to fifteen minutes."

I tried to do the math. So, if they made two hundred loaves, twice a week and there were five of us . . .

"The division of labor around here is pretty sexist if you ask me," Mary said. "I have a goddamned engineering degree from Berkeley, for Chrissakes. But it's the dudes that get to come up with the ideas while we're tasked with most of the practical work to realize those ideas."

Behind me, I heard a male's voice, low, yet lush. "Yeah, we're just out there socializing." I turned to see a striking young Black man in a slim mustard-colored cardigan. He stepped into the kitchen and started to roll up his sleeves. "Promotin', mixin' and minglin'," he said in a velvety voice as he flourished his arms, "while all y'all women are out there collectin', mixin' and minglin' the food and then servin' it up."

"That's right." Mary held up a rolling pin.

"I help out the best I can, ya know," the man said.

"Yes, I know. You're a different sort," Mary added with a giggle.

"And it ain't just cuz of the color of my skin." He rested the back of his hand on his cheek, his other hand on his hip.

"A modern-day Renaissance man, you are. So many talents. What happened to your face?" He had a reddish bruise around his swollen eye.

"I fell off my horse during a jousting competition."

I stopped laughing when I thought he looked familiar, but I couldn't place him. By now, I'd seen so many new faces I'd be unable to remember. He bowed his head slightly toward me, peering up, and then he said. "I know you. My name's River."

"My name's Anna."

"As I was saying," Mary said. "The men end up taking credit for everything, while the women provide most of the organization's income from welfare checks and social assistance."

"Y'all provide the dough," River said, and everyone laughed.

"Well, I don't have any money to share," I said. "I had a job, but it didn't last."

"Yeah, that bum was an asshole," River said.

I stopped pushing the ball of batter and looked up. "Wait, you, you know him?" I was careful not to use the past tense.

He arched a manicured eyebrow. "Sure. I recognized you right off."

Mary, stretching the dough, looked up.

River didn't volunteer anything else. Terrified, I looked back and forth between Mary and him, not knowing whom to trust.

He reached for a small mound of batter, slapped it down on the table, and rolled it out, and then he rolled out a familiar tune: *I wanna be wicked!* At once, I recognized those lips. He slapped down the dough . . . *and throw mud pies!*

River smiled at me as if to say your secret is safe with me, but was I just imagining that he knew anything about what happened over at Steinway's or Dilbert's death? And if so, why would he even keep a secret like that? In the meanwhile, I needed to try and act cool, before deciding whether it was time to run again.

CHAPTER 12

A Wild Duet

I was the boy my father never had. I loved the ocean where he and I spent a lot of time together. He told me our last name LeMar meant the sea. The young people flocking around us in Panhandle Park reminded me of the seagulls scrounging for food when Dad used to take me fishing out on a boat full of other fishermen. Sometimes, I thought my life would have been a whole lot better had I been born a seagull or a boy, not that I couldn't do anything a boy could do, except pee standing up, but I believed my father's life might have been better had I been the son he wanted. Actually, it might have been a whole lot better if Grandma had just stayed out of our lives.

The next morning, I accompanied Mary to the park to deliver the bread that got carried off in no time. All the while, I kept a close eye on River who ran ahead of us back to the Haight with the others. My mind got tangled up trying to figure out if he knew anything about what happened back at Steinway's. It didn't seem like he'd been talking to anyone about it, or maybe that was because he knew nothing. Walking back with Mother Mary, I tried to focus on anything else as I carried empty baskets and donated coffee cans.

When Mary spoke, I just wanted to sop up every bit she said as if she were a hearty soup full of knowledge. I loved listening to the way she talked, so smart, like one of those news anchors in business suits and ties on the six o'clock news.

"Many of these young people are straight out of college and come from upper-middle-class backgrounds," she said.

"Like you?" I asked, and she turned to me. "I mean, you mentioned you went to the university."

"See that guy there?" She pointed to a skinny, pimply kid in Clark Kent glasses. "His dad is probably chairman of the board of a large corporation." She pointed to another young girl wearing beads and striped bell bottoms, making out with a boy also in bell bottoms, at least I assumed he was a boy. I couldn't see his face, but he had enviable luxurious long hair. "Her father is a successful lawyer. And his father is a rich stockbroker."

I stared at all the souls, maybe not lost, but happy-looking, anticipating something wonderful to come up over the horizon—something revolutionary. Couples of different races holding hands, families pushing strollers, older people carting their groceries along.

"We're a diverse group, ranging from professionals to runaways, from abusive or repressive families," Mary said.

I should probably call home, I thought suddenly.

"Yes, I am sure everyone is worried about you," Grandma said. "Let's go home."

I raised a hand to squeeze my temples. I can't go back.

"You okay?" Mother Mary asked.

I nodded, dropping my hand.

"The streets aren't safe for young girls like you—or boys. There are some out here as young as fourteen. How old did you say you were?"

"Eighteen."

She peered at me. "Rape's as common as bullshit around here. Thugs and pimps. You need to be careful."

"Listen to her," Grandma said.

Mary looked at me and I put my hand over my mouth, just in case Grandma might want to say more.

"And drugs," she said. "Beware of the callous drug dealers roaming the streets."

* * *

River sat at the house on a shabby green couch rolling a joint. He sealed it with his tongue, admiring his handywork. The bruise around his eye looked more purple. He took a hit, holding it in as he offered some to Mary. He exhaled. "Your reward for a job well done."

She set down her baskets and cans and took a hit. River then offered me the joint. Without hesitation, I reached out. I needed to look cool. By now, I'd watched others; they hadn't gone all reefer mad. I'd been sneaking Dad's Camels. How different could it be?

Grandma blared, "No!" and I inhaled, stifling her. River peered at me as I handed the reefer back, blasting smoke at the same time. "No way you recognized me."

He nodded and smiled as he held in more smoke and then he put on a record.

"You've got an unforgettable face," he said.

"Your eye looks better."

"Magic of makeup."

After a couple of hits, and a bit of a coughing fit, Grandma was but a memory—not dead and gone like I wished, but I thought she'd left me alone for the time being.

River and I were by ourselves. I recognized Bob Dylan's song, "Blowin' in the Wind," on the record player as River got up and started swaying to the music. I sat back, taking another hit, watching him move, graceful as a cat ballerina.

"He'd sound better with a piano," he said.

"You think so? Is that all it would take?" Grandma said, and River paused to look at me. I shrugged my shoulders. I knew Dylan wasn't her favorite, but I dug him. I sprung up to dance, hoping to drown her out and let the music take me away. And it did. I sat down and took another hit.

I don't know how long I'd been lost in the moment when I heard River talking to me, as if I were under water, about something that seemed like a total non sequitur. "I loved 'Empty Bed Blues.'"

"What?" The record had changed. "Who's this?" I asked, piercing the surface.

"Jefferson Airplane. As I was saying, her vocals and keyboard are pretty good."

"They are," I said, bobbing my head to the music.

"You don't know how my fingers were itching to come up and play the piano over at Steinway's," River said, pretending to play piano. I froze in place. Finally, the moment of truth.

"Oh, that Dilbert didn't mind putting his hands all over me," River said, fluttering his fingers up and down around his body, "but he wouldn't let me touch his piano. And then when I heard you, it was better than playing myself."

"You play?"

He nodded. So far it didn't seem like he knew what happened over at Steinway's and if he did, he wasn't making a federal case out of it.

I started to dance again. "And when I heard you sing, I wanted to cry. I loved your get-up, especially your sparkly earrings."

"Thank you, again," he said. "Sorry it's not what you would have preferred."

"What?"

"You just said you loved my singing, but that you would have preferred something from Bessie Smith."

"No, I, I didn't. Who's Bessie Smith?"

"I think she was a blues singer from the twenties jazz age."

Oh no! The music and the pot had literally taken me away, leaving me vulnerable to Grandma's impulses. "Did I say anything else?"

"Just that you once saw her in Paris while you were working with the Red Cross during the war."

Oh shit, she's back. So much for letting my guard down. No more pot for me.

River smiled, motioning for me to follow him upstairs. "Speaking of all that jazz, I want to show you something jazzy."

I followed him, wondering what else Grandma might have said during my brief lapse in consciousness. River shared a room across the hall from Mary. I stepped in behind him, over a small mattress and looked around. He opened up an armoire. Hanging were ordinary girl's clothes, and then off to the side hung the glittery dress he'd worn over at Steinways. I reached for it but then a boa draped over a hook caught my attention and I tugged it out and wrapped it around my neck.

"Why do you have all this stuff?" I asked.

"I'm a performer across town," he said, reaching into the bottom of the wardrobe where there were girls' sneakers and sandals. "Today, I'm feeling a little more Diana Ross than Josephine Baker."

"Who's Josephine?" I asked.

He smiled at me as he pulled out a shoebox. "I did think it was sort of strange when you told me I reminded you of Josephine Baker." *I said that, too?* "You said you'd gone to one of her shows at La Revue Nègre in the Champs Elysèe Theatre." I sucked in a tiny breath. "She was also from the twenties. Girl, I love your imagination." Yeah, that's it, my imagination, alright. He opened the box, removed two pairs of giant stilettos, and handed a shimmering silver pair to me. "Let's play." He slipped on some red ones.

I reached for the high heels, sliding them on as he dragged out another box and carried it over to a dressing table where he extracted a wig, some false eyelashes, and makeup. Good for hiding bruises? He pulled out a chair for me to take a seat. I clomped over in the big shoes and sat down. Lifting my chin, he applied some lipstick and some eyeliner. "Close your eyes." I felt the cool swipe of a tiny brush across my lids and then a soft puff to my cheeks as he applied some rouge. "Okay, now open."

I gasped not recognizing the beautiful young woman in the mirror staring back at me. At home, I'd never experienced anything like this. At the most I'd tried on Mom's red lipstick, but sampling the rest of this extravagant stuff thrilled me. It made me—well, after the weed, I supposed I felt sexy. I got up and tried to sashay around the room in those humongous heels. I nearly tripped as I pivoted but then I saw how he'd applied his own makeup and the wig, not the same as the other night at Steinway's. This one had a flip, but he still looked like a movie star. His lips were cherry red and I stumbled over to kiss him. His mouth, soft and warm, tasted like all kinds of sweetness.

I'd never kissed a boy. But River had been dressed like a girl, a girl who wasn't kissing me back. He asked if I wanted another hit and I said no, thank you. Confused, I backed away, stepped over to the armoire and pulled out a sparkly dress. I slipped out of my skirt and wiggled into the gown. "Can you zip me, please?" I asked, turning to see him buttoning up an ordinary dress like something a sorority girl might wear to a frat party. He zipped me and then lit a cigarette and handed it to me. In a tall floor mirror in the corner of the room, we looked like a couple of teenagers sneaking a smoke. We giggled, made faces and struck poses. Afterward, we lay on the mattress blowing smoke rings.

"Miss Anna, what are you doing here?"

I sat up. "You're right. I should be out there helping with the others."

He kicked off his high heels. "No, I'm asking what are you doing here, in San Francisco? Where are you from? We all got a story. What's yours? Did your parents abuse you? Your father rape you?"

"No! Hell, no!"

"So then why are you here?"

Now was the time to use my imagination or an overused cliché. "I guess I couldn't believe that's all there is. There's got to be more to life."

He rolled over onto an elbow, resting his chin on his fist. Appearing unconvinced, he narrowed his eyes at me. "It's really a shame what happened over at Steinway's."

I choked. I'd smoked enough pot to be paranoid. "Yes. A real shame." I stood, and kicked off the heels. Was he trying to trap me into a confession? Was there a reward out for my arrest? I looked toward the window. I could always jump. I slipped out of the dress. "What about you? What are you doing here?" I asked, hanging the dress back up. Are you a spy? I wondered.

"I'm cursed," he replied.

I eased up. Cursed like me?

"You see," he said, sitting up on the mattress, one leg crossed over the other thigh. "All my life I been searching for a place where I could find others like me."

"Where you could perform as a girl?"

He smiled. "Before coming to San Francisco, I read about a place in New York called Casa Susanna where I might live out my secret fantasies and meet others who had similar ones and wouldn't think I was crazy. But the more I researched, the more I realized there wasn't anyone like me."

"Black?"

"Methodist." He laughed, pressing his thumb into the ball of his foot.

"I'm Catholic," I volunteered, taking a seat at the dressing table.

"And I'm probably the only Black Methodist from Iowa."

"Oh, my grandfather was from Iowa," I added. "Apparently, he came out West to seek his fortune. He used to say, 'Oranges for your health, sunshine for your wealth.' And then he met my grandmother, but then he died and transferred his consciousness."

"He what?" River asked, switching legs, to massage the other foot with his thumb.

"It was a religious thing."

River laughed. It seemed to go over his head. I'd dodged a bullet not having to explain my history.

"So, we're probably related," he said and off my confused look, he added, "with your roots from Iowa and all."

"Oh right," I said. No explanation about Grandma needed. "My mother's family came from Mexico."

"Cool. Before I got here, I'd never known a Mexican person."

"And I'd never met a Black Methodist from Iowa with a Southern accent." But the truth was I'd never met a Black person, period. Only in movies or on the recent news with all the talk about Civil Rights, had I even laid eyes on one. I thought about how my father would say he had nothing against coloreds, but then he'd utter things like, "It's starting to get a little dark around here" when we'd go into town. I hated how he acted all superior, the way he treated my mother, too, like he was the mighty white savior of anyone a darker shade of color. And before River, I'd never known a boy who wanted to be a girl. "What about your family?" I asked.

"I'm an only child," he said. "My mother's white and I never knew my father." River smoothed back a brown strand of straight hair from his wig. "So lucky for you that you knew your father."

I looked away. Even though Dad was horrible, he didn't deserve to be stabbed.

"I always thought my mother left me because I wasn't born a girl." He stood.

"I know my dad wanted a boy," I said, sensing my situation wasn't the same as River's.

He smiled, shaking his head. "I think it's time for you to choose a new name, a name to reflect the real you."

"You mean I get a choice."

He nodded.

"Well, I guess I am looking for choices. So, is River your Christian name?"

"No, it's my chosen name. I've always loved the water."

I showed off my knowledge of geography. "You grew up near the Mississippi, right?"

"Closer to the Raccoon River. Mississippi would have been too hard to spell and Raccoon would have been a silly name."

"Yeah, not as cool as Sun, or Ocean, or Leaf," I said. "I love the water, too, mostly the ocean. My last name means 'the ocean.' But I also love the moon."

"Hmm. What about Sailor Moon? No, with your hair it should be Strawberry Moon. But then again, you're pretty sweet. I've got it. Honey Moon, Honey for short."

I laughed, liking the sound of it, but doubting that I'd ever answer to it.

"Honey Moon," River said, and I turned my head like the moon tide. "You answered to it. Now it's stuck on you like—honey." I wouldn't argue.

River stood and reached out to take my hand, pulling me up to dance with him.

Face to face, I tried to mimic his moves, mashing potatoes and twisting my hips, like we were enacting a scene straight out of the *Patty Duke Show*.

One pair of matching bookends, different as night and day, we sang from the theme song. And what a wild duet we were just a couple of extraordinary teenaged girls leading dual lives wanting to live ordinary teenaged lives.

Finally, I'd found a friend, someone I thought I might confide in. River shuffled to the vanity to remove his wig, his matted Afro springing to life. I looked into the mirror, feeling safer talking to his reflection. "I'm also cursed."

He looked up before dropping the wig back into the box.

CHAPTER 13

Have Another Hit

In the morning, I anxiously waited to talk to River about my curse. I stood in the kitchen with Mary, Indigo, and the others getting ready to make bread. I would tell him everything I hadn't the night before, including how I'd killed Dilbert, but then a young man stumbled in.

"What's your name?" River asked the stranger, his hair freshly cropped like a Marine jarhead. "Tony. Tony Hatchet."

Indigo offered him some bread. "When we're finished, you can come help me over at the free store around the corner," she said.

River poured two cups of tea, handed me one, and sat on a stool at the counter.

"Thank you."

"Awfully quiet this morning, Honey Moon. You okay?"

I liked my new name. "Yeah, just thinking about stuff." I took a sip of my tea.

"Well, I'll leave you to your thoughts," he said, picking up a newspaper, something my father would do when Mom wanted to talk. I wanted to talk, but it would have to wait. There were too many people around.

In the meanwhile, the girls set out the ingredients on the big table to make the bread. I looked around, thinking about my sisters at home and how, except for Baby Josie, I'd been envious of them for so many reasons—because they had a bond with each other, because they'd been able to go to school. But I was more jealous of Maggie because by age fifteen, she'd already been kissed at least a thousand times. Even Patty had a boyfriend. At first, I'd been eager to hear how their day went at school. But when they started sharing about all the cute boys and bragging about their crushes, my envy grew into an inside-out sort of rage. As I spread some flour onto the table to make some dough, I wondered why I had to stay home. Why couldn't I go to school like the normal kids? Stupid questions are when you know the answer. I grew to hate Grandma Phoebe even more. My anger eventually drove my sisters away. Every afternoon, they'd tiptoe past my bedroom to do their homework. When they'd go down to play, I'd slip into their rooms to steal their school books and read about things Mom, with her limitations, couldn't teach me. Soon, I also read their journals about all the silly stuff, including how Patty was going to marry Ted and they were going to have three children. Unfortunately, all the reading I'd done couldn't teach me how to read people, much less how to read boys.

I slapped the dough, thinking how I didn't understand the relationship between a man and a woman, much less making out. Before hitting the road, I'd never been kissed. I'd watched my parents kiss. I'd watched them fight. Sometimes, it seemed they'd fight only to end up kissing and then they'd disappear up the stairs.

I thought about when Dilbert planted that gross kiss on me and I'd felt a fierce repulsion. "For that alone, he deserved to die," Grandma whispered.

"Oh my God, Phoebe. Get out!"

River peered at me probingly. I waved my hand over my head. "Oh fly. Get out!"

Last night when I kissed River, it felt nice, but I didn't feel any sparks or fireworks like I'd imagined, like I'd read about in

Wuthering Heights or *Anna Karenina*. I wanted the passion I'd seen on the big screen, like in *Casablanca* or *Gone with the Wind*, the way they stared into each other's eyes as if they could see into each other's souls. I watched Indigo walk out of the kitchen and gasped when a man about mid-twenties came in.

"Hiya, Everett," Indigo said on her way out the back door. "See you later."

Everett looked like Jesus—the white one, not like the one at Cristo del Rey Church—slender face, full lips, and straight nose. I instantly felt like a sparkler being waved around on the Fourth of July and then suddenly shameful, for if he was Jesus, I shouldn't be feeling the feels where I felt them. I squeezed the dough, taking a deep breath before slapping it down onto the wooden tabletop. Pressing the heels of my palms into the dough, I pushed and pulled, mechanically. Out of the corner of my eye, I noticed his dusty brown sandals inching closer.

"Who have we here?" he asked. My heart jackrabbited inside my chest. I took a deep breath, getting ready to respond, but nothing came out of my mouth as I gathered the dough into a ball to stuff into the two-pound coffee cans.

"This is Anna," Mary volunteered for me, thankfully. "Anna, this is Everett Grady. He runs the operation."

His eyes lingered on me, his face easing into a grin. I smiled sheepishly, drowning in his clear eyes, the color of the water I imagined he walked on. He extended his hand, and I reached out, quickly retracting mine when I noticed the glove of white flour. I dusted off on my apron. He then took my hand in his like a hand sandwich. "Welcome." A current of electricity rushed up my arm, circled my heart, and then pooled into my—as Grandma called them–"nether regions."

Maybe it was only chemistry on my part, but I imagined what Mary Magdalene might have felt when first encountering Jesus. "My Lord, may I wash your feet?" I yanked my eyes away from his, calmed by the sight of a spray of freckles splashed across his nose. I couldn't imagine Jesus had freckles.

I tried to blow the hair out of my burning face, but when that didn't work, I pushed my hair with the back of my hand, but then like a benediction, he swiped my forehead. There must have been flour on my brow. I felt my face flush redder than cayenne pepper, my whole body burning even hotter. I wanted to stretch the ball of dough over my head and then jump into the oven.

Mary checked the stovetop as River pulled out a loaf of bread from the oven and then dumped it down on the table.

"Careful there, boy," Everett said.

River glowered at him. You could cut the tension inside the warm kitchen with a butter knife, but I didn't think Everett even noticed River storming out.

★ ★ ★

In the living room later that night, people gathered, smoking and drinking up what Everett had to say. Standing in the doorway, sipping some wine from a jelly jar, every once in a while, I'd catch him looking up, as if searching for one of his lost sheep. And then as Everett was on the tail end of his tale—something about fascism and how we had no business in Vietnam—he locked eyes on me and beamed. He was like the fisherman throwing out a line and I was the little fish being lured by a shiny object. When he finally came over and touched my shoulder, I was hooked, but then someone pulled out a tambourine, someone else a guitar, and then River grabbed my hand. "Anna plays piano. I heard her over at Steinway's. She's pretty good."

I glared at River and he shrugged his shoulders, palms up.

"Steinway's?" Everett said. "You mean the place where that guy croaked."

"It was in this morning's paper," River added, as if it were old news.

My stomach contracted like I'd just been whacked by a bat. Too bad I wasn't a ball getting hit out of there. News sure traveled fast. Everett grinned. "You must be a killer piano player. Show us what you got."

I looked around the room, growing more nervous as I recognized some of the musicians on the scene lately, some from posters hanging on the walls.

Trying to act all cool, I took a seat and pulled back the piano lid. After my brief stint at Steinway's, I thought I knew what people wanted to hear and then just recently, there'd been a song on the radio being played over and over while we worked in the kitchen. It was by a local group and the words resonated with me. I played the first notes of "Somebody to Love" and this time I sang the words out loud.

I finished and the room fell silent. Mary stepped up and hugged me. Tears dripped down River's cheeks.

And then Everett clapped and the others joined in. "Well, obviously you can sing," he said, taking a seat next to me.

"What else you got?" asked a man I recognized as John from Lazarus Rising that played over at Kezar Stadium the day of the march. Everett stood and I played the next song, the one the band had performed about a girl taking a hit of fresh air.

John said, "It does sound better with piano." He sorta creeped me out with his greasy long hair and beady eyes.

"And I think it sounds better with a girl," Everett said, and I blushed.

"And she plays the guitar, too," River added.

Soon, the group got to talking about what was happening out on the street and Vietnam, but River wanted to sing, so I accompanied him on the piano. We made quite a duo. Me playing straight man to his eccentric style of singing and dancing, stirring something wicked in the crowd.

Later, up in my room, as I journaled about how everyone around talked about love and how I thought I'd finally found it, I was interrupted by clapping and turned to see River leaning on the doorjamb. "You were amazing down there," he said, staring at my closed journal.

"Thank you. New lyrics," I said off his look.

"A love song about Everett?" He stepped into the room.

Is he jealous? I wondered and then Grandma added, "I've warned you not to confuse lust with love."

River searched my face. "Anyway, we made a good team. The whole thing just blew me away, like a psychedelic trip."

"Thank you. A trip, huh?"

"I take it, you've never done LSD?"

I reached for the jelly jar of wine I'd brought up to the room with me. "No, I don't need drugs to take a trip." I sipped. I'd barely had my first experience with pot and that didn't go so well. "What's it like?" I asked, setting down my guitar.

"Well, it's not just a trip. It can be kind of a spiritual search." He plopped onto the bed, hands behind his head. "It's a way of expanding your consciousness, embracing a higher one."

"I already have two and the last thing I want is to embrace or expand another consciousness. I'm looking for a way to ditch one."

He peered at me and laughed. "Two? You're funny."

"So, seriously, what's it like?" I asked.

He sat up, reached into his pocket and pulled out a pack of cigarettes before getting up to walk over to the dresser to pick up an ashtray. He lit his cigarette, shaking out the match as he inhaled and then he stepped over some blankets to offer it to me. I'd rather have the matches, but I took the cig.

"The last time, it was really a beautiful trip, like an evolutionary journey."

As he spoke, I exhaled, noticing the *Shroud of Turin* on the wall behind Mary's bed. The image of Jesus, the real one I'd learned about in catechism. Next to it sat a picture of Buddha, Saint Francis of Assisi, a Red Indian Chief, and some swami. I passed the cigarette back to River who took a seat in a chair across from me.

"I sort of felt paranoid," River said. "I started running and then the trip really hit me." He then exhaled. "It was like I lay down and died. I heard beautiful music, sort of like a choir of angels singing. It was a beautiful trip." He laughed. "But I did a number on myself when I rolled in the dirt and fell in the ditch and went under a car where I kicked in the tires. I scarred up my feet and hands and my chest and back. It's going away now." He held out his hands.

"That sure doesn't sound like any kind of trip I want to go on."

"All I can say is if you do, be sure you're in the right place to do it and try not to overdose. Have friends to watch you and keep you from hurting yourself. Then you'll have a trip that's out of this world." He sank to the floor, sitting cross-legged at my feet.

"Wow. Thanks, River, I'll keep all that in mind, but like I said, I don't need drugs to take a trip. Besides, I'm already cursed."

"That's what you said the other night." He leaned in, looking up at me. "Do tell."

"You won't believe me."

"Try me. Come on. What are you talking about?" He slipped off his shoes.

The moment had come. Except once I let Grandma out of the bag, there would be no putting her back in, but I was desperate to unburden myself. My gut told me I could trust him. "Can I see your matches?"

He didn't hesitate to reach into his pocket.

I struck a match, shook it out, taking in a breath of not just comfort, but courage. I closed my eyes, trying to gauge the words I'd use, but when I opened them, he examined me like I was some sort of foreign object.

"So, you know the other night when I told you I was in Paris working for the Red Cross during the war?"

"Yes."

"World War I. Come on?" I stared at him. "I wasn't even born yet."

He scrunched his eyes. "You're right, but I wasn't going to say . . ."

"But my grandmother was and she was the one talking through me."

"And you say you've never done LSD?" Eyes widening, he laughed and then quickly turned somber. "Go on." Elbows on his knees, he rested his chin on his fists.

I rubbed the used match between my fingers. "I'd always heard a voice in my head that wasn't mine. I was four when I first heard my parents talking about how my grandmother had transferred her consciousness to me at my birth. Before that, I really didn't know the difference. I mean, how was I to know that all the people in the world didn't think the way I did—didn't have multiple consciousness. After a while, I was kept at home for my own protection. We never knew when or where Grandma was going to pop in."

"So, it's like reincarnation?" River asked.

"Not exactly. It's actually an eastern religious ritual called Phowa, but next level; sort of like the last rites given in the Catholic Church just before someone dies. Like a priest, or anyone really, prays over the dying person. It's their last chance to be forgiven for their sins, so they can get into heaven and not go to hell."

"Oh Lord. Sorry but I was raised Methodist. To me it all sounds like mumbo jumbo. I'd need a whole church full of priests to do their voodoo magic on me," River said with a laugh.

"Darling, I told you he wouldn't understand." Grandma only needed to whisper for attention.

"Wait, there's the voice again. How do you do that?" He peered into my eyes.

I stood and reached for the cigarette. I held in the smoke. "It's not me." I blasted out the vapor wishing Grandma would disappear with it. "Anyway, there's not much written about it, but there was a book at home, probably Grandma's. I've done a lot of research at the library, but there's nothing except I guess if you believe in Albert Einstein's speed of light theory or his theory of relativity, then you've got to believe in his law of energy conservation."

"I wasn't the best student in school, but please go on." He looked at me as if I were a mad scientist. "This is all just fascinating."

"Anyway, Einstein says energy can neither be created nor destroyed, but it can change forms. It's the 'law.' So, it's like we're all light, energy, and somehow, Grandma transferred her energy over to me."

"But how, exactly?"

He didn't interrupt me as I described to him what I knew of the process, including the piercing of the fontanel, at which I detected a slight flinch in his demeanor.

"You see babies are pure at birth, so lucky me. I inherited more than just her ear for music, and I can tell you right now, the only thing that's pure is the hell she's put me through." His mouth opened to suck it all in. "So now, I just need to find a way to send her back."

River nodded, then looked off to the side, squeezing his lips with his hand and then using a pointer finger as if deciphering a math problem in the air, he asked, "What about anyone else in your family? Do your siblings share a consciousness?"

"Just my father with his father," I said. River arched a dubious eyebrow. "When I was around eight, in a moment of atonement, my father told me that he'd also been cursed and that he'd suffered because his father had used him the same way my grandmother used me." It was one of the reasons I'd forgiven Dad for hurting me, one of the reasons I felt sorry for him—sometimes even more sorry than I felt for myself—it's probably the main reason for the stabbing—but not the only reason as it would turn out.

River cocked his head. "So, your grandma uses your voice to talk. How—what does it sound like, in your head? Is it like a thought or like someone whispering in your ear?" His eyes widened as he focused on me, elbows on knees, chin resting in his hands.

"It's difficult to describe, especially if you've never heard voices yourself. It's like she's standing right next to me or like her voice is a thought. Sometimes it's both. You know how sometimes you'll hear a tune and later you find yourself humming that tune and you never made a conscious decision to start humming that tune and then you can't get it out of your head?"

River nodded. "It's so annoying, especially if it's Bob Dylan."

I laughed. "I happen to like Dylan. But yes, exactly. Sometimes we have a conversation."

"Like what? Does she ever make you do things you don't want? Like things that could hurt you?"

Can I trust him to tell him about Dilbert or my father? That's a lot to dump on him right now.

"Never. I would never hurt my Anna," Grandma yelled.

River peered at me.

"It's more like she tries to stop me from myself. But she has done things that end up hurting me."

"What do you mean?"

"It's hard to explain. It's why I'm here and not home anymore. It's why I'm here and not playing piano anymore at Steinway's." I peered at River hoping he could just figure everything out without me having to say anything more? But, how could he?

"Wait, did Dilbert hurt you? Were you there when he killed himself?"

Bam! I got a burning pain in my lower stomach that rose like a flame into my head that became too heavy to meet his eyes anymore. I looked down at the used match still in my hand, blackened by soot.

"Well, tell you what, if I had the courage, I might have killed him myself."

Was River setting up a trap by downplaying the act of murder? Trembling, I'd said too much, and yet there was still so much more I wanted to unload. But I wasn't ready. I didn't know whether I could trust River so I tried to change the subject. "Her voice has been present day and night since I can remember."

"Sounds like an acid trip to me," River said.

My voice shook. "Even while I sleep, it's like I have the most vivid dreams and in color. There are memories buried in my bones from the past, but who's past?" Sometimes, I wondered if I hadn't fallen into one of her dreams, the red and purple parade of her passion, rage, and regrets; a display of her fertile green desire, even the blue smoke from her Chesterfields seemed to drift through my esophagus. "I used to dream I lived in France. I had to teach myself French to try and understand why I was making love to some French soldier. It was so intense."

"Oh, that was Guillome," Grandma said with a raspy girlish giggle. "You're old enough now. I can tell you."

"Gross. You see?" I said.

River, wide-eyed, shook his head.

"I could even smell the manure on his boots and then I woke up, my whole body aching, and it felt like a death."

"That's because he died," Grandma added with a bit more solemnity.

"This is why I shouldn't talk to anyone about my dreams. You're the first person I've told about anything. It's the reason I'm so lonely sometimes. The reason I'm so isolated and withdrawn. It's the reason I'm full of rage. I don't want to be that way." I started to cry. "I want to be normal. You think I'm crazy like everyone else."

River sprang up and threw his arms around me, rocking like we were doing some sort of slow sad dance, my head on his shoulder. "Oh, sugar, I don't think you're crazy. I think you're better than normal. Honey, you're marvelous."

"I want her to go away," I sobbed into his collarbone. More than the fear of being linked to Dilbert's death was the idea of a prison sentence with Grandma. A death sentence might be better. "I need to find a way to get rid of her." I sensed some rumbling, but she said nothing.

River pulled away. "You know, you mentioned something about it being an Eastern religious practice. Maybe, Mother Mary can help."

So, he believed me!

"I think she's Buddhist or Hindu or some shit like that," River added. "She's always meditatin' or sneakin' next door to hang out with these bald Krishnas who listen to lectures by some guru." River pointed to another poster on the wall of a swami sitting lotus style, dressed in orange with a matching turban and a colorful flower lei.

Beneath the poster was Mary's stack of books. I picked up the one I'd noticed earlier titled *Tibetan Book of the Dead*.

"Indeed, perhaps she can help us," Grandma said.

River took the book from me. "I'm just going to borrow it," he said, and headed toward the door, stepping over pillows, but before he walked out, he turned to me, holding the book out to make a point. "And one more thing. Mother Mary's cool, but stay away from Everett. He's the devil, a wolf in sheep's clothing. He speaks with a forked tongue."

"Okay, I get it already." My gut, Grandma, and now River were all telling me the same thing.

Sharing my story with River felt as if I'd taken a hit of fresh air after being buried alive for centuries.

In the bathroom and as I brushed my teeth, I looked into the mirror. My eyes seemed brighter, even the worry ripples on my forehead looked less worried. I couldn't wait to hear what advice Mother Mary might give me.

CHAPTER 14

Dreams

Not a bread-making morning, we lazed in the bedroom. The sun streamed in, illuminating Mother Mary sitting lotus-style on top of her bed, meditating, eyes closed. I tiptoed in reverently, but tripped over one of the pillows scattered across the floor, and the towel fell off my head.

"Sorry." I stepped over to the nightstand and touched her stack of books.

"Are these all yours?" I picked one up.

She nodded as Indigo came in from her shower, wet black hair cascading to her hips. She noticed the *Book on Dreams* I held.

"Outta sight," Indigo said. "Can you interpret my dream for me?" Her towel tumbled to the floor and her breasts, large as cantaloupes, jiggled as she flapped her arms. "I was a bird, this time flying over the Bay."

I turned away. I don't believe I'd ever seen another completely naked person in my life. In my house, we were all very modest, screaming loud enough to scare ghosts out of the room if we were caught in our underwear.

"I don't need Freud to interpret this," Mary said. "You're either feeling free or you want to escape."

"Well, since I've already escaped, I must be feeling free," Indigo said, wiggling into her jeans.

"Wow, so dreams have meaning?" I asked.

"Of course, they do and there are plenty of typical dreams," Mary said. "For instance, I'm sure you've dreamt about flying or being chased, or being naked in public."

River appeared at the doorway. "Those are dreams?" He strode into the room and plopped onto a pile of blankets.

"They sound like nightmares to me," I said, combing fingers through my tangled wet hair.

"Sounds more like my reality." River laughed, and then, gently cradling his still swollen face, he said, "Tell us about your French dream, the one with Guillome."

I glared at him as Grandma said, "Not funny!" He put a hand over his mouth just as his eyes darted toward the doorway. I turned to see Tony standing there, leaning on the doorframe. "Hey man. What's this a big slumber party?"

"Mother Mary's interpreting our dreams," Indigo said.

"Way out. I always dream that my teeth are falling out," Tony said, crossing his arms.

I laughed nervously, remembering I'd had the same dreams.

"That just means you've lost personal power, the ability to be assertive and protect yourself," Mary said. "On the other hand, it can also indicate a desire to flee or escape from the realities of life."

How could I have anything personal, much less power, with Grandma plaguing my mind? And, weren't we all escaping something? I wanted to escape Grandma before I became her. I'd fled home for good reason and I sure didn't want to think about what had happened to Dilbert. I wanted to hope it would all go away. I knew his mother was dead, but I didn't want to know if he had any other family that would miss him. Thankfully, so far, I hadn't had any nightmares about him, but I did have some crazy dreams, lately.

"Can you interpret this one? I had it last night," I said, testing the waters, and soon all eyes were on me. "I was in this swimming pool filled with sparkling turquoise water. I was splashing around and then some sharks started chasing me. I was so scared and then one circled me and opened up his jaw to swallow me and I woke up in a cold sweat."

Mary laughed. "Cool, two symbols in one dream. First, let's start with the swimming pool, which in general means passionate love. There's someone you wish to start a relationship with."

I looked at Tony, close-set eyes, pock-faced, and short. Not my type—not that I had a type. I looked at River—not his type. And the scary feelings I had for Everett confused me. The sensations swung from one side of the metronome to the other—good or bad, it was too powerful to tell.

"A shark may represent a person in your life who is draining you emotionally. But more than one symbol, that's something to pay close attention to."

Bingo! And duh! Grandma was the deadly fish here and definitely a drain on me.

"Instead of being frozen in fear, you must confront it in order to move past it. Everyone carries a shadow." Yup, she's definitely talking about Phoebe. "There's a part of you that you're not acknowledging."

I don't want to acknowledge her. I don't even want her around.

"A swimming pool represents danger which leads to this shark you dreamed about. I know you're eighteen and can make your own life choices, but I'd say just be careful around Everett," Mary said.

Everett? I had been thinking about him day and literally night.

"Shark dreams are associated with negativity and conscious or unconscious threats."

Dilbert is a dead shark fish chum and the threat of him has no teeth, speaking of teeth, I thought, as I heard a knock on the door downstairs. We all turned our heads.

"More runaways," Mary said, inhaling deeply as she stood.

"Or the FBI," Indigo added as Tony moved out of the doorway to let Mary pass on her way downstairs. "Everett's paranoid that the house is being watched," she said, tossing some pillows onto the bed.

"But, but why?" I asked.

"He's been warned about contributing to the delinquency of minors by harboring runaways," she said and the alarm clanged inside my chest. She then peered at Tony. "Also, it's illegal to harbor anyone who's gone AWOL." Tony beat feet across the hall to hide.

Mary called for us to come down. "There are a couple of policemen here who'd like to ask some questions." It was too late for me to run. Indigo, Willow, River, and I came downstairs. Two burly cops stood in the living room.

All at once I'm nine years old and the officers are in my living room trying to settle Dad down. I wished I could run to my room like my sisters and cower, but Grandma held me hostage again, hijacking my voice. She and Mom had ganged up on him for the millionth time about his drinking. Dad grew into such a rage again, punching holes in the wall, throwing furniture. The police did nothing to help except watch as Mom loaded my siblings and me into the car. We stayed in a hotel that night, three to twin beds lying sideways. Grandma sang a lullaby through me that night to calm us.

★ ★ ★

"This is Honey Moon," Mary said, turning to the others. "River, Willow, and Indigo."

"Anyone else live here?" the taller cop asked.

"People come and go," Mary said, dismissively. And without turning to us, she added, "These officers are investigating the death of the man from Steinway's."

With sweaty hands, I clutched the sides of my dress. *Instead of being frozen in fear, you must confront it in order to move past it.* "Death? What happened?" I asked. "When?"

"That's what we're trying to find out. So far, it looks like suicide."

The shorter cop narrowed his eyes at me. "Or, maybe it was made to look like suicide."

"So, you suspect foul play?" Mary asked.

"We're just out canvassing the neighborhood."

They weren't volunteering much information. And neither would I.

"Anyone here ever frequent Steinway Café?"

River and I answered yes at the same time. So much for not volunteering. I wadded up the fabric at my side. Indigo and Willow were free to take a seat on the couch.

The tall cop peered at River. "Well, River, what's your real name?"

"Levi. Levi Smith."

"Where'd you get that black eye?"

"I was born with it."

Willow and Indigo giggled. The cops weren't having it.

"I walked into a door."

"Do you happen to know any female Black singers?"

River looked like he didn't know whether to laugh or be serious. "In person?"

"Why?" Mary asked.

I wondered if everyone could hear my heart beating. Someone over at Steinway's must have seen or heard something. Or maybe River hadn't told me everything.

"Someone saw her arguing with the owner just before she walked out the night before the incident." I remembered Dilbert going after her. "We just want to ask her some questions," Tall cop said, turning to River. "I'll need to see your ID."

River didn't hesitate, as if this was routine, and pulled out his wallet to hand over his identification. Taller cop jotted down his information.

"And you, Honey Moon, what's your real name?" he asked without looking up.

I clenched my teeth from chattering, but didn't hesitate to answer with false confidence, "Susan Glass."

The officer gazed at me and I prayed he wouldn't ask for my ID. All I had was a Glendale library card with my name Phoebe Anna LeMar. But instead, he turned back to River as if he'd already found his man, convicted him, and sent him to the gas chamber. I panicked, ready to turn myself in. "Calm down," Grandma shouted.

Taller cop cut a glance at me. "Do you know anyone named DeeDee?"

I shrugged my shoulders.

He then addressed River. "Levi Smith, where were you Tuesday night?"

"I was here," River answered.

"I can vouch for him," Mary said.

I wanted to take the attention off of River. "I was out partying on the street and then crashed over in Panhandle Park."

"Not that he asked you," shorter cop said. "Out past curfew? So, you were loitering?"

"You can't prove it," Grandma said, and I slapped my hand over my mouth. I must have looked scared.

Taller cop said to me, "I'm going to need to see your ID, too." I froze.

"On what grounds?" Mary asked.

Tall cop stared at her and then jotted down some more notes in his pad, peering at River and me. I wondered what DeeDee might have told them.

"What's this all about?" Mary asked.

"Mr. Moss was found dead. Almost looks like a suicide, except for the fire and the busted open safe in his office." I could understand a fire, but I knew nothing about a busted open safe. I wondered about DeeDee.

Fire? River watched as I reached into my pocket to feel for the pack of matches. He scrunched his face and subtly shook his head.

And then the officer asked, "Do either of you own a knife?" All my blood drained to my feet. How could I have left it behind?

"I thought you said it was a gun," Mary said, whipping out her knife, and the cops slapped their hands on their holsters faster than a speeding bullet. She laughed. "Are you kidding? Everyone around here owns one."

Tall cop's nostrils flared big as tunnels as if he knew he'd come to a dead end.

"And what about the fire?" Mary asked.

"It was contained." He closed his notepad. "If you hear anything, here's my number. "And if you come across any Black female singers—" He handed Mary a card.

She locked the door behind them and then turned toward us. "Honey Moon, you're white as flour."

I saw chartreuse. "I'm not feeling good," I said, taking the stairs up two at a time.

After puking in the bathroom, I splashed my face and stared in the mirror. What am I going to do?

"Go home," Grandma said, and I hurried to the bedroom to gather my belongings. Sure enough, I couldn't find my knife, the knife with so many bad memories.

River walked in as I packed up my things. "What are you doing?"

"I gotta split."

He took my hands. "Look at me, Honey. What's the matter? You can tell me."

Hot tears sizzled down my cheeks. "I feel like I'm naked and being chased by sharks, and all my teeth are falling out," I blubbered, pulling my hands away to swipe my runny nose with the back of my sleeve. "I want to swim away."

"Sounds like quite a nightmare." River chuckled. "You know, like I said before, if I'd had the courage, I would have killed Dilbert myself."

Morbidly curious, I peered into River's dark, soulful eyes, the skin around the left one already healing that yellowish green color. I knew the different shades of bruises from experience. I wiped my eyes and then sunk onto the bed.

He sat down next to me. "After I sang the other night, Dilbert came up to offer me a job singing there."

"Yeah, I remember."

"He asked me to come back to his office and then he came on to me. First he put his hand on my chest." River chuckled. "You should have seen his freaked-out face when he realized my bra was stuffed with socks. I backed away, but then he grabbed my crotch. He punched me in the face, before throwing me to the ground and kicking me."

"Oh my God! So this was all happening as I was out front playing the piano?"

"When he finished pounding on me, he went to his desk drawer and pulled out a gun and yelled, 'Get the fuck out of here, you nigger faggot, before I call the police.' I wanted to kill him right then and there."

"I'm so sorry." I reached out to touch River's arm, still bruised from where Dilbert had kicked him. "I wondered where you'd gone and then I saw you limping out the front door. Do you think he called the police?"

River shrugged his shoulders, got up, and walked to the window, his back to me. I wondered if I could trust him.

"You can trust him," Grandma whispered.

"He tried to rape me," I said, and River pivoted toward me. "And then the gun went off."

Head cocked, River stared at me dubiously. "Did you shoot him?"

"Not exactly, and I know what it looks like."

"I'm not sure I do."

I explained quickly how it happened.

"What about the fire?"

I shrugged. "I have no idea." I wasn't ready to tell him about another of my quirks. I wasn't a pyromaniac.

"Aren't you tired of running? How long can you keep this all in?"

"So, you think I should turn myself in?"

"No, but—it's just that I know what it's like."

I held my head. "I know. Mary said something about confronting my fears so that I can move past them. I thought she was talking about Everett."

"Yeah, you need to talk to Mother Mary, but not about Everett or Dilbert. You need to talk about how to get rid of your Grandma."

"Excuse me?" Grandma squawked out loud. "Darling, cut me off and you'll have no connection to the past."

"Whose past?" I responded. "I don't care about your past. I'll create a new future for myself."

"Darling, no woman is an island."

* * *

My heart raced as I stuffed my knapsack wondering if Mother Mary could help me. I needed to get out of here sooner than later. I looked around the bedroom to make sure I hadn't missed anything.

"Well you certainly mustn't tell her anything," Grandma said. "As evolved as you may think she is, she won't understand. She'll turn you in. Don't be naive."

"I'm not naive. You are. Besides, you told me to listen to my gut."

I turned to find Mother Mary standing in the doorway. "New lyrics?"

I couldn't hold it in anymore, and why should I? What did I have to lose by telling Mother Mary? I didn't want to run anymore. I shook my head.

"River says you need to talk to me."

After I'd confided in River, it felt like a haunted house had been lifted off of me. I imagined how much better I'd feel if I did talk to Mother Mary.

"I um—my um."

"No, Anna!"

"Well, I'm just going to say it. I share a consciousness with my grandmother."

Mary stared at me, leaning her head as if she wasn't hearing straight.

"You know those times when you've caught me talking to myself, well—I'm actually talking to her."

"Her, your grandmother?" Mary smiled as if I were a two-year-old talking about my imaginary rabbit friend, Harvey. "And is she talking back?"

I huffed, crossing my arms over my chest, thrusting a hip. This was a bad idea.

"How exactly is that happening?" Mary asked.

For the second time in two days, I'd have to explain the whole Grandma Phoebe phenomenon. River had been quite understanding and I hoped Mary would be, too. As I spoke, Mary simply nodded.

"It's sort of like when Jesus died and then on the third day, he rose again. She didn't exactly die, she just waited until the day I was born and transferred over to me. It's a thing called Phowa."

Mary's brow crinkled. Whether she believed me or not, by just sharing this with her, a weight had been lifted. But it also felt as if Grandma were a pressure cooker about to explode. I'd been taking my time getting to the point when Grandma spoke up in an octave lower than mine. "Darling Mother Mary, you're quite an intelligent young woman with all of your Eastern religious teachings. Are you sure you've never heard of it?"

Mary drew her head back slightly, searching my face. "An offshoot? No, but I don't know everything. I can certainly ask."

"Anna, this is exactly why I told you not to tell."

Mary peered even closer at me. "Why do you sound so hoarse?"

"So, Mother Mary," Grandma said.

"Puh, please, just call me Mary," she said with a wary smile.

"Very well and you can call me Phoebe. Mary, whom might you query and what might you say precipitated the inquiry?"

"I can talk to my swami," Mary said without skipping a beat.

"One of your modern-day teachers," Grandma Phoebe said, dismissively. "How much can he possibly know?"

"Well, he's studied the masters."

"Ah, yes, I myself studied the divine wisdom of the masters back in 1908. Divine wisdom being the common tree trunk from which religions sprout as branches."

"Wait, you said 1908." Mary finally seemed to pick up on the lapse in time, the change in diction, and the lower C-sharp in my voice.

"Indeed, I traveled to India after the death of my dear father. I was searching for answers and a connection. It is there that I learned about the transference of consciousness."

I wished you'd go back and unlearn it, already, I thought, and as soon as I did, I knew I needed to find a way to get to India. Maybe I can meet Mary's swami. Or go to India and find Grandma's, if he's still alive.

"I was there until April, 1910 during the grooming of the New World Teacher, Jiddu Krishnamurti. I taught him music. He wasn't very good at piano, all thumbs, poor dear."

"Wait, you were there the same time as Annie Besant?" Mary said, eyes widening as if the British social reformer Besant herself had stepped into the room. Mary had once again swallowed the line, bait, hook, and sinker.

"You've heard of her?"

"Of course, I admire her writings on female activism," Mary said, reaching over to grab a book from her nightstand. "I'm reading from this book," she said, holding up *A Dirty Filthy Book*.

"Ah, yes," Grandma said. "Quite informative. Her talks on birth control."

"Yes, and women taking agency of their own body," Mary said.

And now I'd found myself sucked into the conversation and couldn't resist adding, "So much for control. You still had my father."

"What are you talking about?" Mary asked, peering at me.

"I was talking to her," I responded to Mary, pointing to my temple.

Mary scrunched her brow and shook her head, clearly confused.

I waited for Grandma to say something, but she remained silent on this subject. I knew how she hated airing dirty laundry.

Besides I already knew the story, something about how her music always came first. And then I added a zinger: "So, he *was* a mistake, after all!"

Mary sucked in a breath and then slapped her hand over her mouth, muffling what she said next. "But I didn't know he was married." She lowered herself onto the edge of her bed, tears springing forth. Some sort of scab had obviously been picked off. I wanted to step in to help Mary and tell her we weren't talking about her, but covering up for Grandma Phoebe usually got me into more trouble.

"I gave the child up for adoption. It was a mistake." Mary sobbed.

"Darling, there are no mistakes, only opportunities to evolve," Grandma said.

So why hadn't I evolved, I wondered? Why did I still feel like a tiny plankton unable to swim against the ocean's current of Grandma? Unable to see the sun? How could I to grow when she always stood in my light? I grabbed a tissue from the nightstand and handed it to Mary.

"Thank you. Phoebe." She blew her nose. "Sorry, may I call you Phoebe?"

"Why certainly, Mary, darling."

Mary blew her nose. "This is all so fascinating. I have so many questions. You know, there was this study at Berkeley, about the future of teleporting information—machines called computers, but this discussion would be way more advanced. I don't know if we're even ready for—"

"Oh my God! How is this going to help me?" I asked. "What about your swami? When can I meet him?"

"Maybe. What if I invited you—and Phoebe—to come and lecture next week over at—"

"Are you fucking kidding me?" I yelled. "This isn't what I— how is this helping me?"

Mary stared at me in what I imagined to be a cocktail of shame, disbelief, and confusion.

The police are snooping around asking questions about a murder. I don't have time to worry about Grandma and swamis and other people's mistakes! I grabbed my bag and stormed out of the room, down the stairs, and out the front door. I'd miss my chance to talk to Mary's swami, besides Grandma probably would have charmed the robe off of him anyway.

CHAPTER 15

A Church Along the Way

I ran past a line of shivering hippies huddled together under blankets on Clayton Street, near the corner of Haight, right in front of where I'd thrown up the day I first met Mary. Waiting to get into the free clinic, they'd come from all over the country thinking it would be sunny in San Francisco in the middle of summer, but it wasn't and they'd catch colds and even pneumonia. The clinic was also a place where runaways could get help with stuff like gonorrhea and cut feet. There were also injuries from botched abortions, stomach problems from eating rotten food, not to mention hallucinations and bad trips from all the drugs. The clinic's motto was "Healthcare is a right not a privilege."

Hugging my coat tighter, head down, I kept walking, guitar and knapsack strapped to my back, hoping I'd never find myself in need of such a place.

"Hey, it's the Guitar Girl!" I recognized the voice and froze in place, staring into his eyes, like magnets drawing me in as Charlie, the creep from the van, smiled at me, a strung-out girl hanging on each of his arms.

"Run!" Grandma said.

I hurried toward the park, a shadow of paranoia following and then catching up to me, seeping into my pores, poisoning my mind. He can't catch me and why would he want to? I mean, he only had two arms. How could he possibly handle more than two girls? But what about the police? Overcome with terror, I imagined the police had somehow made the connection between my father's stabbing and Dilbert. I took a right turn and before long I could see a twin set of church steeples practically piercing through the puffs of clouds. I ran toward the church.

Out of breath, I stood on the church steps surrounded by silvery pigeons soaking in the filtered rays of sunlight on their wings. The bells sounded and another flock of birds scrambled out of the towers. It didn't look like anyone was following me and I needed a moment to rest and come up with a plan.

"Find the bus station," Grandma said. "And get on a bus. Go home."

St. Ignatius Church, the sign read at the entrance. I remembered learning about Ignatius the Spanish saint with lots of reddish hair like mine and Grandma's.

To spite Grandma Phoebe or maybe just because I'd run out of answers, I stepped into the church. Wasn't a church, after all, sort of like out of bounds for the authorities? An olly, olly oxen free zone? I remembered my Old Testament catechism mentioning something about safe havens at the altar for criminals who commit accidental murder. Under the domed ceilings, rainbow prisms of light streamed from the arched stained-glass windows. It felt cool inside and the familiar smell of incense infused me with a sense of peace, luring me back in time. I braced myself as I moved forward up the red-carpeted aisle, and when I reached the altar, I knelt down and called upon all the saints and angels I'd ever prayed to in my whole life.

I looked off to the side where a statue of the Virgin Mary stood. I walked over to light one of the penny candles at her feet. *You can light them all, but it's not going to work, darling.* I lit a votive anyway and then kneeled down to pray to St. Joan, my patron saint I'd chosen at confirmation when I was twelve.

I closed my eyes. "*Dear St. Joan, please help me hold up my sword against my assailants and this invader of my thoughts.*" I pictured myself in armor holding up a sword, jabbing at the air. I was never good at praying, my mind was always flitting all over the place like a captured beetle bug in a mason jar. Soon, all I could hear over the silence were my thoughts. I opened my eyes to look around as I adjusted my knees, remembering my First Holy Communion. I closed my eyes again, to squeeze out the memory, but still my mind drifted to that picture of myself resembling a little seven-year-old angel in my virginal mantilla, like a halo over Shirley Temple curls.

We're all lined up, boys on one side, girls on the other clicking in white patent-leather shoes over the cool, snow-colored tiles up to the altar. Ahead, penny candles flickered from little strawberry jelly jars, the color of the blood dripping from Jesus' palms up on the cross. And there, in the pew, sat Mom, wearing her Coty red lipstick and sporting a pair of sunglasses to shield eyes that weren't just brown, but black and blue. In Mom's lap napped baby sister, Patty.

"There she is!" Maggie shouted as I made my way up the aisle, little white-gloved hands steepled together in front of my nose in silent supplication. I haven't seen my father yet and pray he won't be a no-show.

Absent for my birth, and my baptism, I'd learned, why would this sacrament be any different? But like the traces of frankincense that permeated the church, my father would only be a hint of a memory.

I hadn't eaten the morning of my First Holy Communion so by the time it's my row's turn to stand and make our way to the altar, my stomach growls like Dad with a hangover. This time the scent of the burning incense nauseates me. I stand and wobble like a drunk before staggering up to the Communion rail where I genuflect, look up to Father Reynoso, and stick out my tongue. The wafer tastes like a tortilla. I'm so hungry.

In the name of the Father—*touch your forehead*—and the Son—*touch your heart*—and the Holy Spirit—*touch each shoulder.* I return to my pew and bow my pin-curled head.

That morning, I'd floated out of the church into a brighter world with all of God's newest little saints-in-the-making. In the span of an hour, I'd transformed into Saint Anna, patron saint of drunken fathers. At seven years of age, my only mission had been to make Dad stop. I'd felt an energy so powerful that if I only prayed harder, he'd never get drunk again. It didn't work.

But now maybe if I only pray harder, Grandma Phoebe might leave me alone. I had a new calling as I walked out of St. Ignatius Church. I looked up at the sound of squawking seagulls, imagining myself as part of the flock. I followed them until I hit the dock of the bay.

★ ★ ★

The Golden Gate Bridge loomed large to my left and I wondered if that might be a sign from St. Joan. My father once told me how he'd tried to jump off the Colorado Street "Suicide Bridge" in Pasadena. "It's the only way I thought I could get rid of the voice," he'd told me. "When you die, they die."

I'd need to find a different sign.

CHAPTER 16

Don't Jump

A briny smell blew in from the bay evoking a memory of the fishing trip with Dad before everything took a dive. What was it about mixing all of these smells with disasters that unearthed these memories? I shook my head, trying to wash away the echo in my mind as I drifted toward the bridge, the mist cooling my face. I reached a boatyard where a sign read 'Point Golden Gate' and found a bench where I set my bag down. I took a seat to catch my breath, resting my guitar on my lap. Boats of every type, size and shape sailed, chugged and cruised back and forth beneath the bridge and then the memory bubbled up.

On our fishing trip, Dad had shared how the police showed up at the bridge just before he was going to jump. Someone had reported the car he'd been driving as stolen. He was saved by the red flashing lights, he said.

I wondered what it would be like to jump. Would death be instantaneous, painless? Or would I hit the water only to slowly drown?

I felt a scratch in my throat. "Not a good idea, Darling. Besides you know it is a sin in the Catholic Church. And nothing changes, except that you are on the other side, even more miserable than here on Earth."

"Years later, Dad did eventually succeed in getting rid of his father's consciousness."

"Yes, and if those brave surfers had not rescued him and then brought him back to life, he wouldn't have survived. He would have died like Wesley. I would advise you not to do anything crazy."

Apparently, sometime after the bridge fiasco, Dad drove out to Santa Monica and swam out past the breakers where he got spun around as if he were in a giant washing machine. The next thing he remembered was a couple of surfers performing mouth-to-mouth on the shore.

I strummed my guitar. "Yeah, you mean, don't be like Dad, be more like you."

"Must you be so contrary?"

"Must you always butt in?" I sang, plucking the strings.

"You would only be worse off on the other side. You are not prepared. You would not have time to transfer your consciousness should you end it all here."

I thrummed so hard I thought I might have sliced my fingers. "Oh God, why on Earth would I want to transfer my consciousness?"

Silence. I'd won this debate. Chalk one up for me, I thought as a man in a blue uniform marched toward me out of some white government-looking building. I couldn't tell if he was a cop or not. I wanted to bolt, but he stood close enough to shoot me and not miss. I twanged the strings. "Grandma, someone's coming. Be quiet." He got closer and I noticed he wore navy blue bell bottom jeans and a light blue chambray shirt. Not the police, thank God.

"Hello." He tipped a little blue ball cap. His face tilted up and the spotlight above his blond head seemed to shine on him alone as if he'd been cut out of sunshine and pasted onto a watery background. Close enough for me to see an eagle sitting in a "V" on his upper sleeve; he appeared to be as tall as the bridge in the background.

"Hi." I removed my hand from my mouth.

"Come to look at the bridge?" he asked.

"So that's the infamous Golden Gate."

"That's it," he said and, still floating from my earlier church experience and speaking of drowning, I almost drowned in his ocean blue eyes sparkling behind a pair of black-rimmed, military-issue glasses.

"Looks more orange than gold," I said. "How tall is it?"

"Around seven hundred fifty feet to the top."

"If someone were to jump, would they survive?"

He searched my face. "We encounter them pretty frequently. Sometimes, we can intervene. But, to answer your question, odds would not be in the jumper's favor."

"I suppose that all depends on what the jumper's favor is," I answered, giggling nervously. He didn't crack a smile. I noticed his jaw muscles constricting. "So, what's that emblem on your sleeve?" I asked.

"Coast Guard."

"Hmm. So, is that all you do all day is rescue pole vaulters?" I asked.

"Mostly, and boaters who get into trouble."

"Sorry, but that sounds pretty boring."

"Well, I might be getting shipped to Nam, so that ought to be exciting."

"Vietnam?" All I'd heard about that place was that they were killing innocent women and children. "But why?"

"Part of a military assignment," he said.

"Like what?"

"It's top secret. If I told you, I'd have to kill you," he said with a mischievous grin, and I smiled.

"So, you're military?"

He nodded. "Coast Guard is military. I know how to shoot straight."

"With what, a water pistol?" I laughed. "Do you arrest people?" I asked and then the eerie sound of a horn made me jump up from the bench.

The Coastie pivoted quickly. "Excuse me, gotta go," he yelled, bolting away, his long legs scissor-cutting a swath toward a boathouse.

I scanned the wind-whipped waters but couldn't see any sign of imminent danger and snugged up my sweater. Walking away, I wondered why anyone would give his life to fight and possibly be killed for our country so corrupt. Why were we even in Vietnam? I was ashamed of myself for not understanding everything going on in the world, but if I were fighting for something besides autonomy from Grandma, I might be a better, more evolved person.

★ ★ ★

By the time I reached the base of the bridge, I heard quick footsteps snapping behind me. I panicked, turning to see the Guardsman gaining on me. I sucked in a brackish breath. Had he heard about Dilbert? Had he come to arrest me? Did he have that authority?

"False alarm," he said. "Do you mind if I walk with you?"

"It's still a free country," I said, calming myself as I looked up to see how he blocked the sun like a mountain at sunset. *Oh my, he's as tall and handsome as that actor, John Wayne. Grandma!* "I don't even know your name."

"Thomas Steele. My friends call me Tommy."

"Nice to meet you, Thomas."

"My friends call me Honey—Anna, actually. My Dad was in the Navy."

"Oh yeah?"

I grew quiet. Why had I volunteered that? Except that even after the gulf separated Dad and me, I'd always be part sailor, by blood. I wouldn't mention how he ended up over in the psychiatric ward of the Oakland Naval Hospital before being medically discharged with a lifelong prescription of lithium. He would go for long periods without taking them and then a couple of years ago, Mom made me take the pills. She'd read somewhere that it worked on migraines. It didn't. It made me twitch and pee a lot.

Finally, we made it to the top of the bridge. My brain kept going back to how my father said he tried to jump. Again, I wondered what it would feel like to just jump off, not to die necessarily, but to be a girl flying through the air without a care. Not that I would jump because girls don't fly.

I looked across. "What's over there?"

"Just a sleepy little town called Mill Valley."

I stared at the vessels coming and going. "I wonder where it's off to," I said, noticing a tall cruise ship pass underneath us.

"Some place exotic, I imagine," Thomas said.

"Like Hawaii? That, sounds exotic." I imagined being a stowaway off to see the world.

"Yeah, I hope to get stationed there someday. Listen, I should turn back. Have you eaten?" I shook my head. "Why don't you come back with me to the base and grab a bite to eat? You know, until you figure things out."

It sounded like a good idea, but I'd come this far, nearly crossed the bridge—the bridge of no return. *Listen to your gut, darling. You are hungry. He seems decent. The bridge will still be here. You can jump later.*

"Okay."

★ ★ ★

The seagulls gathered like the hungry hippies in Panhandle Park as soon as we took a seat at a picnic table just outside the barracks. Thomas broke off some bread and flung it far enough to keep them at bay.

"That was nice of you to watch over me," I said, bringing a spoonful of soup to my mouth. "But for your information, I wasn't going to jump. I just wondered what it was like on the other side."

"No problem. You might be the last female civilian I get to talk to for a long time." He gulped his coffee. "Where's home?"

I put my hand over my heart. "Right here."

He smiled. "Of course."

"How about you?"

"Good question. As a child I was uprooted so many times, sometimes I don't remember," Thomas said.

I'd been stuck in the same place for sixteen years, my roots had grown deep until Dad, the final tornado, ripped me out and hurled me away. Even Grandma wasn't strong enough to hold me down anymore. But was I strong enough to stand on my own, I wondered?

"Seriously, I was born in Philly, but my family is scattered. I miss them."

"Are you scared?" I asked. "I mean—of going to Vietnam?"

"Oh, hell yeah."

I slurped some more soup, noticing the birds had returned. This time I tore off a piece of my bread and tossed it. "I guess sometimes we have no choice except to face our fears," I said, mimicking some of the grown up talk I'd heard through the years. *Don't be a sissy. This will make you tougher*, Dad had said, teaching me some boxing moves that left me with bruises. I finished my soup. "Thank you so much." I pushed the bowl away. "Where's the nearest bus station?"

Thomas's smile faded. "Over on Mission Street. Where are you headed?"

"Not sure." I looked away from his kind eyes. "I'll decide when I get there." I wrapped the rest of my bread in a napkin and slipped it into my pocket.

"I could give you a ride as soon as I'm finished here in a couple of hours."

I stood. "That's okay. You've been very nice, Thomas."

"You can call me Tommy."

And with that invitation to familiarity, a hug seemed in order, like I was leaving someone very close to me, but I'd only just met him and besides, I wasn't a hugger. We shook hands and said goodbye. I walked a few yards, before looking back over my shoulder. He stared at me. And then he waved.

"Goodbye, Tommy."

I reached the Mission Street station where the next bus wouldn't be leaving until six a.m.

CHAPTER 17

Homing Pigeon

In a telephone booth, outside the bus station, I held extra coins in my clammy hands prepared to go over the time. There'd be a lot of catching up, a lot of explaining, and so I made sure I had plenty of dimes and nickels. As the phone rang, I picked at a dried piece of gum stuck to the glass. By the third ring, I'd twirled the cord around my finger. I could barely stand I was so nervous. Mom can scold me for as long as it takes, I thought. I deserve it. Pigeons gathered outside. I'd give them the rest of my bread the Coastie gave me as soon as I finished my call. I smiled as the phone rang a fourth time. Silly to think they could be the same birds I'd seen at the church earlier, like St. Ignatius homing pigeons. And then after a couple more rings, a recording came on saying the number I'd dialed had been disconnected and that there was no new number. I dropped the receiver and watched it spin around at the end of the cord.

I panicked, but then just in case I'd misdialed, I tried again. I got the same recording. This time I was the one spinning at the end of a disconnected lifeline.

"Hold on, darling. I'm still with you," Grandma said, as I got too dizzy to hang on. I wondered what had happened at home. "We'll find out when we get back," Grandma said. At once, I felt a sick sort of comfort in being held hostage by my mental captor and I felt an urgency to connect with a human being. I put another dime in the phone slot.

"Hello?" I knew Willow by the bouncy sound of her voice.

"Willow, it's Anna."

"Who?"

"Honey. Is River there?" I asked.

"No, the police came and took him away in handcuffs."

"What?" I squeezed the receiver. "Why?"

"For killing that dude over at Steinway's."

The phone booth closed in on me. I needed air and wanted to throw up. I pushed the little door open and spilled out, the pigeons scattering. River had been arrested for something I'd done. No, for something Grandma had done.

"But it was an accident, darling," Grandma said. "The police are just fishing."

"Well, I need to fix this."

The bus would be leaving in the morning, but I couldn't go home now.

"They'll have to let him go," Grandma said. "Let's just wait for the bus."

Bent over, hands on my knees, I tried to catch my breath. *But what if—?* I dared to imagine. *What if River turns me in?*

"Darling, you and he are kindred spirits, he wouldn't do that."

"Grandma, you and I couldn't be more kindred, and look at the mess you've gotten me into." I stood straight, noticing a skeletal homeless man staring at me. Surely, he'd seen plenty of strange people talking to themselves, so I couldn't be any different. "I need to find River. I'm going to turn myself in. I'll explain how it was in self-defense."

"That's not a good idea."

"Sir, where's the police station?" I asked the poor man, handing him my coins.

About half an hour later, I trudged up a slight incline toward the Tenderloin Police Precinct. Classy apartment buildings lined the streets with a mix of houses that looked as if they were run by slumlords. Walls of graffiti-plastered seedy bars and hotels sprouted up on either side of the street as well as plenty of liquor stores and little markets. People doing drugs in broad daylight, I stepped over cigarette butts and used needles and syringes tossed onto the sidewalks. I sidestepped an emaciated, ropy-haired junky and a vacant-eyed prostitute hanging out underneath a giant pink leg suspended over a sign advertising "Live Nude Girls." The whole street nauseated me with the smells of rotten garbage, vomit, pee, and poop. I wanted to take a shower and burn my shoes and clothes, but first I wanted to find River. And then some creepy guy with shocking wild hair who was wearing tattered rags grabbed me by the shoulder, but I kicked him in the shins and took off running.

As I neared the police station just around the corner, I stepped into a laundromat to catch my breath and look for a bathroom. I followed a sign for one in the back where someone camped out on the floor at the entrance. Inside a filthy restroom, I didn't recognize my guilty face as I looked into a smudged cracked mirror. I reached into my pocket for my matches. Lighting one, I blew it out and then used the black sulfur to line my eyes like River had taught me. I wanted to look older.

But as soon as I walked out and turned the corner, I felt like a scared little girl again. Headed toward the police station, I'd stepped back into my childhood, back to the Glendale Police Department where they'd been holding my father for driving drunk for something I used to think I'd caused. Never mind what he'd done to us at home before he drove off and crashed into the "Welcome to Glendale" sign on Verdugo. And now here I was again, but this time I was here for River and for something I'd caused. I would turn myself in.

Sucking in a breath of courage, I approached the counter and stared into the balding head of a clerk bent over some paperwork. I cleared my throat. "Excuse me, sir?"

Without lifting his shiny dome, he peeked up over his glasses and furrowed his caterpillar dark eyebrows like he didn't want to lose his place, like he didn't have time for me.

"I'm looking for Riv—I mean Levi Smith. Is he being held here?"

He pushed back in his chair, looked around his desk, and then under it. "I don't see him here. Do you?"

He treated me like a stupid little girl. I could feel Grandma itching to say something. I dropped my bag, but it was too late to slap my hand over my mouth and stop her. "Oh my, we are in the presence of a comedian, a regular Groucho Marx." *Grandma, no!* "This must only be your day job," Grandma added.

I smiled through clamped teeth as the clerk pushed his glasses to the top of his head studying me. "What's he in for—this Mr. Smith? And what is your relationship to him?"

I should have been more prepared as I stood there staring into his rheumy eyes. I suddenly lost the courage to turn myself in for the murder of Dilbert Moss, especially to this clown of a cop. "I'm not sure. He's just a friend."

"What's your name?" he asked.

"Anna Jones."

He jotted something into his notepad. "Levi Smith," he muttered, looking up over his glasses. "Anna Jones. Sit down over there. I'll let you know."

I turned to see a line of people forming behind me. A giant clock on the wall read four-ten p.m. This sure was a busy place for this time of day. I wondered who and what they were all here for. I took a seat and tried to push the bloody image of Dilbert Moss out of my mind: the hole through his neck, his eyes that would haunt me forever as he stared at me before he died. Maybe if I squeezed my eyes hard enough, I could shut out the memory—imagine it didn't happen.

Someone shouted and I opened my eyes to see a woman pound a fist on the counter in front of the clerk. She had matted black hair and wore pink slippers. What sort of emergency had prompted her to forget her shoes? As she turned sideways, I saw a baby slung in her other arm. The baby had a bruise on his forehead. I trembled, and remembered waiting for my father and how my eye had been swollen shut and in the early stages of dark blue violet. No one at the station had asked about my puffy face. I wished they'd kept him there forever. Sure, he'd acted all sorry and was on his best behavior, promising it would never happen again. Still, I was afraid of him coming home, but I was even more afraid of upsetting Mom.

Damn it! Why did all of my memories have to be about them? And why did I think I needed to go home? I needed to make new memories, happy ones. But first, I needed to find River and come clean to the cops about the death of Dilbert Moss.

The baby cried, and the mother slapped her hand over his little face. The clerk stood up, clearly frustrated, and then the young woman shoved a bottle into the baby's mouth. Poor little thing hadn't yet learned that children were to be seen and not heard.

I looked around the station. Above a bulletin board spackled with pictures of missing children and already-chewed gum, a round clock read four-fifty p.m. as the sun disappeared behind the buildings. A scruffy dressed young person wearing a crown of dried leaves and little sticks walked in spewing Bible quotations about the "fearful, and unbelieving, and the abominable, and murderers, and whoremongers, and sorcerers, and idolaters."

A short cop came rushing out from a back room to handcuff the man who wouldn't shut up. "A second death all in the lake of fire and brimstone." Another burly cop came out to help escort the screeching man away.

I remembered the time Dad saw the Virgin Mary in the backyard. What was it about crazy people that turned them to religion? He'd been arrested for public intoxication, never mind what he'd done in private intoxication. Mom had tried to convince the police that we couldn't bring Dad home, that he was sick—suicidal—and he needed to go to the hospital. And so, after ushering him into a small room, they asked Mom to go in to ask some questions. She refused, pushing me forward. "Mija, go on. You talk." So, all of a sudden, I was not to 'shut up' or mind my 'own business,' even though most of the time it was Grandma Phoebe pissing Dad off with her preaching. So, all of a sudden, it was okay for a kid to be heard.

By five-thirty, there'd been a shift change and a new clerk sat behind the desk. I got back in line to make sure I hadn't been forgotten. When I reached the counter, the new clerk looked up. "There's no record of Levi Smith," he said. "What's he in for again?"

"I think it was because—there was a—a man was stabbed over at Steinway's," I said, and the clerk's eyebrow lifted. "That's not in our jurisdiction." He then picked up the phone and dialed. After a short conversation, he looked up and said, "He's not at Northern. He might have been booked and transferred over to Central." I felt the air in my heart leaking out and then I pushed my luck by asking him to please call there for me, too. He hesitated but then he did. River wasn't at Central either.

I didn't know what else to do, where else to try. I schlepped back to the station to wait for the bus leaving for Los Angeles. I'd be that proverbial dog returning home with my tail between my legs. I sat down on a hard bench and when I curled up to try and get comfortable, I recalled another time I sat in a cold steel chair at a table across from Dad in a tiny, windowless interview room at a jail on the Tijuana border.

He'd been gone for months to we didn't know where until the call came in from the Tijuana jail. He sounded crazy like he'd been having another of his manic episodes. The authorities would only release him to family. I drove Mom down to the border to try and convince them not to release him and to help us get him into the VA hospital. He needed help. A couple of male cops stood behind him as if he were a violent criminal, ready to pounce. Unshaven and gaunt, he was missing a front tooth. My tears wanted to escape the bars of my eyelashes. I felt powerless and hopeless; a good-for-nothing, bueno para nada. It hurt me to see my dad looking so desperate, and yet I took comfort knowing he was no longer a danger to anyone, including himself. He quieted for a few moments and as I backed away to leave, he looked at me and shouted, "When I get out, I'm putting your mother into the blender." Within moments of making the threat, I was shepherded out of the room, and as I walked down the short hallway back to my mother, it shocked me to hear him pleading, "Anna, tell them to let me go! I'm sorry. Don't leave me here."

I hadn't been able to help Dad then and now I couldn't help River, either. Physically exhausted and emotionally drained, I cried myself to sleep in the cold hard truth of my failures.

I sprang up in darkness. I'd been dreaming that Mother Mary had answers for me about River. I knew I'd be waking everyone up back at the house in the Haight, but I didn't care. I hurried over to the phone booth.

"Hello?" a welcome, familiar voice asked.

"River," I screamed. "You're back."

"Girl, you okay?" he whispered.

"Me? How about you?"

"I'm good." I could hear him smiling.

"I called earlier to say goodbye, but then—"

"You can tell me in person," River said. "I've got the best news."

What could be better than River being out of jail? Better news would be that the cops had dropped the case of Dilbert Moss. "What news?"

"It can wait 'til you get back."

"But, that's why I'm calling. I'm not coming back. I can't get hold of my family and I'm worried. I'm going home."

"Wait. Where are you?"

"I'm at the bus station on Mission Street."

"Let me come to you."

★ ★ ★

As the sun poked its face up over the bay, I sat outside on a bus bench watching a couple of pigeons pecking around my feet and remembered I still had some bread from yesterday. I unwrapped my napkin and tore off some pieces, stale by now, and soon a few more gathered. Little runaways who always made their way back home. I'd lost my connection home and I'd run out of breadcrumbs to help me find my way back.

I looked up thinking I saw River, an oasis shimmering toward me out of a dry desert. Bathed in the morning sun, it warmed my heart when he waved. "Here you are," he shouted. Even through his little round lilac sunglasses, I could see his eyes crinkle up when he smiled. Dressed in purple and green striped bell bottoms, and a camel-colored leather jacket, his trim Afro glistened like moonlight on a dark sea.

"What's with the Cleopatra look?" he asked, pointing to his eye.

"I was going for Twiggy."

The palm of his hand spread over his face, he shook his head, like he was trying not to laugh. He then reached for my bag. "They want us to leave with them tonight."

"Who wants us?"

"The band. Lazarus Rising. Their keyboardist got popped for drugs, so they want you. Plus, they liked our little performance the other night back at the house. You know, me singing and swinging. You backing me up. We'll be the opening act. We can call each other Asphalt and Patchouli."

"Are you serious?"

"First show is Friday night up in Eureka. Are you in?"

"What about my family? What about Moss? What about my father?"

"This is a journey only made heavier when you carry your past on your back. Let them go. This is your time. Someone probably just forgot to pay the phone bill. You can try again at the next stop. As for Moss, remember, it was self-defense."

He sounded persuasive and yet Grandma shouted, "We need to go home." But her voice was drowned out by the sound of the church bells chiming in the distance, a streetcar clanging, and then a foghorn. The signs were everywhere.

"Yes! Eureka, here we come," I shouted, trying to convince myself that this was a sane way to go.

CHAPTER 18

Lazarus Rising

All but three rows of seats in the front of the bus had been removed. There were a couple of bunk beds on either side in the back and a small lounge area with pillows on the floor. The rest looked like the inside of an empty garage with the equipment, a couple of bikes, some suitcases, and sleeping bags. On the bus was our driver, Abe, a big burly guy who would also fill in as bouncer, the manager Ralphie, River, and me. John would fly out and arrive late Friday around the same time we'd come pulling up to the Eureka Municipal Auditorium.

River sat across the aisle from me wearing an open, purple and green velvety vest, underneath his brown abs so tight I could practically see his ivory ribcage. I wondered what it would be like to run my hand across his chest. I wondered if he'd let me.

"I went to the Tenderloin police station looking for you," I said, peeling my eyes off his torso.

His eyes sparked up. "Girl, the Loin's my old stomping ground." He scooted closer to me from across the aisle.

I recalled how I'd passed all the drag bars along the way to the police station, the glazed looks of hookers like aimless carousel horses hanging out of hotel fronts.

"Seriously, I used to pass through there on my way to church." River laughed. "The Church for the Fellowship of all Peoples over on Larkin. Tenderloin's no place for a girl like you," he added.

"Like me? It's no place for a human like me. What happened with the police? I mean, why did they come back for you?"

"Someone reported seeing me run out of the Steinway Café the night before Moss was killed."

"But you were in drag," I said, remembering him that night adjusting his wig as he scrambled out of the cafe. "How would they know?"

He strummed his cheeks with his fingertips and arched a manicured eyebrow. "I suppose I've become a little notorious." He then smoothed his hair with the back of his palm. "A celebrity of sorts."

True. I'd heard people referring to him lately as a cross between Little Richard and Liberace, but I was reminded more of that movie with Tony Curtis and Jack Lemon dressing as women to hide from the mob. I peered a little deeper at River; the way his eyes twinkled, definitely Tony Curtis, my childhood heartthrob. We were both in transit, running and hiding from something—a couple of angsty teenage gangsters.

"Did, did they ask about me? I mean, at the police station—did anyone report seeing me at Steinway's?"

"Nope. They obviously thought they had their *man*," River said, crossing his arms over his hairless chest.

"They called the other precincts for me, too," I said, "but there was no record of River or Levi Smith at any of the stations."

River moved over and sat next to me, leaning in conspiratorially, "Oh, Honey, you really believe my last name is 'Smith'?"

"Obviously, I don't know everything about you, Levi Smith. Whatever your name is."

"Anyhow, Everett contacted one of the Panther's lawyers who threatened the cops he'd file some sort of writ of habeas corpus mumbo jumbo," he said. "I guess they had bigger catfish to fry and so they let me go." River laughed. "Never did like that Everett. Always talking about how he understood the Brothers and how he respected them in the same struggle. White Boy, don't understand shit. And now, damn, I owe him. It's a good thing we're getting outta dodge."

I got up and staggered to the lounge at the back of the bus to get something to drink. I gasped when I found Tony sitting on the giant ice chest. A chill ran up my spine.

"Hiya, Honey." He stood so I could grab a couple of Cokes.

I then careened back up the aisle to my seat. "You need to learn to dance with the bus," River said as I handed him a drink.

"Hey, what's Tony doing here?

"Oh yeah, he's handling the equipment," River said.

"And whatever else the band needs," Tony said with a grin as he took a seat behind me. "At your service."

I had a bad feeling and so did Grandma. "I didn't think draft dodgers knew anything about service," she said under my breath.

Grandma! I inhaled deeply, hoping I'd made the right choice about the direction of the next part of the journey on which I was about to embark.

★ ★ ★

Another mile marker ticked by as the bus carried me further away from the only world I'd ever known. I'd never been farther north than San Francisco. Geographically, I'd never been this far from my family. After five hours plowing through fog as thick as oatmeal, we arrived at the hotel in Eureka, still with plenty of time before going on stage. River remained seated as everyone else deboarded. "What are you waiting for?" I asked, backpack in hand.

"Why let this perfectly comfortable bus go to waste," he said. "Besides, I can save some money sleeping here."

I didn't have the strength to argue about how the band should cover the cost, and how Tony was supposed to be the one guarding the equipment. I'd learn later that sleeping on the bus was just easier for people like River. "Just let me use the phone," I said, "and a shower. Then I'm coming back to stay with you."

In the lobby, I called home again only to get the same recording. I wished I'd gotten to know our neighbors on Fernbrook better, but my mother was always too embarrassed to socialize with any of the white families; it wasn't just because of the color of her skin, but because Dad was a drunk, an embarrassment, plus she hated our neighbors. I thought about calling the church. Maybe they'd know something.

The church receptionist picked up the phone. She told me she was sorry she wasn't able to help me, but that she'd ask Father Reynoso after Mass the next morning. She asked if she could take a number where I could be reached. I told her I'd call back later.

Inside the Eureka Municipal Auditorium, River and I warmed up the crowd of about two thousand with me at the piano and him singing songs by Marvin Gaye and Otis Redding. I knew he'd rather be strutting around the stage singing like Etta James or Nina Simone, but this wasn't that type of crowd. They'd come to see Lazarus Rising, after all. And then, before everyone grew restless, the band came on.

Over the heavy jazz and classical influence, the band had more of a strong folk background. I played keyboard which I liked because I could hide behind it and also watch River on rhythm guitar and John on lead. They were totally in sync. Their swing and twanging tempos sounded like divining rods humming at some heavenly source. What a high being surrounded by Joe on drums, the amps, the rumbling stage, and the echoing audience.

After the concert, River and I returned to the bus. He shared his Bota bag filled with wine. Grandma, quite chatty, pulsated a yellow aura. "This was almost as thrilling as the time I played for the troops during World War I." She paused for a moment reminiscing. "Oh, darling, what a magical night. I was in heaven."

I laughed. "So, why didn't you stay there?"

★ ★ ★

The next morning, I woke up wishing I could tell my mother about the concert. I could just imagine her face smoothing out around her big, toothy smile. Even though Grandma said I shouldn't think it's the "cat's pajamas" to sing back-up for an all-male ensemble, I was just grateful for the opportunity.

I called the church. There was no information for me other than Father Reynoso had recalled seeing the family last Sunday in the second row, same pew as always where Mom insisted that we all sit tall and proud. They'd all been there, except, of course, Dad and me. Father Reynoso asked if he could relay a message to the family. "Just tell them I'm okay and I love them all . . ." The bus honked. "I'll try again, soon." I took comfort in the information Father gave me and boarded the bus headed to Portland.

★ ★ ★

The ride was so smooth that if it weren't for the difference in the height and density of redwood trees, I'd swear the bus wasn't moving at all, and even though my seated body was at rest, my train of thoughts drove me crazy. But I'm not on a train, I thought with a laugh. Maybe if I were, my thoughts could connect like little boxcars of memories to make some sort of sense of my life. I rested my head on the seatback near the window where my breath fogged up the glass. I drew a smiley face on the clouded glass and then swiped it and closed my eyes, hoping to wipe away the image of me stabbing my father. The stunned look on his face. I wanted him to know I was sorry for what had happened. As for Dilbert Moss, nothing I could do would bring him back from the dead. Sadly, the bus couldn't outpace the impressions springing up mile after mile. "This is all your fault, Grandma. You've ripped me away from home." And just by whispering her name, she took it as an invitation to speak.

"But you can always go back," she said. "Although, I believe we're finally on the right track." More like Grandma had switched tracks. She loved being on stage again.

I reached into my purse for a pack of cigarettes. Not just drinking, but I'd started smoking as a way to drown out the sound of Grandma or blur her out of existence. How could her voice come through if my ears were numb or if I always had something in my mouth?

I felt a change in the road. I stared out the window and watched my world slip further away.

* * *

After breakfast in a Boise diner, I stepped into a phone booth. This time, I tried the operator and asked if there were any new listings in Glendale under "LeMar." She said, "Nothing, except for a Magdalena Le Mar in Monte Vista."

My sister!

Maggie answered the phone after two rings. "Maggie. It's me."

"Anna!" she said, and, suddenly, a combination of familiarity and homesickness blendered my insides. "Are you okay? Where are you?"

"I'm fine. In Idaho."

"Where? What's in Idaho besides potatoes?"

Maggie always joked—we all had to—but this time I couldn't help but laugh and then quickly sombered, "How's Dad?"

"I guess he's fine. You can't really see the scar," she said.

"How about Mom? Is she there? Can I talk to her?" Hearing the muffled sounds in the background, I braced for her to lambaste me.

"She doesn't want to. She says you made your choice. You really hurt her this time," Maggie said as a flash of guilt rushed through me. "Anyway, what about you?"

"I'm okay." I switched gears to tell her a little about what I'd been up to.

"You're lucky, you got away," she said. "Monte Vista is as far away as we got."

"Monte Vista? What are you talking about?"

"Dad got really bad."

"Because of the knife wound." My voice shook. I wanted to cry.

"Who knows?" Maggie said. "Supposedly, it all started way before you left. Mom said we couldn't stay anymore. He really wants us to come back, but Mom says it's not safe. He promises he'll change, but now he's in debt up to his ears. He owes so much money."

"To who? For what?"

"He lost his job, so besides the regular bills to live, I don't know. The credit people kept calling, so that's why the phone number was put in my name, to put them off until we could figure something out. Now, we're all squeezed into a tiny apartment."

"But the house was paid off long ago," I said.

"Apparently, he borrowed against it so I'm not sure how much of the loan is left."

Grandma would no longer stay silent. "After all the pain and suffering I endured to save that place!"

"What are you talking about, Anna?" Maggie asked. "How'd you save the place?"

I cleared my throat, warning Grandma to stay quiet. Growing up, Maggie had seen and heard me talking to myself, but had never understood my bizarre behavior and I'd been warned by my parents not to talk about it. Again, it had been hard for me to explain and I wasn't about to try again now.

"It would just be really sad if we lost the place. Is there anything I can do? Are you okay?" I said, stifling Grandma.

"I'm okay just waiting until I can make like a banana and split myself."

"I got a job working at the Bank of America. I'm also saving up so I can move the hell out of here."

I laughed. "That's great, but you're only fifteen."

"That's not what I told them," Maggie said. "Desperate times call for desperate measures."

I smiled, wishing I had Maggie's self-confidence. "So how is Mom?"

"She took a job cleaning houses. It got really scary, and he didn't want Mom working. So, we finally just packed up and left."

"Can I send some money?"

"Sure. And I'd tell you to come home, but honestly, I don't know where you'd sleep. I share a room with Mom. Josie and Patty share the other. Michael sleeps on the couch in the living room. It's pretty cramped."

"What about Bella?"

"We left her with Dad for company."

Even though I shouldn't have cared, I was happy he had a companion.

"You're probably better off wherever you are," she said.

I wouldn't tell her I'd been sleeping on the cold floor of a stinky bus full of rock and rollers and before that on the floor of a flophouse in the Haight with three other hippies.

"How long will you be in Idaho?"

"Just until tomorrow."

"Anyone famous like the Doors?"

"Not yet. Anyway, I should get going. I'll call again when I get the chance."

"Okay. Hey, so when do you think you might come home?"

Without thinking, I told her Thanksgiving and then the thought warmed my heart like the kitchen on a holiday morning, until I remembered our house was gone and I was pretty sure so was that giant table we'd gathered around when we tried to act like a normal family. The table had a button to call the maids and butlers—not that we ever had any help—and the chairs were covered in royal blue mohair. My grandparents had imported the set from Normandy after their honeymoon. Rumor was, it belonged to the Medici. "Maybe Christmas," I said. "I'll let you know. I've got to go."

My head throbbed. Stuffed with nostalgia and painful memories, I stepped outside of the phone booth with a lump in my throat and a knot I my stomach. I then boarded the bus, stumbling to the back to crawl into my sleeping bag. I covered my head with a blanket and prepared to ride out a migraine.

CHAPTER 19

Blonde Indians

Christmas 1967 was just another day on the tour. We'd been on the road for a couple of months giggin' in different venues. I'd learned to play different instruments, like the sitar that was hooked up to a Fender amp driving a couple of Wurlitzer horns. On stage at the Tulsa Assembly Center, we played a couple of Christmas carols. Dressed as an elf, I imagined being on a magic winter sleigh ride with the psychedelic sounds vibrating through my fingers to my boots. As the drumbeat pounded a sensual rhythm with my heart, I looked over at River. Wearing a jeweled headband and a red and green sequined pantsuit, he outshined long-haired John who wore a pair of boring brown corduroys and a tan chambray shirt. As egocentric as I thought John was, he didn't seem to mind being upstaged by River who shimmied and shook around him, the sparkles lighting up John's bearded face; as a matter of fact, there'd been a moment when I thought I picked up on something electric between them. The crowd cheered and the collective roar buzzed enough energy to light up all of Oklahoma.

During a side trip the next day to a trading post out in Broken Arrow, River and I strolled the dusty aisles shopping for souvenirs. Even though it would be late, I wanted to send home some

Christmas trinkets. As I finished paying for a turquoise bracelet for Mom and some matching turquoise rings, one for me and for each sibling, I looked up to see John and River ambling away head-to-head, acting like a couple of conspiring, giggling school girls on a shopping spree. I was so confused and a little jealous. River turned to me and held out his hand. "Hurry up, slow poke," he said. "John has some ideas," he added. Ideas that include me?

Within a couple of months, the band had fine-tuned their set and regurgitated the same arrangement as the night before, except for a couple of new additions. By the time we reached Oklahoma City, John had arranged to fly in a couple of loud, well-endowed, bleached platinum back-up singers, Cindy and Cheryl, from Los Angeles. There wasn't much for them to do, except wiggle their hips and look sexy—not hard for them to do.

From a stage in Norman where every seat in the arena had been sold, no one sat as John strutted across the stage, lashing a beat on his guitar, flipping his hair back, whipping the fans into a frenzy. The drummer receded into the background, the beat pounding inside my ribcage as River crow-hopped on, bare chested with warrior paint on his face. The crowd went wild as the girls, including me, came on dressed in the short leather fringed dresses he'd purchased for us back at a trading post in Tulsa. We also wore feathers in our hair. I took my place at the keyboards, my hands flying. A couple of white-faced blonde Indians, Cheryl tapped a small leather-skinned tribal drum as Cindy slapped the tambourine on her butt.

Set in position on stage, drenched in sweat, chests heaving, including River who dropped back behind the mic near me, Cindy and Cheryl sashayed around John. They crouched, chins up, arms extended in worship. He stood in the middle strumming his guitar, the band behind them lit with just a faint glow of blue light. The devotees knew every word, their voices swelling and soaring, a unified flock in musical formation. The arena crackled in anticipation of the show's climax.

After the break, the fans stirred into a sufficient fever, we sauntered back on stage, John all strut and arrogance, hands in the air, demanding more applause.

One by one, the band dropped out leaving only John and his guitar on the dark stage, but for a halo of light. His fans adored him.

And then the chanting started. "River! River! River!" John stormed off.

★ ★ ★

On the road out of Norman, Oklahoma, mighty gusts of white-capped breakers of snow tumbled across the plains, lulling me as the tires beneath the bus thudded rhythmically with a sound reminiscent of a boat splashing through waves. Other than the noise, I enjoyed bobbing along the miles of human silence.

Asleep now, the girls and John would be traveling with us on the bus throughout the tour. Earlier they'd been laughing and chatting incessantly behind a makeshift curtain, the Indian blanket I'd purchased at the trading post, where they also cuddled up with John, keeping him company from town to town. My mind still raced, but I wasn't ready to turn in. River and I sat up a bit longer to digest the night's experience.

"I'd say that went off pretty well," River said.

"Are you kidding? They loved it." Wherever we went, everyone loved River. "Do you think you might have upstaged John?"

"Nah, he likes it when everybody lets loose. We were just diggin' the beat."

"It really was pretty groovy. I wonder what he'll will come up with next."

"Cowboys and cowgirls on horseback."

"Or, you and John could come out in chaps with those cheek cut-outs." I laughed. "They loved you and your gyrating around, all glistening bare-chested. Upstaging John until he stormed off."

"Truthfully, I don't think he minded. Anyway, I wasn't gyrating."

"Whatever, it was all pretty far out."

"You know, I've written some songs, I'm thinking about asking John if I might perform one."

"Honey, that's fantastic!"

Ever since the girls joined, I started thinking I had something they didn't. Turns out I was a little competitive, after all.

"Bravo!" Grandma said, "It's time you take control of your music."

"Control? Are you serious? You know you can't wait to grab the music baton."

She ignored my response. "The drumbeats are reminiscent of music I performed with Charles Wakefield Cadman during his American Indian song phase."

"Who?" River asked.

"Land of the Sky Blue Waters," Grandma responded.

"Never heard of it, Grandma," he said, sitting up now.

"You know, that Hamm's beer commercial," I added.

"Oh, right. Of course."

★ ★ ★

Grandma and River loved to talk. Besides her interfering now in my friendship and my new career, she would be getting in the way of my love life, such as it wasn't. Every time I'd get close to hitching up with someone, she'd be right there to tell me to respect myself and to get back on the bus where it seemed everyone had hooked up, including River, I'd find out.

CHAPTER 20

My Love Story

February 14, 1968: Sweet seventeen and still I'd never been kissed, except for whatever that sloppy mess was that I'd instigated with River back at Steinway's. John, who probably thought River and I were an item, and even the band members treated me like a little sister which I did appreciate. It was definitely about time to find love and write my own love story. I'd been on the pill already a few months, thanks to the free clinic back in the Haight, so I was prepared for amour.

Sadly, every night on the news was all about hate. I remained alone in my hotel room most of the time, respecting myself like Grandma admonished, while the others went out partying. If River came to my room at all, he'd get all nervous and return to the bus because of the "segregation laws," he said. "I don't wanna get lynched."

The nation reckoned with changes that would make it a fateful year. But pathetically, all I cared about was finding love. Missing home in a crazy world, loneliness clutched at my insides and I grew even more heartsick. I didn't want to die before I found love. And so far, I wasn't sure about either sex. I'd fallen in love with River when I thought he was a girl, so what did that tell me? And now he didn't even want me, making any excuse to keep away. I was desperate, but why should I have to feel pain, suffer and cry, before I could feel love?

There's nothing sexy about a reign of terror, but in January 1968, as the news reported that the North Vietnamese communists had launched something called the Tet Offensive, I couldn't help but notice young couples in Seattle holding hands, dodging the bullets of rain, like they were Gene Kelly and Debbie Reynolds singing, *The sun's in my heart and I'm ready for love.*

February, the month of love, came filled with hate. In Memphis, the death of a couple of African-American sanitation workers would lead to a civil rights movement. But, what did that have to do with me?

I picked up a newspaper before boarding the bus. In Vietnam there was the "justified" destruction of another village full of innocents. At the South Carolina State campus, three protesters died and twenty-seven more were wounded when police opened fire on students protesting segregation at Orangeburg's only bowling alley. I put down the paper. I felt sorry, but even guiltier because selfishly, all I could think about was not having a Valentine in my life. I wanted to choose love over violence and vengeance.

Talk about rose-colored glasses: when we got to Albuquerque, I bought River a silly Valentine's card, two little bears on the cover holding paws, and presented it to him after the concert one night. Isn't that what you do when you like someone?

"Honey, this is so sweet," he said, moving in for a hug. "Which bear am I? I'm sorry I didn't get you . . ."

"That's okay." I didn't want to put him on the spot. "It's nothing, really."

"Tell you what," he said, slipping the card into his back pocket. "Tomorrow, let's do something. You know today every restaurant in town has gotta be booked, besides this ain't the sort of town where two little bears like you and me should be seen together."

Back at the hotel later that night, I stepped out for a smoke and when I saw River drift out of John's room, I was crushed. He saw me, too, and took a seat next to me.

"Are you okay?"

The chilly night air made it hard to tell the difference between smoke or my breath. "I don't want to talk right now." I hugged myself, staring into the distance where a three-quarter moon lit up the snowcapped Sandia Mountains. It would be nice to find a little cave up there and then morph into a bear and go into hibernation. "I've been lied to my whole life, kept in the dark. I hate secrets." I felt betrayed. Why had he kept this from me? The real question was: Why had I refused to open my eyes?

"I haven't lied to you, Honey. I've wanted to tell you."

"Tell me what? I don't understand." I remained stiff. "I don't understand why you can't trust me enough to be honest."

His voice cracked. "No matter what, I will always love you."

★ ★ ★

I was ready to glom onto just about anyone who smiled at me. I set a goal to lose my virginity sooner than later. I figured it might be the right of passage that would transform me into a girl more like Cheryl or Cindy; a girl people crushed on. I tried to pick-up or get picked up everywhere we landed, but I was so awkward and then by the time we traveled over the highway through red and green scrubbed mesas and reached the dry plains and tumbleweeds of El Paso, Texas, I was derailed by menstrual cramps and a migraine. I was in no condition for love.

By the time we got to San Marcos, I'd become a new girl with more determination. After the concert, I sat at the bar smoking a cigarette and acting all confident like Lana Turner in *The Bad and the Beautiful.* I was just about to order something to drink when a beefy boy in a cowboy hat, a tie-dye T-shirt, and Wranglers with a belt buckle the size of a barn, offered to buy me a beer.

"Remember, you're not of age to drink," Grandma scolded.

I dragged on my Marlboro, holding it as I turned my head to exhale; and then raised my arm across my mouth as if sneezing and talked into my shoulder. "I'm legal here in Texas, Grandma, and so are guns." I turned back around to find myself staring into a pair of big brown eyes, like a rodeo calf about to be roped. I smiled at the strapping baby-faced cowboy and, feeling confident, I asked if he had anything stronger back at his place. I thought I was being smart (more of a smart ass), but as I followed his rawhide boot steps through the front entrance, a blast of cold air bucked me in the face, infusing me with enough oxygen to quickly sprout some new brain cells. I chickened out and ran back inside for shelter.

The next week, after a concert at a smaller venue on the outskirts of Des Moines, a cute, straw-haired hayseed zeroed his large Tony Curtis eyes on me the whole night. With a short nose, chubby cheeks and a few corn silky whiskers sprouting out of his recessed chin, he had the innocent face of a prepubescent boy, like someone you could trust, nothing like those entitled Baylor boys I'd met in Dallas. I took a seat at the bar to order a Coke and then noticed River walking off with some tall "drink of water." Before when he'd tried to explain how we could never be that kind of a couple, I couldn't understand. Wasn't I good enough, pretty enough, smart enough, sexy enough? But watching him now with another man was a sobering sight. He looked happy and I tried not to look jealous.

The country mouse finally walked up and offered to buy me a drink. I figured I could practice on him the art of conversation and get to know him a little better first. I started the dialogue: "I'd dig a beer, please." And then when Grandma reminded me once more that I wasn't old enough to drink, I put my hand over my mouth. "As long as you're my guardian, it's okay. Besides it's not like I'm doing drugs or smoking pot or having sex." I then ordered a double rum and Coke, the drink of courage.

He told me his name, Mason, and after another drink, the conversation seemed to flow as if I were his tipsy barber or career counselor.

"So, what line of work are you in, Marcus?"

"It's Mason and I'm a farmer."

"Groovy." Elbow on the bar, fist under my chin, I tried to come across as if I were interested. "So, what do you grow?"

"Right now, it's corn. We also raise cows and pigs."

"Far out. So where do you see yourself in five years?"

"Farming." He peered at me. *Duh.*

"Hmm." I nodded before taking another sip. "So, what's fun to do in Dallas."

He looked at me as if I were some sort of stupid scarecrow. "How would I know? I've lived in Iowa all my life." He slammed down his beer.

"I'm sorry." I gulped the rest of my drink and it didn't take long before I was having fun making out with the corn husker at the bar. I'd passed the foreplay test. But when he took my hand to lead me out to his truck, Grandma landed on me like a Midwestern tornado.

"Young lady!"

"Grandma, not now. Blow away!" So much for keeping Grandma a secret.

"Anna, you're drunk. I don't want you ending up like your father."

"Low blow, Grandma," I yelled out loud. "Don't forget you're the one who fucked him up." My crying didn't deter Mason.

Under the blurry lights in the parking lot, I could see the big boy's confused face as Grandma and I argued back and forth. The impatient cornjerker grabbed me around the waist and hoisted me onto the hood of his car, my face just missing the hood ornament, but my dress snagged it and I heard it rip.

He yanked off my panties like he'd husked an ear of corn. I twisted around, punching and smacking, until finally I kicked him in the balls. He curled into a ball before springing up, grabbing my wrist and then slapping me across the face. "Cockteaser."

Well if I was a cockteaser, then Grandma was the cockblocker. "Young man, your father never seemed to mind the oral titillation," she said, just as another boy in a cowboy hat appeared and grabbed my assailant's arm.

"Hey, dude. Not cool," cowboy hat said.

The boy, barn owl-eyed, backed off and away yelling at me, "You're fuckin' crazy."

I dashed off to the bus hoping to find River, but when I boarded, calling out, I only heard the echo of his name. I made my way to the back and stripped out of my torn dress into my long T-shirt. The chilly temperature sobered me up like a slap across the face. Crawling into my cold sleeping bag, I broke into a sob, wishing I'd checked into the hotel with the other girls. "Why did you have to say you worried that I'd be like Dad?"

"I'm sorry, darling. But in the moment, it was all I could come up with."

"But do you really believe that?" I blubbered, shivering.

"Of course not. You're nothing like your father. You're a good person; kind and gentle, thoughtful and full of compassion. But like him, you just want to be loved."

"And is it a sin to want to be loved?" *Love?* Dad sure went about it the wrong way. I'm done with boys. I wiped my nose on my sleeve and then cinched my covers close to my strained heart.

"Darling, remember, you must not confuse lust for love."

Not in the mood to listen to Grandma and her version of love, I pulled the blanket over my head. I knew it was futile, but maybe she'd get the message. She didn't.

"I remember when I was just about your age—" Oh, for God's sake. "All the beaus; all the heartache. And then I met your grandfather and it was a forbidden love."

"Why?" I was sorry I'd asked. She made this all about her, again.

"Well, because, as you might remember, he was married with three children." No, I didn't remember. "I was the piano teacher. Being around him was agony. Finally, I left the country. How I mourned the separation. But grief is the price we pay for love."

"Obviously, it worked out for you or I wouldn't be here."

"If it had worked out for me, darling, I wouldn't be here."

"What does that mean?" Again, sorry I asked, but then I heard someone boarding.

I sat up to see River heading toward me as Grandma whispered, "Get some sleep, darling. When the time is right and when the right person comes along, I promise to get out of your hair."

Hmph.

"I'll disappear, I swear to you."

River turned on a light. "You're back early," he said.

"And how was your quickie?"

"You've been crying. What's wrong?"

Where to begin? "I'm trashed as in, I'm trash. Just a horrible person," I said, rolling over to hide my face.

"Look at me."

By the time I turned to face him, he'd already crawled into his sleeping bag.

"There's nothing wrong with you, except that you're shivering. Come over here," he said, inviting me into his sleeping bag. "I read where families in the Arctic sleep naked together to keep warm."

"Gross. I'm not getting naked," I said.

"Me neither." He pulled back his bedroll to show he wasn't naked. Finally, I climbed in and he laughed as he rolled away from me.

"Why can't you love me?" I whispered, "If only you could, it would make our lives so much easier."

"Honey, you're my soul sister. Of course, I love you," he responded. "Now go to sleep."

But sleeping was torturous with his warm body next to mine. Before long, he was snoring softly into the night and as I burrowed my head into his back, his shirt soaking up my tears, my breathing in concert with his, I was embarrassed at how I ached for his arms to reach around and hold me. But all I had to keep me company were my questions about love and a Grandma who seemed to hold the secrets.

★ ★ ★

Regrettably, my lust story wasn't quite over. One night after a concert in Montrose, the Greenwich Village of Houston, River and I waited at the back exit for John. We'd planned to go to one of the many bohemian clubs in the area.

"Why did John make you fade into the background?" I asked.

Montrose, also known as "gayborhood," would have eaten up the act with River in it if only John hadn't made him stand back. In cow skin skirts and psychedelic fringe tops, cowboy hats and boots, Cindy and Cheryl had done their dancing thing around John as if he were a Jesus cowboy in a leather vest and chaps. Off to the side next to me, stood River, dressed down and singing back-up. I caught John's furtive, seductive looks directed back at River as he sang the song I'd written. I wondered how the words tasted in his mouth. *Love me like you do your amigo. Hold me closer or else let me go.*

"He just wanted to try something out," River said.

"Something like trying on your words for size and listening for the applause," Grandma said out loud.

"I'm sorry he stole your song," River said.

We stepped outside where a group of teenage fans shouted for John. "We want John!" Finally, he stepped out, flashing a smile as he waved a pair of pink panties over his head. "Someone missing these?" The crowd went wild, hooting, hollering, and whistling. Earlier during the concert as he sang, the underwear came flying up onto the stage, and as he now signed an autograph, he looked up, immediately catching River's eyes. The way River looked back confused me. Hadn't John just put him in his place on stage, a more submissive role? Or maybe the girls wouldn't have gone as wild with the two men on stage who only had eyes for each other. Suddenly, I saw how they could practically rip each other's clothes off with just their eyes. I just knew I'd be in the way. I didn't want to be a witness to whatever this was, whether it was love or maybe they were horny for each other or just playing some sort of twisted game. I wanted to head back.

"See you later," I said, dusting off my hurt feelings. I don't even think they heard me as they cruised away.

Truth was, I knew it was normal for a boy, but I wondered if feeling horny was normal for a girl.

"Of course, it is, darling."

"Grandma, what do you know about normal?"

Left standing amongst a throng of teenagers, most probably older than me, I soaked in the silly chatter. Thick with the syrupy Southern drawl, I found it even more difficult to understand what the big deal was, but the teen spirit was infectious.

"I'll bet Lazarus is hung like a horse," a tall girl said.

A blonde-headed boy added, "It's the motion of the ocean, not the size of the boat."

"And only someone with a small dinghy would say that," said another button-down boy.

Small dinghy had a sense of humor. "Your mama doesn't seem to mind," said blond boy.

I hooted with everyone else.

"Must be how you got out of the draft, you know, like having flat feet," button-down boy said.

"Not everyone has a daddy who plays golf with LBJ," said tall girl.

"Vietnam is senseless anyway," short girl said. "Why would anyone want to go? It's so humid."

The Houston night felt pretty humid.

"Say, my parents are spending the weekend down at the beach house in Galveston," she added. "They said we could have some friends over. I can get Maria to whip up some nachos."

They invited me to tag along.

"Anna, not a good idea," Grandma said.

Why the hell not? Didn't I need to be around kids my own age? Besides, I reckoned there'd be safety in numbers. They seemed nice and blond boy was sort of cute.

The next thing I remember was being in the back of a car yelling, "Take me home! I want Mamá!" Despite the breach in my memory, I did recall ending up back at the bus in the parking lot slumped down on the bottom step of the bus, feet planted on the curb as if I could stop the world from spinning.

A Blue Norther had blown in overnight plummeting the temperature to thirty degrees. At dawn, River returned to find me shivering and wet, my lashes tinged in frost. He carried me onto the bus where I woke up two days later in a new town. It's a wonder I didn't come down with pneumonia.

"It's a wonder you're not pregnant," Grandma added.

"Oh my God! What? Oh Grandma, please stop. I don't want to know."

"You had a bad reaction to something you smoked. You kept screaming to be taken home until frat boy finally drove you back. You'd passed out by the time he got to the parking lot. He tried to have his way with you first."

"Oh, no! Did he take my virginity?"

"No. I told him I hoped my lady blisters were healed by now and that the penis on the last boy had shriveled up like a slice of fried bacon. You should have seen his face. Alas, he kept your panties as a souvenir or for bragging rights. Imagine what he might have told the others; that he had relations with someone famous from the band."

"I'm not famous."

"Not yet, darling. And not if you keep up this type of behavior."

"You're right. I'm so stupid."

"I said you weren't street smart. You're also a teenager, whose prefrontal cortex hasn't fully formed."

And then, after the Texas-sized headache, full of enough shame to pack all of the Roman Catholic confessionals around the world—you'd think I might have learned a lesson, but I'm sorry to say I hadn't.

CHAPTER 21

The Flying Unicorn

The winter high plains had been flat and desolate, but now the approaching giant oaks and crabapple trees dotted the scenery like a French Impressionist painting. I gazed out the bus window, imagining the smell of the lilac bushes that would bud soon. As February exhaled the remnants of winter, no matter where we traveled in March, the promise of spring perfumed the air and with spring came the promise of amour.

The next morning, refueled for the trip with a hot cup of coffee, a donut, and a copy of the *Houston Chronicle*, I took a window seat and wrapped myself in my bedroll as the rest of the band boarded after being out God-knows-where all night. Abe closed the door. I looked around. "Where's Tony?"

"He's been warned," John responded, making his way to the back of the bus.

River shrugged as I looked at him for answers. He took a seat across from me. *Warned?* I just always knew Tony was trouble.

* * *

Cindy tossed me an issue of *Redbook* magazine. I browsed through it but stopped when I came across an article about an orthopedic surgeon who'd been to Vietnam and said, "Nothing could have prepared me for my encounters with Vietnamese women and children burned by napalm. It was shocking and sickening, even for a physician, to see and smell the blackened flesh." I set the magazine aside remembering my march to Kezar Stadium and how Betsy had said, "They're killing our babies." I closed the magazine thinking about how naïve I'd been; how totally consumed with the matters confined inside my own head.

I opened up the newspaper and read how all across America even more university students were protesting the Dow Chemical Company, the principal manufacturer of napalm. In New York, around five hundred students picketed a university-sponsored recruiting event for Dow, holding up signs reading, "Dow Shall Not Kill" and "Dow Deforms Babies." I turned the page to read how in Los Angeles, some fifteen thousand Latino high school students walked out of classes to press their demand for a better education. I thought about my family and worried how that might affect them. But now, I'd realized that everything centered around finding love, and not just the kind between a man and a woman. Humanity needed to find some love.

In Delano, California, Cesar Chavez had been on a hunger strike, and when he broke his fast, presidential candidate Robert F. Kennedy was by his side. Kennedy had asked how he could help. Something pulled at my heartstrings and I looked out the window, terraced fields rolling past, and remembered Mom telling me that she'd met Chavez while working the fields up North and that's where she reunited with Dad while he was up there working, too. My mother wouldn't have been out there picking strawberries, I thought, if it hadn't been for Grandma Phoebe first getting her deported.

"It all worked out. She found love."

"Yeah, rub it in. Even those two were destined to get struck by cupid's arrow."

I set down the newspaper when I noticed Cindy, in the corner of my eye, handing River a book to read. "Someone gave me this back in Montrose," she said, her earring still dangling after she pushed a golden strand of hair behind her ear. "Apparently, *Emmanuelle* is all the rage in Europe, but I don't read French," she said, and I thought good luck, Cindy, he's not into girls. Then for a second my insecurities took over and I wondered, maybe he's just not into me.

"Neither do I," River responded, "Parlez-vous français?"

"Je fais," I said, snatching the novel from him. "I know some French."

"Well, Honey, now as you practice your French, maybe you might even learn something about sex," Cindy said, sashaying her way to the back of the bus.

"En efet, c'etait lors de mon passage in France avec la—" Grandma said.

"Oh my God. Yeah, I know, Grandma. You were in France with the Red Cross during the war and fell in love." I settled into my seat to open up to the first page.

"Chapter One, 'The Flying Unicorn.' Emmanuelle boarded the plane in London that was to take her to Bangkok."

River laughed, pulling out a book to read. It seemed River had his hands on a new book every few days.

"What are you reading?" I asked.

"*Jesus and the Disinherited.* I picked it up at my church in San Francisco."

I didn't want to think about Jesus at the moment, so I returned to my own book, which would surely land me in hell. By the second page, I'd stopped reading aloud, my temperature rising and burning through to my Catholic core. The inside of the bus warmed to the temperature inside a virgin's womb and the engine vibrated beneath me like a heart beating on speed which caused my vagina to feel sinful things I had no control over. The protagonist was having sex with a complete stranger on the plane. I was grateful Grandma hadn't made an appearance so far. I peeked across the aisle. River had his head buried in *Ebony*, the "Best Dressed Women of 1968" issue. Fat chance. The only sex I'd be having would be in my dreams, and it wouldn't be with River.

After several miles and several pages of sex with strangers, I heated up enough to ignite the book on fire. Toes curling, I set down the novel and wiped the drool from my swelling lips. I rubbed my eyes and opened them to see River staring at me, a mischievous grin plastered on his face.

"Ooh la la?" he asked.

"Wouldn't you like to know?" I tossed him the book. "How's it going with John? Why aren't you back there having an orgy with the others?"

"Not my thing." River laughed, tossing the book back. "He's still trying to find himself. I'm more monogamous. Besides, I do have my standards."

I grinned, suspecting the truth was that River proved too much competition for John.

Tony, who had apparently passed out last night in the space behind me, popped up from underneath a mound of tarps and blankets. "Did someone say 'orgy'?"

No such luck losing Tony. I wondered why he'd been warned. I stuffed the book into my sack. *Emanuelle* would be part of my future sex-ed class, but still I'd never figure River out, much less the whole concept of sex. Was I confusing lust for love as Grandma put it? I pulled my leather-fringed dress out of the bag to mend the tear before the next show. You'd think I'd learned my lesson by now, but I was seventeen and the mixed cocktail of rum, marijuana and raging hormones had cut off oxygen to my brain, making me lose precious smart brain cells. Also, it didn't help having to watch everyone else in the band hook up.

★ ★ ★

At the end of March, we made a quick trip into New Orleans for a concert at the Stash House, a place practically right on the Mississippi River. After the concert, River said goodnight and I took a short cab ride back to my hotel room at the Hotel Saint Vincent up on Magazine Street and turned in. The next morning, as I waited for room service to deliver my breakfast, I called home.

Maggie answered.

"It's only Thursday. Why aren't you in school?" I placed my clothes from the night before onto pink cushioned hangers.

"It's closed. A bunch of the Mexican kids from the local high schools had a walk out as part of the Chicano Movement. I marched the first day, but it's not really my thing."

"Being Mexican isn't part of your thing?" I hung up my velvet blue fringed top.

"The only way to get ahead is to work hard. I got a promotion at the bank."

"You're on your way." I heard a knock on the door. "Hold on a sec." I set down the phone. A bellboy pushed a cart into my room and then lifted the lid to a silver serving dish. He poured me a cup of coffee. "Thank you." I picked the phone back up.

"Who's that? One of your many lovers? Mom says that's why you don't want to come home. That you're living in sin shacking up with a paramour. You know all that free love everyone's talking about. Where are you anyway?"

"Paramour, that's a fancy word for Mom."

"She probably picked it up in one of her romance novels," Maggie said.

"I wish I had at least one paramour," I said, pouring in some cream and sugar. "I'm in New Orleans. That was room service, not a lover." I stirred.

"Look at you! There's working hard and then there's doing what you do."

I laughed. "Speaking of working hard and love, how's Mom?" I blew into my cup.

"She's good. She's been spending a lot of time over at Uncle Teodoro's house. That barrio is so depressing."

"I guess." I took a sip.

"But I do remember they made it fun."

I didn't remember having fun over there. What I remember was the spot under a pepper tree in a nearby field full of mustard plants where I'd escape to read books like *Gulliver's Travels* or *James and the Giant Peach*.

I told Maggie I'd call her back later. I couldn't wait to eat my breakfast without going down memory lane and developing indigestion. I didn't want to think about not having someone to love me.

★ ★ ★

After breakfast, I strolled along the banks of the Mississippi River. A cool damp air blew in, carrying a salty sweet smell, and when a big steamboat floated by, a bittersweet moment surfaced. I remembered the ships in San Francisco that day I walked along the bay, thinking about what it would be like to jump off the bridge, and then I met that Coastie and my life took another turn before I boarded the bus with River.

★ ★ ★

I met up with the band right before the concert and went to the dressing room where River got ready.

"Hey River. Did you have a good day?"

"Girl, I love this town," he said, pulling down his lower lid to line his eye. "It's a mecca for people like me." I hadn't seen him this happy in a while.

This town did have everything. All sorts of elegant mansions and fancy shops, libraries, churches, and the museum, even the little Audubon Zoo with all the cute animals where young families visited. River and I could be very happy here, I dared to dream.

"Did you know the Stash House used to be a brothel, a gym, and a gambling house?" River asked.

Now it was mostly a residential area peppered with a few businesses. We could raise a family there.

"There's this place over on Lasalle. Man, the rhythm and blues, the rock n' roll," he said. "And get this, this town has the best colored drag show, the most beautiful queens I've ever seen this side of Mississippi."

That sounded funny, being that we were literally on the banks of the old muddy river and River had grown up just on the other side.

River laughed, patting his short Afro. "Believe me, I know the difference."

★ ★ ★

March 31, 1968, Missouri: Even though discrimination in public locations had been outlawed a few years, I still didn't see too much mingling of the different races, even out on the sidewalks. And some places like Kansas City still frowned upon interracial couples, married or not. I remembered Mom telling me about all the bad looks she'd gotten in Glendale for being a Mexican married to a white guy. I hadn't paid attention being mostly focused on my Grandma problems. Most places still wouldn't give River a place to lay his head, so sometimes I hung out with him on the bus. Sometimes I worked on my lyrics.

Why can't you love me
the way I love you?
Make your heart love me
the way mine loves true
I see how you see
we are not free
to love one another
more than a brother
My heart breaks in two
halves. Make us a whole
lotta love, my soul
Please love me true.

A paper airplane landed on my pages.

"Hey, wanna go to a show?" River asked.

"You mean like a date?"

He looked at me as if I was serious. I laughed. "Right. I don't mind being a third wheel."

With a look of relief, he said. "Just you and me, kid."

The idea of a big screen and a tub of hot buttered popcorn in an air-conditioned theater sounded heavenly. And to hang out with my best friend, I didn't care what was playing, but I secretly hoped it might be *Romeo and Juliet*. I still naively hoped River and I could be more than friends.

Just around the corner on Troost Avenue stood a two-story brick building with a rippled square glass tile front and a double door entrance decorated with a flashing neon marquee that read *The Jewel Box Lounge*. Standing outside, River explained how this place had been here since 1945 but didn't start showing drag shows until around ten years ago and mostly white performers to mostly heterosexual white people. I recalled the movie I'd watched with Mom, *Some Like It Hot* with my favorite actor Tony Curtis who dressed like a woman to escape the mob. Someone else running away?

River stared at a poster. "It's like when I look at other drag people, I see a mirror of my real self."

I looked closer at the beautiful women in the posters, men in drag like Dorothy from *The Wizard of Odd* and Maria from the *The Sound of Misogyny*.

River pointed to a poster of Mae West in *Go West Young Man* and laughed. "That's what I did, except there wasn't enough makeup to hide my Blackness, so I was never officially hired, even though people would come from all over just to listen to me sing not just Eartha Kitt songs, but Dina Washington's 'Salty Papa Blues' and Sara Vaughan's 'I'm Crazy to Love You.' So, I moved west to San Francisco and the rest, as they say, is history."

"And I'm glad you did. Go West, that is."

The next show would come on later. Squeezing into a room full of white men in suits and ties and (from what I could tell, men dressed as women), we made our way over to a long bar where we ordered some drinks. Already there were couples seated at little candlelit cocktail tables. The smell of perfume and cigarettes filled the space. We found an empty table off to the side and took a seat as the house lights went down. And then a tiny light pinpointed onto the face of the first female impersonator reclined on a divan, a voluptuous person in a bouffant wig and blackface. The singer did a good acapella getting the crowd settled in for the next act. The light grew bigger as he opened his mouth and crescendoed "I Just Want to Make Love." River sat rigid in his chair. "What the hell!?"

I shook my head. "What's wrong?"

River leaned over. "That's my act. He stole it! I used to do Etta James."

I reached over, placing my hand over his, but Grandma spoke up first. "Imagine what Etta might say about everyone stealing her show."

River peered at me, brows furrowed. He gulped back his drink and went back to the bar.

The next acts were more campy but hilarious. River had been right, though: there were no Black performers except for the blackface person who'd become part of the satirical act where she played the maid in *Gone with the Wild*.

As we walked back after that act, River couldn't let go of his anger. "My performance always came at the end. And there he was right at the beginning, and in blackface!"

"So, a man impersonating a Black woman?" Grandma said. "It was done all the time in vaudeville."

"I don't got a problem with that, but why not leave it to a Black man to do? I miss performing, but not like that." River stopped and faced me. "My art is serious. How can I explain that it's not just about gender and entertainment, but a lifestyle that's not cool, especially if you're Black? But blackface, that's an insult! Impersonating the Black woman and then casting her through a distorted lens is plain wrong. It's just a way for white people to make fun and get out their feelings and fears about race and sex and control. And why does a white man get away with this!"

I was the last person River had to explain anything about impersonation and control. We boarded the bus where we'd spend the night. River took his place at the back of the bus.

CHAPTER 22

Memphis Blues

April 4, 1968: After traveling all night, I was excited to finally roll into Memphis, home of my heartthrob Elvis Presley. Back home, Mom had all his records and together we watched all of his movies from *Love Me Tender* to *Jailhouse Rock*. If I were to bump into the King, I'd do more than just let him buy me a beer. I was still waiting for a hunk of burning love to love me tenderly. Oh, a girl could dream!

Fortunately, the city of blues seemed a little more tolerant and at least catered to Blacks, but still I saw no mixed couples. Even when the old Black clerk at the Lorraine Motel arched a wiry eyebrow, River and I felt comfortable checking in together a couple blocks away from the others. Now that things between John and River had cooled off, some, including Tony, thought River and I were a couple. Still, I believed I could turn him straight. What did I know? Pretty much everyone left us alone.

In the lobby, I'd freaked out a little when the old clerk let on that Martin Luther King, Jr. was staying here. How cool would it be to run into him?

After dinner at a diner across the street, we settled into the room to rest up before getting ready for a ten o'clock show. River picked up the book and stretched back on the twin bed, one leg crossed over the other. I carried the phone with its long extension cord to the bathroom and called home.

"Hey, where are you, anyway?" Maggie asked.

"Memphis."

"It sounds like you're peeing."

"I am." I laughed. "In a Memphis hotel bathroom."

"Gross, but I guess I'd rather be in a Memphis bathroom than this dump."

"Maggie, this place is not exactly a palace. Can I talk to Mom?" I thought I heard Mom in the background.

"She's not home," Maggie said.

I didn't believe her but didn't want to press her. Let Mom stay mad at me. "Well, gotta go. Say hi to everyone for me." I hung up the phone, put it back on the nightstand, and plopped onto my bed.

"You might find this interesting." River set down his book and sat up. "Sort of reminds me of what you might be going through with Grandma."

"You mean hell?" I could see the streetlights flashing outside.

Speaking of whom, I hadn't heard from her in a couple of days. I picked up a book. Only a few pages in, I grew drowsy and lay back on my pillow.

"This cat uses the term 'double-consciousness' applying it to the idea that Black people must have two fields of vision at all times." River read from the book, "'They must be conscious of how they view themselves, as well as . . . how the world views them . . . an American, a Negro; two souls, two thoughts, two unreconciled strivings; two warring ideals in one dark body . . .'"

"Interesting. Two warring ideals." I could barely keep my eyes open, but River was on a roll.

"But what if you're someone like me, an American, a Negro, and a homosexual?"

Finally, he admitted he was gay. I could dig deeper, but to what end? I already knew and suspected he knew I did, too. So, "What if . . ." Was this a rhetorical question about who he was or did he really want my answer? I had no answers at the moment. I turned toward him. "What's the book again?"

He showed me the cover. "*Souls of Black Folk: Essays and Sketches* by W.E. Burghardt Du Bois. "I need to find a place where I'm free to be who I am."

"At least you know who you are." Groggily, I realized I honestly didn't know who I was or who I wanted to be. Yes, I was Mexican and American but also cursed with an alien grandmother who weighed in on a lot of my thoughts and conversations. River and I shared something in common, a trifecta of consciousnesses. I'd challenge anyone to find a book on that. Plus, I still hadn't ruled out the possibility of being lesbian because I'd liked kissing Betsy that time, and River when I thought he was a she, so maybe it was more a superfecta of identities, which could be good if you're betting on a horse.

River rolled onto his stomach. "In the first chapter he uses the metaphor of a veil worn by all African-Americans because their view of the world is way different from those of white people. The veil can be a gift of second sight for Blacks, so it's both a curse and a blessing."

"Seems more like a gift of denial." I laughed. "The only veil I ever wore was in church."

"Indeed, to shroud the truth," Grandma added.

"And she's back." River laughed. "Sometimes, I do see Grandma as a gift."

"Well, I've looked this gift horse in the mouth my whole life and her presence—pun intended—I'd rather not have."

With that I rolled over to shut my eyes before the alarm clock went off for the next concert.

* * *

Later, after our gig at a club filled to the rafters with fans, Tony came into the small dressing room to tell River there was a man outside who wanted to see him—probably someone who wants to hook up with him. I felt that pang of jealousy and told River I sensed a migraine coming on and wanted to head back to the room.

"I don't want you walking back alone," he said, turning to Tony. "Walk her back to the room."

Before I could object, Tony had slung his arm through mine. I wasn't afraid of him so much as he annoyed the hell out of me. For some reason, River got along with him, but he didn't know everything, as it would turn out.

"Listen to your gut," Grandma said as I peeled Tony's arm away.

"I don't get how River could possibly tickle your ivories. Don't you wanna be with a real man?"

"Like who?" I side-eyed him. "Flake-off Tony."

He laughed as we passed a bar. "I was at Steinway's that night, you know. River told me it wasn't him who killed the owner, but I saw everything." My blood drained to my feet. "I was there, too, and I know more than you think."

"How 'bout a little nightcap and we solve this mystery?"

I could see the hotel by now only a block away. "Not tonight, Sherlock." As much as I wanted to know what he thought he knew, I walked away, picking up the pace, constantly checking back over my shoulder until I saw Tony walk into the bar. When I got to my room, I locked my door and wedged a chair under the doorknob.

Taking advantage of my quiet time, I pulled out some matches from the club, inhaling the sulfur smell as I struck one. I thought I'd just about broken the habit, but oh the smell of comfort as I lit some candles. I pulled a bottle of beer from the small fridge and poured some before running a bath with lavender-scented oils. Tony had been fishing and I just needed to wash away his stench.

I lay back remembering scenes from that French book and as I let the warm water from the spigot rush between my legs, I sensed Grandma and immediately shot up. I turned the water off and pulled the plug, but my frustrations would not disappear down the drain. I climbed into my bed and tried to clear my mind, but now I thought of River and wondered who he was with. I thought of Tony and how I'd dodged a bullet and how I was lucky he liked his booze more than he liked the ladies. As I reached over to turn off the light on my nightstand, I noticed the copy of the *Life* I'd bought at a newsstand on Main Street. I came across an interesting article about the guru to the Beatles, the Maharishi Mahesh Yogi. Before long, I fell asleep.

I dreamed I sat lotus-style with Elvis before a giant altar. The dream played out in living Technicolor. Wearing a vivid orange and red lei like he wore in his movie *Blue Hawaii*. Fire licked my body. His music flooded my dream as my temperature rose higher and higher, burning through to my soul. We levitated to the sounds of tambourines, sitars, and cymbals, his kisses lifting me higher, making love as we ascended over the blue-green ocean which turned out to be a giant bathtub with a spigot spewing like a waterfall. I'd just about reached orgasm when I heard a crash.

Someone had bolted into the room knocking over the chair. I sprang up, the *Life* slipping off my heaving chest.

"Shhh! Sorry," River whispered. "Were you sleeping?"

River had interrupted my fantasy and I certainly didn't need Mother Mary or Freud's *Interpretation of Dreams* to decode my dream about my hunk of burning love, but then I realized it wasn't Elvis with me in *Blue Hawaii*. Who was it? I couldn't see his face.

"No, I—I thought you were Tony."

"Tony?"

"Yeah, we need to talk."

"But first, you'll never guess who I ran into," River said.

"Elvis?" I panted.

"No."

"Martin Luther King, Jr.?" I rubbed my eyes.

"Not him."

"Well then, who?" I asked.

"My father."

The subject of Tony would have to wait. River sat on the edge of his twin bed telling me how after I left the club, a man named Marvin Monk came backstage, claiming to be his father and told him the story about how he and his mother had been together one summer in New Orleans. "He was a jazz pianist. I just knew it," River said, quite charged up. "It makes sense. My mother couldn't play anything but a radio. Anyway, he said that when she went back to college that fall, she discovered she was pregnant. When her parents found out she was 'knocked up,' forget marriage, they sent her to the farm in Iowa to live with her grandparents. The bigger surprise was when I turned out to be a Black grandbaby." River smiled and then quickly sobered. "Later, she married a farmer who didn't want me around, so I ended up living with my great-grandparents, and after they died, I hit the road, did drag shows and that's how I ended up in San Francisco."

"Wow."

"Marvin told me that my mother wrote him about how she'd made a mistake."

"But back then, they couldn't have gotten married anyway," I said.

River shook his head. "After a while, she did let him know about me. He told me that if he'd known from the beginning, he would have found a way to marry my mother or at least see me. She let him know she'd seen me perform recently in Iowa."

"Wait, she was at our concert in Des Moines and she didn't come say hi?"

He shrugged. "Apparently. He told me that when he saw the billboard up on Beale Street advertising the band, he just knew he had to see me," River said. "I can't sleep now." He picked up the magazine I'd dropped to the floor and started pacing the tiny room.

I couldn't imagine what River was going through. "So, how did you leave things? Will you see him again?"

River shrugged his shoulders, "Not sure." He riffled through the pages. "Says here," River said, pointing to the page, "the Swami 'tells acid heads that LSD is nowhere, informs young rebels that they owe obedience to their parents and advises draft protesters to serve because it's the law.' Bullshit. I wish I had some LSD to counteract the trip I've been on tonight."

"Is that how it works?" I asked. "It counteracts?"

He shrugged his shoulders and then reached for his shoe under the bed and pulled out a fat joint. "What the hell, we don't have to be anywhere until tomorrow night."

"You mean tonight." I pointed to the clock that read four-forty-eight a.m.

He lit the doobie, took a hit, and passed it to me. We sat up in our twin beds talking until noon, listening to the Beatles' "White Album" on the little record player we'd purchased in Tulsa. We talked about life and the crazy families we were born into. We tried to interpret the lyrics and what it would be like to visit India like the Beatles had, to meditate and to compose songs. "Let's do it!" River said.

"Do what?" I handed back the joint. He toked on it and held it in. "Let's go to India." He blasted out the smoke. "Did you know Martin Luther King, Jr., was influenced by Gandhi?"

"That sounds like a lovely idea," Grandma said. "I remember the time—"

"Oh shit, Grandma. Not now," I said with a laugh, but then the notion of going to India to learn how to be free of her crossed my mind. I pulled the covers over my head and closed my eyes to see if I could chase Elvis down in my dreams, and pretty quickly I drifted off into a deep sleep, but by then Elvis had already left the bedroom.

★ ★ ★

Twilight, and I woke to the sound of River singing in the shower. It was time to get ready to go out and grab a bite to eat before our next gig. Towel wrapped around his trim waist, he dripped out of the bathroom in a fog of steam.

"Did you get any sleep?" I asked as a light flashed outside the window, the sound of a loud pop following. I heard someone yelling as River dropped his towel, turning toward the window. Of all things to recall during a crisis, I remembered looking and thinking, *Lord have mercy!* before he shouted, "Get down!"

★ ★ ★

As the nation reeled over the death of Martin Luther King, Jr., River and I sobbed packing up our things as the police, FBI, and news people swarmed all around our hotel. We needed to vacate immediately. The assassination took me back to the assassination of our President, John F. Kennedy, only a few years ago. My whole family had been in shock and I was left terrified about the future. I couldn't believe something like that could happen again. And now another great man of peace had been murdered. River was inconsolable about Martin Luther King, Jr., his grief compounded by the fact that he'd finally met his father. Sadly, things were left unfinished and unsaid before we moved on. There'd been no closure.

And then in June, the news about the assassination of Senator Robert Kennedy sent the nation reeling.

Love was just the fuel that hate needed to burn the world down to ashes.

CHAPTER 23

Commencing Countdown

July, 1969, we rolled through the city of Brotherly Love. I couldn't believe we'd been on the road crisscrossing the country for almost two years. Lazarus Rising had a new live album climbing the charts and hopefully it would be as big as the Beatles' "White Album" which by then was all the rage. Speaking of Beatles, Paul was still my favorite, with those big sad eyes. Grandma was happy I had River as a sort of chaperone. And, as it turned out, every once in a while, River was happy to be regaled by Grandma about her quaint history, i.e., her travels to India, and, get this, I did not know her French lover Guillome was a Black man.

All of the motels we'd checked into looked alike with their sparse lobbies, linoleum floors, potted plastic rubber plants, and stiff-looking furniture left over from the '50s. But it did feel like I'd stayed here before. After the clerk at the Lazy Daze Motel handed me the key, I moseyed out into twilight where the temperature had dipped to something tolerable. Earlier, so hazy and humid, I thought I'd melt into the bus seat. The bus was parked toward the back of the lot where River, still more comfortable sleeping, stepped off to join me. After the tragedy in Memphis, the world seemed a little scarier, especially for River. Besides, I didn't want to leave him alone. We headed toward the room.

Inside, over a green matted carpet, were the typical side-by-side beds with Amish rust-colored quilts. I flipped on a switch and smiled when I saw a lighthouse in a seascape—sort of out of place for this part of the country—light up above the headboard. When I get my own house near the ocean, I'm getting one just like that. Surprised, this was the first time I'd thought about settling down or even owning a home the same as normal people. That would never happen with Grandma still in residence. I dumped my suitcase on the floor, too tired to unpack.

We were like an old married couple on TV who didn't sleep together—Lucy and Ricky without the matching pajamas who slept in twin beds. "Which side do you want?" I asked River.

"Do you mind if I take the one near the TV? *Ice Station Zebra* with Rock Hudson is playing tonight."

Closest to the bathroom on the dresser up against a dark wood-paneled wall was a Motorola television set. "Be my guest," I said, kicking off my shoes and plopping onto the bed nearest the window.

"You know he's a homosexual?" River said.

"Don't you wish?"

He turned up the volume. The local news reported some trouble in the next town over. Race riots between white and Black gangs had raged now for a couple of days. There'd been tension all around the country for some time. Apparently, it all started when someone shot a Black boy in York and then a police officer was killed. As the heat rose in the city, more firebombs hit businesses, more rocks hit windows, and the toll of injured climbed in the emergency room. Liquor stores and taverns were closed. A state of emergency was declared with state police coming in to try and stop the violence. Curfews were being set in place. Anyone twenty-one or younger had to stay inside between nine p.m. and six a.m.

"I'm glad you're not sleeping out on the bus."

"Yeah, I'm much safer inside this hotel room with a white female."

The race riots had become all too common, and yet I feared it would only get worse. I didn't want to close my eyes to the problem, but I was having a hard time staying awake. I lay back on the pillow, hard as the sad truth about brotherly love, but not too hard to dream.

The next morning, I could see through my eyelids just how bright everything appeared to be on my outsides. River sang to me, "Sun is up, Dear Prudence—" How could he always be so cheerful? Since I was a little girl, even after a good night's sleep, I tended to wake up on the wrong side of the bed. My whole life, I'd ended up on the outside side of things—not just on the fringe, but far out in outer space. And then I heard the scraping of the curtain rods as he pulled back the drapes. "Wakey, wakey. Eggs and bakey."

As soon as I smelled the sweet aroma of coffee, I opened my eyes to a room swimming in a soft shade of morning light. He'd set down a couple cups at the small table near the window. I pulled back the covers, got up and took a seat. "Thank you, River." I sipped my coffee as he adjusted the TV, and then I turned to gaze out the window.

The desolate, sparkling swimming pool looked inviting and yet so sad, and then I had a déjà vu moment. "The pool just reminds me of the plunge on Verdugo where we'd go swimming every summer," I said, blowing into the cup of coffee, already cool by now.

"Sounds like someone's missing her family," he said, turning on the radio.

"Maybe, but I don't miss all the chlorine and my eyes getting so red. Anyway, I figured the lifeguards could watch my sisters so they wouldn't drown while I played Marco Polo with kids more my age." I turned toward River.

"So, you were a *normal* kid, after all. I knew it."

In the background, I heard the lyrics to "Space Oddity".

"The pool was the one place I actually made friends every summer. It was a place where I didn't feel like an alien or a space cadet."

"Speaking of which, suit up," River said. "We'll take a dip and then come back to watch the moon landing."

"Oh, is that today already?"

"Why do you think that Bowie song is playing?"

We listened to the rest of the song before stepping out for a swim.

★ ★ ★

As I turban-toweled my hair, I heard River from the other room. "This TV isn't working. There's one over at the diner. And it's in color."

Tony had already taken a seat at the counter, slugging down an Old Milwaukee. The patrons didn't seem to notice the mixed couple, who weren't from around these parts, walk in, but I could feel the hair-raising static electricity in the air. Quiet as the sound in space where there are no molecules to vibrate noise, all eyes were glued to the astronomical episode on TV.

Tony slid over, making room for us at the counter just in time to watch the landing on the heavenly giant golf ball. A rush of anticipation surged through me. "The connection keeps getting dropped," Tony said out of the side of his mouth. "They're almost out of fuel."

What? My heart stopped. *But they've come this far! I've come this far.* Since take off a few days ago, I'd made up a sort of heads or tails little game where I'd compared the Apollo space journey to my life and so if something were to happen, I'd be jinxed, too. And then within a few seconds, I heard, "Houston, Tranquility

Base here. The Eagle has landed." The whole earthly diner erupted into cheers and loud applause.

In one giant stride, the no-nonsense waitress in a starched pink uniform and a tightly corkscrewed cinnamon-colored bun, stood in front of me blocking my view of one of the most historical occurrences of a lifetime, but suddenly I felt famished, as if I'd raced to the moon and back.

"I'll take a cheeseburger, some fries, and a Coke," I said, remembering how Dad used to joke with us that the moon was nothing but a big ball of moldy cheese—Dad, never serious except when he hung out on the dark side of the moon. And today on a brighter side, in a flash, the world seemed to have transformed. Could this be the change needed to bring the country together, the light needed to enlighten, to wash away the sins of the world? The waitress finished jotting down my order and without looking up asked, "What about your boyfriend?" her phony smile, a severe slash above her chin.

"He's not my—I don't know." I was St. Peter denying Jesus. "Why don't you ask him?"

Hand on hips as wide as the galaxy, she stared down at me and I knew it would take more than a moon landing to shift her attitude. River's look told me not to make any trouble.

"He'll take a 7Up and a burger without onions." A burger, the way he told me his white grandpa Elroy had grilled for him back in Iowa before he'd blasted off and changed his name to River; before we ever met, to float together like Huckleberry Finn and Jim through this odyssey in time in a tin can of a bus where through the windows, I'd seen the stars shine brighter from the deserts, the plains and the mountains, brighter than they ever did beyond the lamp lights of home.

On the television mounted up on the wall, the scene had broken away to the newsroom. I couldn't believe that in just a few more hours, Neil Armstrong would step out onto the moon.

Unreal. The stiff-starched waitress brought our drinks and set them down just as someone behind us shouted, "Anthony Hatchet!" I turned to see the tall silhouette of a cop, gun drawn, striding toward us. "You're under arrest."

Tony, seated to my left sprang up and in one giant leap, took off for the exit where another cop stood ready to intercept him. One of the cops handcuffed River and suddenly, I felt someone grab my wrists.

"You have the right to remain silent—" the tall cop said.

"But, what's this about?" River asked as we were escorted outside.

I could understand that the law had probably caught up to Tony for going AWOL, but it terrified me to wonder why we were also being hauled in.

"We'd like to ask you some questions, about a murder," the tall cop said, and I lost feeling in my legs. Dilbert Moss?

"It was an accident," Grandma said.

Holding me up by my elbow, the tall cop asked. "What was an accident? What do you know?"

Shit. I turned my head away from the policeman. "Grandma, I've got this."

We were led to the police car. "Get in."

When we arrived at the police station, River and I were taken into separate rooms to be interviewed. By then I was eighteen and not a minor. Except for my name, I had no proper identification.

"Would you like to call someone?" the tall cop asked me.

"Why? Am I under arrest?"

He wouldn't answer. "Where's your home?"

"California." Off his cold look, I added. "Glendale."

"Where were you last November?"

I shook my head and shrugged my shoulders. Last November?

"You've got a family, don't you? Weren't you home for Thanksgiving?"

"No." That I knew for sure. I'd told Maggie I hoped to come home then or maybe for Christmas, but that never happened. I racked my brain. We'd been all over the place. Was this a trick question? What did it have to do with Dilbert Moss?

"When's the last time you saw your mother or father?"

Oh, my God! My body prickled.

"It's been awhile. Why? Are they okay?"

"Is Charley alright?" Grandma asked.

"I wouldn't know. Who's Charley?" Tall cop asked.

"My dad," I said, recovering quickly. "I call him Charley."

The cop shrugged. "I'm just trying to establish—corroborate—again, where were you last November?"

My heart quaked. "Let me think. I keep a little diary in my purse."

The shorter officer left the room.

"When did you, Mr. Hatchet, and Mr. Nolan first hook up?"

"Mr. Nolan?"

"Levi Nolan."

So that's River's name. "A couple years ago in San Francisco."

"What do you know about Levi?"

Apparently, not enough. "He's from Iowa."

And what do you know about Anthony Hatchet?

"Tony?" I wouldn't tell them I knew he was AWOL. "I think he's from Philadelphia, right around here some place. I think he's got friends and family here."

The short cop returned with my purse and handed it to the taller cop who then handed it to me. Hand shaking, I took out my little diary and opened it up, flipping through the month of November 1968. I looked up into the interrogating cop's face and closed the little book. "It shows we were here. We had a gig over at Eagle Tavern."

We'd performed in front of some soldiers who'd just returned from Vietnam. Grandma had been so excited. She said it reminded her of the time she performed for some troops in France. I'd pounded on the piano to shut her up.

The tall cop then pulled out a picture of a soldier. "Do you recognize him?"

I looked at the picture of a young, dark-haired man in uniform. "No."

I did remember how after the concert, Tony had stayed behind, I'd assumed to catch up with an old friend over a couple of beers. The rest of us packed up our stuff and went back to our hotel.

"Marine Corps Cpl. Corriveau was found dead along the Pennsylvania Turnpike with a stab to the heart."

I spiraled down, confused. What did this have to do with me?

"Allegedly, he was a friend of Anthony 'Tony' Hatchet. We think Anthony had something to do with it."

My lips parted, but no words came out. Again, what did this have to do with me? Oh my God. Had River been involved? I'd never know what Tony thought he saw at Steinway's.

★ ★ ★

After several agonizing hours, River and I were released, but River had been beaten and bruised, his eye swollen, a cut on his forehead.

"What happened?" I asked River.

"Don't ask?"

They'd retained Tony, placing him under arrest for the murder of the young Marine. While we waited for one of the crew to come pick us up in the van, River and I compared information.

"With the riots going on, they must have rounded up all the Blacks in the area. So, after they slapped me around for a while and for good measure, one of the cops came in to say they had their man. It seems somebody recognized Tony. He and this Marine had gotten into an argument about him being a coward and a deserter and Tony ended up stabbing the guy."

"But in the heart?"

"It's not the first time he's been in trouble with the law. Remember when John said he'd been warned?"

"Yeah?"

"Apparently, after a concert, John and some of the other band members came across him getting a little rough with a girl. They pulled him off her before things got way out of hand."

"What? And John didn't kick him to the curb? He let him on the bus with us?"

"John said he pleaded. He apologized. He said he was drunk and that he'd never done anything like that before and he'd never do anything like that again."

"As far as we know, until now, except murder a soldier."

River nodded looking off, quiet for a while. "He begged for another chance and John gave it to him." He turned to me.

"What is it?" I asked.

"Apparently, the Marine didn't have any family," he said as the van pulled up. River remained silent all the way back to the hotel.

★ ★ ★

I filled a bucket of ice just outside our room and then went in. I handed a towel with ice to River just as a news story broke on the television. A young Black woman named Lillie Belle Allen had been visiting her sister when she was shot and killed on Newberry Street. The governor had called in the National Guard.

"I'm tired of turning the other cheek," River said, holding the towel to his cheek.

It was time to get out of town. We hoped the next stop would be more peaceful, but the race riots were taking place all over, including our next destination, New York. We were on our way, but there would be two fewer people on the bus.

CHAPTER 24

'Til Death Do Us Part

August, 1969, felt like a double heartbreak. The memory of River, my only friend and brother on this journey, would remain imprinted like a footprint on my heart forever. Paralyzed, I sat on the bus hugging my pillow. Through the blurry window, the skies, rumbling with thunder and cracking with lightning, slurped up the wet road ahead.

Earlier that morning, I'd awakened to the sounds of a thunderstorm. River had taken a seat on his bed, turning his head away from me. Usually, I was the one who remained silent. I hated seeing River like he couldn't hold his head up. I got out of my bed and sat next to him. "Talk to me, River." I placed a hand on his shoulder.

"I've been doing a lot of thinking," he said, facing me now, his eye swollen shut.

He didn't even flinch when lightning cracked in the distance. Out the window, the tall ash trees bowed to the elements. "Yeah, I can see that," I said, returning to face him.

"The cops asked if I wanted to call anyone. All I could think of was you."

"Me, too." Smiling weakly, I saw my wavy reflection in his one red, watery eye.

"But you have family and you can at least call a sister," he said. "While I sat in jail, I thought about who I could call. I'd just met my father in Memphis. He'd begged me to call him if I ever needed anything. But how would it look if my first call came from the jail. My mother didn't even bother to come say hello when we were in Iowa. I was right in her backyard—the place I once called home. My grandparents are dead." River looked so sad. "I think I need to get to know my family," he said.

"But we're family. You and me."

He smiled at me. "I think it's time I got to know all the cousins and half-brothers and sisters in New Orleans." He smiled. "Apparently there are dozens. I need to find myself, but first I need to know my history. I read where DuBois says, 'The History of the American Negro is the history of this strife—this longing to attain self-conscious manhood, to merge his double self into a better and truer self.' I simply wish to be both a Negro and an American, without being cursed and spit upon by my fellows, without having the doors of opportunity closed roughly in my face."

I couldn't argue that.

"I think I might find answers to my being if I were to return."

I nodded, hand over my mouth, suppressing the urge to cry.

"I dug the music vibe in New Orleans." He smiled. "I loved everything about that place. I'm going back."

"What!? But what about New York? The Statue of Liberty, and SoHo, and Casa Susanna."

River shook his head. "Don't you remember what happened last month when we were in Greenwich Village?"

"But you could dress normal." I reached out to take his hands.

"Normal? And what about the color of my skin?" He pulled away.

"Isn't New York supposed to be pretty liberal? I thought it was hip," I answered, but he disappeared into the bathroom.

"Remember what happened last time we stayed in Greenwich Village?" he asked. River had stumbled back to the room in the early morning a bit shaken up. He told me he'd escaped arrest but that others weren't as lucky. After a small gig over at the Bitter End, he'd gone a couple blocks up to a bar called Stonewall Inn where they had drag shows. Just after midnight and the place was packed. Apparently undercover cops came in and raided the place, starting with employees, and then singling out drag queens and other cross-dressing customers. He told me the police roughed up a woman dressed as a man and then from outside people started throwing coins and bottles. The tires on cop cars were slashed.

The next day River had read to me from the Village Voice how the police had difficulty "keeping a dyke and a dancing faggot in a patrol car."

"Homo Nest Raided, Queen Bees Are Stinging Mad" blared the headline on the front page of the Daily News. "Lilies of the valley pranced out to the street" when the cops showed up, the paper said. The rebellion lasted six days.

As offensive as the media coverage was, it would be the beginning of a change, but as progressive as I thought New York might be, things were still pretty tense. River was right, New York wasn't safe for a person like him, and he didn't have the strength to fight back anymore. I couldn't argue his decision.

River walked out of the bathroom. "I'll go with you," I said, even though settling in New Orleans wasn't exactly a dream of mine, I'd follow him to the end of the Mississippi.

"No, Honey. This is not your path. I see great things for you."

Tears gushed from my eyes. "But you're my best friend. I can't live without you." I reached over to wrap my arms around him and sobbed, my mascara and Twiggy eyeliner running down my cheeks.

He handed me a piece of paper with a number where he could be reached. "Remember, I'll always love you, Honey Moon," he said, lifting my chin, peering deeply into my soul, "and you, too, Grandma."

I couldn't bring myself to tell him the same and turned away before Grandma could say anything. He set his suitcase on the bed and I ran out into the pouring rain.

★ ★ ★

On the bus to New York, Grandma, always looking for double rainbows, tried to make me feel better. "Darling, every crossroad you've come to on your travels so far has brought you to where you need to be. Think about it. You never would have met River if you hadn't walked into Steinway's."

"Yeah, never mind that Dilbert would still be alive," I said. "And now River's gone. What's that all about?"

"Darling, I do know how it feels. I had this friend once, a great composer, Charles Cadman. We traveled together through Europe—that is, we and his mother—"

"Oh, for the love of God! This is not helping." I massaged my forehead. "Why do you always have to compare your life to mine?"

"You've made a great friend. Just because River's gone—"

"No! He was more than a friend and now I'm on this bus with a big hole in my heart and an insensitive leech."

"It will mend itself," she said.

"God dammit, Grandma. I didn't just tear my dress."

"Please don't use that language. It's not becoming of a young lady."

I wished she had a face so that I could throw that half-full glass of water onto it. "Fuck you! Is that more becoming?"

"You're hurt. You sound so much like your father when he's angry and hurt."

My body tensed with rage. I thought my insides might rip through my skin. I put my pillow over my face to scream my brains out.

Finished purging, I removed the pillow and spoke as calmly as I could, as coolly as Grandma always did. "Now I can understand why he wanted to get rid of you, why he called you a bitch." I waited for her to respond. In the lethal silence I knew she'd been gearing up for a muted blast off.

She didn't respond, but I knew the debates would continue.

I rolled down the bus window for some fresh air as we bumped along through fertile rolling hills and valleys. I took in the cloying fragrance of the sweet grasses and tobacco fields as we entered the dairy and horse farm country.

I didn't know what was worse, the smell of manure or the inside of the bus reeking of pot and sweaty humans. I reached into my pocket for the book of matches River had left me. I struck one, shook it out, and inhaled. As the scenery sped by like some sort of emergency, I remembered Maggie telling me that after the ambulance had taken Dad away, Mom raced to the hospital to sit next to him—forever, as she promised, even while some doctor stitched him up. I'd been the one who fought him off and left him with a scar, a reminder of me. And Mom, probably the only person I'd ever truly loved, was there to tend to his scar just as she tended to her vows, forsaking all others, even me. Never mind my scars. I'd tend to them myself. I'd mend. Grandma even said so. At least now I was free. No one could hold me back by promising to love me until death did I part.

Devastated at losing River, I wanted to die. *I'll always love you, Honey Moon.* But it wasn't to the moon and back. He hadn't promised to love me forever until death did us part, like married people do. Grandma was right. Grief was the price you paid for love. I lit another match, waved it around, trying to inhale some comfort.

The bus lurched as the gears changed and I bolted up, my book dropping from my lap. "Where are we?"

"For God's sake, Honey," Cindy said. "Pull your head out and pay more attention. We're headed to New York."

"Cool." It didn't register. After River, life had gone on and the wheels on the bus still went round and round, but now that all the air in my life had hissed out, I lived deflated as a flat tire hiding behind my books, never taking the time to get to know the rest of the band members traveling with us, much less bond with the girls.

I reached down for my book.

"Did you ever finish *Emmanuelle*?" Cindy asked. "I heard about the scene with the banana?"

"What are you? Twelve?" I said.

Cheryl stuck out her tongue and I rolled my eyes. She then made a "V" with her fingers and flicked her tongue through it.

Cindy and Cheryl seemed nice enough, if not intimidating. Besides lacking social skills, it was a chore making connections. Besides, hovering Grandma had always been there to keep me company. But then, I met River, the one friend I'd learned to trust. He'd opened my eyes to a whole new world and then left me to wander alone.

"You need to call home," Grandma said.

I pulled a book up to my face and whispered, "I'll call when we get settled in New York. Besides, what's the hurry?"

"Very well," Grandma said, sounding more ominous. "I suppose there's nothing I can do anymore. What is done is done."

What's that supposed to mean? What had she ever *done* but make trouble for me? I turned the page and read: "the enormous difference between the relationships you need, and the one you deeply want. The need is created out of an accumulation of negativities, planted by traumatic experiences: fears, doubts, anxiety, dependence, weakness in certain realms, inadequacy, incompleteness . . ." Anaïs Nin.

I closed the book. I'd call home as soon as I could.

★ ★ ★

In New York, I saw no tall buildings as the bus traveled out in the boondocks somewhere in the middle of rolling green hills, fringed by forests, corn stalks, and cows. We slowed enough to read the sign. Had I blinked my eyes, I would have missed the 'Village of Liberty' altogether. We pulled into a Holiday Inn.

"Woodstock?" It came back to me then, but I'd read how the event had been canceled up in a place called Wallkill, and this wasn't Wallkill.

Cindy told me how Ralphie, the manager, had gotten a call while we were in Philadelphia. "Apparently, a lot of bands, like Mind Garage and the Doors, are canceling for whatever reason," she said. "We don't have to be in Manhattan until next week, so here we are. Come on. Let's get checked in and then go check things out."

But before I could even set down my suitcase and guitar in the lobby, Ralphie ran up to me. "Honey, grab your guitar and follow John."

I turned to see John walking out the front door.

"Where's he going?"

Cindy shrugged her shoulders and I followed John around the back where the wind nearly knocked me over. A helicopter settled down for a landing. John faced me, his hair whipping up, and shouted something I couldn't hear as he motioned for me to hurry up.

The next thing I knew, I, with three other male band members, Lazarus, and the pilot, were lifting off and then flying over patches of cornfields and farmlands bordered by ribbons of people, cars, buses, motorcycles, and bicycles like microscopic, psychedelic-colored blood cells traveling through a bucolic artery heading toward a body where I imagined everyone's heart beat as one.

★ ★ ★

The chopper landed in a field behind a stage.

After disembarking, the helicopter took off again, mud churning beneath it. I wiped my face with the back of my shirt and tried to smooth my hair back just as some curly dark-haired man took me by the elbow.

"I'm Artie, one of the promoters," he shouted, and led me onto the back of the stage where soon I heard someone performing, his voice booming out of a couple of giant metal speaker towers. "He's on his third encore," Artie said, throwing his arms up in exasperation. "The band is stuck in traffic."

I recognized the voice of the singer from shows where we'd both opened for other big-name bands. He was singing some sort of spiritual song.

"He's run out of songs to play," Artie said, lighting a cigarette. "You're up next."

I looked out at the sea of glistening humans and thought I'd drown. I hugged my guitar as if it were a lifesaver.

"Let's open with 'Why Can't You Love Me?'" John said, knocking me out of my trance. I'd composed that song with River in mind, a song we both sang while I played the piano. "I'll sing River's part," Lazarus said.

"Oh, darling," Grandma said. "This is our—pardon me, this is your big opportunity."

"Grandma, I don't—" my voice cracked. Suddenly my tongue seemed to be tied in a knot. "I can't sing without River," I said, noticing some crew guy rolling in a keyboard right after Richie left the stage.

"You will sing without him," Grandma said.

I took a deep breath and held it as if I were diving into the frigid ocean. There was no time to swim away, only time to paddle if I wanted to survive.

"Hey man, that was far out," John said, reaching out to shake hands with a sweaty, ecstatic Richie Havens walking off the stage.

"Yeah, I played everything else I knew. I had to improvise," Richie said as another helicopter came into view.

Within moments the chopper landed and when the doors finally opened up, the world pulled away from underneath me. Out stepped the guru from the article I'd read in *Life* magazine.

The promoter lifted his arm to look at his watch. "Oh shit, he's right on time," he said, flicking his cigarette. "We probably shouldn't have Swami Satchidananda wait. He'll go on next, before you," he said, stomping the still-burning cigarette with his boot and then hurrying over to greet the special guest.

Saved by the Swami, I wouldn't have to play—just yet—several musicians and crew swarmed the guru and escorted him up to the back of the stage where I'd been standing petrified at the thought of performing. His followers gathered for a blessing before he took to the stage where he sat lotus-style on a bench before addressing the crowd:

"My Beloved Brothers and Sisters, I am overwhelmed with joy to see the entire youth of America gathered here in the name of the fine art of music. In fact, through the music, we can work

wonders. Music is a celestial sound and it is the sound that controls the whole universe, not atomic vibrations . . ."

I felt a collective unifying vibration, and by the time the crowd chanted, "Hari OM, Hari Hari OM."

Lazarus Rising finally took the stage and the thought of performing no longer terrified me. "Darling, you are going to be simply fabulous," Grandma said.

"Yeah, Grandma, I've got this," I responded, taking my place behind the piano.

Still mesmerized after listening to the Swami, the crowd stayed quietly respectable as I struck the first notes of "Why Can't You Love Me?" John harmonizing River's part, I realized I'd only come on this journey because of him, and by the time John and I finished the song, the helicopter buzzed up, taking the Swami away to wherever he came from. I pushed away from the piano, leaving John to sing solo and walked to the end of the stage, watching the helicopter disappear into the sky. After a moment, the crowd started chanting, "Honey Moon, come back!"

"Darling, go back and finish," Grandma said.

I looked at John, a true showman, who glared at me, motioning with his eyes for me to come back. I shook my head and without missing a beat, he picked up his guitar and started the next song.

"I'm finished, Grandma," I said, stepping off the stage. I then parted my way through the crowd, making my way out onto the road.

"Anna, go back!"

No one would ever remember I'd been on stage. I wouldn't stay for the rest of the festival. If I had to, I'd follow the guru to the ends of the earth.

CHAPTER 25

The Big Apple

Unfortunately, I would have to stick it out with the band a little longer. My big plans called for big money. As I packed up back at the Liberty Hotel, John showed up and begged me to stay on; promising to pay me more and even letting me perform some of my own music. I couldn't say no.

* * *

We arrived at another hotel on 57th just a few blocks from Carnegie Hall. Before unpacking, I took a seat on the bed to phone home. After five rings, I hung up. It was around three o'clock Pacific time. My family was still not home. I'd try again later. Meanwhile, I unpacked my things and decided to try the number River had given me. I wanted him to come visit me.

A man answered. River was out, he told me. I left the number where he could reach me.

Exhausted, I grabbed a book and turned in. I fell asleep but then awoke with a feeling of dread. A memory had been buried in my bones from the past, but whose past? It wasn't the first night I'd fallen asleep into Grandma's vivid dreams, into her cravings. Sometimes I felt a sorrow so profound as if someone had been killed; perhaps, my grandfather. But last night I dreamed about a young boy who'd died. He'd been related to my father. I woke up heartsore.

I sat up in bed. "Tell me what happened, Grandma. Who was this boy?" With a dogged persistence, I continued to interrogate her before the memory might slip away, before it might get buried again. Grandma remained silent as she had been for some time now, hiding somewhere in the mossy folds of my brain.

★ ★ ★

Days later, returning from the studio, the phone rang down the hall. As I neared my room it became even more distinct. At the door, I fumbled with the key. It could be River! On the nightstand, the phone vibrated with panic. I picked it up.

"Anna, thank God you finally answered," Maggie said, anxiety in her voice. "Dad's dead."

My heart plummeted. Gasping, breath trapped, I'd forgotten to exhale. "Oh Daddy!" I burst out crying surprised at myself and then I caught my reflection in the dresser mirror across the room, the little girl I used to be. Embarrassed at my emotional outbreak, I sucked it up before apologizing to Maggie. "I'm sorry. What happened?" I wiped my tears.

"He shot himself."

"No!" The child in the mirror stared back at me. Dad was dead now, but still she wasn't free. I felt dizzy, swirling downward, as if I might pass out; as if I were looking down from a helicopter watching the world being sucked away. I slumped onto the bed and closed my eyes, cradling my forehead. He'd finally accomplished what he'd threatened to do so many times, like he was the Boy Who Cried Wolf. "When did it happen?"

"They found him last Friday."

Last Friday? That's when Grandma insisted that I call home, but I'd refused and then she let it go saying there was nothing she could do anymore. *What is done is done.* I couldn't remember hearing from her since then.

High-pitched noises sounded in my skull like sirens or wolves howling. I clutched the bedcovers to keep from lifting off, but the traffic noise outside called to me to spring up and storm out. Suddenly, I wanted to blend into the cacophony of sound as if the melody of the street and the disharmony in my head might transform into some sort of soothing new music of my soul.

"Who found him? Where? In the house?"

"I guess life just finally got to him," practical Maggie said.

Does she feel nothing?

"It's time to come home. You'll be safe now."

Now? I sobbed out loud. What does she know? And if she knew anything, how long had she known and why hadn't she told me?

"When's the—is there going to be a funeral?" I stammered, planting both feet on the floor to stop the room from spinning.

"Not for a couple weeks," Maggie said. "The church frowns on suicide, but Mom insists on having it in the church, even though she also wanted him excommunicated."

Is this a joke?

"We'll have to see what Father Reynoso has to say. Anyway, I'm thinking the Rosary should be on Monday or Tuesday night and then the service the next day," she said. "It would be nice if you could get here to help. I'm hiring some Mariachis. You know how Dad loved them?"

Yeah, Dad loved them so much that Mom grew to hate them and all they represented; drunken, lonesome ballads of loss and heartbreak. "You could do a reading or even the eulogy."

I blew my nose.

"I'll have Patty be in charge of ordering the food. I should probably say goodbye. There's so much to do and Mom is sort of useless right now, but she insists we give him a proper Catholic send-off."

As if I could hang on to a perfect life that never existed, I listened to the beeping sound after Maggie hung up. Why was everyone going through so much trouble for him? Acting like it was some sort of Hollywood production. Dad couldn't care less. He's dead. Never mind that he wasn't even a real Catholic; he only got baptized as an added measure to prove to Mom he was going to quit drinking. Why couldn't you stop, Daddy? I swiped my tears. There were so many more questions swirling in my head; so many I'd been afraid to ask. Why couldn't you love me?

★ ★ ★

Again, I found myself running out of breath as I sprinted along the sidewalk, not knowing where I was headed, dodging throngs of pedestrians, dogs on leashes, hot dog vendors, and plenty of protestors. The last time I took off running, I ended up in a San Francisco bus station just before River came along to stop me from returning home. Maybe I should've gone home. Things would have been different, for sure. Dad might still be alive.

"It was his fate." Grandma spoke up finally.

"Oh my God, Phoebe," I shouted. "Everything would have been different had you just died without transferring over to me. Am I next?"

Behind me a mother pushing a stroller rushed past me as a few pinstriped Wall Street types carrying briefcases strode toward me, seemingly not bothered about my carrying on a heated conversation with myself. Heads lowered, they simply stepped around me, hurrying off to their important jobs.

The sun beat down on me through a sky the color of a week-old bruise. Steam rose up off the asphalt and ascended through the grates in the sidewalks. Noisy garbage trucks scooped up the trash leaving the streets still smelling of urine and rotten food. I felt like vomiting. Not only had my father died, but the whole nation wobbled on the heels of a turbulent time. All of the highways across America fumed noxious gases. The assassinations and the Vietnam War still raged like an out of control forest fire. Around the country, people protested in the streets with a fanatical sense of anger and loss. And then River left me with my insides the same as the outside world, sticky and humid; the air and my veins swollen with toxicity and yet I pushed myself along.

Racing across Central Park reminded me of Griffith Park and Panhandle Park where people played music and the pungent smell of pot and patchouli packed a punch. Today, there were young families picnicking in the shade; fathers playing catch with their kids; all normal stuff ordinary families did. A little boy threw a Frisbee for his dog who looked a lot like my Bella. The child looked a lot like my father as a little boy in a picture of him—playing with his three-legged dog, Mel—that hung on the wall at home. I didn't know I had any tears left as I slumped to the ground and sat on the grass. Now that Dad was dead, the seeds that had been planted in darkness were free to grow and I wouldn't let Grandma throw dirt on them anymore. She wasn't telling me to go home now, and why should she? Home sure as hell never existed for me. And now that Dad's gone, what's the point? I didn't want to go to Dad's funeral, but wondered who might show up for him if I didn't. His friends? Neighbors? We were his only family. I felt sorry for him, but then as I plucked blades of grass, one elusive memory after the other sprouted up, one blade of truth at a time.

Dad has slapped me across my face before it hits the wall.

There'd been a work party he wanted to get to where the families from the plant were invited, but I didn't like some of his smelly friends with their bo, beer, and cigarettes breath. I refused to go.

"Grandma, where were you that time he gave me the black eye?"

She fell silent as I yanked a handful of grass, remembering, I'm only eleven and Dad has staggered home unexpectedly, drunk again, yelling for Mom, "Teresa, where are you?" She'd left me alone to attend to some school event for my sisters. Had he run out of money? Was he in trouble? My body convulsed as I hid in my room hoping he'd just go to his room and pass out. I got up to bar my door with my desk chair. Too late. He barged through as I backed away, grabbing me before throwing me onto the bed. Even still, I can smell the stinky beer on his hot breath, and now a memory, I'd stuffed down before losing consciousness, bubbles to the surface and bursts—the stench of his rough Camel-cigarette stained hand on my small, insignificant breast. As trivial as I was made to believe this had been, I knew now this "accident" was monumental.

His hand a branding iron, my chest burns. "Oh my God, Grandma! Why didn't you do anything? Why did everyone downplay this moment? Why was I made to believe it never happened? Why did I think I'd done something wrong?" I remembered how he finally removed his hand to slap it over my mouth. I see his red-rimmed, cold steel metal grey eyes widen, the big pupils, black holes bursting through an explosion. Rolling off of me, he creeps away like the Hunchback of Notre Dame. Until the day I stabbed him, I never looked into his eyes again and I crammed the memory in the back closet of my memory.

"You say you wanted to keep me safe from him and now he's dead," I sobbed.

Still no sign of Grandma, but I felt her hiding in the shadows of my mind.

The little boy with the dog and the Frisbee ran past and I recalled the morning after the incident. I'd heard a gunshot coming from the garage and ran in to find my father lying on the ground. I knelt by his side, choking on the smell of firecrackers and sulfur, thinking he was dead until he turned and lifted his head. "I'm so sorry, Mouse." He begged me to forgive him, telling me he'd been out of his mind; that he'd gone out drinking after being haunted by his stepbrother who'd killed himself. What? What stepbrother? Last time he was sad because of his murdered father. I was so confused. Wasn't I too young to hear all of this? And then he cried and I felt sad for him. He stopped talking as if he'd passed his heavy burdens onto me.

Later, when I asked Mom about it, she basically told me to mind my own business, which I did. At the time, I put the whole ordeal out of my mind only to feel sorry for Dad and the dead stepbrother. To bring anything up might send my father into either a rage or melancholy. Later, Mom said he was drunk and had mistaken me for her. Grandma said he was angry with her, not me. What was I? The human punching bag? Everyone made excuses for my father's horrific behavior; my mother, my grandmother, society, and the church told me to forgive. Even I tried to justify his actions. But why? Why was he more important than me? Why should I go to his funeral? I'm not going!

"You're right." Grandma finally spoke up. "He's long departed. There's nothing for us back home anymore."

I could keep running, but whether she chose silence or not, she would always be with me like a squatter who'd taken up residence, invading my soul. I knew there was only one way for me to be free. Suicide.

★ ★ ★

I wept, not so much for my father, but for the kid who'd suffered his abuse. After stumbling blindly out of the park onto the West End, I drifted along for several blocks, landing on the steps where a sign read, *Universal Church*. I wandered in to find white-gowned bodies strewn everywhere in all sorts of pretzel poses, slowly rising to dance and chant and clap their bangle-wristed hands. Finally, exhausted, they sunk to their knees, bowing their heads to the floor and the silence. At the sound of chimes, the followers sat up crossing their legs to face the front of a small stage. And then the hall went dark.

The smell of incense comforted me, wafting its way through my veins. And then on the raised platform, a heavenly light shone on a golden harp, behind which sat a regal, ebony-colored woman. Over the jingling, I heard a young women's voice say, "Ladies and gentlemen, please help me welcome Alice Coltrane." Alice's hands and arms fluttered like dark ribbons across the glistening strings, creating a sound like raindrops to soothe my scorched soul.

"Envision yourself floating on a sea of love." Her music was spiritual, vibrant, and jazzy. A snare drum joined in and then bells. More lights came on illuminating other musicians. I felt a magnetic pull and a momentous push from Grandma before I edged my way closer to the stage. I sat down and crossed my legs, focusing on the short-necked, pair-shaped stringed instrument called the oud and a long-necked, stringed instrument called the tamboura that sounded like the drone of insects. Someone played a soprano saxophone, and someone else, a bowed bass. The vibrations made me feel like a little bee in a field of mustard plants. As the saxophone wailed, a mind-blowing, colorful vibrancy mixed with exotic overtones created a music so divine. Reverberating throughout the hall rang a sound I'd never heard. The jazz I'd known had been loud and bombastic, almost a protest, but this music seemed to speak even louder in a more delicate, graceful, articulate way. More than just jazzy, the music seemed to go beyond the boundaries of both Eastern and Western music. Hypnotic. Transforming.

Outside, while the noise of the streets, the protests, the shouting to be heard, seemed to be quelled; inside, I floated along a cool, peaceful river.

And then for the next piece, Alice got up to take a seat at a grand piano and turned to the audience. Grandma insisted, in her yellow voice, that we scoot up closer. And then what an orchestra of celestial music, if this was what heaven sounded like, I was ready to go. All of a sudden, my world didn't seem so small. A foreign sense of joy washed over me. This new, eccentric music reminded me of my journey so far across the country where I'd discovered the beautiful parks, rivers, lakes, and rest areas, stopping a moment before going on. It seemed like all of my life I'd been restricted to a couple of octaves and now I discovered all the ebony and ivory keys, I could use the whole piano. I grew excited and looked forward to where my journey was going to take me next. Suddenly I wasn't afraid of what might be around the corner.

When the music stopped, the pretty woman walked to center stage. "And now Swami Satchidananda will bless us on our way out to love and serve the world."

Had I heard correctly? The Swami from Woodstock? What are the odds of this? My spirit wanted to leave my body.

The bearded man walked out, raised his arms, his orange sleeves swaying as he spoke. "Welcome my brothers and sisters."

"Welcome," we responded.

He took a seat and sat cross-legged to speak of many things, but this next part stuck. "Remember the goal of Integral Yoga, and the birthright of every individual, is to realize the spiritual unity behind all the diversities in the entire creation and to live harmoniously as members of one universal family."

Does that mean Grandma, too? How am I to learn to live in harmony with Grandma bogarting space in my head?

"Be here now." He seemed to be addressing me. "Mind over matter. Remember, the body is only the vehicle you are using."

My whole body revved up, the moist hairs on the back of my sweaty neck standing at samasthiti. "Body is not the real you," Swami said. "Death is taking the body away, not the soul." I listened intently trying to absorb everything he said. "Yoga is a pathway to non-dual or unity consciousness. We all have unity and, at the same time, diversity. Physically, mentally, and materially we are all different. We do not think the same way. Although we sometimes say we are thinking alike, our thoughts are never one hundred percent the same. Even when we gather for a common purpose, our thoughts are still different. No mind is exactly the same as another mind. Nature never makes duplicates. Scientists say that not even two snowflakes are exactly alike. There is constant variety in creation. Mentally we are different; physically we are different. The only thing in which we are not different is our awareness, our consciousness, the light within or, as the Bible calls it, the image of God. In that, we are all one. The same light shining through many different colored lamps."

And then, if speaking directly to me, he peered my way. "Let go of the anger. It is possible to live in harmony with your dual consciousness. Treasure your gift."

I could have died right there. My dual consciousness? I couldn't stop the deluge of tears.

On a natural high after meeting the Swami, I shyly approached Alice. "I've never heard anything quite so beautiful."

"Are you a musician?"

"I play piano and guitar. I can also sing."

"You are blessed, indeed."

I nodded.

"Did you enjoy what the Swami had to say?"

"I sure did. It's been a magical night of music and words."

"Indeed. Enchanting," Grandma added.

"Where did you learn such sounds?" I asked.

"India. As a matter of fact, as soon as I spend some time recording here in New York, I'm headed back to finish up a new album. You should make the trip."

India?

* * *

A red light blinked on the phone as soon as I walked into my hotel room. River had left a message. I dialed him back immediately. He picked up on the first ring.

"River! Thank God!"

"Honey, is everything okay?"

"My dad's dead." I choked on my tears. "He shot himself. The family wants me home for the funeral, but I'm not going."

"Oh, Honey. Of course, you have to go home. Tell me what happened."

I stifled tears. "I'm not sure. I haven't processed everything. I really miss you."

"I miss you, too. When you're ready. I'm here for you."

"You'd really love New York. The band is on a hiatus until early next year. It's a good thing, because I just need a break from everything." I filled him in on what took place after he left me and how I'd met the Swami. "And then you'll never guess who I met. You'll never guess. Call it synchronicity, karma, whatever. I stumbled into this yoga place over on the West End. And there was this beautiful Black woman on stage, playing the piano and then the harp. John Coltrane's wife."

"Get out! Alice Coltrane?"

"Can you believe it? And you'll never believe, she's a follower of the Swami and she introduced him to me tonight."

"Wait, she introduced you to *the* Swami?"

"Yes. And her music—it's out of this world and she's working on an album right here in New York. She's so nice. She said I must make it to India. Isn't that what we talked about? Oh, River, I so wish you were here with me. Come with me to India!"

"Well, first of all, take a breath. You need to go to your father's funeral."

"But I think finding the Swami is a sign. I need to go to India."

"India will always be there."

I didn't want to argue. "You're right, River. Enough about me. How are you? What's it like knowing your father? How is the rest of the family? How are your shows?"

"Sounds like I'm missing out, but getting to know my family has been a trip. My father introduced me around so I've gotten some work. I know New York's a little more liberal than down here, and someday I'll end up there, but right now it's a little too cold for my blood. Speaking of real or not, how's Grandma handling all this?"

"Pretty quiet since we got the news about Dad. I think her job is done and she's finally leaving me alone. She says there's nothing left for her at home anymore."

"But there's plenty left for you at home. You still have family."

"I've made family and a home on the road. River, I miss you."

After we said goodbye, I lay back with the phone receiver to my heart. The off-the-hook beeping sound gave me the sense I'd always stay connected to those I loved.

BOOK TWO

CHAPTER 26

Homecoming

October, 1969: "Ladies and gentlemen, welcome to Los Angeles where the local time is three-twenty p.m. and the temperature is a warm ninety-two degrees," our airline pilot announced. "The Santa Ana Winds are coming out of the north-east twenty to thirty miles per hour."

The winds make me nervous. Joan Didion wrote about the *season of suicide and divorce and prickly dread, wherever the wind blows.* My parent's trial separation (divorce wasn't allowed in the Catholic church) had been imminent and my father had taken his life.

I stood out on the curb waiting for my ride in my lace up leather moccasins and a knee- length purple wool coat. The October weather in New York had been the opposite of Los Angeles. I took off my coat and sat on my one piece of thrashed luggage. The air, zapped of any moisture, turned my skin lizard-like.

An empty bag of Bugles chips, a snack we never had at home, floated by. The bag, like a body having served its purpose, now just useless garbage, was being blown back toward the ocean. I felt like useless garbage and just wanted to go down to the beach. I was more surprised than nervous when Maggie finally appeared. I didn't recognize her until she removed her Jackie O sunglasses, but then off my look, she said, "Blue contact lenses." Her eye shadow matched the color of the sun-bleached sky. Bleached also was her hair which looked strange next to her skin, a darker shade than mine. Wearing a short polyester paisley dress and black vinyl boots, she looked like she'd just stepped out of the cover of *Seventeen* magazine.

"Sorry, the traffic really blows," she said, moving in for a side hug, one of those tentative greetings or farewell half embraces our family gave, if any at all.

The syrupy scent of Windsong perfume lingered as she pulled away. Welcome home, Anna and—" she said, her eyes probing mine. "Grandma Phoebe."

Taken aback, before I could ask what or how she knew anything about Grandma, Grandma, being all about manners and such, said, "Thank you, Margaret. You look nice."

"Thanks, Grandma, and I can't wait to hear more about this transfer of consciousness thing. Mom filled me in. It all makes sense now, weirdo. With you coming home, she thought it was best I know."

"What about the others?" I asked.

"Not yet. It's going to be a rite of passage sort of thing. Not 'til they're mature enough to grasp this hippy-dippy shit." Maggie raised her hand, salute-like, to measure our heights, from the top of my head to hers. "Hey, I'm taller than you now."

"And so? Are we still competing?"

"No, just saying."

Back home, nicks on the kitchen wall marked our height. Always a competition, I'd notice Maggie's subtle tiptoeing. We'd race in the backyard to see who could run the fastest, who could throw a rock the furthest, who could jump the highest. We'd stick our arms out to compare who was tanner.

"Anyway, no fair. You're wearing heels," I said, "but your boobs look bigger."

"It's the pill." She smiled, pulling her shoulders back as I followed her to the parking garage where she stopped next to a new compact white Ford Falcon sedan.

"Yours?"

"Bought it with my own money."

I put my luggage in the back seat and then slid onto the vinyl passenger seat. It was the first time I'd ever smelled that new car smell. "Nice ride. You must be doing well at the bank."

"I am," she said, adjusting her glasses as she looked into the rearview mirror from where a string of rosary beads hung. "It's also how we got the apartment we're living in."

She must be dating the bank president, I thought, unfairly, as she backed out.

Ahead of her, she had her whole life planned out. I envied her vision for her future. She'd work for a while longer at the bank while she finished college—going to college had never been in the cards for me—and then she'd buy her own place with her own money. I'd already dashed any of Mom's hopes that I would be the perfect Mexican daughter who waited for marriage before leaving home. And now Maggie wasn't about to marry anyone, much less anyone who didn't come to the table with his own income. He had to have a college degree like she was working toward, he had to wear nice shoes, and he couldn't be a drinker.

She caught me noticing the turquoise ring on her finger. "I love it, thank you again. So now tell me about this phenomenon where you share a consciousness with Grandma," she asked as we drove past the entrance to Griffith Observatory.

"It's complicated. It's like–remember that time we went up to the observatory?"

"You mean when Michael walked off holding another woman's hand thinking it was Mom." Maggie laughed. "It was dark. He couldn't tell."

"Maybe he did know. Anyway, I remember looking through that giant telescope, seeing all the stars and finally those weren't just shadows on the moon, they were mountains. Only with time and distance—"

"I wonder if now you can see the flag Neil Armstrong planted?"

So much for trying to explain Grandma and how until recently it had been like looking through a kaleidoscope of loud colors.

★ ★ ★

We turned onto Brand Avenue. "So that's why I need to go to India. I think it might hold the answers as far as finding a way to undo what Grandma has done."

"I'm so sorry you have to go through all that. That would explain you being such a strange kid."

"And what's your excuse?" I asked, braiding my hair that had been whipping around with the windows rolled down.

"You look like a red-haired Pocahontas," she said.

"And you look like a bleached blonde Dolores del Rio."

She laughed. "With my new hair color, the cops leave us alone when we're cruising Whittier Boulevard, except the one I ended up dating. You know what they say about a man in uniform. Anyway, it didn't last. Are you dating anyone?"

"No."

"Ah, come on. No one in the band?"

"Especially no one in the band."

She side-eyed me. "So then maybe you'll go cruising with me one of these nights, since I lost my partner in crime."

"The cop?"

"No, Patty, who by the way is pregnant."

"What! She's only sixteen. Who's the father?"

"It's all just breaking news. She's about four months along. His name is Alan Duncan. He's a senior over at Glendale High, wants to be a professional surfer. We haven't met him, yet. They were all set to get married and drive to Vegas when Dad suddenly interrupted their plans."

As we headed north on Brand Avenue across Colorado Street, Maggie told me how Patty had recently moved in with Alan and his mother, a recent divorcee. I'm sure Mom was mortified, citing all the metaphors she could think of: putting the cart before the horse; why buy the milk when you can get the cow for free? Sin verguenza.

"Patty was her last hope of having one of her daughters take care of her in old age," Maggie said.

"But there's still Josie and Michael."

"She says she'll be dead by then."

"Right, she's going to outlive all of us. How's Patty feeling anyway?"

"Pretty good. No morning sickness, really. She's starting to show. If we had time we could stop by and see her, but we'll see her tomorrow."

North Verdugo Road split off onto Canada Boulevard. "Where are we going?"

"I want to stop by the house to pick something out for Dad to wear."

"What!?" I panicked. "I thought it was going to be a closed casket."

"It is. But he can't go into the next world all naked."

I laughed nervously. "No, just missing half his face. So, you think he's been hanging around waiting for his clothes? He came into this world buck naked, for God's sake."

Both hands firmly positioned at ten and two, Maggie stared ahead. "Anyway, Mom wants him to wear a suit. The one they were married in."

The two things Dad hated in this world, and probably the next, were suits and church, both things Mom had insisted he get on board with.

We pulled up to the place that looked so much smaller than what I remembered. Above the roof of a Tudor-style mini mansion, the sun melted like yellow butter onto the amber hills of Verdugo. Shades of pastel streaked the evening sky as the Santa Anas whistled through the canyon. Beyond the border of river rocks, a desert full of tumbleweeds took over what used to be the front lawn. A push mower off to the right side of the house looked like it didn't have the strength to make it back to the garage. The place appeared to be even more dilapidated, the screens missing on the windows, the shutters hanging on like loose teeth.

Grandma Phoebe spoke up in her smoky voice. "For shame. We worked so hard to keep this home. I fought even harder to keep it nice for the generations to come."

"Is that you or Grandma talking now?" Maggie asked.

I pursed my lips before speaking and raised an index finger. "You'd think she didn't care about such things, but remember, there's still a part of her consciousness that is stuck in this world. It's like she's got one foot in this place and one foot in the other."

"And what about Dad? Wasn't she torn up?" Maggie asked, searching my eyes. "Aren't you torn up about him, Grandma?"

"Why? He's no longer in this realm," Grandma answered in her smoky voice.

"But can't you, like, talk to the dead?" Maggie asked.

"Only if they contact me. Charley never wanted me around when we were alive. I'll never hear from him again."

"Wow, Anna," Maggie said with a nervous giggle. "So how soon do you plan on going to India?" I shrugged my shoulders. "But seriously, Grandma, we're going to do everything we can to fix it up and move back in. It's just going to take some time and some money."

"Just let me know how I can help," I added. "I've been able to save a little."

"It's going to take more than just a little. Just wait until you go inside."

★ ★ ★

Maggie yanked off the yellow crime scene tape and inserted a key into the weathered, splintered front door lock.

My nerves were as exposed as the years of lies I'd been told. Standing in the foyer, it felt dank and cold, yet reeked like that hot August day when I'd first arrived in Manhattan during a garbage strike. But now through it all, I smelled something sweet and distinctive—gardenias? Like memories, some nauseating fragrances are hard to mask, even with a dead body rotting for at least a week and months of piled-up waste. I reached behind the withering potted plant to switch on a light. Nothing. I flicked it on and off. I went for my matches and then panicked when I came up empty.

"There's no electricity. Hasn't been for months," Maggie said, handing me a tissue from a pack in her purse. She wadded one up and shoved a piece up to her nose. I did the same.

"I don't need light to see the destruction that took place," Grandma said. "My poor son rotting here all alone."

"Like we should have all stayed and rotted with him?" Maggie said.

There was still enough sunlight to see the clutter everywhere–like two years' worth of trash. The next thing I knew, a black cat slithered around my ankles.

"Igor," Maggie said as I reached down to pet him, all fur and bones. He purred. "Feral. Dad tamed him to come in and eat the mice. Comes and goes through a hole right there near the fireplace."

"What about Bella?"

"She died last spring."

"No! Why didn't anyone tell me?"

"If you loved your dog so much, you should have stayed or at least taken her with you." As if those were the most practical answers to my dire situation. I glared daggers at my sister. "Anyway, she was old," Maggie said. "We buried her under the lemon tree out back."

"Near Grandpa?"

"What are you talking about?" Maggie asked, disappearing upstairs. She apparently knew nothing about how Grandpa ended up there, and didn't care to learn how Phoebe had the folks at Forest Lawn Memorial deliver his ashes home seven years after his death. Talk about control. I wiped my tears, stepping into the living room to look around. The last remnants of daylight illuminated the cobwebbed silver-framed family photos of us lined up across the mantel, including Mom and Dad's wedding photo, their young faces so full of American dreams. As sycamore shadows danced across the Oriental rug, I remembered my sisters pirouetting from embroidered flower to flower as I played the piano, which I turned to see still stood in all her dusty glory across the hallway in the chamber room.

"Cleopatra," Grandma Phoebe whispered. "Let's go play something."

Outside, the sun slipped behind the Verdugo hills, but I didn't need light to play as I tiptoed toward Cleopatra. Off to the side of the piano sat a crystal bowl with no water and the withered gardenias I must have smelled. I raked my fingers over the black piano lid, leaving prints like music staves without the notes. I sat to play the first few notes of "Ode to Joy," stopping abruptly as I was accompanied by all the questions.

"Don't stop. That's lovely," Grandma said.

I switched to Chopin's *Funeral March*. "Why did Dad's step-brother kill himself? You were his piano teacher?" Grandma didn't answer. I played a little softer, rushing through my interrogation before Maggie came back down. "What happened to him? Was he also cursed with a dual consciousness? Did Dad believe this? Did you have anything to do with that? Oh my God, did Dad ever know why?" I pounded out my next question. "Grandma, am I fated to kill myself, too?"

"Oh, darling, no. As you know, his father had a family before us. Leland, Charley's half-brother, had just turned fifteen years old when he suffered a terrible automobile accident. He lost his arm and grew despondent."

"And then you broke up the marriage and married his father? Mom told me you were a homewrecker."

"Darling, it's complicated."

"Did Dad know?"

"We never talked about it. It happened years before he was even born. Charley was very sensitive. It was hard enough getting through the death of his father, my beloved Wesley, and then the seven-year probate."

Maggie yelled from upstairs. "Anna! It's getting dark. Come help me find it."

I wanted to hear more, but scrambled to the top of the stairs. The ceiling had a giant gaping hole, as if a meteor had struck the roof. I didn't need a telescope to see the first stars already popping in the sky. Buckets and pots lined the hallway to catch the rain that had poured through.

"They say last winter was the rainiest season we had in history," Maggie said as she stood waiting for me on the catwalk. "It's a good thing we'd already moved out."

I hugged myself, rubbing my arms, imagining my father and Igor all alone in this big, cold house. "I guess he would have frozen to death this winter, if he hadn't shot his brains out first."

"Anna, quit being so macabre," Maggie said, switching on a flashlight. She'd come prepared.

"But it's true," I said, walking toward the bedroom he shared with Mom for all those years.

"The same bedroom Wesley and I shared," Grandma thought-whispered.

"The same bedroom I ran out of years ago, and yes, the same place I stabbed him, or rather you stabbed him," I thought-whispered back. I hesitated, bracing myself before entering the room smelling of bleach and mold, but also still the stench of unfiltered Camels and Pabst Blue Ribbon. And then there in the middle of the room, under another hole in the ceiling, in front of the smoke smudged fireplace surround—had he tried to keep warm? Was this evidence of his final moments on Earth? I looked at the bed he'd shared with my mother, a ghostly impression of him preserved in the stained mattress. It would take more than just new carpet, plaster, and a fresh coat of paint to cover up this tragedy. I burst out crying.

Maggie did a one-arm side hug around me. "Go ahead. I'm done crying," she said, as if she were yielding over her reserve of tears. I bawled over Bella, too.

My sister pointed the flashlight toward the closet and then after mustering some courage, I followed her in, immediately inhaling the must of mothballs and cedar. Rummaging through the sparse amount of clothing after Mom had cleared out her stuff, Maggie found a suit, the same one in his wedding photo. She held it up to the light before handing it to me and continued to look for a shirt. I felt the fabric and then slipped my hand into the pocket, afraid what I might come up with. I pulled out a plastic coin like a poker chip. I took the flashlight from Maggie and shined it on a white AA chip. My heart cracked. I swiped a tear leaking from the corner of my eye and then recognized a shirt next to where the suit had hung. I beamed the light onto the guayabera shirt Dad had worn on the last Easter Sunday I'd ever seen him alive. Yellow now, but still holding Mom's starch, I grabbed it and walked out. He would be buried in this shirt, also. Under his suit, Mom would never know.

★ ★ ★

We pulled into a dead-end road surrounded by apartment buildings. The sight of five or six kids running around startled me, but then the squeals of laughter under the light of the streetlamps made me smile. "I'm going to drop this stuff off at the mortuary. Let Mom know. It's upstairs, 9B, the one on the end," Maggie said, and sped off.

Even through the dark, I could smell the oleanders as I passed through a metal fence made up of what looked like seven-foot spears surrounding the building. The aroma of arroz con pollo wafted out of the apartment as I made my way up to the porch decorated with potted geraniums and hanging ferns. My stomach lurched when I saw the silhouette of my mother through the screen door. She swung the door open, making way for me to step through. Her reluctance like a shield, I moved in for a hug, catching the clean, cool smell of Noxzema. Stiffly, she patted my back and then pulled away. "You're so bony. Hurry, don't let the flies in." The door slammed behind me as if to prevent me from running away again.

"Maggie had to drop stuff off over at—" Mom took my suitcase and walked away. "She'll be back soon."

Talk about bony, the house dress she wore seemed to swallow her. She'd aged since I'd seen her last, and the vision shocked me. I used to help her cover her roots, but now she'd stopped coloring her hair altogether, her grey hair like a steel-wool Brillo pad.

All this time, and still she couldn't look me in the eyes. I wanted to cry. I wanted to be comforted. He was my father, too. I wanted to talk. I didn't know where to start. Maybe I could have said: *I'm sorry about Dad. Or, how've you been? Or, I like what you've done with the place*, except I didn't know what it looked like before. I recognized some things from the Glendale house, wondering what Grandma might say, but other stuff looked new to me.

Beyond a wood-framed, green nubby couch, the distant city lights shown like fireworks through a picture window. "Like a street scene out of Paris. What a view." I said, before looking around the small space. "Cozy."

"La-di-da. We got most of it from the Goodwill. Nothing fancy."

"I like it."

Mom peered into my eyes searching for Grandma. "Not that I need your approval anymore, Phoebe."

"My dear, you did your best under the circumstances."

"Now that Charley's gone, why are you still hanging around?" Mom asked.

I heard footsteps outside coming up the stairs and turned to see Michael and Josie storm in like excited puppies, all sweaty and out of breath, the screen door slamming behind them.

"Anna," Michael squealed, wrapping his wiry arms around me, then pulling away. "I'm as tall as you now."

Josie, seven and a little more reserved, let me hug her.

* * *

As I hung outside the galley kitchen watching Mom add the finishing touches to the simmering pot, steam rolling out and fogging up the window to make the kitchen smell delicious, it warmed my heart when I noticed the turquoise bracelet I'd sent her from Oklahoma. "Smells wonderful." She looked over her shoulder; the steam had also fogged up her glasses.

"Siéntate. You must be hungry."

At the small yellow and gold-speckled Formica-topped dinette, Michael and Josie sat doing homework, Josie counting on her fingers to do her math problems.

"Maggie found this set at a garage sale over in Glendale," Mom said, stepping out of the narrow kitchen carrying a pot of scrumptiousness. "People over there like to get rid of stuff to make room for the new."

I felt Grandma like an itch needing to get scratched. "Please let it go," I whispered, scooting in my matching chair.

Mom pulled out a little mound of masa and rolled out some tortillas, her hands knowing what to do without the need of her attention. In between the flipping, she ladled a plate with Mexican rice, the way I remembered it with cumin, green peas, and carrots. Flip. She then served some shredded chicken simmered in olive oil and salsa and topped with lime juice. Flip. Finally, she set down a tortillero full of hot tortillas, took off her apron, pulled out a seat across from me, and stared down at the plate. "We already ate."

I took a bite before my salivary glands might explode. Nowhere on my travels throughout the country had there been any better Mexican cuisine than what my mother made and with whatever ingredients she could find.

"I've missed your cooking."

"Hmmph," she said.

"I've missed you," I added. I couldn't see her rheumy eyes through her fogged-up glasses—no different than the times she chose not to look at me at all. Those times when she just didn't want to acknowledge that other person taking up space behind my eyes.

"Didn't you miss me, Mom? Weren't you worried about me?"

"What could I do? You made your choice." Using her apron, she wiped her glasses. "Kids, there's ice cream in the freezer."

"Yay," Josie squealed, and got up to race past Michael into the kitchen, returning with the tub of Neapolitan. Michael followed with some bowls. Mom scooped some for me.

"Oh, no thank you. I'm full. It was so delicious."

"Just leftovers," she said as if she'd gone to no trouble for this prodigal daughter of hers. She stood, picking up my suitcase. "It's late for you. You should go to bed. I made up my bed for you."

"That's okay, I'll take the couch," I said as she walked away.

"That's where I sleep," Michael said.

"I'll sleep with the girls," Mom said.

"But, I don't . . ."

"Ya basta."

Bossing me was another way Mom showed affection. And when she did it with those big infinite black eyes magnified by her reading glasses, looking just off to the side of my face, it frightened me into submission.

I kissed her cheek. "Good night, everyone."

She closed the door.

Overwhelmed, I could barely keep my eyes open as soon as the weight of the world hit my pillow. A puff of eucalyptus-scented wind fluttered the window curtains. Dogs barked and crickets chirped as I stared out toward the star-filled sky. The day had been electric, hot, and dry, but now the temperature had dropped and I smelled the rain coming. It would be damp and chilly in the days to come. I felt it to the marrow as I sunk down into the firm mattress. It didn't matter the place, we were all under one roof again. "Except your father," Grandma Phoebe whispered. And Patty, for that matter, but I was too tired to argue over semantics. Even she knew life was more peaceful when he wasn't around. If only she weren't around. Mom had asked why Grandma still hung around even though we knew there was only one way out for the voice.

★ ★ ★

The following night at the wake, more people than I would have imagined attended, mostly men and no wailing women, thank God.

I stood at the front of the small salon, casket behind me, with my stiff-lipped, black-veiled Mom and four siblings, including Patty who looked like she'd swallowed a giant watermelon and her guy looking like he'd swallowed more than he could chew. It wouldn't be easy raising the baby.

The coffin, flanked on one side by a giant photo of Dad in his Navy uniform (Maggie had picked out this respectable photo even though he'd been discharged within his first two years) and a wreath of sweet-smelling flowers on the other, but it was the bold, citrusy scent of Brylcreem that cloyed my heart. Dad used to slather that stuff on his head, and as I turned to make sure the casket was still closed and that Dad wasn't sitting up, a handsome young Mexican man, black hair slicked back into a ducktail—a Mexican Jesus—stepped up to offer his condolences. I checked again to make sure Dad hadn't risen from the dead.

"Most of us knew your dad from AA," he said, gesturing to the other men. His apostles? "Good guy, always volunteering.

Made some strong coffee." His broad smile showed large white teeth, free of coffee stains. Surprised, I never knew Dad to help anyone but himself. Being of service was apparently one of the important principles in that program, like making amends.

"Thank you for coming," I said as he shook my hand.

He then reached out to shake Mom's hand. Clutching the rosary beads that had been hanging in Maggie's rearview mirror, she nodded as she took his hand. "Si, gracias."

And then a taller, darker male version of Mom, my Uncle Teodoro came up and one-arm hugged her. At the same, cousin Teddie snuck up on me from the other side. "Boo!" she said, and I shrieked as she pulled me in for a bear hug.

"Inside a mortuary, really, Teddie? Have some respect. Sin verguenza. You almost scared me to death."

She laughed. A year older than me, and now standing at least two inches taller, Teddie used to try and scare the crap out of me until I learned that her "Boo!" was more intimidating than her bite when she'd make herself big as a bear; a Teddy bear more like it with her amber-hued skin and long raven-colored hair parted down the middle. Looking past the black eyeliner into her dark almond-shaped eyes, I saw her hibernating kind soul.

"We'll catch up later," she said, kissing me on the cheek before taking a seat in the row behind our pew with three of her younger brothers whose names and ages I couldn't quite remember at the moment. But I knew who was missing. My cousin Frederico "Freddy," killed recently in Vietnam, and I'd learn nothing more than he died a hero in combat. The family liked to talk about everything except death.

After the wake, Mom was in good hands. I wasn't up to any gathering and asked Maggie to drop me off back at the apartment.

* * *

In New Orleans, River picked up the phone. "Remember, I'm there with you in spirit," he said before hanging up, and yet I felt terribly alone.

Still jetlagged, I passed out on the living room couch before taking off my shoes.

When my family got home, Michael woke me up. "Goldilocks, you're sleeping in my bed."

"Anna, go to the room," Mom said, and I felt like a kid being punished again.

* * *

I bawled during the Mass at Cristo Del Rey the following morning unable to read what I'd prepared, so Maggie took over:

Let love be the answer

Let us not die with Dad

Le us think of death as a second birth.

Let him transcend.

And we can keep on living.

Maggie finished by talking about how much fun Dad was sometimes and it was true. All the camping trips, the outings to the park. I even remembered the trips to the Pike in Long Beach where I was brave enough to go on the roller coaster. I was the boy he never had until Michael, "a softie" who, according to Dad, would grow up afraid of his own shadow, but I was the one afraid of my shadow.

Michael hugged me, and then when the lone singer sang "Amazing Grace," I lost it, my whole body quaking.

"You had everything you needed, I tried to make sure of that," Grandma whispered. "He loved you and only did his best."

His best? I didn't have the energy to argue in church and so I would lose ground again by staying silent. Father Reynoso held the chains connected to the incense thurible, and after three swings, the smoke hovered over the first few family pews.

I felt faint and cradled my heavy head burdened with the guilt of thinking badly about my father, the remorse about his stabbing and the events leading up to that night, for running away and breaking his heart, for setting things in motion leading to the day he killed himself. *Oh Dad, I hope heaven gives you a second chance.*

We followed the casket down the aisle, shuffling out into the mottled daylight where Mom stood under the dark clouds hanging so low, she wore them like a widow's veil. And then the sky spit onto the mariachi band that Maggie had arranged to perform. I knew Dad loved the Mexican culture, this seemed like overkill to me, but it's what Mom said he'd want. I also knew how much he loved my mother—almost to death. This was all really fucked up.

My gut ached. Except for coffee, I hadn't eaten anything that morning, even though Mom had gotten up before everyone else to make breakfast.

But now, I couldn't stomach being around people anymore and didn't feel like going to the burial. Grandma Phoebe didn't push me to go either. We both knew he was already partying with the dead somewhere else. After some heavy sprinkles, an umbrella appeared over my head like my own personal black cloud. I turned to see the handsome Mexican man with the nice smile from the wake holding the handle.

"Thank you. Do you have a car?"

CHAPTER 27

The Funeral

The '57 Chevy Bel Air had been his dad's car. A set of dice hung from the rearview mirror, swinging sideways as the car hydroplaned across a wet, oil-slickened road. I braced myself, grabbing the armrest. A blaze of red brake lights and a boulevard of amber lights flashed all the way through downtown. I heard sirens.

After he slowed the car and pulled over to a stop, I turned toward him.

"I guess I should introduce myself, Anna."

"Yeah, if I'm gonna die in a car crash, today, I guess I should at least know your name first." I turned to look into cinnamon eyes, lashes like long black lacey mantillas. Not fair.

"I'm Ruben Moya," he said, raising a right hand to make the sign of a cross and then he signaled to get back on the road.

Streaks of dirt slid down the windshield, the wipers smearing a muddy rainbow across the glass, blurring the remnants of the afternoon.

"I was going to wash the car before—"

"Can you take me to the beach?"

"You're not thinking about drowning yourself, are you?"

"Don't you dare think about it," Grandma whispered. And then I couldn't stop thinking about how I'd finally be free if I were to drown.

Just as suddenly as it dumped on us, the rain stopped. Heading west, the sun played peekaboo behind the breaks in the gray clouds.

"Any particular spot?" Ruben asked.

"Not really."

The traffic on Wilshire Boulevard slowed. The streets gleamed, the grit and grime on the city's surface washed clean for now.

"He seems like a nice fellow," Grandma whispered. "A real sheik. Your mother would be pleased."

For sure. That would satisfy her need for at least one of her daughters to find a nice Mexican boy to marry, even though she'd married a gringo. But then again, maybe she'd learned her mistake.

"So, you met my dad at AA?"

"In jail, actually."

So much for "nice Mexican boy," but then I thought of Jesus behind bars before he was brought to face Pontius Pilate. "I'm not assuming anything," I said.

"I was arrested during one of the student walk-outs. Your father was in for a DUI. We became fast friends. After he got released, he bailed me out. I went with him to an AA meeting. He wanted to be able to show the judge he was a changed man. After that, I'd go with him every week. I got a lot out of those meetings. Like I said, he made some good coffee."

"So, you're not an alcoholic."

"It's a label, but I suppose. I mean, that's one of the prerequisites for attending, admitting that you are one."

"Hmm."

"Anyway, we ended up going once a month down to the VA hospital in Long Beach. We pushed wheel chairs around. He'd play the piano."

"My Dad was a vet."

"Yeah, he told me, but that he never saw any action. Never left the port in San Diego."

I wondered if Dad also told him about his hospitalization up in Oakland because everyone thought he was crazy—because he was. Because when you grow up listening to your dead father talk to you and using you to exact revenge for his murder, you sort of lose it. Because when you try to explain your situation to a head doctor that you share your father's consciousness, you're only going to get a lifetime supply of lithium. That's why I kept my mouth shut.

"What about you? Did you see any action?" I asked.

"I'm more of a pacifist." He laughed. "I'm in college so I didn't get drafted. At least, not yet anyway. Freddy didn't have it so lucky. It should have been me. He never had a chance."

"Freddy, my cousin?"

Ruben nodded.

"He was my compadre."

"I'm so sorry. I was on the road when I got the news and couldn't make the funeral."

"It was quite a turnout. A popular kid. Drafted as soon as he graduated high school. He'd barely turned eighteen. Hadn't decided on college yet. He loved working with his hands. Wanted to be a mechanic. He worked on this Chevy," Ruben said, tapping the wheel.

"You must have some sort of survivor's guilt? Is that why you drink?" I tried to make a joke in light of the topic.

"More or less," he said, chuckling. "But I'm trying to make a difference. I don't want his death to be in vain."

"What can you do?"

"By educating people, getting the word out, protesting the war—"

"Going to AA meetings?"

"That, too." He signaled to turn onto a major highway. "You know an unequal number of Mexicans and Blacks have been killed in Nam. The draft, including the entire social, political, and economical system of the United States of America has been created so that Mexican youth are sent into Vietnam to be killed and to kill innocent men, women, and children. Many more Chicanos are sent to Vietnam, in proportion to the total white population."

I'd heard this before, but now Freddy's death made it real. Even if I'd only hung out with him a little bit, he was still my blood.

"I'm also going to miss your dad. Quite a funny character." Ruben laughed. "Like how even though he's a gringo, he thought he was the son of Pancho Villa."

"It's possible," I tried to normalize the conversation. I'd heard the same crazy story. "Did he tell you how he used to see the Virgin Mary standing out in the backyard?"

Ruben laughed. "And Juan Diego?"

"No, just Mary."

"Interesting guy. He knew a lot about the world and the history of this whole area. Stuff they don't teach in the schools. Like how this land belonged to the Gabrielino Tribes way before the Spanish, way before the Treaty of Hidalgo ended the war between the US and Mexico. He told me how a land grant was given to the Verdugo family, the same land where you all grew up. Supposedly, there's an oak tree up there where General Pico and General Fremont had some peace talks. I want to go check it out. And then he told me how his stepfather stole property from the Verdugos. I really think it bothered him."

"Talk about survivor's guilt," I said.

"The truth is America is a country built on the mass genocide of tens of millions of my ancestors, slavery, and the theft of an entire hemisphere."

"True." I remembered what I'd been told about Dad's family and stepfather. Still, I wondered how Grandma Phoebe didn't know. One day your cook and your gardener don't show up. Wouldn't your world stop working? Wouldn't you want to investigate?

"I'm the one who found your father," Ruben said. "When he didn't show up at the church to carpool down to the VA Hospital, I drove up to the house. The back door was open. I smelled death before ever stepping in. He must have been gone already about a week."

I looked out the window as a tear escaped my eye and slipped off my shoulder. Ruben wasn't Mexican Jesus, after all, or he would have saved my Dad.

We didn't talk the rest of the ride until we got to Santa Monica where he pulled into a parking lot and turned to me with that smile.

"Thanks for the lift." I don't remember having any inkling to do anything, but what happened next seemed like a natural thing to do, as if I'd known him for a long time, after all he knew my father, the good side of him, which might sound sort of weird, but I felt a certain intimacy as if he were more than a friend. I leaned in to kiss him and his eyes widened. He didn't have a chance to back away, and kissed back, tasting of clove gum, but that was it. No more. No roving hands. No signals to read.

"You're welcome," he said. "I just started seeing Teddie. I let her know I was driving you, I thought, to the cemetery."

Laughing out loud and then starting to cry again, my emotions were all over the place. "That's great. She's great. You're great. Everything's great. I'm an idiot."

He reached over and cupped my face, swiping my tears with a thumb. "No, you're not. You've lost your father. You're confused. You need time."

The rain stopped and so did my crying. I took off my shoes and then rolled down my pantyhose, stuffing them into my purse. Ruben stared at me, back rigid against his door like he was afraid I might pounce on him again. He could have been right, I needed time to sort through my confusion. Only a small connection to my past, Ruben wouldn't be able to help me understand my father and he was nothing like him, thank God. I reached for the door handle. "Thanks for the lift." I opened my door and stepped out. "I'm just going to walk."

"Would you like me to go with you?"

"No, thanks. I think I just need some time alone. I'll call Maggie to come get me when I'm ready."

★ ★ ★

The cold, windy shore welcomed me with a brisk, sandy slap across the face. I made my way down to the water, taking in the smell of the briny salt and sand, bird shit, and everything left of the earth after it's been washed clean. Dozens of sandpipers skittered back and forth in a synchronized choreography as if they were dancing with the tide. A seagull squawked and I watched it scavenge the shore, taking what he wanted and leaving the rest. That's all I want. I don't need much. I don't ask for much. All I want is to be left alone.

I felt as if I were falling into some sort of trance. *Can't you hear them calling?* Grandma said, luringly. *Listen to them.*

What? Who? I covered my ears. I won't listen. I'm tired of standing, jumping and sitting for you. I won't do it anymore. You've made me your lap dog and I'm through. I stripped out of my clothes. Barefoot, I followed the imprints of the seagull's webbed feet to the water's edge where they disappeared. I stepped into the frigid water, but couldn't feel it. Standing knee-deep, the thought of swimming out past the breakers entered my mind, past the waves of no return.

You do hear the call, Grandma said.

And it's hard not to hear the call of the wild—the music of the untamed. What are you asking me to do? Is this the call Dad heard? Or his half-brother, Leland?

Listen to the orchestra of the ocean.

Numb, I stared out at the horizon, picturing my whole life plummeting off the brink of despair. I couldn't imagine or even dream of a future. If only I could get into the rhythm of the ocean. Aren't we after all just children of the sea—part of the tides to return again?

A rogue wave slapped me down and I swallowed the ocean. I threw up and snapped out of my spell.

Turning back, I sloshed to the shore and plopped down onto the sand to wait for the sun to set.

The sun had gone down, stealing away all of the color with it and leaving me behind in a dark, cold world. In the distance, the Harvest Moon rose above the mountains. Next month, the Mourning Moon, and a time for this Honey Moon to let go of past troubles and look forward to a new season and soon, a new year. I got dressed.

★ ★ ★

Under the moonlight, I staggered into a little dive bar near the pier and took a seat at the bar. I ordered a burger to soak up the double vodka tonic I'd also ordered. In the corner, a small band was just setting up as a television blared the news from a counter across from me. I brought the drink to my lips and stopped when I recognized the face of the man named Charles Manson. He and his followers had been arrested for the murders of actress Sharon Tate and others. He looked straight into the camera as if he recognized me, too. I lost my appetite. Those poor people.

"We dodged that bullet," Grandma said.

"Seriously? I would never have been in that van if it hadn't been for you in the first place. None of us would be in this position," I replied, speaking into my drink, as the television reported how about 500,000 people marched in Washington, DC for peace. It would become the largest anti-war rally in US history. Performing on stage were Arlo Guthrie, Pete Seeger, Peter, Paul and Mary, Richie Havens, and Lazarus Rising. I knew I needed to eat and struggled to take a bite.

"Hey, Honey Moon." Surprised, to hear my name in this place, I turned to look into the smiling face of some long-haired dude from the group getting ready to play. "Why aren't you in DC with Lazarus?"

I chewed, then swallowed. "I came home for my dad's funeral."

"Ah man, that's a bummer. Sorry," he said. "I was going to ask if you'd come up and play something for us, but I understand."

"Yeah, thanks." I took another bite, thinking about it for a second. Maybe it's what I need. "Yes, darling."

I wiped my mouth and then stepped onto the tiny stage. Setting my drink down on a dinged up upright piano, I took a seat, looking out to a handful of inattentive patrons. "This has been laying on my heart for a while."

Rain falls through the hole in the ceiling
Stars shine through and I have a feeling
There's a world for us somewhere out there
A peaceful place for spirits who share
The need for a quiet home to lay
No wars or hate, only love and play
A place at long last to rest in peace . . .

By the time I finished, the small crowd had hushed and now clapped. I took a bow. "It was what we needed," Grandma whispered. "The music."

I drained my drink, needing another, but before I could order, Ruben walked up. "That was beautiful," he said, all glassy-eyed.

"Thanks. Don't look at me like that. Even God can see the necessity of getting drunk on a day like today."

"I'll drive you back when you're ready. It's what your dad would have wanted."

"What my dad would have wanted? Fuck."

"He did love you and his family."

I stepped off my seat and tried to run, but now my legs wouldn't cooperate.

CHAPTER 28

Campo Corona

Except for an excruciating headache, Ruben had delivered me home safe and sound. I ended up hanging around with the family a few more weeks while I decided my next course of action. In the meanwhile, Grandma and Mom got into it about whose fault it was that Dad's life had ended the way it did. And whose fault it was that I'd ended up the way I was. I mean, how was I?

I felt overwhelmed, yet excited about getting to celebrate Thanksgiving with my Marquez family. With the fading distraction of Dad, Grandma's power over me weakening, I felt this could be my opportunity to connect with my Mexican roots, at least that half of me. I wore a simple mid-length orange dress and my fringe boots. The moisture in the air had frizzed my hair, so I wore braids.

Uncle Teodoro had stayed in Mexico so as not to get drafted into the gringo guerra. Later, when my uncle did arrive in the States, he settled in Los Angeles and ended up working in a walnut factory in the eastern part of LA where he met my Aunt Othelia. They married and moved into a little bunkhouse next to her family in a section of Monte Vista called "Campo Corona." And there they raised their family.

The neighborhood, so different than the manicured one where I grew up, had changed since I'd been there last and not in a good way. The Campo looked like an old man's open mouth missing most of his teeth and what were left were rotting and ready to fall out. The dusty red tongue of a road was now paved over in asphalt. Only a few of the houses, more like sheds for large families, remained. The others had been razed and bulldozed to be redeveloped into industrial areas and more modern suburban houses that could be sold to families that would be part of the first generation of the Mexican-American middle class. But most families here couldn't afford to stay and just moved away.

The tiny home, originally one shoebox-sized bedroom, had a tiny kitchen and a small living room to house their family of eight. My aunt and uncle slept behind a curtain in the living room while the five children—four boys and one girl—were stuffed into a room with no window, literally like sardines in a can. Even though there was running water inside the house, there was still no local fire department, so if there'd ever been a fire, no one would have survived. Eventually, my uncle added a back bedroom made of cast-off railway wood. He'd knocked out a back wall extending the kitchen out onto the back porch and finally added an indoor bathroom, the plumbing having been salvaged before the destruction of one of the neighboring properties. He painted the home a cheery American peach pie color, as if he needed to prove some sort of patriotism in order to stay.

Even now, looking onto the postage stamp patch of grass bordered by a chain-link fence, there was still dirt all around and shriveled plants left over from when Abuela Antonia also lived with my cousins after my grandfather died. Before Abuela died, also of diabetes, she'd gotten along pretty well with her assimilated daughter-in-law who couldn't roll out a tortilla to save her life—much to my uncle's chagrin—but she knew how to roll out a good time.

"Come in, come in," I heard Aunt Othelia say from the other side of the front door. We stepped into the room, my eyes adjusting to the dark. An outside picnic table had been dragged into the small kitchen and adjoined to the dining table, part of it hanging in the living room, so that we could all fit.

"Everything looks so pretty," I said, noticing the same set of dessert rose and apple Franciscan ware we had at home.

"Your Abuela Antonia gave us two settings as a wedding gift. Same as your mother. I added to them."

I remembered Mom saving S & H Green stamps from the market and then me licking the backs and pasting them into the little book in order to save enough to add to her set. Mom preferred those dishes to the French Haviland Chinaware we inherited from Grandma Phoebe. She said Phoebe's dishes were too fancy to use even on special occasions, which had become fewer and further in between as the years went by.

I asked how I could help and when my aunt set me to heating the rolls, I recalled my time at Diggers and suddenly I missed Mary and the others, most especially River. I wondered if he was celebrating with his newfound family in New Orleans. I'd try to catch up with him soon.

And then after some catching up and pleasantries, my uncle took his place at the head of the table. My mother was next to him and then to her right sat my little brother. I sat to the right of him with Maggie to my right and then Josie. Across from Mom and my brother were my three teenaged boy cousins. Directly across from me sat Teddie. If memory served me, she had always sat at the grown-up table, even before her quinceañera, the celebration of her transition into womanhood, before she tweezed her eyebrows thinner than frown lines. Maybe it had been just because of her size, always a big-boned girl, that she never fit at the kid's table with the rest of us, or because she was the only girl in her family.

Across from Josie sat Aunt Othelia next to the silver-framed photo of her dead son Freddy in uniform propped up at the head of the table. Freddy who would have been nineteen, had been killed six months ago over in Vietnam, but right now, no one was allowed to talk about it or him even though he'd finally made it to the grown-up table. As I stared at the picture, I squeezed my brother's hand unable to fathom the pain of losing him. I remembered back when I sat at the kid's table with Freddy and the others. I was sorry/not sorry I'd missed his funeral. Missing also was Patty who'd gone to live with the father of her baby due anytime now.

Uncle Teodoro led us in prayer and then stood to carve the turkey, the boys rubbing their hands together as my aunt got up to retrieve bottles of Coca Cola and 7Up. There was already a pitcher of fresh squeezed lemonade which I'd watched her dump tons of sugar into earlier. Vases of roses and sweet-smelling carnations from my aunt's garden were pulled off the table to make room for the platters of food. I got up to help my aunt, her brow glistening red. I carried over platters of mashed potatoes, green beans, and a yellow Jell-O salad with chunks of pineapple and cottage cheese blended in.

When the casserole dish full of yams was passed to my uncle, he raised his voice. "Te dije que si nunca vi otra nuez en mi vida . . ." He complained about the yams loaded with walnuts, brown sugar and scorched marshmallows on top.

"It's not like you had to shell them like I did as a little girl," Aunt Othelia said, turning to the rest of us. "By the time he came along there were machines at the factory."

"Ni modo, no los como."

"Suit yourself, hombre. More for me," Aunt Othelia said, and everyone laughed. She'd obviously been eating more portions than just hers and his.

Pretty soon everyone, except Teddie and me, was chattering and laughing. I'd been gone so long, I'd fallen out of the loop, but did help pass the food. Aunt Othelia wiped the back of her forehead with the edge of her apron before finally sitting down. Pouring herself a glass of lemonade, she looked at me and said, "Bueno, Anna, tell us more about your adventures? Your Mamá, makes it sound so enviable."

"Sin verguenza. Living like a loose woman," Mom said.

Before I could answer, my uncle had ripped off another piece of tortilla and told my aunt to go get the chili my mother had made."

"Why don't you get up and get it yourself, old man," Teddie said, raising her voice. I'd never heard her talk back to her father like that.

Red faced, Uncle Teodoro choked, grabbing his throat, his eyes bugging out. I looked back and forth between him and Teddie, who pushed her chair back and rushed over to pound on her father's back. The boys sat helpless as newborns. Aunt Othelia sat frozen until my uncle finally spit out a slimy piece of turkey. Everyone seemed relieved to see he wasn't going to die from choking or a stroke. Teddie waited until he drank some 7Up to calm down and then she stepped toward the front door.

"Teddie, sientate." Uncle Teodoro pounded a fist on the table. "Hay, mira no más!"

"Yeah, just look. Don't you see it's a sign? Bunch of hypocrites sitting around celebrating the white man's holiday while our brothers are being slaughtered like turkeys in Vietnam," Teddie said. "And when are we going to talk about what happened to Freddy!"

"Mija, don't talk like that," Aunt Othelia said. "He was a hero and we are celebrating the freedom he fought for our country..."

"And, Mamá, don't forget that extra dose of insulin after stuffing yourself with the all-American apple pie."

The front screen door slammed behind Teddie. The scene was similar to others I remembered when something always pissed her off and she wasn't afraid to let everyone know about it.

"Never mind her. She gets that way," Aunt Othelia said, walking over to get the spicy salsa from the counter and then stepping over to her husband. She held it over his head and smiled at the rest of us. "Shall I pour it for you, too?" He waved her off and she then returned to her place and reached over for a roll which she proceeded to liberally spread with Parkay out of the plastic tub.

The little house had heated up hotter than Mom's habanero salsa, so after I helped clear the table, I stepped out for some fresh air and found Teddie seated on the porch stoop smoking. I squeezed in next to her.

"Teddie, I'm really sorry about Freddy."

"And I'm sorry about your dad."

"Can I have one?" I asked, motioning toward her cigarette.

"It's been years," she said, slapping one out of the pack.

"I know." I lit up.

"Girl, you were always a strange kid. Always with your head in a book or talking to your Grandma. Scared the shit out of me."

"Wait. You knew about Grandma?"

CHAPTER 29

Brown People in Berets

I'm ten sitting on a tree stump in my cousins' backyard where Abuela also has a garden, coffee cans and lard cans full of red geraniums and sweet-smelling carnations. Colorful puffs sprout from the prickly nopales. In a pink eyelet dress, I purse my lips, so Grandma Phoebe can't say anything about getting dirty as I watch the kids at my cousin Sal's birthday party take turns swinging a bat at the piñata filled with candy.

Grandma Phoebe had warned me to act like a lady, reminding me how much better I had it in the house built for her. But I didn't think so. I couldn't recall any kids hanging around our house, except my siblings. I had no memory of playing kick the can, or having a piñata filled with dulce. "You have a piano you can play with at home," Grandma had whispered.

"Yeah, I remember you talking to your Grandma Phoebe," Teddie said. "We're Mexican. We talk to our ancestors. Nothing new. I talk to Freddy all the time and Abuela Antonia. Now that your dad's gone, you can talk to him, too."

I didn't think Teddie understood. "Oh, hell no." I took a deep drag wondering why Phoebe hadn't popped in lately.

"Anyway, back then I sensed your pain, so I'd try to talk to you, but you'd go all quiet and run off."

"You're the one who scared me," I said, exhaling.

"Why?" Voice booming, she sat straighter, twisted toward me, and then laughed. "Afraid of my brownness?"

"Not at all." I always envied the color of her skin, wishing I could be her color, that way I thought I might fit in better, not stand out like a strawberry milkshake. It was more her voice and her size that she used to intimidate others, but never me. "You knew how to be seen. You knew how to be heard."

"Even though you were little, you sat there like you were the Queen of Sheba. Just staring, like you were looking down at us. Like you were all high and mighty living in that big castle. Like your caca didn't smell."

That wasn't even close to the truth. "My caca does smell. I remember sitting in this very spot staring out at a bunch of kids having a good time. I really wanted to join in so badly and just act like one of the kids running around and not caring about getting all dirty, but—"

"But what? Afraid of getting down in the dirt?"

"No."

"Too bad your family can't hang on to the castle your grandpa built," Teddie said.

"On stolen land."

Teddie looked at me curiously. "What do you mean?"

I blinked, wondering if she knew anything at all about the family home over in Glendale. "What do *you* mean?"

"Your mother's been talking to my dad. Apparently, your father borrowed against your casa to pay off some gambling deuda or something," she said, emphasizing the Spanish words.

A gambling debt? This was new to me, but not unbelievable. But then I wondered if maybe Teddie might have gotten something lost in the translation. "Are you sure they were talking about my father?"

"Even though I don't speak Spanish, I can understand, especially when it's put in context or, cuss words. Funny, Dad and I used to argue. He'd say to me. 'You're a Chicana.' I'd say 'No, I'm American' and yet we never spoke Spanish in the house."

It surprised me that except for a few words, she never learned Spanish. Her father spoke it fluently, but my aunt, born in the US never pushed it on my cousins and, as a matter of fact, forbade any talk of their Mexicanness.

"What about your family?" I asked. "Will you be able to stay?"

Teddie shook her head. "Papá's been a hold out, pushing his luck as if he can just dig deeper roots into the ground he doesn't even own. Like, he thinks he can fly an American flag from the porch and they'll just let us stay. Thank them for their service. The flag they gave Mamá at Freddy's funeral. As if some big excavator won't just come up and sever the house from its roots. Or, like some big bad white American wolf won't just come huff and puff and blow the house down."

"And then where will you all go?" I asked, noticing the American flag fluttering in the Santa Anas.

She blew smoke into the wind. "I don't know. Maybe, I'll hit the road like you did. Let them figure it out. This ain't my problem. Anyway, I'm sorry you're losing your home."

"I'm more sad that we lost Freddy."

"Yeah, he was going to buy my parents their own castle someday. Get a GI loan, finish school. He had big plans."

I inhaled and held it in a few seconds. We sat in the dark in awkward silence and then a crow squawked from the telephone wire strung along the street.

"Whatever happened to Grandma Antonia's parrot?" I asked. "I heard they can live up to fifty years."

"We buried Pauline with her up at Rose Hills." I stared at my cousin. "Freddy and I snuck into the cemetery and dug a little hole. Had a little parrot ceremony." She inhaled, and then started laughing and coughing at the same time. "He died the same week she did. I guess no one paid attention to him."

I thought about my dad. And how the family had moved out leaving him in that big, fancy house, all alone.

Aunt Othelia stepped out onto the porch with two plates full of apple pie à la mode. "We need to fatten you up, Anna."

"And me?" Teddie asked.

"You're already perfect. We can just let the seams out a bit in the wedding dress."

"In your dreams, Mamá."

Aunt Othelia walked back inside.

"You're getting married?" I asked.

"No! You heard what I said. After my first year, I dropped out of college and then she started bugging me again. Getting married is what all the good Mexican girls do." Teddie laughed. "I got news for her, I ain't that good and marriage ain't part of any plan of mine. I was her only hope that her daughter would wear her dress. So, what have you been up to?"

"Oh, not too much."

"That's not what Mamá tells me."

"Oh yeah?"

Mexican mothers love the chisme, especially when it comes to their kids. Whether it's good or bad. To brag, complain, it doesn't matter.

"So, you ran away with a band."

I laughed out loud. "Yeah, I'm still running."

"Good for you. I'm so jealous. Like I said, maybe I'll run away with you. I want to travel the world. Starting in Mexico. I hardly know anything about my own roots. I don't know anything about my ancestors."

I wondered how Teddie might do if we traded places. If she had her abuela taking up space in her head. Oh, there would be hell!

"My parents insisted I assimilate. It wasn't until I joined the Brown Berets that I knew anything about the history or culture of my people. Like, what did I care about the past?"

"I've heard of the Berets. It was started by a bunch of young Chicano students, right?"

"Right." She gave me a little more of the history of the Berets and how she'd been learning to reject assimilation into European American society and to stand against the Vietnam War and police brutality. Just last year, they helped lead massive walkouts at high schools on the Eastside and sit-ins that went on for days as part of the demands for better education, including Mexican American studies and relevant bilingual education and college prep. Before the Berets, she had no idea about her family's journey to the Eastside of Los Angeles. She, much less her brothers, never dreamed of college.

"So, yeah, that's why I'm fired up about it. Anyway, I know my father's family is from Mexico and my mom was born here. Her family is also native Gabrielinos (Tongvas), the people that were first here hundreds of years ago. But that's about all I know."

"Did you know the family lived up on La Cañada in Glendale?"

"Yeah, you and your LeMar family."

I was scared. Maybe I should have kept silent about it, but I couldn't. "I mean your dad, my mom, their parents."

"No shit," Teddie said. "You mean like they owned it?"

"Yeah, it used to be part of the Verdugo Land Grant. They were pushed out. You could probably learn more about it at the library. All I know is what happened more recently like when our parents were little."

"Anna be careful," Grandma whispered, but I ignored her.

"My father's stepfather had something to do with them being repatriated, sent back to Mexico."

"What the fuck! All that time I shared a room with Abuela and she never said anything." Teddie stared off. "Everyone thinks if nothing's said, then nothing happened. That's pretty fucked up. It's like erasing our history."

"Yeah, I know."

"How'd you find out?"

"Anna!" Grandma screamed out loud, startling Teddie.

"*Anna* has her sources," I said. "Honestly, there are things I wish I never knew."

⋆ ⋆ ⋆

The sun set beyond the city of Los Angeles, the buildings looking as if they were newly arrived immigrants lined up for questioning. How'd you get here? Up and down the street, the lights flickered on, a sign of home and security, of warmth and feasting families stuffing themselves like turkeys on this American holiday. A couple of people strolled by, walking off the remnants of the day as a car pulled up in front of the house. The headlights turned off, but I recognized the blue Chevy before Ruben Moya ever stepped out of the car.

He opened the gate and walked up the path. "Hi Teddie. You ready?"

"Yeah." She turned to me. "It's a pinche coffee shop and they don't even know how to make their own coffee." She stood. "We're making some plans for our first demonstration next month to protest the war and the drafting of Chicanos and some other shit."

"Remember, our struggle is not in Vietnam but in the movement for social justice at home," Ruben said.

"We don't have time to just sit around like hippies, all peace and love, make pretty music and take drugs." Is that what she thought I was doing? "We gotta make shit happen," Teddie added. "Take a bat and swing at life's big piñata."

"Prima, you wanna come with?" Teddie asked. "Learn some shit about your brown people."

"Yeah, I guess."

CHAPTER 30

Who's the Güera?

During the ride over, Ruben explained just how important Teddie, seated in the front, was and how much she'd done for the Berets. "Teddie, she's a fighter, man." I could sense his pride. I was proud of her, too. I always knew she'd make a difference in this world.

"With four brothers, I had to learn," Teddie said. "But I also learned to serve."

"This is a good group of young people wanting to make changes," Ruben added. "We're all tired of the police brutality, the bad jobs, no college, no health care."

Quickly, Teddie got worked up. "And the young people are very attracted to this, and I'm passionate about the work we're doing. You know, even though it's really dinky, I come from a comfortable home, but I need life experience. Even though I could have gone if I wanted to, I figured out college isn't for me. I want to protest everything that is unjust. Other groups are doing the same thing. Look what's happening in the south with the Blacks."

I'd seen firsthand what happened in Memphis. I thought of River.

"I joined because it seemed like an alternative to what was going on at my high school between the white and brown students. A lot of fights and we're the ones being disciplined more severely and jailed. The police ride up on campus on their motorcycles and arrest the Chicanos, not the white kids, not the surfers."

"Surfers?"

"Yeah, it's a white thing. There's a lot of prejudice. Like in class, the teachers never call on the Brown kids, they never call on me."

"She's way smarter than any surfer," Ruben said.

"Thanks, babe, but you know, I'm drowning, and unless things in the group change, I'm gonna swim away. I believe in what we stand for, but there are some things that gotta change."

"Like what?" I asked.

"The sexism. The machismo. If I wanted that, I could stay home with my father and my brothers. The men treat us worse than nothings, worse than the pigs treat us."

"Well, Teddie, I appreciate you. And the others do, too. They just need to be taught," Ruben said. "Just be patient."

"I don't have time for that shit. There's so much work to do. It's a wonder their mothers taught them how to wipe their own colas."

"Teddie and some of the other girls helped start the free clinic. They got the doctors, equipment, volunteers, and the labs," Ruben said.

"There's nothing we can't do. That's the easy part. The hardest part's going into the community to introduce the clinic to the people. They're afraid of the Brown Berets."

"Why?" I asked.

"We're looked at as a militant group. And there's been some trouble with the police. Like I said, the pigs are out for us."

Ruben parked his Chevy up the street from the coffee shop, which looked dark from the outside. "The police like to make their house calls every once in a while, so we keep the lights off," Teddie whispered.

I could feel all eyes tracking me as we inched into a dark room. Eventually my eyes adjusted. A few young men had gathered around a table. I followed my cousin to a back little room like a kitchen where there was some light but no windows. A couple of girls stood off to the side sizing me up and down. And then one of the girls, slim with long black hair and steely dark eyes, blocked us as we made our way to the coffee pot brewing on the stove. "Who's the güera impersonating a Mexican?" she asked. I clutched my left braid.

"She is Mexican, half," Teddie said. "She's my cousin, Anna."

The girl, arching a thin eyebrow, put a hand on her hip.

"Don't be stupid," my cousin said. "My aunt married a gringo."

Once again, I felt out of place wishing my skin was less pink.

"You sure she's not a snitch for the pigs?" a big-boned woman asked as she walked in to wait for the coffee still percolating.

"And how do we know you're not one?" Ruben asked moving in, cup in hand.

"Funny, pendejo," the woman said.

Teddie walked up to the woman who was even taller than she. "Gloria, this is my cousin, Anna. Anna, this is our female minister, Gloria Arellanes."

"Nice to meet you." I curtsied as if I were meeting royalty.

Gloria didn't have time for me and seized the pot of coffee, taking it with her into the front room. Ruben followed with his empty cup and joined the other men. I followed my cousin and stood silently, back against the wall with the other girls as the men discussed what seemed to be some serious political stuff.

"Hey, after you're done pouring coffee . . ." the male leader said to Gloria.

"Hay is for horses, cabron," she responded, pulling the coffee pot away. Teddie quickly stepped up to take the carafe from her.

"Sorry," the leader said, sounding not sorry at all. "Anyway, we need a letter to LAPD asking for permission so we can march down the streets of East LA."

Gloria, surrounded by a bunch of macho males, took a seat. She then took notes, scribbling away like a glorified secretary, and then I saw lights flashing across the front window like a shooting star.

"Quiet. Down," the leader whispered loudly, everyone dropping onto the floor, duck and cover, like a nuclear attack drill.

My heart dropped faster than I fell to my knees. I crawled toward the back and Teddie grabbed my arm, stopping me. "They're just checking." And then a light beamed into the shop through the closed blinds. I sprang up ready to run, like I had from my home, like I had from Diggers, like I'd been doing for a few years now.

"No. They're probably at the back door, too," Teddie said. "Stay still."

Forget about duck and cover, we were sitting ducks. I'd been arrested in Philadelphia and even thrown in jail, but there was no guarantee that I'd be released this time. Besides my cousin and Ruben, I had no idea who these people were or what they'd done. I knew some of them had already been in trouble with the law for such things as breaking curfew and protesting and I'd be guilty just by association.

After some time, Ruben rose out of a crouch and tiptoed to the front where he looked out a peephole in the front door. "They're gone." He held a penlight up to check his watch. Six o'clock shift change, probably headed home for a nice turkey dinner."

Everyone returned to what they were doing. "Teddie bring us some more coffee," the leader said.

On the ride home, I thought about what I'd just witnessed. My takeaway, besides the police scare, was that the whole scene at the coffee shop reminded me of the women of Diggers doing the same work while the dudes took all the credit. And it wasn't just the white man. The Spanish took from the Tongvas and the Mexicans. George had taken from my grandmother and my family. Men throughout history just took from women what they wanted, lording their power over anyone who might have seemed weaker. And then I thought about my role in the band. The lyrics I'd written, the song's I'd scored—all the credit going to a dude. That would have to change if I were to ever go back.

★ ★ ★

John called from New York just before Christmas to see when I was coming back. They missed their "girl." Rather, they needed someone to make coffee, write their songs, and clean up after them. Besides, Duncan had left the band and they needed me, John said, and the new album *Bumpy Roads Live* was coming out, an album with a few of the songs I'd written. They were to begin their 1970 tour at the Fillmore East in New York and needed me for vocals and keyboards and some studio time to overdub. In other words, they needed me to clean up someone else's mess, again.

I'd go back, but I wanted to see some changes. John assured me there would be. It was also an excuse for me to leave home again. I flew out before the New Year, but I told my family I'd be back in February for a couple of concerts coming up in California.

★ ★ ★

The day after the February 23, 1970, concert in San Francisco, Patty went into labor. I flew into Los Angeles to meet my new niece who was beautiful as far as newborns go. I'd picked up some flowers in the hospital gift shop.

"What's her name?" I asked, placing the flowers into a plastic water glass.

"Lindsay Teresa. Teresa after Mom."

"Nice."

"Yeah, hopefully, that will soften Mom up a bit—welcome me back into the fold like you," Patty said.

"Really? So, I'm the prodigal daughter and I didn't even have to give her a grandchild? Groovy."

We both laughed.

"I'm not so sure about the name Lindsay, but Teresa is definitely a saint's name."

She nodded. "And she should be happy that we finally got married, so we wouldn't bring a 'bastard' into the world."

I laughed. "Congratulations on both accomplishments."

"Someday we'll take that honeymoon to Hawaii and stay in that pink hotel," Patty said.

"The Royal Hawaiian?"

"Yes, and lay out at the pool and order buckets of Mai Tais."

I wished that for her. Even though my sister lived in a fantasy world with no clue about how the real world worked, who was I to judge? We'd both learn what we needed to know as we took our different paths along our life journeys.

"That does sound like a dream," I said and then kissed baby and mother before saying goodbye.

"How long are you sticking around this time?" she asked.

"I'm not sure, but I'll come visit."

★ ★ ★

That evening I met up with Teddie. Chilly, sitting out on her porch, she shivered. "It's just nerves," she told me. "Tomorrow is going to be a big day."

They were getting ready for the march the next day and expected thousands of protestors. "There's so much that can go wrong."

I wasn't sure I wanted to be a part of trouble.

"Remember how I told you there was a plan in place. A letter got sent to the Berets telling them that the women and some of the younger men have resigned."

"Seriously?" I asked.

"Yeah, we let them know how we felt that we were treated as less than nothing."

"Way to go, prima! Way to stand up for yourselves and fight."

"They didn't believe Gloria when she said we would leave, but we did."

"What about Ruben?" I asked.

"They need him. We need him there. He's our go-between."

"Yeah, he seems like a super good guy."

"Wait, are you crushin' on him?" Teddie asked.

"Hells bells, no. He's way into you."

"Fine by me. Besides, why would you, when you've got your pick of rock stars. I heard that you performed with Santana up in San Francisco. Did you hook up with him? My dad told me we could be cousins because he's from the same part of Mexico," Teddie said.

"We've said hi in passing."

"He played at Woodstock, too, right?" Teddie asked.

"Yeah, but I cut out before they ever came on stage."

"You're so lucky, chingona. If I had half your talent and your looks, I'd use it to get the message out."

"What do you mean 'my looks'?"

"You're güera. White. You've got a foot in the door. They'll listen to you."

"Not really. I'm still just a girl. I can't say anything."

"But it's also about what you don't say. When's your next concert?"

"Next month downtown at the Olympic Auditorium. Speaking of gifts, prima, I'll get you tickets. Santana won't be there but you can come back stage. I'm going to stick around for the show and then the band's heading back to New York."

"Can't wait," Teddie said. "So now let's talk about the plan for what's happening at tomorrow's march. I'll bet you haven't marched before?"

"I did up in San Francisco a couple years ago, to protest the war and women's rights, and civil rights. Even some Black Berets marched along with us. That's where I heard Coretta Scott King speak."

"Mira no mas," Teddie said, arching an impressed eyebrow. "Well, since we left the Brown Berets, we formed a new group of Chicana activists, who want to push for women's rights, better working conditions, and still protest against police brutality. But our place is not in the kitchen making coffee and sweeping the floors. It's not having to get pinned down in the bedroom, either. The group is named Las Adelitas de Aztlan after female soldiers who fought in the Mexican Revolution. Fifty years ago. Imagine that. Some things never change. Like us, they did everything from cooking to cleaning, but they also fought in the front lines with real rifles. And now we want to take our place in the front lines."

"You're going to shoot real guns?"

"No, but we do have real bullets." She laughed nervously. "Tomorrow we'll march and demand our rights as Las Adelitas de Aztlan!"

"Cousin, hopefully, you can make a difference and in the next fifty years, this will all just be ancient history to tell the grandkids."

* * *

On a street corner in East Los Angeles with a backdrop of palm trees and rain clouds, I recognized some of the men from the coffee shop. A crowd had gathered to listen to a young man shout into a loudspeaker. I didn't recognize him.

The physical killing off of our people through the war in Vietnam while we are dying is twice the rate of all other soldiers of Vietnam. We are protesting against the discriminatory draft laws that give deferments to all the Anglo middle-class people of this country and make the heaviest burden of the war fall on the Mexicanos. So we are here today saying: 'Ya Basta!'

The Brown Berets lined up to lead the march down the boulevard and the Adelitas followed behind with at least 3,000 other men, women, and children. I pulled the hood up on my raincoat and stood behind my cousin ready to march under the group's banner, holding a white cross, representing Freddy. Some of the other girls also carried crosses. I held the silver-framed photo of my cousin that I eventually slipped under my coat to protect it from the rain. One of the girls wore a couple of bullet-filled bandoliers slung sash-style across her shoulders and chest. The sound of drums beat as the leader marched in step, shouting, "Chicano!" and the protestors replied, "Power!" shielding themselves from the rain, which came pouring down, with umbrellas, sheets of plastic, and all sorts of head coverings, including berets and even giant sombreros. Police on the sidelines and at the ready stayed dry in their cars. As the thunder cracked overhead we crossed under an overpass and came through the other side. Still, we kept marching in the driving rain, holding up soggy signs, the letters dripping, but the message clear: *Que Viva La Raza, que viva vida . . .*

The march had started off peacefully and ended that way.

I came away overwhelmed. I came away changed. By the end of the march, I felt a unity with that side of me that wasn't white. I understood that here in the United States there was also a struggle for social justice. I understood that man had been destroying our Raza in Vietnam, Raza in the jails, the schools, the factories, the fields . . . it had to stop. It was up to the Raza, up to us.

"Bring them home!" I shouted with my family. "Hell no. We won't go. Que viva la Raza, que viva vida . . ."

I felt muy orgullosa marching with my Chicana cousin, my Chicano family.

★ ★ ★

Invigorated for days after the march, I'd come to realize that just like Vietnam wasn't the Chicano's war, just like Stonewall wasn't a clash River had wanted to enter, this was not a battle I wanted to choose. My war still raged inside the walls of my head where the voice constantly nagged. 'Anna, why are you still here? You were born to do so much more. You have your music. You need to take control of your life.' Which was totally ironic, because how could I control my life when she'd taken over and colonized my brain? I wished I had the fight in me, but I was just a pale-faced coward who'd climbed the hill, but wasn't prepared to die on it by pulling others up. At least not yet.

★ ★ ★

Grandma had either pissed me off or emboldened me because a couple of days before the concert, I approached John. "This is my home town. These are my people. I've written something I'd like to sing." He surprised me by agreeing so quickly. He must have been on drugs.

From the stage of the Olympic Auditorium, I looked out to a river of brown faces, my family in the first few rows, and then the lights dimmed. A grand piano had been pushed out to center stage. I would be singing my own song.

Mi corazon, an ivory-veined granite rock
tossed into the Rio Grande moons ago.
I want to float up, pierce the muddied waters
with a machete and fight for what's right;
for mis hermanas, but I'm only half, not real.
Can I be one with you if I'm güera,
If I'm still fighting my own guerra at home.
where the embers lie waiting to ignite the flames,
tears ready, listening for La Llorona, pleading,
leave me asleep at the bottom of the Rio Grande
where you drowned me moons ago.

I looked out to a field of flickering lights, like brilliant stars across a desert sky. The crowd, on their feet now, whistled and applauded for about five minutes. I'd climbed the hill, now what?

"Thank you all!" Without asking for John's approval, I shouted. "We'd like to dedicate the proceeds from tonight's concert to Las Adelitas de Aztlan."

CHAPTER 31

India

I could not live in any of the worlds offered to me—the world of my parents, the world of war, the world of politics. ~Anaïs Nin

But how could I recreate a world of my own as Nin had written? I could keep running, except I'd still be stuck not just with myself but with Grandma who'd represented all that was wrong with my home, the establishment, and the world. I wanted to be part of the rebellion, the protests, the activists, and the freedom riders, but how could I relate truly when the gurus of the times were telling us to look within for happiness. So, you know, not super helpful. Young kids were running away, but I'd swim the ocean in search of answers, in search of peace.

I returned with the band to New York. Angry about the donation, John took it out of my payment. He made it pretty clear that I'd never be given the same opportunity as that magical night at the Olympic. "Those were your homies," he said. "Of course, they'd cheer someone homegrown."

I'd never be anything more than a keyboard player, a back-up singer, a songwriter, and a coffee maker. Not with John in control. The band had been named for him, after all, Lazarus Rising, after he'd OD'd one night in San Francisco and then recovered miraculously. Oh, he hadn't minded taking credit for my lyrics, most of which had become hits on the recent album, *Bumpy*

Road and which would be certified gold within the next couple of decades.

I left the band.

★ ★ ★

I spent my time at the at the West End center practicing yoga and meditation. The music and chanting would take me away, but my mind had not settled. How could it be when I had two of them occupying the small space of my skull? Grandma floated around heaven in this environment, but how long could I remain? I'd moved in with some of the members from the center, surviving on what little I'd earned playing with the band (the men had taken most of it), trusting that money would continue to come from somewhere, and then one day a letter arrived from home. Inside, I found a copy of my birth certificate that I'd asked Mom to send me. Folded inside the letter was also a check for five hundred dollars. I called home to thank Mom for the copy of my birth certificate and the check.

"Mom, that's a lot of money. You must have cleaned lots of houses."

"Well it was a house. Ours. We had to clean out the Glendale place after it was sold."

"What?"

And Grandma yelled, "What? My house!"

"The money is so you can buy a ticket home, and other incidentals."

"Thank you, Mom, and I'll come home just as soon as I get back from India."

"India?" Mom asked in a tone of disappointment. "You've lost your mind?"

"That's the goal."

"You may as well go to the moon."

* * *

At the end of 1970, by the time I caught up with Swami Satchidinanda in Bombay and his young American followers, they'd already traveled through Europe collecting more young devotees like souvenirs. They'd even met the Pope who blessed them on the holy path they'd chosen under Swami's divine guidance.

I remained on the fringe watching as women in colorful saris and men in white cotton tunics and dhoti loincloths or lungi sarongs greeted him wherever he arrived with leis and fruit. Children rushed to touch him and help him with his bags as followers bowed their heads and folded their hands prayer-like. Satchidinanda, dressed in an ochre-colored kasaya, laid his hands on the group to bless them. Later, as he sat, an older woman with a bindi on her forehead began the ritual of anointing Swami from his head to his toes, offering milk to cleanse the surrounding aura.

Sometime after, we devotees accompanied the Swami through the marketplace. As he purchased some fruit, huge crowds swarmed around him like bees to honey, their sweet faces an indication of their deep spiritual heritage. After he made the way to his car, his driver had to be careful not to run anyone over.

The next day, in the home of another host, friends and relatives gathered for a puja at his feet as a sign of worship and then Swami began with songs and devotions as some, legs crossed, listened to his words. "Yoga is the master key to open everything. If you want to open the heart of your beloved, we have yoga. If you want to open the heart of the scriptures, we have yoga. Health, wealth, strength, everything can be opened with yoga. That is why it is universal."

Afterward, the disciples came one by one to receive his blessings and to ask his personal advice.

Thinking I'd have more opportunities when he wasn't around devotees or family, I never approached him. Instead, I absorbed everything he had to say and waited for my chance.

The next day we followed his car to another hometown where he'd lived and gone to school as a young boy. We gathered in the home of an uncle to listen to Swami speak his consoling words late into the night. "There's a divine plan behind everything, if we allow ourselves to be used by that unseen force. As good instruments many things can happen in a mysterious miraculous way. If we interfere with that plan by introducing our own plan, the egocentric plan, tension will be created, for in any event ultimately the divine plan will beam out."

I listened intently from the doorway of the crowded room, hoping Grandma was paying attention, too. As far as I was concerned, she'd introduced her selfish plan into my life. And I now sought the Divine plan that would escort her out.

When he stood preparing to leave, my hands grew sweaty, my heart flapping like a hummingbird. I'd finally mustered the courage to approach him, but as he reached into his pocket and pulled out packets of gum, the children all squealed, glomming onto him like Double Bubble. I'd try again at the next occasion.

That night in a new place to lay my head, I wrote home and then I started a letter to my friend.

Dear River,

I really miss you so much. The travel by bus reminds me so much of our time on the road. I wish you were in the seat next to me . . .

* * *

The next morning, Swami spoke at a college where hundreds of Tamil poetry students had gathered to listen. This time I remembered the little tape recorder I'd packed and turned it on. "Always try to serve like this. Don't even call it helping, call it service. You are benefited by that. If a man begs from you and you give him something, you shouldn't think you are helping him; instead, he is helping you."

From there we traveled some more, passing a shrine of the elephant-headed aspect of God. All along our travels, pedestrians, monkeys, and brahma bulls crisscrossed the dusty roads. We also had the great fortune of visiting many holy places significant to his early life as well as ashrams so incredibly stunning. When I walked in they seemed to be filled with an intense vibration of deep peace. Everywhere, there were crowds, men and boys, beating drums in celebration of Swami Satchidinanda. Alice Coltrane eventually joined us on this leg of the trip, but I didn't get to hang with her as she followed Swami pretty closely as part of his inner circle.

That night I sat down to add to my letter to River:

You would have loved today's journey. We entered the inner sanctum of this Hindu temple surrounded by all these little altars. We walked around them clockwise paying respect to the different aspects of the Lord. I'm still confused about the differences between Hinduism and Buddhism. So far, I've learned that Buddhists don't believe in a god and, apparently, Buddha is not a god. As opposed to Hindus who believe in many.

Besides journaling, I'm carrying this little tape recorder everywhere so I don't miss anything. You'd really find what the Swami says so interesting. He says, "There are not many gods. There is only one and that one has no name, no form, and no place," he said, and the next part is so cool. "He is everywhere and in actuality he is neither a 'he' nor a 'she' nor 'it' but such abstractions cannot be grasped by our limited minds." So, in other words, limited minds can't understand the breadth of gender. He said, "Only when the mind expands to a greater capacity, can we understand the infinite things. That's why according to our capacity the infinite one reduces himself to a lower level." Doesn't it all sound really far out?

In New Delhi, we attended a conference where there were talks and seminars for several days. We traveled up to Masuri where we could see across to the peak of the Himalayas deep in Tibet.

In the meanwhile, I'm learning so much. Swami says, "Everybody present on Earth has to realize he has a hand someplace in making corrections. We can't save ourselves. We can't save the world, it's already decided." My question, of course, is what about Grandma's hand?

Tomorrow we head south. I'll write again when I'm settled. Love you to the Honey Moon and back!

Om shanti, shanti, shanti. Me

★ ★ ★

At last the moment arrived. We were all in Bonaris and had just plunged into the sacred river to be purified. As I lay on a giant rock drying myself out in the sun, trying to meditate, Grandma wouldn't shut up about the whole experience. "Isn't it all so exhilarating?"

"Indeed, it is, Anna," a man's voice said.

I opened my eyes and turned my head to see Swami on the rock next to me. Legs crossed, face up, he had his eyes closed.

"Meditating?"

"Trying." I rolled onto my side and cut to the chase while I had the chance. "Back in New York, I heard you speak about how it was possible to live in harmony with your dual consciousness."

He smiled, lifting his chin to the sun, as if he were proud of me, his Young Grasshopper.

"I share a consciousness with my grandmother."

"Ah, yes. What a gift."

Maybe he hadn't heard me right. Maybe he didn't understand my being literal. "My grandmother lives in my head."

He nodded slightly. "You can learn to live in harmony with your dual consciousness, but you must first learn to let go of the anger."

He'd said that before, but I hadn't understood what anger had to do with it?

"Perhaps, he was talking to me," Grandma said. Oh, I hadn't thought of that. Even if she'd done a decent job trying to control her anger, she had a lot to be pissed about and she'd for sure passed it on to me, traumatizing me with anger from who knows how many generations.

"Indeed," he said. "We have the ability to control our thoughts, instead of being controlled by them. We want to avoid the pain and grief that comes with accepting a relationship is over, and so we hold on and continue to keep getting hurt forever. However, once we let go, the pain will ease over time."

"She's the one not willing to let me go. I just want her gone so I can finally be happy."

"It's not that easy," Grandma added. "I've been trying for quite some time."

The Swami didn't seem to notice the low tinted voice. "Run toward the light and your shadow will stay behind you," Swami said. "Some people want to be happy quickly, so they take shortcuts and get temporary happiness. But borrowed joy comes and goes." He looked as if he were speaking to the heavens. "We keep trying to find that happiness and we keep missing it. When we finally tire of searching for happiness, we sit quietly and wonder, "What is this? Why am I unhappy? Happiness simply is. Our true nature is peace and joy, a duality, if only we don't disturb it."

With that, he became silent and I didn't want to disturb his peace.

Later, I wished I'd had my recorder with me so I could go back and listen between the lines. I was sure I'd missed something again.

But the funny thing, as time went on, was that Grandma seemed to be at peace and more importantly, I seemed to be at peace with her. My mind seemed focused, not flying all around. Could it be Grandma and I were now truly one, no longer just parallel beings, but united? Not discordant, no cacophony? A beautiful duet? I wondered whether it would be possible for Grandma and me to live in harmony as "peace" and "joy." I'd make it my mission to gather the tools for this to happen. She was a part of me; it would be like cutting off my head to spite my thinking (believe me, the thought had crossed my mind before). I soared with elation. Ebullient, I was on my way to a spiritual awakening I'd never experienced before. It felt as if I'd arrived, seated on the edge of a peaceful lake—but this couldn't be the end of my journey.

And it wasn't. Grandma wasn't quite ready to let me go, but for the first time in my life, I wasn't motivated to let her go. I just needed to learn how to harmonize a little better.

A few of the devotees had planned to follow Swami on to Ceylon, but as we neared Madras (Chennai), I felt Grandma's excitement growing. "We're so close to Adyar. We must visit." She was right. I hadn't come this far not to.

CHAPTER 32

Just Breathe and Lessons Learned

Madras proved a more difficult city to drive through than LA during rush hour.

"It has certainly changed since I was here last," Grandma said as our bus rolled in, horn blaring, through the suffocating city.

Drivers and pedestrians seemed to ignore the traffic policemen in khaki and white baggy kurtas. Vans full of passengers whizzed by, including half a dozen men and boys sitting lotus-style on the rooftops. Buses stuffed with passengers hanging out the open windows bumped along. Festively decorated tiny rickshaws with two rows of seating tuk-tuked up and down the sooty streets. People, laden with packs on their backs, peddled bikes back and forth. Women dressed in bright saris clutched their children's hands along the dusty sidewalks as they made purchases from the fruit stands and shops with colorful signs in English. Brahma bulls pulled carts full of feed or grain.

Makeshift billboards hung on poles and lattices made of timber from the mahogany trees. The city, sitting on what used to be a marshy forest, still maintained some green that had not been totally choked out by development. Lined with curtains of palm trees, the streets gave one the hospitable feeling of a Hawaiian tropical vacation. But as I stood on the top step of the hot, humid bus, there was no relief, no welcoming smell from any leis of plumeria. Instead, auto exhaust and the stench of dung and sewage from the open sewers stung my eyes. The air looked smoggier than any day back home and sultrier than a steam room.

I deboarded into a balmy day across from the mouth of the Adyar River, where its brackish currents swirled into the Bay of Bengal. As I made my way from the bus stop to the headquarters of the Theosophical Society, there was no mistaking the contrast in the midst of all the urban chaos.

An older sentry stood guard at the entrance to what looked like an enchanted forest. "Do you have an appointment?"

"Do I need one?"

He laughed and then welcomed me onto the grounds where I asked for directions to the main building. Sitting on 250 acres of garden space on the banks of the Adyar River, the buildings were flanked by ancient trees that were probably around even before Grandma's last visit. The aroma of fragrant flowers greeted me and a chorus of birds sang as I took in the surroundings, a lush jungle full of mangroves, coconut groves, and banyan trees.

"Now we can breathe," Grandma said. "We must walk the grounds. I remember now what air, what nights, what marvelous quiet, no street noise. I just know we'll find the answers here."

"Settle down, Grandma." The idea of being free of her at last seemed less elusive. I knew she also wanted to be free of me and her earthly ties. "I need to see if I can get a room."

At the main reception area, an old guide in short white hair asked me to state my purpose. After telling him I wanted to do some research on an ancient religious practice toward enlightenment, he escorted me to the Leadbetter Chambers building, a hostel for visitors. The ceilings were vaulted and the light from the high windows sliced down, casting oblique shadows like I might be in jail. The ventilation ports above the windows and overhead fans offered a bit of relief. I wasted no time unpacking before I left to find the library.

"It looks the same," Grandma said as I crunched along a loamy path filled with dried bean pods. "Except for that new building."

I stepped into the main hall surrounded by the symbols of the world's major religions. On the northeast section of the hall were emblems of Zoroastrianism, Islamism, Sikhism, Daosim, Confucianism, and Hinduism. A statue of Krishna stood with his flute and sacred cow. Another sacred cow.

"As you can see, darling, all religions, all castes. I was free to attend whichever service I wanted, whichever lectures," Grandma said. "Because I'd recently been heartbroken over the death of my father and when I stumbled into a lecture on the transference of consciousness and learned how one could assist even after the loved one had gone, I knew I had to do something."

So where do I find that class where I can learn how to undo what you've done to me? I thought, but I don't think Grandma paid me any attention.

"I took time to study and after time, I just knew Father made it to that pure land because of me."

* * *

Wandering into the west side of the north wall, it seemed all the gods that ever existed were represented. Silently, I thanked them all for bringing me here and prayed that one of them might help me find the answers to my being.

Feeling hopeful, I entered a more modern structure, and stepped up to a dark young man in a white cotton tunic sitting behind a desk. He had a broad, smooth forehead, lush wavy black hair, a slender nose, full lips, and the beginnings of a five o'clock shadow. As he jotted some notes on a piece of paper, I noticed his long, brown slender fingers as if he was born to write and work in a library. I instantly knew he could help me.

"May I assist you?" he asked, revealing a big arresting smile that captured my breath. He set down his pen and folded his hands.

I took a deep breath. "I hope so."

"Have you visited before?"

"No, I've never been here."

"Well then allow me to welcome you." He nodded, opening his hands, palms up cordially. "This is the newest facility. It is climate controlled in order to preserve ancient manuscripts and books."

"Quite impressive," Grandma said. "While here last, I studied the works of the Master Kuthumi with the young Krishnamurti. Might you have copies of any of their works?"

The librarian peered at me. "You appear too young to have studied here with Krishnamurti. And you said you'd never been here before."

"Oh yes, well I mean, my grandmother. The last time my grandmother was here."

I turned my head and thought-voiced, "Grandma, be quiet. Let me do the talking." I turned to the librarian and smiled. "Can you please help me? I'm looking for a book about transferring consciousness, a practice called Phowa."

His eyes widened. "Very well, do you have the name or the catalog number?"

"More specifically, I'm looking for anything written about transferring a consciousness back to its source."

He brought his hand to his mouth and squeezed his lips, his gold watch glinting in the lamplight as he dropped his arm back onto the desk. "Ah, you mean something on spiritual suicide."

I went cold, not knowing how to respond. Both my father and Grandma had tried to explain that the only way to rid myself of Grandma would be by death or suicide. I felt a scratch in my throat. "Remember, not a good idea, darling. Besides the fact that it's a sin in the Catholic Church, I remind you again, nothing changes, except that you're on the other side, even more miserable than here on Earth."

Spiritual suicide seemed a bit more palatable. "Grandma, let me handle this." I looked at the librarian. "Yes, please, something on that."

"Very well, but still I must have a name or catalog number," he said, returning to his writing. "Feel free to look through the catalogs," he said without looking up and pointing a long finger to a wall with rows upon rows of directories. "Once you've found what you're looking for, I will retrieve the book for you. We close in thirty minutes." He returned to his note taking.

Frustrating and frightening. I didn't even know where to begin as I opened the first long narrow index box. Some of the print was in English, but most was Greek to me. Saved by the sound of the dinner bell, I stopped.

★ ★ ★

The next morning, I awoke to the sound of another bell signaling breakfast. In the hall, I tried the crispy-thin wafer dosa like one of Mom's tortillas served with sumbar and chutney.

I needed to go back to the library for research and to get to know that young man better, but first I wanted to tour the grounds where I came upon so many flowers in every shape and color I'd never seen before. I wanted to bottle the fragrances. There were shrubs and herbs and trees I didn't recognize except for the bottlebrush and the pepper trees and the palm trees, short and tall. And then canopied within a coconut grove grew a five-hundred-year-old banyan tree, considered a holy site. Directly adjacent stood the School of Wisdom in the Blavatsky bungalow where Theosophical lessons were given every day. A class had just started. What are the chances they'd be discussing transference of consciousness? I wondered. I walked in and took a seat.

The leader of the day, a slim older woman, with silver threaded through her charcoal colored hair, led us in meditation. She mentioned something about inward turning and contacting a subtler, deeper order. At first, I resisted. My goal had been to get out of my head, but by the end of the session, I did end up leaving in a more peaceful state.

I continued touring the grounds, coming upon a Garden of Remembrance, an elevated grassy area in the shape of a six-pointed star.

"Let us sit there awhile," Grandma said. "Perhaps if we remember . . ."

I'd grown so tired of remembering her life. I kept walking until I noticed a Bodhi tree representing the Lord Buddha's enlighten-ment, across from which sat a temple dedicated to Buddhism. The moment I stepped into the cave-like dwelling, the air seemed to be sucked out. Everything stood still, including the giant thousand-year-old statue of the Lord Buddha himself. It was just that giant idol and me. My skin prickled as I remembered my catechism where I read something in the Bible about false gods. "For the Lord your God, who is among you, is a jealous God and his anger will burn against you, and he will destroy you from the face of the land." Now, that's the god I remember. I was more afraid of the punitive one than the enlightened one. I hurried out into the garden where I stopped to catch my breath before tripping and falling down onto a patch of grass.

A gong sounded. Lunch already? But the sun had dipped below the tall trees. The breeze blowing in from the river that had chilled my skin as I looked at my watch on the goose bumped skin of my wrist. Six o'clock. I'd even missed the dinner bell.

But I wasn't hungry. I'd been in the garden all day, humming a tune I'd never heard before, at the same time listening to all the sounds outside my head, birds and insects, the garden vibrating through my body with the energy of the surrounding wildlife. For the time, I'd become one with nature, breathing in the essence, the fragrance of all the flowers, nature's incense. Had I taken a nap? I didn't want to leave. Neither did Grandma, whom I hadn't thought about all day.

"I didn't think about you either, my darling."

After a breakfast of vada, a savory donut-shaped fried lentil fritter served with coconut chutney, I headed over to the School of Wisdom where I would make the morning classes and my garden visit a daily ritual, putting off the return to the library for another week or so. I felt a calling on the outside of things and outside is where I thought I might finally find the answer to the Grandma situation.

But then one evening as I sat in silence watching the miracle bugs and fireflies put on a mesmerizing light show, I heard a voice and turned to see the young man from the library. "You haven't returned to the library."

"Hi. No, not yet."

He extended a hand, "I am Vihaan." With still enough twilight, I could see his smile transform his face, his cheekbones shining like big polished obsidian marbles and his white, large teeth highlighting his fine features.

"I'm Anna." I stood, dusting myself off. "I am 'overdue' (I laughed at my own pun) to return to the library, but for now it seems I might find the answers out here. I'm not even sure a book exists for what I'm looking for."

"Unfortunately, from what I've learned, once you've arrived in that Amitabha, that pure place without ego, one does not return to the circle of life."

Without holding back anymore, I'd run out of time, and at the risk of sounding crazy, I said to Vihaan, "I share a consciousness with my grandmother—go ahead, Grandma, say something."

"Greetings, Vihaan," she said in her smoky voice.

He looked me in the eyes, wobbling his head slightly. "Hello, Anna's Grandma."

"You can call me Phoebe," Grandma responded.

I knew he doubted us, but I didn't have time or the desire to explain anymore.

"And so, I thought I could find what I'm looking for in a book. I'm hoping to reverse the transference of consciousness."

"I see," Vihaan responded, humoring me, no doubt, as he took a seat on a nearby bench. I sat back down on the grassy ground where I'd been seated, now, at his feet.

"There is much to learn," he said. "But, unfortunately, much wisdom has been passed down from the masters by word of mouth, not much is written. Sometimes, it is only through the accumulated energy of the lineage or the oracle itself, and the blessings of the teacher. Only then is a qualified lama able to directly transfer the blessing of a practice to disciples."

"I see, and where might I find a qualified lama?" I asked. "The sooner I can be free of her, the better off I'll be."

"So says you," Vihaan said.

I opened my hands like a lotus flower, palms up. "Even now, we're not alone. She's sitting with us here in this garden."

He scanned the area. "Oh, right. Right."

"You mentioned something about spiritual suicide. Is there a book on that?"

"Again," he laughed. "I would need a catalog number."

We sat in silence, the cicadas growing louder, the sky a little duskier. I picked a blade of grass and twirled it between my fingers.

"There was a time a couple of years ago," Vihaan said. "I had the opportunity to study the teachings of Machiq, a Tibeten yogini from the eleventh century. That's the cool thing about working here. I can study as much and whatever I want."

"I had the same experience back around 1910," Grandma said in her grating voice, "when I studied the works with the young Krishnamurti."

Vihaan side-eyed me. "Anna, do you know the parable of the water snake?"

I shook my head, flicking the piece of grass.

"Basically, the moral of the story is that the trick lies in grasping the teachings properly so as not to get bitten and suffer death or death-like suffering."

"I do believe I was bitten," Grandma said, Vihaan side-eyeing me again.

"What I've learned from my grandmother, and the only things I've read on the subject of transference of consciousness, was that if you did it wrong, like if you didn't let go of everything, you would suffer the consequences." I was proof of what had gone wrong. Grandma had been on a fast track to enlightenment and it failed.

Vihaan confirmed what I'd read—that it was unwise to undertake the practice without initiation, oral transmission, and instruction from a lineage holder. So now what?

"I gather you are on a journey to undo what has been learned?"

"Now we're talking."

"Well, here is another story for you."

I hadn't come here for stories. I'd come here for the truth. Grandma had told so many tales leaving an imprint on me the size of an elephant's foot, I wasn't sure of the truth about anything.

"I had a teacher who taught me about this girl, Machiq, who was born as an Indian prince turned monk, and had achieved both spiritual and scholarly accomplishments at an early age. At twenty, he entered a cave where he left his body and merged his consciousness with a wrathful blue-black dakini, entering the womb of her mother."

"Wait, he came out as a girl? Sorry, please go on."

"Basically, her teachings have to do with, rather than emptying our mind or sending this 'shadow' off somewhere, we must learn to live with it. Bringing it to light through acceptance."

"So, rather than let go, accept?" I asked.

"Real love is accepting the shadow and letting it evolve into something else. The more we deny the shadow, the more our lives are ruled by it."

"Oh yes, indeed," Grandma butt in. "This is what I've been trying to teach you all along, Anna. Things you won't find in a book. You have to live it, go through it, and as the Swami said, let go of the fight. You can no longer deny that I exist."

"And you've gotta stop controlling me."

Vihaan stared at me and then stood as if he didn't want to get involved in a domestic squabble. "I must get home to my family, but if there's anything more I can tell you, I can meet you here again tomorrow evening."

"Oh yes, thank you." I stood, bringing my hands together, prayer-like. "Same bat time, same bat channel?"

"I love Batman," he said, under the moonlight, his brilliance bouncing off his large, white teeth. He turned to leave, arms flapping as if he were a bat.

The next day after class, while I waited for Vihaan, I took a walk, in spite of the baking weather. Many different species of trees were in full bloom. There were just as many different bird sounds as well. I thought about nature and how I was part of this grander world I'd traveled, meeting different people of various races and religions. I was just a freckle on this big planet.

Vihaan showed up. "Shall we go for a walk?"

"Sure, I've already hiked around. There are so many trees and birds."

"Yes, and I have names for all of them." I listened as he listed them all.

"Impressive, you sound like an encyclopedia. Those were just the trees?"

"Shall I name the birds?"

We laughed. "No, that's okay. I'd rather hear more stories like the one you told yesterday." I liked Vihaan and the soothing sound of his voice. "Like the one where Machiq enters a cave. It sort of reminds me of my catechism and one of the Bible stories about how Jesus left the tomb and made an appearance to Mary Magdalene and some of his disciples and when they told Thomas, he said he'd need to stick his hand through the hole in Jesus's side where the sword had pierced through."

"Yes, Doubting Thomas. Actually, Saint Thomas was martyred here in Madras."

"Really?"

"Yes, apparently, he came to India to do missionary work and ended up in Madras where he was eventually killed back in 72 AD."

"That's hard to believe."

"Well, you can doubt it if you like, Anna," he said with a laugh.

I looked forward to our meet-ups. We met a few more times and as I listened to his stories, I watched his face light up in the telling. I imagined kissing his full lips. I imagined being his wife and listening to his peaceful, yet alluring voice, morning, noon and night.

But then on what would turn out to be my final evening, we walked to the shore. The thought that this part of my journey was coming to an end made my stomach flutter as if I'd swallowed all the butterflies in the garden. We ended up at a gate that was slightly ajar. I pushed through and found myself standing on the shore.

"You know, Vihaan, I grew up believing so many things that have proven to be false, like about life and love." I dug my feet into the sand. "My grandmother seemed certain of so much, telling me stories about how the world existed and how I was to exist in this realm. I believed in things within my own family, about my ancestors, the ghosts, my religion, my country, whether or not miracles really happen like in the Bible? Is there a heaven and hell? Was Mary really a virgin? Things my Grandma tells me. Seems to me stories are just a form of instruction. Call me Doubting Anna, but I really have a hard time trusting so many of the stories I've been told."

"There are gifts and blessings in all these things, but they can all be made absolute and used to defend the ego. Have you heard the parable of the raft?"

"Another story?"

He smiled. "One of the principles behind Buddha's sense is that spirituality ought to be practical. In other words, don't speculate on theological debates. None of these things can be known, and we waste our time and energies pursuing them, often fighting over them. Spirituality ought to be practical. Use the truths that are given to you as a raft, to carry you across the raging waters, through troubled times, to help you find your way to safety and blessings. The time will come when you will cross the river and gently set your raft down on the banks and move on."

I looked out across the ocean, sparkling and shoreless. On the other side was home. "I'm going to miss you so much, Vihaan."

"I'll miss you, too, Anna."

Suddenly, I wanted to return home to apply all that my personal lama had taught me.

"I understand, Anna, but I like it here," Grandma whispered.

"Believe me, Grandma, if I could, I'd find a way to leave you here." And as soon as the words left my mouth, I felt something akin to remorse.

So that's all it took. Simple. While it takes nine months before a baby is ready to come into this world, it had taken me almost twenty years to reach this stage of enlightenment. They say it takes what it takes. I felt the lotus flower in my heart blooming. I'd come to comprehend how going forward there would be no benefit in denying the existence of my wise old Grandma, no use trying to figure her out.

At last, it seemed that while I hadn't found the answers to my quest, I'd finally lost the questions. I'd been through the process of a transformation, a human revolution. On this journey, I'd been looking for ways to ditch Grandma—finding love would have been the bonus or the reward for having put up with her my whole life. By accepting the gift of Grandma Phoebe, I'd found a way to treasure my gift. I'd started to breathe again during this expedition. But still on a quest to find love, I also had a new question to ask of the universe. What is my purpose?

CHAPTER 33

Layover in Paradise

With the freshly minted optimism I'd gained during my stay at the Society, and especially from Vihaan, and, of course before that, my travels with Swami Satchidinanda, I was ready to go home and practice co-existing with my dual consciousness. Grandma wanted to stay, but understood the pull for me to finally return to my family. But during my layover in Tokyo, the trajectory of my life would change forever.

As I waited to board my plane, I picked up a newspaper to catch up on what was going on at home, but Grandma wanted to talk, so I held the paper up close to my face.

"Thank you for the lovely trip, Anna."

"Yes, it's been quite a journey. I should be thanking you, Grandma. I definitely feel a transformation, like I've changed for the better. It's like I have some new tools to live in harmony with you. I might have learned how to handle you."

"I'm delighted."

"I said *might* have learned," I chuckled. "Time will tell if we can exist out in the real world."

"Darling, we've survived thus far."

"But I want to thrive."

I flipped through the paper. Back home, the National Women's Political Caucus, a grassroots organization established by women such as Betty Friedan, Shirley Chisholm, and Gloria Steinem, would focus on supporting women who sought offices at all levels of the government. Yes! We need more women in government. The voting age had been lowered from twenty-one to eighteen, which made sense—if you could get drafted at eighteen, then you should be able to vote. "Joy to the World" was the number one single. I read that Nixon had declared a war on drugs. I laughed at the irony when I read that Mick Jagger and Keith Richards were sentenced for two drug offenses. But then, my heart took a dive when I came across the caption: "Leader of Lazarus Rising Dead of an Overdose."

"Of all the gin joints in all the towns in all the world," I heard a man say.

By now my heart was in my throat. Rest in Peace, Dear John. I wiped my eyes before setting the paper down and looked up. His face looked familiar, but his uniform was the dead giveaway. United States Coast Guard. "Well, here's lookin' at you kid," I said. "Tommy, right? What are you doing here?"

"Just finished a tour of duty in Nam. Headed for some R & R and then I'll start my next tour in Hawaii."

"The most exotic place in the world."

"How about you?" he asked.

"I'm headed back to Los Angeles." I pointed to the empty seat next to me.

He sat. "Where've you been since that day I saved your life?"

"India, on a sort of self-reflecting journey." I peered into his eyes for emphasis.

"So now that you've seen how the other half lives, you can appreciate your life at home."

"Maybe, but I think I'd rather be heading to Hawaii like you."

"Well, why not? You seem like the kind of girl who would do that sort of thing."

"Do what?"

"Fly with the wind."

Hawaii did sound tempting. Just then there was an announcement. My flight to Los Angeles was delayed due to mechanical issues.

"There's your sign. Come with me." Tommy seemed sweet and with his deep-set blue eyes, ski-slope nose, and chiseled jawline—he even had one of those dimples in his chin. He was also pretty easy to look at, but what did I know about whom to trust?

I smiled. "It is a tempting idea."

"I'm sorry. I didn't mean to cross the line." He stretched out his long legs. "So, seriously, what were you doing in India?"

"Looking for peace."

"World peace would be nice."

"I was looking for inner peace."

"Yes, of course, it all starts there."

"This coming from a man who's just been fighting in Vietnam."

I walked over to the counter to find out when the mechanical issue would be fixed. Before the counterperson could tell me anything, the loud speaker announced the flight cancellation.

I changed my flight and ended up on my way to Oahu with Tommy.

CHAPTER 34

The Royal Hawaiian

The smell of sweet plumeria greeted us as soon as we landed in Hawaii. Our cab stopped in front of the big pink hotel I recognized as the Royal Hawaiian. I'd only seen pictures of it, but now up close and in person, it seemed even more grand. It was a honeymoon destination for those so inclined, like my sister Patty who talked about it and how it had been a dream. Too bad, as Mom put it, she'd put the cart before the horse as far as marriage went. Their only honeymoon celebration was in the hospital after she gave birth. The candy stripers had served up a nice dinner to the new parents, including a glass of Champagne.

I side-eyed Tommy and then turned to face him. "This is not part of my budget."

"Well, it's not part of mine, either, but I'll be living in the barracks soon enough, and for now I'm on R & R and we're gonna live it up. We'll pretend we're married, get a honeymoon suite." Off my face, he corrected himself. "With two beds."

"In a honeymoon suite?"

"You're right."

As it turned out, a room with a queen-sized bed and a sofa was more in his budget. At least it had a balcony facing the ocean.

"I'll take the sofa," he said.

"Are you sure?"

That night I heard screaming and bolted out of bed to run to his side. I nudged him to wake up. "It's okay. It's okay, Tommy." I turned on the table lamp. He stared at me with a look of confusion. "It's just a nightmare." His forehead felt clammy and cool. I brought him some water and a damp towel for his brow. No words exchanged, I wondered what might have happened to him in Vietnam, but I'd never know. I wouldn't press him. I cradled him like a baby until he fell back to sleep.

The nighttime trade winds blew all our troubles away. The next morning the same wind that had fanned the palm trees whispered good morning. Tommy didn't seem to remember having a nightmare; at least, he mentioned nothing. We spent the next couple days exploring the island and each other, nothing physical, though. First, we visited the Arizona Memorial and then the Polynesian Cultural Center.

We hiked up to Manoa Falls. As the falls washed over me, I wondered if he'd kiss me, but he didn't. Later, on the beach, I imagined that kiss in *From Here to Eternity*. Nope. Nada.

The next day, he did take my hand as we climbed to the top of Diamond Head. He inhaled. "Aloha." He turned to me. "'Alo' *in the presence of* and 'ha' *breath of life*." I did the same. "Aloha," I yelled, outstretching my arms.

That evening we went into the hotel bar and ordered a couple of Mai Tais, with umbrellas and enough garnish to make a fruit salad. The place got too loud. "You know we have the best view from our own balcony," Tommy said. *Now we're talking.* Up in the room, we walked out to the balcony and sat like a couple of old people on their silver wedding anniversary, talking about our families (I kept it short: parents, siblings, boring stuff. I didn't tell him how I'd been shortchanged in the childhood department or how my father had offed himself. His was the perfect family, a mother, a father, a younger brother and sister, a dog and a cat, and undoubtedly that proverbial white picket fence.) As I chewed on the cherry, he asked if I'd ever been in love. I spit the stem out over the rail. I thought I'd been in love. He said he had been until he received a Dear John letter. He stripped the pineapple from its rind and tossed the skin. He didn't go into detail except to say he was crushed. "Probably just puppy love," he added. We talked about the world, his views and mine, which so far seemed to be aligned. He asked more about my time on the road. I slurped through my straw before telling him about the band and then how I'd ended up in India.

"So, while I was over there dodging gunfire, you were singing Kumbaya around the campfire." I smiled at him, eyebrow raised, and he immediately apologized. I wondered about his time in Vietnam and whether he'd had to use a gun?

"I was mostly there for search and rescue."

I already knew he was a lifesaver at heart. I couldn't imagine him leaving behind his humanity, even in combat.

"But we also patrolled up and down the Mekong River delta and the coastline where we intercepted sampans, little flat boats that were transporting guns and ammunition. We actually lost quite a few of our people," he said, looking away. "So, unfortunately, I did have to fire my gun."

"Is that why you have the nightmares?"

I'd thrown him off guard. "Thank you for taking care of me last night," he said. So, he did remember. The memories would be something he would keep to himself; something he would want to protect me from. For now, I had my secrets, too.

"So now we're even," I said.

Was this the Mai Tai talking or was I falling for Tommy? Tall, fair-haired, and blue-eyed, he looked nothing like Elvis, Tony Curtis, or Paul McCartney. Besides truly caring for him, he made me feel safe; no need to weigh my thoughts or measure my words. I found more and more in common, or, rather, he had what I thought I wanted in life: a partner in love. But was this all happening too fast or maybe not fast enough? He hadn't even kissed me. Had I come here only to discover another River? Grandma had told me not to confuse lust for love. Trust me, there was no lust here. Maybe she should have warned me not to confuse someone caring for me for love–at least not that kind of love. It took my traveling to the other side of the world to learn that in the English language, there is only one word for 'love.' I learned that in Sanskrit there were ninety-six. The way Ruben cared for me or the way Vihaan took time to explain things was a different sort of love. In that moment, I realized theirs was a love like a father should love his daughter. I *loved* how I'd just come to understand that.

I loved watching the Adam's apple in Tommy's throat bob up and down as he gulped his drink. I loved watching him talk, using his hands, about nature and how there's a connection to the universe and how we share a consciousness with it. I smiled as he spoke, exposing his teeth, so straight now, after his parents had loved him enough to put braces on him to correct the huge gap as a child. My parents had done nothing to correct the gap between us.

"We need to coexist and honor nature," Tommy said. "Leave it a little better than how we found it."

"You don't sound like someone who'd up and join the military."

He shook his head. "I had no choice. My draft number was seven. My mother was Quaker so I could have been a conscientious objector, but instead I joined the Coast Guard never imagining I'd be sent to battle. Believe me, I'm not a fighter. I'm a lover."

I laughed, the drink coming out my nose. So far, I hadn't seen this side of him. He was gentle and kind, but Romeo he was not. He handed me a napkin.

"What? We do need to love one another." He grew serious. "The world is full of so much diversity. We can't just eliminate a whole group of people because we don't agree on everything."

Twirling my little cocktail umbrella, I liked him even more. I thought about what he said and what Swami had said about learning to live in harmony with my dual consciousness. Speaking of whom, I hadn't heard a peep out of Grandma during these past few days and honestly, I hadn't missed her. And then, I remembered how she said that when I found the right person, she'd keep out. Was Tommy the right person or just another man who cared? He'd been the perfect gentleman so far, like that Jimmy Stewart character in the movies. He'd taken the couch like he said, leaving me the bed.

I wouldn't ruin our friendship by making the first move. "I'd like to order another." I stuck the little umbrella behind my ear, feeling mellow around my new buddy.

"Sure, and how about some dinner?"

The next morning, we walked across the beach of Waikiki, me trying to keep up with his footprints in the sand. He wanted to teach me to surf. "It's a real thrill to experience a wave and then when you do, you'll want another. It's like an addiction."

The cloudless azure sky morning couldn't be more perfect as we lined up, the definition of line-up being, according to Tommy who liked teaching me things: taking into consideration the wind current, swell size and direction and other surfers vying for position, the position where you sit and wait. The water lay flat as an ironing board and so we sat waiting.

"Surfing teaches you to be patient. This is when I meditate." He closed his eyes. Serene-looking, a gentle giant, he had a nice profile and a strong chin. I didn't know if I could be as patient as him. Again, was he just another River? Sitting on my board, I closed my eyes, too. I thought about my conversations with my cousin Teddie about the "surfers" vs. the Mexicans. My surfer was nothing like the "surfers" she talked about.

"Paddle!" he yelled all of a sudden.

I paddled like a crazy windmill. A swell picked me and my board up as we slid down the face of a wave.

"Stand up!" he shouted.

I popped up into a stance and turned slightly to ride the wave in.

What a thrill!

"That was great!" Tommy yelled. "Wanna try it again?"

"Hell, yeah!"

* * *

That evening he had a surprise for me. This has to be it, I thought.

"Ever seen a green flash?" he asked, opening my door to the rental car.

I'd never even heard of one. I thought maybe it was a movie like *Flash Gordon's Trip to Mars*. He drove us to the west side of the island, removing his hands from the steering wheel to describe the spectacle I was about to see. "It's a meteorological phenomenon that occurs when the conditions are just right."

We arrived at a place called Sunset Beach. Tommy spread a blanket on the beach. "I promise, you'll be surprised." The sun floated above the horizon and I sensed a change in the temperature and an immeasurably subtle vibration on the shore. I waited as patiently as I could for the green surprise.

And then as the dazzling orb disappeared behind the skyline, I saw an emerald flash mushrooming in the space just vacated by the sun.

"This is incredible! I've never seen that before."

"It doesn't happen all the time, like I said, the conditions have to be just right."

"How did you know?"

"Magic," he said, "Just keep watching."

As I witnessed the spectacular colors in the wake of the flash, I felt his arm slip around my waist and it felt like all the colors of the rainbow had wrapped around me. Surrendering to the energy in his magnetic touch, I couldn't pull away, and then he found my lips and kissed me, finally. It tasted like rainbow sherbet: lemon, orange, strawberry, peach, and, of course, pineapple. But then he let go. "Oh, one more thing," he said, pulling away. He jumped up and ran back to his car. Awkward. What kind of kiss was that? I really liked him. I wanted to cry. Who am I with?

He returned with a picnic basket and pulled out a bottle of wine. "I wanted to toast to the end of a beautiful time with you." He opened the bottle.

I held up a hand. "None for me, please."

He looked crushed and confused, examining my eyes as if he were searching for someone lost at sea. Now that I'd found him, I knew I'd be lost without him.

"I'd like to enjoy this moment with a clear head. I've had the best time with you, Tommy." I needed to figure out my feelings and I didn't want alcohol to cloud my thinking or fool me into believing I was in love, especially with someone who wasn't going to love me back as more than just a friend. I needed to protect my heart and not get hurt again.

He didn't take his eyes off me as he set down the bottle and then pulled me in for a kiss, holding me as if he had multiple arms to clutch my whole body like an octopus, so tight like he didn't want to let me go. I could feel his heartbeat. I could sense the shift in the air between us, fate luring me off in an unknown direction. I didn't want this to end. I'd be on the plane tomorrow headed back to Los Angeles, to a life I had no clue about. I could see the changing colors of the horizon in his blue eyes, tearing up, and then a shadow fell over him as he looked at me. He got down on one knee. What's happening?

"Anna, I love you. Please, marry me?"

But we'd barely had our first kiss.

★ ★ ★

In the military, things happen fast. One must act quickly. Two weeks of R & R had flown by and the kiss, while pretty good, we'd still need to work on it. So, with no time to spare, I answered in the affirmative. "Hell, yeah!"

Was that too fast? "But what about a honeymoon?" I asked.

"I promise our life is going to be one long honeymoon."

The trip back to the base seemed like an eternity. I calmed my breathing and looked out the window, barely noticing the curtain of palm trees gilded by moonlight, the moon also spilling its light like a bucket of glittering diamonds across the water. The anticipation mounted like a tidal wave and as soon as we pulled into the parking lot of the Royal Hawaiian, we rushed into the elevator and made up for all the kisses that had been held back so far—one hundred percent better than that clumsy kiss on the beach. The door opened, slow as a yawn, and before he could unlock the door to our room, I'd pulled my sundress over my head. He fumbled with the key, kicking off his flip-flops as he pushed the door open and then he swooped me up and carried me over the threshold and headed toward the couch. "The bed!" I yelled. He stomped out of his shorts and laid me on the bed. Hungry for his kisses, I grabbed the nape of his neck, pulling him close. He practically devoured me from my lips to my throat to my hardened nipples, chafed from surfing, and finally my inner thighs. I reached down to feel his erection, hard as a surfboard, I thought with a giggle, guiding him inside. Together we let go to enjoy the tsunami that had built up. The most exhilarating experience of my life, when we finished, I wanted to do it all over again.

We lay in bed, spent. "You know my mother always said, 'why buy the cow when you can get the milk for free.'"

"In the military, nothing is free," Tommy answered.

"Are you sure you still want to marry me?" I asked.

"Hell, yeah!"

★ ★ ★

I called home to let Mom know I got married. It was a bigger shock to her than the idea of me going to India, which I'd tried to explain was only because I thought I might finally find a way to get rid of Grandma. "Just ignore her," Mom used to say.

And as a matter of fact, Grandma had been pretty quiet during my time in India and most especially during my time with Tommy. Was this a sign that she thought I was in good hands?

"And I'm moving to Hawaii." I told my mother.

"Well, I can't stop you. Have a nice life."

CHAPTER 35

Life and Death

Perhaps as a way to prepare me for a life of spinsterhood, my mother told me stories about the old country and how the saddest day was when a girl got married and, after that, there were no guarantees it would get better. The day I married Tommy was the first best day of my life, and after that, it only got better and better, one good wave after the other. We spent the next three years in Hawaii in military housing, me adjusting to marriage and easing into a new routine. Tommy got assigned to the search and rescue station in Honolulu, on duty two days and two days off. I got my GED and then signed up for classes at the local college studying music. During his time off, we surfed and soaked up the sun. We visited all the other islands, hiked waterfalls and biked to volcano peaks. We cooked at home and read poetry, discussed world history, listened to music and danced. I even played my guitar and started writing music again.

★ ★ ★

1974: After our time in Hawaii, Tommy got promoted and we were transferred to Terminal Island in San Pedro, California. When I walked into our new house at Fort MacArthur, I broke down and cried when I saw the piano dwarfing the room.

"I figured, now that we're closer to Los Angeles, you might want to get back to your music, seriously. Maybe record some stuff." He then handed me a copy of the *Rolling Stone* magazine. The issue that came out the time John had died. "I found it packed away with your sheet music."

I recognized my face behind John and the rest of the Lazarus band. Tommy read out loud: "The last two songs on the album *Bumpy Roads* were recorded entirely in the studio and are nonetheless the most accurate reproduction of the band's acclaimed live performances. Years later and fans are still talking about Anna LeMar's virtuoso piano boogie which dominates the album giving it a unique sound."

Tommy knew my dreams even if I didn't. He knew I needed to make music. While he was out to sea, my music kept me company. I found myself staying up late into the night and wasted no time filling every moment composing. Sometimes, I'd even forget to eat or get out of my pajamas. Around the time I finally had some music ready to record, Tommy got promoted to BM1 and spent more time ashore. I grew comfortable in our new rhythm, remembering to change into something nice, brush my teeth, and comb my hair before he came home. I looked forward to dinners with him seated across the table from me, sharing my lyrics and his sea stories, getting lost in his loving eyes. Getting lost in my music, life seemed perfectly harmonious.

And then a couple of years later, as careful as I thought I'd been, I found myself pregnant. I didn't know what to do. We'd talked about how I didn't think I'd be a good mother, and how I wanted to devote myself to my music career and how I didn't think it was right to bring a child into this crazy world, but now I couldn't keep it from him. Our relationship had been built on trust and honesty—except for the part about my dual consciousness, the real reason I didn't want children. It was the part of me still connected to the past called Grandma Phoebe, pretty much fifty percent of me. But, other than that, I'd been pretty forthright. Besides, it had been quite some time since Grandma had popped in, years as a matter of fact.

I hadn't found the right time yet to tell him about her. Ever since my father died, she hadn't pushed me so much or pressed me to go home. There was no one for her there anymore. Everyone she'd loved, besides my siblings and me, dwelled somewhere on the other side, somewhere Tibetens called the perfect realm of Amitabha. But now something had been reawakened and I feared this baby might give her a new purpose in this life. I wondered whether in good consciousness I should keep it. And sure enough, Grandma came back.

"Darling, this is thrilling news," she said in a blinding color of sunshine. "You must tell Thomas. I promise everything is going to be fine."

She hadn't wanted anything or anyone getting in the way of her first love, music. I thought about all of the tragedies that ensued once she let anyone else in. Thanks to Grandma, I'd never known what I was passionate about. But, ironically, on my journey to rid myself of her, I'd discovered that I hungered for more than one thing.

Grandma tried to assure me she'd have no part in raising our child. "Darling, on our journey together, believe me, I learned so much. I've made so many mistakes, things I cannot undo. I wanted to shape you. But time and time again, in spite of everything, you proved your strength, your self-will, your perfect heart. I can see how we are both so consumed by the need to feel love, the need to love and be loved back. I would tell myself I was helping, but I learned that it was all about me. I realize that now. You see, consciousness without love becomes need and dependency and control all in the name of love. True love comes with freedom or liberation without any condition, without any hand asking for something back."

"You mean with no strings attached. You mean you shouldn't have acted like my puppet master."

"There is nothing more I can do from here; nothing I will do."

"If only it were as easy as cutting the strings."

"You must learn to trust me."

Maybe, I should have a little faith? She'd proven herself to me by staying out of my relationship with Tommy. She seemed to have evolved. Or perhaps we'd gotten to the point where she'd merely become so familiar to me that I didn't notice her anymore.

"Only you and Thomas can shape the baby now."

"What about my father?"

"His death was by suicide and therefore not a perfect death," Grandma said. "He cannot transfer. Do not worry."

I thought about it, a bit relieved that my father had ended the cycle, but then what about others just lurking out there in that other realm?

"All will be fine. Tell your husband about the baby, so that you can both start loving him unconditionally."

I had no choice except to trust her. "I do appreciate your leaving me alone all this time, but I beg of you to keep out of this."

"And I appreciate you staying out of trouble, darling."

Now, I couldn't wait to give him the news, but Tommy and his crew didn't make it back to port that night. I called the station to learn that it had been all hands on deck and Tommy and his crew had responded. That was nothing unusual. As the wife of a Coast Guardsman, I knew the drill.

By the next day, I felt pregnant. I didn't want to be a single mom.

★ ★ ★

"An oil tanker exploded in the harbor and then split in half," Tommy said, late the next day, as he walked through the door, exhausted but still running on adrenaline. "We rescued nineteen crewmembers and fought the fire until we finally abandoned it. It sank."

I heaved a sigh of relief. "I'm pregnant."

He sank to his knees and kissed my stomach.

He was as excited as I was scared. "Of course, we're keeping it." He looked at me as if I'd grown a third eye. "Why would you even think differently?" He pulled me in for a hug.

I shrugged. I prayed our baby wouldn't be born different, like me. I wanted it to be born "normal" like Tommy. I wasn't sure how far along I was, but the next morning I woke up nauseated, like the cells were dividing and crashing into each other. My breasts hurt as if they'd been used as punching bags.

★ ★ ★

Unprepared to visit the family, my hormones weren't ready to face Mom. Even though marrying Tommy was the best thing that had ever happened to me, and now that we were having a baby, she wouldn't be happy because I wasn't going to bring him up in the church. I dialed up my mother, expecting to hear how she didn't approve, not because Tommy wasn't a nice Mexican boy, but because she'd never forgive me for not marrying in the Catholic Church. She picked up on the first ring.

"Oh, this makes me so happy!" She couldn't stop crying.

★ ★ ★

A couple months later, I got a note from River that sent my spirits soaring to the moon. I'd caught him up on my life in a letter the length of *War and Peace*. His correspondence wasn't as long, but packed full of love.

My Dearest Honey Moon,

You have no idea how happy I am to hear from you. I'm thrilled you've found the love you've been looking for and have created a new love from that. A baby! Congratulations! Please do tell me more about this man!

As for me, it turns out I'm of Haitian descent. My grann is from Haiti and she's teaching me French. I'm learning so much about my culture. It seems I'm related to just about everyone down here. New Orleans is wild and like I said before, it's a mecca for people like me..

I got this new book by Ishmael Reed called 'Mumbo Jumbo.' It's about the spread of this dancing plague which is joyful and undeniably Black like me. You know how I love to dance! Anyway, I had to laugh when I opened up to the page and read his definition of 'Mumbo Jumbo' which is Mandingo 'for magician who makes the troubled spirits of ancestors go away. Grandmother, go away! I got the chills. To think the answers to your quest might be in this little book. I've just started it, so I'll let you know how it all works out.

Speaking of grandmothers, how is old Grandma Phoebe behaving nowadays? She must be (I'd say in heaven, but we know better) delighted she's going to be a great grann. Tell her au revoir for me. Well, I must run (I have a date with my Mandingo warrior. Details to follow.). I love you to the Honey Moon and back.

câlins et bisous, River

I'd never learn about his Mandingo Warrior nor how his book would turn out.

CHAPTER 36

1977: Dear Baby,

The time is getting closer. You're about six months along, the size of a peanut. Right about now, you can hear the sound of my heartbeat and my voice. Your Daddy likes to put his lips up to my stomach and talk to you. You've been kicking. The time is getting close for you to be in the world with us.

A story must begin somewhere and I want you to know yours begins in love. Your daddy and are so excited to meet you.

You might hear some things from my family or others who might have wondered at times about my state of mind, but I want you to hear them from me, or if all else fails, at least read them from me.

As you get old enough to understand, I'll share my story with you, rather your Great Grandma Phoebe's and mine. But for now, just know that I love you to the honey moon and back and more than all the stardust in the galaxy.

We are so excited to meet you. I promise to be the best mama I can.

*I'm feeling a little tired now, but will write some more later,
my little love . . .*

* * *

A couple of months later and eight months pregnant, I felt
the weight of a nation pushing down on my pelvic area. My
hands and feet were as swollen as pork sausages. I put my feet
up to make a call. Tommy had been transferred again this time
to the Channel Islands station on an eighty-two-foot patrol boat.
I wanted to catch River up and give him my new address in
Oxnard. After the second ring, a man picked up the phone.

"Hello, is River there?"

"No, I'm his friend, Etienne. Who is this?"

I smiled wondering if he was the Mandingo Warrior. "Anna,
uh, Honey Moon."

"Oh, dear. I'm so sorry to have to break the news. River is
dead."

It felt as if I lay on a bed of needles. I cradled my stomach.
Sitting up too soon, the pain grew sharper. How could this be? I'd
been thinking about him so much lately. I swear I was just getting
ready to call as soon as I had a minute, just like the time I was
going to call my father as soon as I got the chance, or rather, the
courage. River had died of an unknown virus like pneumonia,
Etienne said. He didn't want anyone to know. He'd been sick for
a while, baffling all of his doctors. Some strange pandemic. Like
the dancing pandemic he'd mentioned? If he were still here, he'd
laugh. I burst into tears.

There'd been a small service in New Orleans, including his
mother from Iowa and his father Marvin. Etienne told me River
had written me a letter but never got the chance to finish it.

"Do you know what it said?" I asked through a deluge of tears.

"I have it right here." Etienne cleared his throat.

My Darling Honey Moon.

I hope this finds you well. Please know that I have loved you since the beginning of time and will continue to love you to the Honey Moon and back.

I'm so proud of you! You're probably the most courageous-girl-turned woman I've ever met, an inspiration, and fearless truth seeker. Your search has brought you to the answers you were looking for. Our paths crossed for a reason and I know they will cross again. At this time, because of what you've taught me, I'm preparing to transfer my consciousness over to that perfect realm of Amitabha . . .

"He didn't finish the letter," Etienne said. "I came across it inside a little book on his nightstand, next to his pills."

"What book?"

"*Tibetan Book of the Dead.*"

I remembered when he borrowed the book from Mother Mary's room back in the Haight. I'd never be the same and it would take time for me to process the loss of my soul brother, all the while wondering whether or not he'd been able to transfer over successfully.

CHAPTER 37

Get Me to an Ashram

The news of River's death coincided with our move. I hadn't been paying attention to my health and then when I learned that Alice Coltrane now "Turiyasangitananda" had opened an ashram over the hill in Calabasas, I thought it might be good to visit in order to come to terms with his death. I wanted to get myself centered and healthy in body and spirit, especially, before visiting my family and certainly before the baby arrived. Tommy dropped me off.

The retreat in the Santa Monica Mountains was magnificent and it was wonderful to see Alice again.

After dinner, I took a walk under a star-filled night beneath the light of a waxing harvest moon, serenaded by the music of crickets chirping and coyotes howling in the distance. I felt a connection to nature again. A star shot across the sky. We are all light. River you will always be a light in my life. A light breeze bussed my cheek. You're walking with me now, I feel you. I touched my face and then tightened my shawl around my shoulders. I experienced the same peace I'd felt in India. Even though I carried the extra weight of a baby, I stepped lighter. Everything was going to be okay. I'd write a song about this night.

* * *

Heading home, the inside of the car roasted hotter than a bus in India. Growing drowsy, I thought about how happy it made me to hear Alice sing again and it took me back to the first time I heard her in New York. I couldn't wait to get home to my piano. Wouldn't it be nice to have a place in my home, like Grandma's chamber room, where I could raise our child and still play my music? I hummed a tune I'd put to my new lyrics. *Let love be the answer.* Soon, I could no longer keep my eyes open and dozed.

I awoke and put my hand down to rub my stomach. The baby had been flipping around.

"Look, Anna," Tommy said, hooking a thumb across my brow, "Griffith Park." It didn't register that we were headed south instead of back home. "Isn't that where you hung out as a kid?"

I'd done a good job keeping some things from him, but the time would come when I'd have to come clean about what happened that fateful Easter after we got home from the park.

"Someday, we'll bring Junior to ride that carousel." He rested his hand over mine.

I turned to face him, and he looked blurry. I blinked and rubbed my eyes with the back of my hand. "Junior, I don't like that name. Besides, what if he's a girl. It's probably about time to nail down a name?"

"Sure, what do you have in mind this week?"

I'd gone back and forth on a couple of names, but finally I couldn't waste any more time. "Dylan."

"After Thomas or Bob?"

"It actually means son of the sea."

"And if it's a daughter?"

"It fits for either a boy or a girl."

"Perfect.

Dylan continued squirming as we sped along the 101 Freeway. Tommy drummed his left hand on the steering wheel and then merged onto the Glendale Freeway which confused me. We, the baby and I, began to get a little agitated. I squirmed, trying to adjust myself in my seat, rolling onto my right butt cheek, perching an elbow on the armrest. And then I felt something, like cool silk being pulled across my tongue out my mouth, like one of those magic tricks.

"Turn right on Cañada," Grandma said in her low raspy voice. She was back. Please don't. Oh, no. Not now. "And then after a couple miles, you'll turn right on—" she said, and I slapped my hand over my mouth before she could finish. I stared straight ahead. Even though Tommy had always been curious about the house I grew up in, I'd done a good job avoiding the subject.

"Come on. Don't you want to go see it?" He scratched his head.

I shook mine and it rattled my brain. I knew if I opened my mouth, Grandma would take over. Besides, I didn't want to visit the place where my grandmother died, where my grandfather was buried in the back yard. I didn't want to visit the place where my father blew his brains out. But I couldn't share any of this with my husband. I didn't want to visit the place I ended up running away from after I'd stabbed my father.

"Well, I do. I'm curious. I want to see this haunted house where you grew up."

It wasn't haunted. The people inside were.

CHAPTER 38

And Still Those Voices

And within moments, he'd taken the next offramp. We were cruising up Cañada Boulevard, I clutched the armrest as the Eagles' "Hotel California" came on the radio. Well, if that isn't just a little too on the nose, I thought, as Tommy sang along. He had no idea what bats in the cave had been disturbed. He turned to me and like an orchestra leader, waved an imaginary baton, encouraging me to sing along. As a US Coastie, he especially loved the part of the song where it mentioned calling up the captain.

And then before I knew it, he'd turned left onto Cañada Boulevard and we were parked outside my childhood home, the institution I'd run away from years ago. Tommy continued to sing about the voices calling from far away.

Welcome to the Hotel LeMar. My family had lost the house. So, there was no chance of them ever going back. Josie and Mom were now living with my Uncle Teodoro, Aunt Othelia, and my cousins who'd eventually been moved out of Campo Colorado to an apartment. I wished I could help out, at least financially, but that was not possible for the time being. Michael lived up at Stanford now on a scholarship studying physics, a complete shocker for someone whose father told him he wouldn't amount to anything. Michael always wanted to be a physicist and study the universe like the dad in *A Wrinkle in Time*. Maggie had taken a job in Arizona as an anchor for the local news station. Patty eventually married Alan and had two more kids.

Tommy reached out to put his hand on my thigh. "You okay?"

I managed to shake my head. No, I'm not okay. It's hot and humid. The car had no air conditioning and it's boiling hot as hell inside. I felt as if I were drowning in molten ash and the deeper I sank, the more I'm lost myself and all sense of time and place. All of my faculties seemed to be washing away. I'd lost the peaceful feeling I'd found back at the ashram. My heart clanged in my chest and I felt queasy. The nagging pain in my right side grew stronger. I rolled onto my left butt cheek trying to get comfortable.

I thought about how the song said you could check out but you could never leave.

I squeezed my eyes shut to try and block the memory of stabbing my father before I ran away—to try and block the image of the carpet stains up in his room.

A blast of citrus-scented Santa Anas came rushing into the car. I felt Tommy reaching over to roll down my window. The radio was off. I took a deep breath, sensing something familiar. "Oh, darling, I can just imagine the remnant fragrance of orange blossoms in bloom, the eucalyptus and freshly cut grass," Grandma whispered. Perched between the telephone poles like music notes on wires were warbling song sparrows and cooing doves. The starlings serenaded each other up in the sycamores. At once, my senses were no longer numb. My ears were no longer blind as they pricked up like a cat on a bird scent.

"Is that better?" he asked. "You look a little green around the gills."

I turned away from him. One eye open, I peeked out the window. The place had been spiffed up by the new owners, a Mr. and Mrs. Jones, Maggie told me. They'd bought it from the attorney Mom hired to help her save the place. Lousy attorney.

And then I heard piano music wafting out from inside the house. I closed my eyes, straining to listen as the music grew louder, somewhere back in the cobwebs of my childhood, in the mustiness of my mind, I could remember hearing those same notes.

There was a knock on the roof of the car. I sprung open the shades of my eyes to see a man. "Can I help you?"

"We're sorry," Tom said, leaning over me to talk to the man standing just outside my window. "My wife's feeling a little queasy. We pulled over."

Standing on a river rock embankment bordering the property, the man stooped slightly, hands on the thighs of his creased khakis. He was wearing a crisp, pinstriped shirt with one of those ponies on the chest pocket. He peered into the VW. "Oh, I see," he said, obviously noticing my huge stomach as he ran a hand through his silver hair, groomed like one of those TV preachers. He took a step back. "You're not in labor, are you?"

"No, no. It's been a long day," Tommy responded. "We were just passing through. She actually grew up here."

That's not true. Any growing up I did happened after I ran away from this place.

The man stood straight, placing one hand on his hip and bringing the other to his mouth. "Here? So, you're a LeMar?"

"Her name is Phoebe Anna Le—" Tom answered for me, as if I were a child. I was getting annoyed. I'm a grown-ass woman for God's sake—with a child on the way.

"It was," I said. I changed my name long ago. "Phoebe was my grandmother's name. I go by my middle name, Anna, and this is my husband, Thomas."

"My name is Roy Jones. But everybody calls me Roy. My wife Judy and I bought the place years ago. "I'm so sorry about your family. Such a tragedy."

"Yeah, well I'd say the real tragedy was how he took the family for all it's worth," Grandma whispered. Mom told me how he stole the house out from underneath us. I'd been used to losing things all of my life, but I often wondered how he was able to steal our house.

Roy appeared to be nice enough though, like a law-abiding citizen and a decent Christian. I looked into his eyes. He seemed sincere.

"Yes, it was *tragic*." I emphasized the word, peering at Roy just to let him know I was onto him and his evil ways. I knew what he did, except, I didn't just yet.

"Are there really ghosts?" Tommy asked and the music seemed to grow louder.

Roy chuckled. "Well, if there are, they're friendly enough. We love it here."

I couldn't help but choke back tears. Despite everything that was wrong about the place, it had been a magical place to grow up. Only later had I learned how the place lost its charm.

"Say, would you like to come in and take a look around," Roy asked, too eagerly. "Judy is off at her Bible study, so I've got this time on my hands and you know what they say about idle hands?"

"They steal from innocent families?" Grandma said and I saw red.

"Pardon me?" Roy said.

"Stop!"

Tommy clicked off the engine, the keys already rattling in his hand. I heard piano music coming from inside the house. Beethoven's *Pastoral*.

And when the music didn't lure me in, Grandma nudged in yellow. "Darling, it will be all right."

"Of course it will," Tommy said and ran around to help me out of the car.

"Who's playing the piano?" I asked, hobbling up the walkway.

Roy turned, peering at me. "What piano?"

I entered the room and my whole childhood flooded back.

Heading toward the living room, my fingers tingled as an unanticipated joy washed over me. I couldn't wait to see her again. But when we got to what used to be the chamber room in the back part of the house where it overlooked the creek, I gasped, chills waltzing up my arms. "Where's Cleopatra?"

"Who?" Mr. Jones asked.

"The piano." My legs buckled and Tom cradled my elbow to hold me up.

"You okay? Here," Mr. Jones offered, pulling out one of the chairs from the dining set that used to be on the other side of the house. "I'll go get you some water."

Sitting down, I clutched the sides of the chair, the mohair tickling the backs of my thighs, and I remember how much I hated this scratchy sensation as a girl like a sunburn. Mr. Jones came back with a glass of water.

"Thank you." I took a sip. "This used to be the piano room," I said, pointing. "The dining room used to be over there, off the foyer."

"Yes, but with no piano—it was a nine-foot Steinway you know, very valuable," Mr. Jones said with a grin. "It was supposed to come with the house when we bought it." He's still beaming, exposing a set of straight ivory teeth. "You wouldn't by any chance know what happened to it—the piano? It was worth more than the house."

He closed the lid on his smile as I shook my head. "I have no idea."

"Anyway, what's a chamber room with no piano?" he said. "So, we turned it into the dining room. Other than that, we really haven't changed a thing."

"Oh." I swear I heard the music. Or was I merely remembering it. My fingers tingled.

"Feeling better, honey?" Tommy asked.

I closed my eyes to ward off one of the eminent headaches that had traveled with me since childhood. And now that I was pregnant and full of strange hormones, they'd practically taken up full-time residence.

"Yes, just give me a minute," I said, thumbing my temples as if that had ever prevented the aura and then the blackness, like a curtain going down on the stage of my brain.

"Migraine?" Tommy asked.

I'd lost my ability to speak. I held up a finger, nodding would hurt too much. I felt nauseated.

"She gets them all the time." I felt his soothing arm wrap around me.

"My wife used to get them, too," Mr. Jones said. "Best thing for her was to be in a dark, quiet place."

I wanted to resist and run, but the tiny lightning-like zigzags were flashing the warning across the back of my eyelids.

"Why don't you rest over here for a bit?" I heard Mr. Jones say.

I pried open my eyes and my vision became limited to only what I could see through the shattered glass of my brain. I reached out for Tommy's hand and he led me to what felt like a small sofa. As I lay down, I could hear the sound of the drapery rings scraping across the iron rods and then everything got darker.

"While she's resting," I heard Mr. Jones say, "I'll show you the grounds outside."

Their voices faded away and everything went black as pitch. But then, in the distance of my mind, a pinpoint of light appeared, slowly growing larger until a tiny bubble came floating up from somewhere deep down in the recesses of my being. And then, within the bubble like a snow globe, a brilliant golden piano sparkled onto center stage.

CHAPTER 39

Cleopatra

As Anna rests, I must break my promise to let her tell her own story, especially about her baby, but it's only to fill in another breach in time. I can no longer remain silent.

With one eye open, I see Thomas returning from his tour outside with Mr. Jones. I call out to him as he tiptoes past, but it's as if he's gone tone deaf while taking in the grandeur of this home. So, throat cleared, I yell, "Thomas, darling, do you not hear me?" He continues to take in his surroundings as he scans the chamber room. "Thomas, darling, it's me Phoebe, Anna's Grandmother."

He shudders, pivoting toward me, eyes wide as the two moons of Mars. "Anna, you're up," he says, narrowing his eyes, cocking his head.

"It's me, Phoebe," I respond. "Didn't you simply adore the grounds outside? And, what about the hybrid orange-lemon tree?"

He nods slowly, understandably confused.

"Wesley grafted it," I say, failing to mention his ashes are also buried under the tree. "Isn't it all simply splendid?" Thomas is taken by the hand and led into what used to be the chamber room. "I remember how this room had become the center of everyone's world, a place so many found solace, if only for an evening."

"Anna, why do you sound weird?"

His hand is let go and her fingers trill across the surface of the polished dining room table. "Oh, the concerts we would have here. Through the table's luster, one can almost see this home filled with all of the movers and shakers of Los Angeles. Right here where the dining table is once stood the most magnificent body of craftsmanship, all nine feet of the regal Steinway—Cleopatra, I'd named her."

Thomas looks from me to the space where Cleopatra once stood.

"I remember the day Wesley surprised me with her," I say, as the memory, muffled for years, plays out like a sonorous sweet melody. "I hadn't owned one this grand ever. It was 1918 and I'd just returned from a year overseas touring Europe with the famous composer Charles Wakefield Cadman."

"1918?" Thomas asks. "Charles Wakefield Cadman?"

"You know, "The Land of the Sky Blue Water." Founder of the Hollywood Bowl. In any event, prior to that, during a break from the tour—a honeymoon, actually," I say, tittering now as I remember, "after all, we were still newlyweds before I left. Oh, I do feel like I'm blushing. Darling, is my face red?"

"Not really. As a matter of fact, you look pale," he says, staring at us now quite tentative, like he was on his first date—a date during which, by the way, I did excuse myself. After all, what grandmother wants to see their granddaughter naked with some naked fellow? During the last several years, I have tried to give them their space—to mind my own business—but it's been a lifetime since I've visited my home and now as the scent from the gardenias fills the room as they soak in the shallow crystal dish I kept on the piano, I can see my golden-haired boy pushing up on his toes from underneath.

"Why do you sound so strange?" Thomas asks.

I hear the familiar creak of the kitchen door swinging open. "Oh, you're awake," Mr. Jones says, walking in from the kitchen holding out a glass of water.

"Yes, thank you, you're such a dear," I say as Mr. Jones sets a glass down on a coaster.

"I was just telling Thomas about the honeymoon and how this home came to be."

"This home?" Mr. Jones asks.

"Anyhow, it was in Normandy where I immediately fell in love with the architecture of the *Château d'Ételan*, the castle where we stayed one summer. Situated on a site overlooking the river Seine, it was originally designed as a castle where kings and queens, even the Medici stayed."

Thomas and Roy exchange looks.

"Finally, the tour ended and I returned home to my beloved where he wasted no time driving me here to Woodside. Goodness was I surprised to see it was no longer just a vacant piece of land. Except for the smaller size chateau, of course, the gargoyles and a few other flamboyant touches, you'd never know we weren't in Normandy. Out front, an emerald front lawn rolled gently all the way down to the creek that trickled through the property. My darling had built me a palace, a peaceful place I never wanted to leave."

"Anna, you're scaring me."

"Darling, I told you I'm Phoebe."

Shoving his hands into his vest pockets, Roy rocks back on his heels, an invitation for me to tell him more.

"It's so wonderful to see how you've kept—how you've managed to care for much of the original furnishings." Her hand taps the surface of the table. "I wonder how it's come to be that Mr. Jones owns my house. As I was saying, Wesley carried me across the threshold into the foyer. He then took my hand and led me through this home filled with antiques bought at auction at Christie's in London. The royal blue velvet drapery matched the chairs in the dining set. You know, this set had been in the Normandy castle and was rumored to have been given as a wedding gift to King Luis XII by Henry VIII after he'd arranged the marriage of his sister Mary Tudor."

"This home?" Mr. Jones does not break his eager smile. "I did not know that."

"And then as we entered the chamber room, I remembered how he caught me as I collapsed with emotion. Standing there, in the center of the room, all regal, shiny and black, stood a nine-foot Steinway."

"The piano was worth more than this house," Mr. Jones responds, and I can almost see him calculate its worth. "And you have no idea what happened to it?"

"Darling, can you hear the music? Can you feel the joy?" Tell me again, Mr. Jones, how you came to steal this house?"

★ ★ ★

The baby kicked rhythmically to Beethoven's "*Für* Elise," but when I opened my eyes, I saw no piano. The baby had stopped kicking. Outside, the watery shadows of the sycamores dissipated as the sun set over the Verdugo's. The air in the house had cooled and mixed with the sweet smoky fireplace remnants, the same fragrance I remembered as the fire crackled in the fireplace, as my sisters danced from flower to flower across the Oriental rug, while I played piano. Moonlight now filled the room like a bathtub; it felt as if the moon might be tugging me home.

"Anna, are you okay?" Tommy asked, bending slightly.

It's late. Tommy, a silhouette tall as a slender pine, stood next to me and I could barely make out his curious face. In the soft light, I thought he could have been Wesley, but I realized I'd never met my grandfather. I was confused.

"Feeling any better?" Tommy asked.

I nodded as Mr. Jones had turned on a Tiffany lamp and then I looked up to see both men staring at me as if I were some sort of bloated goldfish floating around in a bowl. I wiped the drool from my mouth. Tommy's mouth, which in the past had been generous and kind, now slashed across his face in a single straight line.

"What do you mean you'll haunt me?" Mr. Jones asked.

"What?" I asked, mind reeling.

"And who is Wesley?" Tom asked.

Oh shit. Wesley? What have I said? Or worse, what has Mrs. Buttinsky been saying? Every cell in my body woke up to sound off alarms. Sensing Grandma wanted to speak again, I clamped my jaw shut. It hurt me to see Tommy, whose career had been to rescue people, looking so helpless.

Mr. Jones pulled up a chair as if preparing for episode two of the Phoebe Masterpiece Theater. "It's interesting the things you were saying about this house. Like how Dr. Wesley LeMar had been murdered and how you'd been left to fight everyone off to save this place and raise your son."

I said all that?

"Anna, why am I just now hearing about this?" Tommy asked. "Who is this Wesley character?"

I didn't know how to respond. I'd never found the right time to share about all the madness, the suicides and the murder. When would the time be right? But then with the baby coming, I'd felt the pressure of revealing a little here and there about my background and so then that's when Grandma took it as an invitation to draw Tommy a fuckin' roadmap to this crazy house.

"Wesley was my grandfather," I said, scooting toward the edge of the sofa, so ready to get out of there, but then a cramp seized me back.

"Why yes, Phoebe was his wife—your grandmother." Mr. Jones seemed excited to connect the dots.

I felt Tommy's eyes sear into me as I nodded, puffing little short breaths.

"Are you okay?"

I clenched my fists when I felt Grandma wanting to speak, so I offered up just a little more information, talking over her, hoping to keep her stifled. "He's buried out in the back yard under the citrus tree."

"What the hell?" Tommy said, a little louder.

Mr. Jones, eyes wide as grapefruits, leaned in.

"At least his ashes are," I responded, holding my breath.

"You don't say," Mr. Jones said. "I read he was buried at Glendale Griffith Memorial."

Grandma scratched her way up my throat. "He was. After seven long years of probate, I had his ashes brought home. It's where he wanted to be buried—at the home he'd built—a place where he thought he'd remain close to me."

I felt a strong kick and clutched my stomach. "Tommy, take me home now!"

"But this is our home," said the prodigal voice skipping up my esophagus. There'd be no shutting her up now. "Darlings, I'd like to stay a little longer."

"Are you sure you're okay?" Tommy asked.

My heart thudded. Grandma was back and with the new baby coming, I panicked. How could I be a good mother with her around? I needed to calm down and take back control of my faculties, something I'd been unable to do, especially in this environment.

"Let me bring you some more water," Mr. Jones said, disappearing into the kitchen.

"What happened to your grandfather?" Tommy asked.

"George killed him," Grandma said.

And finally, she admitted it.

"I didn't know anything at the time. I swear on a stack of Bibles. He stole everything from me, my dear Wesley, the relationship I should have had with my son, my music—everything except this house. And now this man, Mr. Jones—take, take, take! It's all men have done to me and I'm going to get back what's mine! And then, Anna, you mustn't allow anyone to take from you ever again."

"Anna, what are you talking about?" Tommy said.

I pushed up to my feet and my water broke all over Mr. Jones's—Grandma's—damask sofa. "Tommy! We need to get out of here. Now!" I yelled as the baby kicked harder. Seizing up with another cramp, I realized the last one happened maybe a minute ago. No, this can't be. I won't have the baby in this house!

★ ★ ★

I sunk in and out of consciousness in the ambulance ride over to the hospital. "We're losing her," someone screamed over the sirens blaring down Verdugo Boulevard. And then the last thing I heard was Tommy yelling, "Oh, God, no! Anna, please hang on. Please don't let her die!"

★ ★ ★

I don't want to die. I'm running through the park. I'm out of breath. Now, I'm drifting down the creek like a little leaf until I come to the ocean. *Listen to the orchestra of the ocean*, Grandma shouts over the sonar whistle of a dolphin, and the low groan clicking of a whale. The crash of waves, like kettledrums smashing over my head, and soon I can hear the fish humming on the ocean floor. I sit and cross my legs to listen to the harps and sounds of India, to Alice Coltrane's music. My own music floods my ears, rock'n'roll and then a child's lullaby.

I bob to the surface and above the sounds of waves crashing, I hear what she hears as I struggle to hang onto my own thoughts and separate myself from Grandma.

And then in the midst, I hear her at the piano. The music is accompanied by flutes and oboes, horns and trumpets, timpani and cymbals. Cellos and sounds of violins fill my ears with a fortissimo in D minor. "Isn't this glorious, Anna?" I fly off the horizon, until I reach that space in between the two worlds, that place full of light. That pure place called Amitabha; the place where I've come without my ego, where you do not return to the circle of life. I feel such joy. And then a suction and I see her face and the ancestors who've gone before me. I'm not scared. I want to stay in this pure place. I see my father and I don't hate him. Grandma takes my father's hand and floats toward her place in front of a giant orchestra filled with ancestors from generations. I take a seat at the giant piano, but I don't want to be a part of her ensemble. And yet, I don't want to leave. This is the most wonderful feeling of my life. But this isn't my life. This is my death, Grandma's death.

I can hear Tommy yelling in the distance, "Anna, please come back! I need you."

I feel his kiss on my lips, so warm and powerful, and then I'm back in my childhood home, splashing in the creek, playing with my siblings, playing my music. And then from this perspective, I see all the beauty in my life, all the happiness I've been searching for only to discover there is nothing greater than finding love.

My world is a mirror magnifying my light, overflowing with the love I've been searching for my whole life.

Finally, I've come to understand all of this. Please, don't let it be too late.

I hear a baby crying. And still her voice, but now it's from somewhere outside my head, "Darling, go home. Dylan needs you."

CHAPTER 40

Love, Mom

1977: Dear Dylan,

As I wrote before, a story must begin somewhere. But it doesn't have to end. Mine began long before I stabbed my father, long before I died on the way to the hospital.

I remember praying, 'Please God, I don't want to die. Please, I just need more time.' I can tell you, as you die, it isn't only your life you see flashing before your eyes, your regrets will haunt you during your final brief period of time. And, in the moments I had left, my life played out from my beginning. Memories slowly filled the spaces where blood had vacated; where the cracks and fissures had broken away.

My greatest regret was that I'd never get to meet you, Dylan. My heart spilled over with so many things I wanted to say to your father. I didn't get to say goodbye. I hadn't told him that day how much I love him. I hadn't said goodbye to my own family. Told them how much I love them.

But I had no fear. I wanted to stay, until I heard your distant cry. I felt my grandmother's warm embrace before she let me go and receded into the light. My heart broken in two, losing that part of me. I came back alone with a single consciousness—to be your mother.

I woke up in the hospital and opened my eyes to see your daddy holding you. He told me he would have died if I hadn't made it, but I'm sure after he held you, that would no longer be true. I felt so much lighter, like I had so much more vacant space within, but there was no gap in my memory.

Before this moment, all of the red flags had been waving: the headaches, blurred vision, all the sort of symptoms I'd grown up with, and then the swollen face, hands and feet. But then, after the latest move and the stress of the new baby coming, and the worry about how, when, and what would I tell your father about my history, and then the loss of my best friend, I'd ignored the warning signs. Apparently, I'd suffered a seizure called eclampsia. But here I am to write to you.

Little Dylan, son of the sea, this is the beginning of your story. I don't know when I'll give you this letter, certainly not before you can read. But for now, everything is documented from the very beginning and when you're ready I'll answer any questions you might still have. There will be no secrets like what I kept from your father. I wish to only mirror and magnify your light.

Love and light, Mom.

CHAPTER 41

The Other Side

My second life began when I realized I only had one. In my room by myself, I truly knew what it felt like to be alone for the first time in my life. Grandma was gone. Rest in peace. I imagined her telling me she was having the time of her afterlife and then I realized I could still talk to her. And as twisted as that might have seemed, I told her to say 'hi' to my father for me and that I hoped he'd forgiven me as I had him and her, but this was now my life—let's not forget.

Tommy sat next to me reading Dr. Spock's *Baby and Childcare* and books on surfing. He acted as if he wasn't worried about my mental state after all I'd been through. I wasn't sure he comprehended the relationship I had with my grandmother, or whether he was just placating me, but he told me he loved me and that it would take further explanation, but now was not the time. My day nurse checked on me. She took my temperature as there was a soft knock on the door.

★ ★ ★

After about a week, I received my first visitors. Maggie, Patty, and Mom bounded in with balloons and a bouquet of flowers. Maggie had flown in from Arizona. Tommy hugged them and then left the room to let us women catch up. They stepped up one-by-one to hug me, this time, more than a sideways hug.

"Josie's outside watching my kids," Patty said. "I'll only stay a minute and then go relieve her."

"And Michael's sorry, but he's in the middle of finals," Maggie added.

"Oh, I know. He called to say he'd see us all for Thanksgiving."

"How are you feeling? I heard it was a tough labor?" Patty said.

"You mean beside the part where I died?"

"What?" Patty asked. "You're kidding. What was that like?" My sister apparently had no problems in the baby delivery department, the latest one having been born at home without a single cramp.

"She doesn't remember too much. Let's talk about that later," Maggie said, pulling up a chair.

And it's not true. I remembered everything, but I still needed some time to process the whole death experience. I didn't want to rush through with the details while the nurse was here.

"Shall I bring the baby in?" the nurse asked.

"Oh, yes!" Patty clapped. "So, I heard your water broke up at the old house."

"Que? What were you doing over there?" Mom asked, taking a seat at my side.

"Grandma Phoebe wanted to pay a visit."

Mom's eyes grew huge behind her glasses. She crossed her arms across her chest, blowing air out her nose. "Por supuesto."

Maggie leaned in, peering into my eyes, searching. "Hi Grandma."

"She's no longer with me."

"De veras?" Mom asked, sitting straighter.

I turned to my mother. "Yes. I'll explain later, but right now the baby's on his way."

"Right," Maggie said, looking toward the door.

"Anyway, the house looked pretty good. Mr. Jones kept asking about the piano."

There was a pregnant pause as Mom and Maggie looked at each other.

"I told him I knew nothing."

"Last laugh is on him," Maggie said, winking at Mom who smiled, nodding. "So, after you left for New York back in 1970, as you know, we had to let the house go—with all of the furniture and furnishings. The attorney Mom hired to try and save the house sold it out from under us to a third party, a Mr. Jones. He brought in cleaners and painters and carpenters to fix up the house before he could move in. The piano, covered in a drop cloth, was still there after they completed their jobs."

"Maggie, how do you know?"

She smiled devilishly. "Marquez & Sons Painting."

"Uncle Teodoro?"

"Sal said it was like a magic disappearing act. Once he pulled the cloth—now you see it, now you don't—the piano was gone."

"Are you serious? What happened to it?"

"We needed money. We barely got peanuts from the sale of the house. It wasn't fair. Get this, our cousin knew a guy who knew the owner of the Troubadour Club. Turns out the club needed the piano for this new British rock 'n' roller who would only play on a Steinway. Maybe you've heard of him? Elton John."

I laughed. "Now you're pulling my leg."

"Where do you think Mom got the money to send before you headed off to India? I went to the concert just to check out the piano and just before he came on stage, I had a chance to sneak up and check the underbelly and sure enough, there was your "A" and my "M" carved in the wood. Pretty cool, huh? The place was packed. He put on a good show. Cleopatra never sounded so good."

"Thanks a lot."

"Hey, you were good," Maggie said, "but, I never saw you do a handstand on the keyboard."

I laughed. "I'll bet she's worth a ton now."

"Yeah, just like our old house."

"And speaking of our old house–" Mom said, as the nurse brought in the baby and placed him in my arms. She leaned in to take a peek and I handed him off to her.

"Aye. He looks just like a Marquez, except for the nose. Lots of black hair." She smoothed it back. "What's his name?

"Dylan." I could see my mother's face tangle up. "Dylan River Steele." I'd added the middle name, so that the memory of my soul brother might live on.

There was a knock at the door. Josie peaked in. "Hey, when's it my turn?"

"Where are the kids?" Patty asked, and as Josie swung the door open wide, I could see the excited faces of my niece and nephew.

"Hi Auntie Anna!" they squealed, and Patty quickly sprang from her seat to usher them all out of the room.

My baby sister walked over to my mother to look at Dylan. "Oh, he's like a little doll." She got all teary-eyed. "Can I hold him?"

"Not yet." Grandma bear held the baby even closer. "He doesn't have a Christian name." She lamented as if Josie might drop him and he'd die without a proper name. "Que lastima," she said smiling down at Dylan.

"Just because it's not in the Bible, Mom? It means son of the sea. Sort of like our last name LeMar, the sea."

Mom thought about it and then smiled, her face turning calm as an ocean at dawn as she looked at the baby. "Hola angelito del mar." She rocked him the way I remember being rocked through the ages by all the mothers, grandmothers, and great-grandmothers who came before me, the same way I would rock my children, the same way my children would rock my grandchildren. As it was in the beginning, as it is now and forever shall be a mother's love. A mother will do anything for her children—and her grandchildren.

Dylan had fallen asleep, his tiny chest rising and falling like a little bird. His lids fluttered as he chased angels in his sleep.

And then, as if an afterthought, Mom looked up and whispered, "Oh, by the way, good news." And I thought the moment couldn't get any better. "It's about the house. Mr. Jones called to say we can have it back for what he paid us. He said he didn't want to live in a house haunted by some old woman."

As surprised as I was to hear what happened, I remembered back at the Glendale house how Grandma Phoebe had said so many things using my voice. I had a vague memory of her telling Mr. Jones, in no uncertain terms, that if he didn't give the house back, she'd haunt him and his children and his children's children for the rest of their lives.

My mother bravely examined my eyes. "Thank you, Phoebe." She handed Dylan to me, a gesture as if she could trust us now with my own child.

"Mom, Grandma's gone." A tear escaped my eye, not for Grandma but for the childhood that got robbed. Except, Mom didn't seem to notice or comprehend. I'd have to explain later. For now, I felt the void, the missing half of the person who had been me for so long. I hugged Dylan, another tear dripping silently onto his cheek. I wouldn't let anyone steal his childhood.

"I still have some money saved from selling the piano so after this we're headed over to sign the papers." I couldn't believe my ears, but I didn't want to stop my mother from talking, with her mouth and her hands. "I asked my brother if he would like to move back onto the property, but this time into the big house with Othelia. It's just Josie and me now so we can take the smaller apartment in the back part." I hadn't seen Mom this excited—ever.

"There's plenty of room for you to visit. We'll even get a swing set for the grandkids. Dylan—aye, what a name—can run around and splash in the creek like you used to."

Blinded by tears, I could still see us all splashing in the brook that flowed alongside the house, running around the backyard as the children we once were, the child I once was before I drifted away. But then on the other side of the narrow river, I saw the raft had been laid down gently on the bank, the oars off to the side. I hadn't drowned, after all. I'd more than survived, I'd thrived.

Au revoir, Grandma Phoebe.

ABOUT THE AUTHOR

RUTHIE MARLENÉE, a native Californian with Mexican roots, is the author of *Isabela's Island*, *Curse of the Ninth*, and *Agave Blues*. Nominated twice for the Pushcart Prize, she is a member of Macondo Writers Workshop, Inlandia Institute, Palm Springs Writers Guild, and is a WriteGirl Mentor.

Her poetry and short stories can be found in various publications, including *The Calendula Review*, *3Elements Literary Review*, *Gunpowder Press*, *Kelp Books*, *Shark Reef*, *The Coiled Serpent Anthology*, *So To Speak*, *Detour Ahead*, *What They Leave Behind: A Latinx Anthology*, *Silver Birch Press*, *Slow Lightning: Impractical Poetry*, and *Writing From Inlandia*.

ACKNOWLEDGMENTS

I am forever grateful to the team at Sibylline Press. To Vicki DeArmon and Julia Park Tracey, thank you for creating this divine space where women-identifying authors over fifty are lifted up and celebrated.

Thank you to mentors who fed my imagination: Stephanie Barbé Hammer, liz Gonzalez, Mary Anne Perez, Mary Camarillo, Judith Brenner, Samantha Dunn. To M.L. Krishnan, for sharing some of your experiences in India, and Shanti Norris (especially with Alice Coltrane and Swami Satchidinanda). To Integral Yoga and The Krotona Institute.

To my husband, Jeff, who shared his knowledge of all things Coast Guard, sixties music, and unconditional love, thank you. You kept me nourished and caffeinated, escorting me across the country and beyond for research. While this is a work of fiction, I thank my sisters for indulging me as I stretched some family truths. Thank you to my daughter, Alexandra, for allowing me to be a mother and a grandmother to your littles, and for being my first reader!

STUDY GUIDE QUESTIONS

1. How do the events of the sixties compare to today? Civil Rights, Women's Rights, the Chicano Movement, Black Panthers, Vietnam War, Immigration. Have we "Come along way, baby?" Or are we doomed to repeat history?

2. Have you ever felt like running away from your strange family? Do you understand why Anna ran away in the first place? Do you agree with her decision to flee?

3. Have you ever heard a little voice in your head and thought it could be an ancestor trying to guide you? Or, have you ever thought: I can just imagine what Grandma would say, or, He must be rolling over in his grave?

4. In Chapter 2, Grandma Phoebe tries to explain the concept of transferring one's consciousness. She says, "In death, there is no concept of present, past or future . . . While dying, there is no concept of time, no separation of moments." Is this hard to comprehend?

5. Does the fact that Anna has been homeschooled work toward the description of her as a bit naïve? Is she too naïve?

6. Does the fact that Anna is mixed add to her confusion about her identity?

7. Should Anna have any sympathy/empathy for her father/ Grandma Phoebe/ancestors?

8. Love is the answer is such a cliché. Do you believe it is the answer?

9. Did the end of the story offer a satisfactory conclusion?

10. Can you see another sequel (Book 3)? Will another character inherit an ancestor's consciousness?

Sibylline Press is proud to publish the brilliant work of women authors over 50. We are a woman-owned publishing company and, like our authors, represent women of a certain age.